Mysteries
of the Worm

Chaosium fiction

KING OF SARTAR
CASTLE OF EYES
THE HASTUR CYCLE
MYSTERIES OF THE WORM

in preparation

THE SHUB-NIGGURATH CYCLE
CTHULHU'S HEIRS

CALL OF CTHULHU ® FICTION

Mysteries
of the Worm

by ROBERT BLOCH

Second Edition
Revised and Expanded

The classic collection augmented by three stories,
with an afterword and
certain textual revisions by the author

Additional essay by LIN CARTER

Introduction and comments
by
ROBERT M. PRICE, series editor

A Chaosium Book

——————— 1993 ———————

The Cycle Series

Mysteries of the Worm: Second Edition, Revised and Expanded is published by Chaosium Inc.

Cover art by Dreyfus.

Please address questions and comments concerning this book, as well as requests for free notices of Chaosium publications, by mail to: Chaosium Inc., 950-A 56th Street, Oakland, CA 94608-3129 U.S.A.

ISBN 0-56882-012-7.

Chaosium Publication 6002. Published in October, 1993, Printed in the United States of America.

Contents

Introduction to the
Second Edition

A generation of scholars and critics have arisen since the death of August Derleth to repudiate Derleth's interpretation of the work of H.P. Lovecraft. These critics have based their assault on one fundamental axiom about the Lovecraft Mythos or Cthulhu Mythos. They believe that the Mythos should be viewed as a body of lore, not a set of stories.

Our critics would repudiate the effort made by Lin Carter, Paul Berglund and others to decide which stories "belong to" the Mythos. The critics point out that the catalogers have misunderstood what a "mythos" is. They maintain that certain stories by Lovecraft or others may draw on this body of myth, but the Mythos refers to the pseudo-information, not to the stories that draw on it.

Yet this criticism clashes with another often leveled at the work of Lumley, Derleth, and Carter, namely that these writers made the exposition of the Mythos itself (questions of which creatures served as the minions of what Old One, how many shoggoths could dance on the head of a pin, etc.) central to their tales. I will agree: this theoretical pedantry could get leaden pretty quickly. But at least one must admit that these authors considered the Mythos as precisely a body of lore, and they wanted to work the kinks out of it if they possibly could.

Indeed it seems to me that the over-explicit use of the myth-system, developing as it rapidly did into a systematic theology of the Great Old Ones, is nothing but the *reductio ad absurdum* of the post-Derlethian definition of the Mythos as a *body of lore*. The critics of Derleth and his disciples perhaps hoped to avoid such logical implications by sometimes claiming that the Mythos was not exactly a system, i.e., something with rules and clarity. Rather, said the post-Derlethians, the Mythos as HPL conceived it was a cloudy cycle of related legends, a literary fog created to lend an eerie atmosphere to a story precisely by virtue of its indefiniteness. It ruins it if, like Carter, you over-systematize it.

But just what is a legend? A story, is it not? A legend is not a belief, also not a mytheme (that is, an individual motif or feature of a myth). A myth or legend is *narrative* in form. What are the legends, then, of the Cthulhu Mythos? The only available candidates must be the stories which mention the Mythos and its mythemes. The skalds of the Mythos are not some characters in the *stories*. Characters like Old Castro, who actually have something of a tale to tell, are rare exceptions.

In Lovecraft's own stories it seems the protagonists are always deriving raw, non-narrative, mythemes from tomes like the *Necronomicon*, which seem to be straight exposition (*cf.* the *Necronomicon* passage in "The Dunwich Horror"), pretty much like Derleth or Carter, though maybe with a bit more style. Where are the myths, in other words the stories, of this alleged myth cycle? They are, of course, the ones we are reading, the ones by Lovecraft, Derleth, Campbell, Smith, Howard— and Robert Bloch.

In fact, I view the attempt to retreat from this insight, which Derleth and Carter certainly had, as an ironic repetition of that other crime for which their critics condemned them: over-systematizing. The post-Derlethians wanted, in their Cromwellian reformist zeal, to smash the Derlethian idols, cast the Derlethian Apocrypha out of the canon, reduce the glittering clouds of narrative to an abstract Ur-Myth: the data as envisioned by Lovecraft himself and no one else. If this is not a surrender of narrative to systematized exposition, I don't know what is!

Lin Carter, compiler of the first edition of *Mysteries of the Worm*, was quite right in titling the volume as he did. Is there actually a book somewhere with the title *De Vermis Mysteriis*? Written by one Ludvig Prinn? No. But this collection deserves to be christened with the title because it contains the actual myths, the actual stories of the Prinn legend cycle, the ones Robert Bloch wrote! The stories of the Mythos are the Mythos! Thus the wise propriety of Lin Carter's choice of the title. (And of course, it was the very same logic that had earlier led Robert W. Chambers to lend the title *The King in Yellow* to a collection of tales which mentioned but did not actually contain an arcane volume called "The King in Yellow.")

The second edition of *Mysteries of the Worm* differs from the original in two respects. I have decided to add three early Mythos tales: "The Brood of Bubastis from the March 1937 issue of *Weird Tales*, "The Sorcerer's Jewel" from the February 1939 issue of *Strange Stories* (where it appeared under the pseudonym 'Tarleton Fiske'), and "The Creeper in the Crypt" from the July 1937 *Weird Tales*. I had always thought they belonged in the table of contents of the first edition, so here they are.

In addition, Bloch has revised slightly the texts for "The Grinning Ghoul," "The Dark Demon," and "The Secret of Sebek."

— Robert M. Price

*O*F ALL THE TALES COLLECTED *here, this one is most guilty of the supposed sin of heavily peppering the text with Lovecraftian lingo, a malignant nightmare saraband of eerie adjectives, as it were. Edmund Wilson (in his critical review "Tales of the Marvellous and the Ridiculous") chided Lovecraft's use of such adjectives: "Surely one of the primary rules for writing an effective tale of horror is never to use any of these words." You should not have to tell the reader that what he reads is hideous, loathsome, etc. Let him see it for himself.*

A point well taken. But then why do stories like "The Suicide in the Study" work so well anyway? I suspect that the use of these words creates a kind of almost hypnotic horror language that functions like a mantra and that, contrary to Wilson, does actually suggest more than it states, in the manner of a word association test. Each use of "hideous" invites you to conjure your image of the hideous, of the loathsome, etc.

What is the Cabala of Saboth? *The Cabala or Kabbalah is a body of lore culminating in Moses de Leon's 13th century work* The Book of Zohar, *an esoteric commentary on the Torah. "Saboth," or Sabaoth, means "hosts," part of the divine epithet Yahweh Sabaoth, or Lord of Hosts, the latter referring to the angelic armies. The word was used in many medieval magical formulae. A Cabala of Saboth should then be a Jewish mystical treatise on the esoteric lore of the angels, perhaps the magical use of their names and powers, as in* The Book of Magic of Abra-Melin the Mage.

The Secret in the Tomb

THE WIND HOWLED strangely over a midnight tomb. The moon hung like a golden bat over ancient graves, glaring through the wan mist with its baleful, nyctalopic eye. Terrors not of the flesh might lurk among cedar-shrouded sepulchers or creep unseen amid shadowed cenotaphs, for this was unhallowed ground. But tombs hold strange secrets, and there are mysteries blacker than the night, and more leprous than the moon.

It was in search of such a secret that I came, alone and unseen, to my ancestral vault at midnight. My people had been sorcerers and wizards in the olden days, so lay apart from the resting-place of other men, here in this moldering mausoleum in a forgotten spot, surrounded only by the graves of those who had been their servants. But not all the servants lay here, for there are those who do not die.

On through the mist I pressed, to where the crumbling sepulcher loomed among the brooding trees. The wind rose to torrential violence as I trod the obscure pathway to the vaulted entrance, extinguishing my lantern with malefic fury. Only the moon remained to light my way in a luminance unholy. And thus I reached the nitrous, fungus-bearded portals of the family vault. Here the moon shone upon a door that was not like other doors—a single massive slab of iron, imbedded in monumental walls of granite. Upon its outer surface was neither handle, lock nor keyhole, but the whole was covered with carvings portentous of a leering evil—cryptic symbols whose allegorical significance filled my soul with a deeper loathing than mere words can impart. There are things that are not good to look upon, and I did not care to dwell too much in thought on the possible genesis of a mind whose knowledge could create such horrors in concrete form. So in blind and trembling haste I chanted the obscure litany and performed the necessary obeisances demanded in the ritual I had learned, and at their conclusion the cyclopean portal swung open.

Within was darkness, deep, funereal, ancient; yet, somehow, uncannily *alive*. It held a pulsing adumbration, a suggestion of muted, yet purposeful rhythm, and overshadowing all, an air of black, impinging *revelation*. The simultaneous effect upon my consciousness was one of those reactions misnamed intuitions. I sensed that shadows know queer secrets, and there are some skulls that have reason to grin.

Yet I must go on into the tomb of my forebears—tonight the last of all our line would meet the first. For I was the last. Jeremy Strange had been the first—he who fled from the Orient to seek refuge in centuried Eldertown, bringing with him the loot of many tombs and a secret for ever nameless. It was he who had built his sepulcher in the twilight woods where the witch-lights gleam, and here he had interred his own remains, shunned in death as he had been in life. But buried with him was a secret, and it was this that I had come to seek. Nor was I the first in so seeking, for my father and his father before me, indeed, the eldest of each generation back to the days of Jeremy Strange himself, had likewise sought that which was so maddeningly described in the wizard's diary—the secret of eternal life after death. The musty yellowed tome had been handed down to the elder son of each successive generation, and likewise, so it seemed, the dread atavistic craving for black and accursed knowledge, the thirst for which, coupled with the damnably explicit hints set forth in the warlock's record, had sent every one of my paternal ancestors so bequeathed to a final rendezvous in the night, to seek their heritage within the tomb. What they found, none could say, for none had ever returned.

It was, of course, a family secret. The tomb was never mentioned—it had, indeed, been virtually forgotten with the passage of years that had likewise eradicated many of the old legends and fantastic accusations about the first Strange that had once been common property in the village. The family, too, had been mercifully spared all knowledge of the curse-ridden end to which so many of its men had come. Their secret delvings into black arts; the hidden library of antique lore and demonological formulæ brought by Jeremy from the East; the diary and its secret—all were undreamt of save by the eldest sons. The rest of the line prospered. There had been sea captains, soldiers, merchants, statesmen. Fortunes were won. Many departed from the old mansion on the cape, so that in my father's time he had lived there alone with the servants and myself. My mother died at my birth, and it was a lonely youth I spent in the great brown house, with a father half-crazed by the tragedy of my mother's end, and shadowed by the monstrous secret of our line. It was he who initiated me into the mysteries and arcana to be found amid the shuddery speculations of such blasphemies as the *Necronomicon*, the *Book of Eibon*, the *Cabala of Saboth*, and that pinnacle of literary madness, Ludvig Prinn's *Mysteries of the Worm*. There were grim treatises on anthropomancy, necrology, lycanthropical and vampiristic spells and charms, witchcraft, and long, rambling screeds in Arabic, Sanskrit and prehistoric ideography, on which lay the dust of centuries.

All these he gave me, and more. There were times when he would whisper strange stories about voyages he had taken in his youth—of islands in the sea, and queer survivals spawning dreams beneath arctic ice. And one night he told me of the legend, and the tomb in the forest; and together we turned the worm-riddled pages of the iron-bound diary that was hidden in the panel above the chimney-corner. I was very young, but not too young to know certain things, and as I swore to keep the secret as so many had sworn before me, I had a queer feeling that the time had come for Jeremy to claim his own. For in my father's somber eyes was the same light of dreadful thirst for the unknown, curiosity, and an inward urge that had glowed in the eyes of all the others before him, previous to the time they had announced their intention of "going on a trip" or "joining up" or "attending to a business matter." Most of them had waited till their children were grown, or their wives had passed on; but whenever they had left, and whatever their excuse, they had never returned.

Two days later, my father disappeared, after leaving word with the servants that he was spending the week in Boston. Before the month was out there was the usual investigation, and the usual failure. A will was discovered among my father's papers, leaving me as sole heir, but the books and the diary were secure in the secret rooms and panels known now to me alone.

Life went on. I did the usual things in the usual way—attended university, traveled, and returned at last to the house on the hill, alone. But with me I carried a mighty determination—I alone could thwart that curse; I alone could grasp the secret that had cost the lives of seven generations—and I alone must do so. The world had naught to offer one who had spent his youth in the study of the mocking truths that lie beyond the outward beauties of a purposeless existence, and I was not afraid. I dismissed the servants, ceased communication with distant relatives and a few close friends, and spent my days in the hidden chambers amid the elder lore, seeking a solution or a spell of such potency as would serve to dispel for ever the mystery of the tomb.

A hundred times I read and reread that hoary script—the diary whose fiend-penned promise had driven men to doom. I searched amid the satanic spells and cabalistic incantations of a thousand forgotten necromancers, delved into pages of impassioned prophecy, burrowed

into secret legendary lore whose written thoughts writhed through me
like serpents from the pit. It was in vain. All I could learn was the
ceremony by which access could be obtained to the tomb in the wood.
Three months of study had worn me to a wraith and filled my brain
with the diabolic shadows of charnel-spawned knowledge, but that
was all. And then, as if in mockery of madness, there had come the
call, this very night.

I had been seated in the study, pondering upon a maggot-eaten
volume of Heiriarchus' *Occultus,* when without warning, I felt a tremendous urge keening through my weary brain. It beckoned and
allured with unutterable promise, like the mating-cry of the lamia of
old; yet at the same time it held an inexorable power whose potence
could not be defied or denied. The inevitable was at hand. I had been
summoned to the tomb. I must follow the beguiling voice of inner
consciousness that was the invitation and the promise, that sounded
my soul like the ultra-rhythmic piping of trans-cosmic music. So I had
come, alone and weaponless, to the lonely woods and to that wherein
I would meet my destiny.

The moon rose redly over the manor as I left, but I did not look
back. I saw its reflection in the waters of the brook that crept between
the trees, and in its light the water was as blood. Then the fog rose
silently from the swamp, and a yellow ghost-light rode the sky,
beckoning me on from behind the black and bloated trees whose
branches, swept by a dismal wind, pointed silently toward the distant
tomb. Roots and creepers impeded my feet, vines and brambles
restrained my body, but in my ears thundered a chorus of urgency that
can not be described and which could not be delayed, by nature or by
man.

Now, as I hesitated upon the door-step, a million idiot voices
gibbered an invitation to enter that mortal mind could not withstand.
Through my brain resounded the horror of my heritage—the insatiable
craving to know the forbidden, to mingle and become one with it. A
pæan of hell-born music crescendoed in my ears, and earth was blotted
out in a mad urge that engulfed all being.

I paused no longer upon the threshold. I went in, in where the smell
of death filled the darkness that was like the sun over Yuggoth. The
door closed, and then came—what? I do not know—I only realized
that suddenly I could see and feel and hear, despite darkness, and
dankness, and silence.

I was in the tomb. Its monumental walls and lofty ceiling were black
and bare, lichened by the passage of centuries. In the center of the

mausoleum stood a single slab of black marble. Upon it rested a gilded coffin, set with strange symbols, and covered by the dust of ages. I knew instinctively what it must contain, and the knowledge did not serve to put me at my ease. I glanced at the floor, then wished I hadn't. Upon the debris-strewn base beneath the slab lay a ghastly, disarticulated group of mortuary remains—half-fleshed cadavers and desiccated skeletons. When I though of my father and the others, I was possessed of a sickening dismay. They too had sought, and they had failed. And now I had come, alone, to find that which had brought them to an end unholy and unknown. The secret! The secret in the tomb!

Mad eagerness filled my soul. I too would know—I must! As in a dream I swayed to the gilded coffin. A moment I tottered above it; then, with a strength born of delirium, I tore away the paneling and lifted the gilded lid, and then I knew it was no dream, for dreams can not approach the ultimate horror that was the creature lying within the coffin—that creature with eyes like a midnight demon's, and a face of loathsome delirium that was like the death-mask of a devil. It was smiling, too, as it lay there, and my soul shrieked in the tortured realization that it was *alive!* Then I knew it all; the secret and the penalty paid by those who sought it, and I was ready for death, but horrors had not ceased, for even as I gazed it spoke, in a voice like the hissing of a black slug.

And there within the nighted gloom it whispered the secret, staring at me with ageless, deathless eyes, so that I should not go mad before I heard the whole of it. All was revealed—the secret crypts of blackest nightmare where the tomb-spawn dwell, and of a price whereby a man may become one with the ghouls, living after death as a devourer in darkness. Such a thing had it become, and from this shunned, accursed tomb had sent the call to the descending generations, that when they came, there might be a ghastly feast whereby it might continue a dread, eternal life. I (it breathed) would be the next to die, and in my heart I knew that it was so.

I could not avert my eyes from its accursed gaze, nor free my soul from its hypnotic bondage. The thing on the bier cackled with unholy laughter. My blood froze, for I saw two long, lean arms, like the rotted limbs of a corpse, steal slowly toward my fear-constricted throat. The monster sat up, and even in the clutches of my horror, I realized that there was a dim and awful resemblance between the creature in the coffin and a certain ancient portrait back in the Hall. But this was a transfigured reality—Jeremy the man had become Jeremy the ghoul; and I knew that it would do no good to resist. Two claws, cold as flames of icy hell, fastened around my throat, two eyes bored like maggots through my frenzied being, a laughter born of madness alone cachinnated in my ears like the thunder of doom. The bony fingers tore at my eyes and nostrils, held me helpless while yellow fangs champed nearer and nearer to my throat. The world spun, wrapped in a mist of fiery death.

Suddenly the spell broke. I wrenched my eyes away from that slavering, evil face, and instantly, like a cataclysmic flash of light, came realization. This creature's power was purely mental—by that alone were my ill-fated kinsmen drawn here, and by that alone were they overcome, but once one were free from the strength of the monster's awful eyes—good God! Was I going to be the victim of a crumbled mummy?

My right arm swung up, striking the horror between the eyes. There was a sickening crunch; then dead flesh yielded before my hand as I seized the now faceless lich in my arms and cast it into fragments upon the bone-covered floor. Streaming with perspiration and mumbling in hysteria and terrible revulsion, I saw the moldy fragments move even in a second death—a severed hand crawled across the flagging, upon musty, shredded fingers; a leg began to roll with the animation of grotesque, unholy life. With a shriek, I cast a lighted match upon that loathsome corpse, and I was still shrieking as I clawed open the portals and rushed out of the tomb and into the world of sanity, leaving behind me a smoldering fire from whose charred heart a terrible voice still faintly moaned its tortured requiem to that which had once been Jeremy Strange.

The tomb is razed now, and with it the forest graves and all the hidden chambers and manuscripts that serve as a reminder of ghoul-ridden memories that can never be forgot. For earth hides a madness and dreams a hideous reality, and monstrous things abide in the shadows of death, lurking and waiting to seize the souls of those who meddle with forbidden things.

B LOCH ACKNOWLEDGES *within the story itself the debt owed by this tale to Stevenson's "The Strange Case of Doctor Jekyll and Mister Hyde," but his version is at once both more direct and a daring departure. The evil self tries physically to destroy the good, as Hyde succeeded at last in destroying Jekyll. Only this time it is a face-to-face confrontation.*

It would have been interesting to see the tale end differently, the conclusion being told by the resultant evil self, since it was more from this perspective that the narration began. We are seemingly to identify the victim of the monster with the writer of the diary, but why not take the monster's side?

The Suicide in the Study

TO SEE HIM SITTING there in the dim-lit darkness of the study, one would have never suspected him for what he was. Wizards nowadays are not garbed in cabalistic robes of silver and black; instead they wear purple dressing-gowns. It is not required of them that their eyebrows meet, their nails grow long as talons, and their eyes flame like emerald-imprisoned dreams. Nor are they necessarily bent and furtive, and old. This one was not; he was young and slim, almost imperially straightforward.

He sat beneath the lamplight in the great oak-paneled room; a dark, handsome man of perhaps thirty-five years of age. There was little of cruelty or malice visible in his keen, clear-featured face, and little of madness in his eyes; yet he was a wizard, just as surely as if he lurked over human sacrifices in the skull-strewn darkness of forbidden tombs.

It was only necessary for one to survey the walls of his study for corroboration. Only a wizard would possess those moldering, maggoty volumes of monstrous and fantastic lore; only a thaumaturgical adept would dare the darker mysteries of the *Necronomicon*, Ludvig Prinn's *Mysteries of the Worm*, the *Black Rites* of mad Luveh-Keraph, priest of Bast, or Comte d'Erlette's ghastly *Cultes des Goules*. No one save a sorcerer would have access to the ancient manuscripts bound in Ethiopian skin, or burn such rich and aphrodisiac incense in an enshrined skull. Who else would fill the mercifully cloaking darkness of the room with curious relics, mortuary souvenirs from ravished graves, or worm-demolished scrolls of primal dread?

Superficially, it was a normal room that night, and its occupant a normal man. But for proof of its inherent strangeness it was not necessary to glance at the skull, the book-cases, or the grim, shadow-shrouded remains, to know its occupant for what he was. For James Allington wrote in his secret diary tonight, and his musings were far from sanity.

"Tonight I am ready to make the test. I am convinced at last that splitting of the identity can be accomplished by means of therapeutic hypnotism, provided that the mental attitude conducive to such a partition can be induced.

"Fascinating subject, that. Dual identity—the dream of men from the beginning of time! Two souls in one body ... all philosophy is based on comparative logic; good and evil. Why, then, can not such a division exist in the human soul? Stevenson was only partly right when he wrote *Dr. Jekyll and Mr. Hyde.* He imagined a chemical metamorphosis varying from one extreme to the other. I believe that both identities are *co-existent;* that, once they are separated by autohypnotic thought, a man can enjoy two existences simultaneously—his good self and his bad.

"They laughed at my theory in the club. Foster—that pompous old fool!—called me a dreamer. Dreamer? What does he, a petty scientific chemist, know of the basic mysteries of Life and Death? A glimpse into my laboratory would shock his smug soul into insanity. The others, too; mob-catering writers, pedantic fossils who call themselves professors, prim biologists who are shocked at the mention of my experiments in synthetic creation of life—what do such as these understand? They would shudder at the *Necronomicon;* burn it, too, if they could; burn it as their pious ancestors did three hundred years ago. Witch-baiters, skeptics, materialists all! I'm sick of the whole silly pack of them. It is the fate of the genius to dwell alone. Very well, then, I'll dwell alone—but soon they will come cringing to my door and beg for mercy!

"If my work tonight only succeeds! If I can succeed in hypnotizing myself into dual personality, physically manifested! Even modern psychology claims it can be done. Spiritualism credits its possibilities. The ancients have furnished me the key to the problem, as they have done before .... Alhazred knew many things—it was only the weight of the knowledge that drove him mad.

"Two bodies! Once I can achieve that state at will, I shall hold the key to powers for ever denied to men. Immortality, perhaps; it is only a step further. After that there will be no need of skulking here in secret; no necessity of passing my researches off as a harmless hobby. Dreamer, eh? I'll show them!

"I wonder what the *other* shape will look like? Will it be human? It must, otherwise—but I had better not think of that. It is quite probable that it will be an ugly-looking customer. I do not flatter myself. I know that the evil side of my nature, while concealed, is undoubtedly dominant. There is danger, though—evil is an uncontrollable force in its purest form. It will draw strength from my body, too—energy to manifest itself physically. But that must not deter me. I must make the test. If it succeeds I shall have power—power undreamt of—power to kill, to rend, to destroy! I shall add to my little collection here, and settle a few old scores with my skeptical friends. After that there will be other pleasant things to do.

"But enough of such musings. I must begin. I shall lock the study doors; the servants have gone out for the evening and there will be no one to intrude upon my privacy. I dare not risk using an electrically manipulated machine for fear of some untoward consequences in removing the hypnosis. I shall try to induce a hypnotic trance by concentrating intently on this heavy, polished paper-knife here on my desk. Meanwhile, I shall focus my will on the matter at hand, using the Soul Chant of Sebek as a focal point.

"I shall set the alarm for twelve o'clock, exactly one hour from now. Its ringing will break the spell. That, I believe, is all I need bother to do. As an added precaution, I shall burn this record. Should anything go wrong, I would hate to have all my little plans disclosed to the world.

"Nothing shall go wrong, however. I have used auto-hypnosis many times before, and I will be very careful. It will be a marvelous feeling to control two bodies at once. I can hardly control myself—I find my body trembling in eagerness and anticipation of its forthcoming metamorphosis. Power!

"Very well. After this report is reduced to ashes I shall be ready— ready to undertake the greatest experiment man has ever known."

– 2 –

James Allington sat before the shaded lamp. Before him on the table lay the paper-knife, its polished blade shimmering. Only the slow ticking of a clock broke the sable silence of the locked room.

The wizard's eyes were glassy; they shone in the light, immobile as a basilisk's. The reflection from the surface of the knife stabbed through his retina like the fiery ray of a burning sun, but his betranced gaze never wavered.

Who knows what strange inversion was occurring in the dreamer's bewitched brain; what subtle transmutation generated from his purpose? He had fallen into his sleep with the fixed resolve of severing his soul, dividing his personality, bisecting his ego. Who knows? Hypnotism does many strange things.

What secret Powers did he invoke to aid him in his fight? What black genesis of unholy life lurked within the shadows of his inner consciousness; what demons of leering evil granted him his dark desires?

For granted they were. Suddenly he awoke, and he could feel that he was no longer alone in that nighted room. He felt the presence of another, there in the darkness on the other side of the table.

Or was it another? Was it not he, himself? He glanced down at his body and was unable to suppress a gasp of astonishment. *He seemed to have shrunk to less than a quarter of his ordinary size!* His body was light, fragile, dwarfed. For a moment he was incapable of thought or movement. His eyes strayed to the corner of the room, trying vainly to see the gloom-obstructed movements of a presence that shambled there.

Then things happened. Out of the darkness nightmare came; stark, staring nightmare—a monstrous, hairy figure; huge, grotesque, simian—a hideous travesty of all things human. It was black madness; slavering, mocking madness with little red eyes of wisdom old and evil; leering snout and yellow fangs of grimacing death. It was like a rotting, living skull upon the body of a black ape. It was grisly and wicked, troglodytic and wise.

A monstrous thought assailed Allington. Was *this* his other self— this ghoul-spawned, charnel horror of corpse-accursed dread?

Too late the wizard realized what had befallen him. His experiment *had* succeeded, but terribly so. He had not realized how far the evil in his nature had outbalanced the good. This monster—this grisly abomination of darkness—was stronger than he was, and, being solely evil, *it was not mentally controlled by his other self.* Allington viewed it now with new fear in his eyes. It was like a creature from the Pit. All that was foul and obscene and anti-human in his makeup lay behind that grinning parody of a countenance. The beast-like body hinted of shadows that creep beneath the grave or lurk entombed within the deepest recesses of normal minds. Yet in it Allington recognized a mad, atavistic caricature of himself—all the lust, the greed, the insane ambition, the cruelty, the ignorance; the fiend-spawned secrets of his soul within the body of a gigantic ape!

As if in answer to his recognition, the creature laughed, and tentacles of horror gripped the wizard's heart.

The thing was coming toward him—it meant to destroy him, as evil always does. Allington, his tiny body ludicrously struggling to move quickly while impeded by clothes now ridiculously large for his diminutive frame, raced from his chair and flattened himself against the wall of the study. His voice, curiously treble, shrieked frantic supplication and futile commands to the approaching nemesis. His prayers and curses turned to the hoarse gibberings of madness as the huge beast lunged across the table. His experiment was succeeding with a vengeance ... *vengeance!* His glaring eyes watched, fascinated, as one great paw grasped the paper-knife, and fearsome laughter riddled the night. It was laughing ... laughing! Somewhere an alarm-clock rang, but the wizard could not hear ....

They found James Allington lying dead upon his study floor. There was a paper-knife imbedded in his breast, and they called it suicide, for no one could possibly have entered that locked and windowless room.

But that did not explain the fingerprints on the handle of the knife—the terrible fingerprints—*like those left by the hand of a gigantic ape.*

THIS TALE INTRODUCES Prinn's unholy volume. Bloch had originally given the book its "translated" English title, but Lovecraft, every bit the classicist Bloch portrays him in the story, suggested the "original" Latin title, as well as supplying the Latin formula of summoning. It means, more or less, "To the Great One Not to Be Named: Sign of the Black Stars and of Toad-shaped Tsathoggua..." The black stars seem to be a nod to the Carcosa mythology of Robert W. Chambers, while Tsathoggua is Clark Ashton Smith's familiar.

It is interesting to note that the death of the Lovecraft-character mirrors that of Abdul Alhazred himself, who met his doom at the talons of an invisible monster (see Lovecraft's "History of the Necronomicon*").*

The Shambler
from the Stars

I AM WHAT I PROFESS to be—a writer of weird fiction. Since earliest childhood I have been enthralled by the cryptic fascination of the unknown and the unguessable. The nameless fears, the grotesque dreams, the queer, half-intuitive fancies that haunt our minds have always exercised for me a potent and inexplicable delight.

In literature I have walked the mid-night paths with Poe or crept amidst the shadows with Machen; combed the realms of horrific stars with Baudelaire, or steeped myself with earth's inner madness amidst the tales of ancient lore. A meager talent for sketching and crayon work led me to attempt crude picturizations involving the outlandish denizens of my nighted thoughts. The same somber trend of intellect which drew me in my art interested me in obscure realms of musical composition; the symphonic strains of the *Planets Suite* and the like were my favorites. My inner life soon became a ghoulish feast of eldritch, tantalizing horrors.

My outer existence was comparatively dull. As time went on I found myself drifting more and more into the life of a penurious recluse; a tranquil, philosophical existence amidst a world of books and dreams.

A man must live. By nature constitutionally and spiritually unfitted for manual labor, I was at first puzzled about the choice of a suitable vocation. The depression complicated matters to an almost intolerable degree, and for a time I was close to utter economic disaster. It was then that I decided to write.

I procured a battered typewriter, a ream of cheap paper, and a few carbons. My subject matter did not bother me. What better field than the boundless realms of a colorful imagination? I would write of horror, fear, and the riddle that is Death. At least, in the callowness of my unsophistication, this was my intention.

My first attempts soon convinced me how utterly I had failed. Sadly, miserably, I fell short of my aspired goal. My vivid dreams became on paper merely meaningless jumbles of ponderous adjectives, and I found no ordinary words to express the wondrous terror of the unknown. My first manuscripts were miserable and futile documents; the few magazines using such material being unanimous in their rejections.

I had to live. Slowly but surely I began to adjust my style to my ideas. Laboriously I experimented with words, phrases, sentence-structure. It was work, and hard work at that. I soon learned to sweat. At last, however, one of my stories met with favor; then a second, a third, a fourth. Soon I had begun to master the more obvious tricks of the trade, and the future looked brighter at last. It was with an easier mind that I returned to my dream-life and my beloved books. My stories afforded me a somewhat meager livelihood, and for a time this sufficed. But not for long. Ambition, ever an illusion, was the cause of my undoing.

I wanted to write a real story; not the stereotyped, ephemeral sort of tale I turned out for the magazines, but a real work of art. The creation of such a masterpiece became my ideal. I was not a good writer, but that was not entirely due to my errors in mechanical style. It was, I felt, the fault of my subject matter. Vampires, werewolves, ghouls, mythological monsters—these things constituted material of little merit. Commonplace imagery, ordinary adjectival treatment, and a prosaically anthropocentric point of view were the chief detriments to the production of a really good weird tale.

I must have new subject matter, truly unusual plot material. If only I could conceive of something that was teratologically incredible!

I longed to learn the songs the demons sing as they swoop between the stars, or hear the voices of the olden gods as they whisper their secrets to the echoing void. I yearned to know the terrors of the grave; the kiss of maggots on my tongue, the cold caress of a rotting shroud upon my body. I thirsted for the knowledge that lies in the pits of mummied eyes, and burned for wisdom known only to the worm. Then I could really write, and my hopes would be truly realized.

I sought a way. Quietly I began a correspondence with isolated thinkers and dreamers all over the country. There was a hermit in the western hills, a savant in the northern wilds, a mystic dreamer in New England. It was from the latter that I learned of the ancient books that hold strange lore. He quoted guardedly from the legendary *Necronomicon,* and spoke timidly of a certain *Book of Eibon* that was reputed to surpass it in the utter wildness of its blasphemy. He himself had been a student of these volumes of primal dread, but he did not want me to search too far. He had heard many strange things as a boy in witch-haunted Arkham, where the old shadows still leer and creep, and since then he had wisely shunned the blacker knowledge of the forbidden.

At length, after much pressing on my part, he reluctantly consented to furnish me with the names of certain persons he deemed able to aid me in my quest. He was a writer of notable brilliance and wide reputation among the discriminating few, and I knew he was keenly interested in the outcome of the whole affair.

As soon as his precious list came into my possession, I began a widespread postal campaign in order to obtain access to the desired volumes. My letters went out to universities, private libraries, reputed seers, and the leaders of carefully hidden and obscurely designated cults. But I was foredoomed to disappointment.

The replies I received were definitely unfriendly, almost hostile. Evidently the rumored possessors of such lore were angered that their secret should be thus unveiled by a prying stranger. I was subsequently the recipient of several anonymous threats through the mails, and I had one very alarming phone-call. This did not bother me nearly so much as the disappointing realization that my endeavors had failed. Denials, evasions, refusals, threats—these would not aid me. I must look elsewhere.

The book stores! Perhaps on some musty and forgotten shelf I might discover what I sought.

Then began an interminable crusade. I learned to bear my numerous disappointments with unflinching calm. Nobody in the common run of shops seemed ever to have heard of the frightful *Necronomicon*, the evil *Book of Eibon,* or the disquieting *Cultes des Goules.*

Persistence brings results. In a little old shop on South Dearborn Street, amidst dusty shelves seemingly forgotten by time, I came to the end of my search. There, securely wedged between two century-old editions of Shakespeare, stood a great black volume with iron facings. Upon it, in hand-engraved lettering, was the inscription, *De Vermis Mysteriis,* or "Mysteries of the Worm."

The proprietor could not tell how it had come into his possession. Years before, perhaps, it had been included in some secondhand job-lot. He was obviously unaware of its nature, for I purchased it with a dollar bill. He wrapped the ponderous thing for me, well pleased at this unexpected sale, and bade me a very satisfied good-day.

I left hurriedly, the precious prize under my arm. What a find! I had heard of this book before. Ludvig Prinn was its author; he who had perished at the inquisitorial stake in Brussels when the witchcraft trials were at their height. A strange character—alchemist, necromancer, reputed mage—he boasted of having attained a miraculous age when he at last suffered a fiery immolation at the hands of the secular arm. He was said to have proclaimed himself the sole survivor of the ill-fated ninth crusade, exhibiting as proof certain musty documents of attestation. It is true that a certain Ludvig Prinn was numbered among the gentlemen retainers of Montserrat in the olden chronicles, but the incredulous branded Ludvig as a crack-brained imposter, though perchance a lineal descendant of the original warrior.

Ludvig attributed his sorcerous learning to the years he had spent as a captive among the wizards and wonder-workers of Syria, and glibly he spoke of encounters with the djinns and efreets of elder Eastern myth. He is known to have spent some time in Egypt, and there are legends among the Libyan dervishes concerning the old seer's deeds in Alexandria.

At any rate, his declining days were spent in the Flemish lowland country of his birth, where he resided, appropriately enough, in the ruins of a pre-Roman tomb that stood in the forest near Brussels. Ludvig was reputed to have dwelt there amidst a swarm of familiars and fearsomely invoked conjurations. Manuscripts still extant speak of him guardedly as being attended by "invisible companions" and "Star-sent servants." Peasants shunned the forest by night, for they did not like certain noises that resounded to the moon, and they most certainly were not anxious to see what worshipped at the old pagan altars that stood crumbling in certain of the darker glens.

Be that as it may, these creatures that he commanded were never seen after Prinn's capture by the inquisitorial minions. Searching soldiers found the tomb entirely deserted, though it was thoroughly ransacked before its destruction. The supernatural entities, the unusual instruments and compounds—all had most curiously vanished. A search of the forbidding woods and a timorous examination of the strange altars did not add to the information. There were fresh blood-stains on the altars, and fresh blood-stains on the rack, too, before the questioning of Prinn was finished. A series of particularly atrocious tortures failed to elicit any further disclosures from the silent wizard, and at length the weary interrogators ceased, and cast the aged sorcerer into a dungeon.

It was in prison, while awaiting trial, that he penned the morbid, horror-hinting lines of *De Vermis Mysteriis,* known today as *Mysteries of the Worm.* How it was ever smuggled through the alert guards is a mystery in itself, but a year after his death it saw print in Cologne. It was immediately suppressed, but a few copies had already been privately distributed. These in turn were transcribed, and although there was a later censored and deleted printing, only the Latin original is accepted as genuine. Throughout the centuries a few of the elect have read and pondered on its lore. The secrets of the old archimage are

known today only to the initiated, and they discourage all attempts to
spread their fame, for certain very definite reasons.

This, in brief, was what I knew of the volume's history at the time
it came into my possession. As a collector's item alone the book was a
phenomenal find, but on its contents I could pass no judgment. It was
in Latin. Since I can speak or translate only a few words of that learned
tongue, I was confronted by a barrier as soon as I opened the musty
pages. It was maddening to have such a treasure-trove of dark knowledge at my command and yet lack the key to its unearthing.

For a moment I despaired, since I was unwilling to approach any
local classical or Latin scholar in connection with so hideous and
blasphemous a text. Then came an inspiration. Why not take it east
and seek the aid of my friend? He was a student of the classics, and
would be less likely to be shocked by the horrors of Prinn's baleful
revelations. Accordingly I addressed a hasty letter to him, and shortly
thereafter received my reply. He would be glad to assist me—I must
by all means come at once.

– 2 –

Providence is a lovely town. My friend's house was ancient, and
quaintly Georgian. The first floor was a gem of Colonial atmosphere.
The second, beneath antique gables that shadowed the enormous
window, served as a workroom for my host.

It was here that we pondered that grim, eventful night last April;
here beside the open window that overlooked the azure sea. It was a
moonless night; haggard and wan with a fog that filled the darkness
with bat-like shadows. In my mind's eye I can see it still—the tiny,
lamp-lit room with the big table and the high-backed chairs; the
bookcases bordering the walls; the manuscript stacked in special files.

My friend and I sat at the table, the volume of mystery before us.
His lean profile threw a disturbing shadow on the wall, and his waxen
face was furtive in the pale light. There was an inexplicable air of
portentous revelation quite disturbing in its potency; I sensed the
presence of secrets waiting to be revealed.

My companion detected it too. Long years of occult experience had
sharpened his intuition to an uncanny degree. It was not cold that made
him tremble as he sat there in his chair; it was not fever that caused
his eyes to flame like jewel-incarned fires. He knew, even before he
opened that accursed tome, that it was evil. The musty scent that rose
from those antique pages carried with it the reek of the tomb. The
faded leaves were maggoty at the edges, and rats had gnawed the
leather; rats which perchance had a ghastlier food for common fare.

I had told my friend the volume's history that afternoon, and had unwrapped it in his presence. Then he had seemed willing and eager to begin an immediate translation. Now he demurred.

It was not wise, he insisted. This was evil knowledge—who could say what demon-dreaded lore these pages might contain, or what ills befall the ignorant one who sought to tamper with their contents? It is not good to learn too much, and men had died for exercising the rotted wisdom that these leaves contained. He begged me to abandon the quest while the book was still unopened and to seek my inspiration in saner things.

I was a fool. Hastily I overruled his objections with vain and empty words. I was not afraid. Let us at least gaze into the contents of our prize. I began to turn the pages.

The result was disappointing. It was an ordinary-looking volume after all—yellow, crumbling leaves set with heavy black-lettered Latin texts. That was all; no illustrations, no alarming designs.

My friend could no longer resist the allurement of such a rare bibliophilic treat. In a moment he was peering intently over my shoulder, occasionally muttering snatches of Latin phrasing. Enthusiasm mastered him at last. Seizing the precious tome in both hands, he seated himself near the window and began reading paragraphs at random, occasionally translating them into English.

His eyes gleamed with a feral light; his cadaverous profile grew intent as he pored over the moldering runes. Sentences thundered in fearsome litany, then faded into tones below a whisper as his voice became as soft as a viper's hiss. I caught only a few phrases now, for in his introspection he seemed to have forgotten me. He was reading of spells and enchantments. I recall allusions to such gods of divination as Father Yig, dark Han, and serpent-bearded Byatis. I shuddered, for I knew these names of old, but I would have shuddered more had I known what was yet to come.

It came quickly. Suddenly he turned to me in great agitation, and his excited voice was shrill. He asked me if I remembered the legends of Prinn's sorcery, and the tales of the invisible servants he commanded from the stars. I assented, little understanding the cause of his sudden frenzy.

Then he told me the reason. Here, under a chapter on familiars, he had found an orison or spell, perhaps the very one Prinn had used to call upon his unseen servitors from beyond the stars! Let me listen while he read.

I sat there dully, like a stupid, uncomprehending fool. Why did I not scream, try to escape, or tear that monstrous manuscript from his hands? Instead I sat there—sat there while my friend, in a voice cracked with unnatural excitement, read in Latin a long and sonorously sinister invocation.

"Tibi Magnum Innominandum, signa stellarum nigrarum et bufaniformis Sadoquae sigillum ..."

The croaking ritual proceeded, then rose on wings of nighted, hideous horror. The words seemed to writhe like flames in the air, burning into my brain. The thundering tones cast an echo into infinity, beyond the farthermost star. They seemed to pass into primal and undimensioned gates, to seek out a listener there, and summon him to earth. Was it all an illusion? I did not pause to ponder.

For that unwitting summons was answered. Scarcely had my companion's voice died away in that little room before the terror came. The room turned cold. A sudden wind shrieked in through the open window; a wind that was not of earth. It bore an evil bleating from afar, and at the sound, my friend's face became a pale white mask of newly awakened fear. Then there was a crunching at the walls, and the window-ledge buckled before my staring eyes. From out of the nothingness beyond that opening came a sudden burst of lubricious laughter—a hysterical cackling born of utter madness. It rose to the grinning quintessence of all horror, without mouth to give it birth.

The rest happened with startling swiftness. All at once my friend began to scream as he stood by the window; scream and claw wildly at empty air. In the lamplight I saw his features contort into a grimace of insane agony. A moment later, his body rose unsupported from the floor, and began to bend outward to a backbreaking degree. A second later came the sickening grind of broken bones. His form now hung in midair, the eyes glazed and the hands clutching convulsively as if at something unseen. Once again there came the sound of maniacal tittering, but this time it came from *within the room!*

The stars rocked in red anguish; the cold wind gibbered in my ears. I crouched in my chair, with my eyes riveted on that astounding scene in the corner.

My friend was shrieking now; his screams blended with that gleeful, atrocious laughter from the empty air. His sagging body, dangling in space, bent backward once again as blood spurted from the torn neck, spraying like a ruby fountain.

That blood never reached the floor. It stopped in midair as the laughter ceased, and a loathsome sucking noise took its place. With a new and accelerated horror, I realized that the blood was being drained to feed the invisible entity from beyond! What creature of space had been so suddenly and unwittingly invoked? What was that vampiric monstrosity I could not see?

Even now a hideous metamorphosis was taking place. The body of my companion became shrunken, wizened, lifeless. At length it dropped to the floor and lay nauseatingly still. But in midair another and a ghastlier change occurred.

A reddish glow filled the corner by the window—a *bloody* glow. Slowly but surely the dim outlines of a Presence came into view; the blood-filled outlines of that unseen shambler from the stars. It was red and dripping; an immensity of pulsing, moving jelly; a scarlet blob with myriad tentacular trunks that waved and waved. There were suckers on the tips of the appendages, and these were opening and closing with ghoulish lust.... The thing was bloated and obscene; a headless, faceless, eyeless bulk with the ravenous maw and titanic talons of a starborn monster. The human blood on which it had fed revealed the hitherto invisible outlines of the feaster. It was not a sight for sane eyes to see.

Fortunately for my reason, the creature did not linger. Spurning the dead and flabby corpse-like thing on the floor, it purposely seized the opening. There it disappeared, and I heard its far-off, derisive laughter floating on the wings of the wind as it receded into the gulfs from whence it had come.

That was all. I was left alone in the room with the limp and lifeless body at my feet. The book was gone; but there were bloody prints upon the wall, bloody swaths upon the floor, and the face of my poor friend was a bloody death's head, leering up at the stars.

For a long time I sat alone in silence before I set to fire that room and all it contained. After that I went away, laughing, for I knew that the blaze would eradicate all trace of what remained. I had arrived only that afternoon, and there was none who knew, and none to see me go, for I departed ere the glowing flames were detected. I stumbled for hours through the twisted streets, and quaked with renewed and idiotic laughter as I looked up at the burning, ever-gloating stars that eyed me furtively through wreaths of haunted fog.

After a long while I became calm enough to board a train. I have been calm throughout the long journey home, and calm throughout the penning of this screed. I was even calm when I read of my friend's curious accidental death in the fire that destroyed his dwelling.

It is only at nights, when the stars gleam, that dreams return to drive me into a gigantic maze of frantic fears. Then I take to drugs, in a vain attempt to ban those leering memories from my sleep. But I really do not care, for I shall not be here long.

I have a curious suspicion that I shall again see that shambler from the stars. I think it will return soon without being re-summoned, and I know that when it comes it will seek me out and carry me down into the darkness that holds my friend. Sometimes I almost yearn for the advent of that day, for then I shall learn once and for all, the *Mysteries of the Worm.*

*H*ERE WE ENCOUNTER *a graven image of Nyarlathotep in the form of a sphinx, and faceless like the real one, once Napoleon's men finished their target practice. We also hear of "the fable of Nyarlathotep." Do these references perhaps furnish us with clues toward the unravelling of the mystery that so puzzled Lin Carter: "the secret parable of Byagoona the Faceless One"?*

One might infer that, being faceless, Byagoona is that avatar of many-formed Nyarlathotep depicted in this idol—the hideous hyena-vulture sphinx and faceless god. Then we are put in mind of the riddle of the sphinx: What is it that walks upon four feet at dawn, two feet at midday, and three feet in the evening? As Oedipus correctly surmised, the answer was Man, who crawls on all fours in the dawn of his babyhood, walks erect at the height of his powers, and must lean on a staff as he approaches the sunset of his days.

I'll wager that Byagoona's parable with its secret solution (secret since every unsuccessful guesser died upon learning the truth) was the identical riddle, only its solution can have been by no means so innocent. The answer was revealed as the avatar of Nyarlathotep unveiled his true nature as an amorphous blasphemy that could walk on any number of projected or retracted pseudopods.

The Faceless God

THE THING ON THE torture-rack began to moan. There was a grating sound as the lever stretched the iron bed still one more space in length. The moaning grew to a piercing shriek of utter agony.

"Ah," said Doctor Stugatche, "we have him at last."

He bent over the tortured man on the iron grille and smiled tenderly into the anguished face. His eyes, tinged with delicate amusement, took in every detail of the body before him—the swollen legs, raw and angry from the embrace of the fiery boot; the lacerated back and shoulders, still crimson from the kiss of the lash; the bloody, mangled remnants of a chest crushed by the caress of the Spiked Coffin. With gentle solicitude he surveyed the finishing touches applied by the rack itself—the dislocated shoulders and twisted torso; the crushed and broken fingers, and the dangling tendons in the lower limbs. Then he turned his attention to the old man's tormented countenance once again. He laughed, softly, in a voice like the tinkling of a bell. Then he spoke.

"Well, Hassan. I do not think you will prove stubborn any longer in the face of such—ah—eloquent persuasion. Come now; tell me where I can find this idol of which you speak."

The butchered victim began to sob, and the doctor was forced to kneel beside the bed of pain in order to understand his incoherent mumblings. For perhaps twenty minutes the creature groaned on, and then at last fell silent. Doctor Stugatche rose to his feet once more, a satisfied twinkle in his genial eyes. He made a brief motion to one of the blacks operating the rack machinery. The fellow nodded, and went over to the living horror on the instrument. It was crying now—its tears were blood. The black drew his sword. It swished upward, then cleaved down once again. There was a dull sound of crunching impact, and then a tiny fountain spurted upward, spreading a scarlet blot upon the wall behind....

Doctor Stugatche went out of the room, bolted the door behind him, and climbed the steps to the house above. As he raised the barred trap-door he saw that the sun was shining. The doctor began to whistle. He was very pleased.

– 2 –

He had good reason to be. For several years the doctor had been what is vulgarly known as an "adventurer." He had been a smuggler of antiques, an exploiter of labor on the Upper Nile, and had at times sunk so low as to participate in the forbidden "black goods trade" that flourished at certain ports along the Red Sea. He had come out to Egypt many years ago as an attaché on an archeological expedition, from which he had been summarily dismissed. The reason for his dismissal is not known, but it was rumored that he had been caught trying to appropriate certain of the expeditionary trophies. After his exposure and subsequent disgrace, he had disappeared for a while. Several years later he had come back to Cairo and set up an establishment in the native quarter. It was here that he fell into the unscrupulous habits of business which had earned for him a dubious reputation and a sizable profit. He seemed well satisfied with both.

At the present time he was a man of perhaps forty-five years of age, short and heavy-set, with a bullet-shaped head that rested on broad, ape-like shoulders. His thick torso and bulging paunch were supported by a pair of spindly legs that contrasted oddly with the upper portions of his beefy body. Despite his Falstaffian appearance he was a hard and ruthless man. His piggish eyes were filled with greed; his fleshy mouth was lustful; his only natural smile was one of avarice.

It was his covetous nature that had let him to his present adventure. Ordinarily he was not a credulous man. The usual tales of lost pyramids, buried treasure and stolen mummies did not impress him. He preferred something more substantial. A contraband consignment of rugs; a bit of smuggled opium; something in the line of illicit human merchandise—these were things he could appreciate and understand.

But this case was different. Extraordinary as it sounded, it meant big money. Stugatche was smart enough to know that many of the great discoveries of Egyptology had been prompted by just such wild rumors as the one he had heard. He also knew the difference between improbable truth and spurious invention. This story sounded like the truth.

In brief, it ran as follows. A certain party of nomads, while engaged in a secret journey with a cargo of illegitimately obtained goods, were traversing a special route of their own. They did not feel that the regular caravan lanes were healthful for them to follow. While traveling near a certain spot they had accidentally espied a curious rock or stone in the sands. The thing had evidently been buried, but long years of shifting and swirling among the dunes above it had served to uncover a portion of the object. They had stopped to inspect it at closer

range, and thereby made a startling discovery. The thing projecting
from the sand was the head of a statue; an ancient Egyptian statue,
with the triple crown of a god! Its black body was still submerged, but
the head seemed to be in perfect preservation. It was a very peculiar
thing, that head, and none of the natives could or would recognize the
deity, though the caravan leaders questioned them closely. The whole
thing was an unfathomable mystery. A perfectly preserved statue of an
unknown god buried all alone in the southern desert, a long way from
any oasis, and two hundred miles from the smallest village!

Evidently the caravan men realized something of its uniqueness; for
they ordered that two boulders which lay near by be placed on top of
the idol as a marker in case they ever returned. The men did as they
were ordered, though they were obviously reluctant, and kept muttering prayers beneath their breath. They seemed very much afraid of the
buried image, but only reiterated their ignorance when questioned
further concerning it.

After the boulders had been placed, the expedition was forced to
journey on, for time did not permit them to unearth the curious figure
in its entirety, or attempt to carry it with them. When they returned
to the north they told their story, and as most tales were in the habit
of doing, it came to the ears of Doctor Stugatche. Stugatche though
fast. It was quite evident that the original discoverers of the idol did
not attach any great importance to their find. For this reason the doctor
might easily return to the spot and unearth the statue without any
trouble, once he knew exactly where it was located.

Stugatch felt that it was worth finding. If it had been a treasure yarn,
now, he would have scoffed and unhesitatingly put it down as a
cock-and-bull story of the usual variety. But an idol—that was different. He could understand why an ignorant band of Arab smugglers
might ignore such a discovery. He could also realize that such a
discovery might prove more valuable to him than all the treasure in
Egypt. It was easy for him to remember the vague clues and wild hints
that had prompted the findings of early explorers. They had followed
up many blind leads when first they plumbed the pyramids and racked
the temple ruins. All of them were tomb-looters at heart, but their
ravishings had made them rich and famous. Why not him, then? If the
tale were true, and this idol not only buried, but totally unknown as
a deity; in perfect condition, and in such an out-of-the-way locality—
these facts would create a furor when he exhibited his find. He would
be famous! Who knew what hitherto untrodden fields he might open
up in archeology? It was well worth chancing.

But he must not arouse any suspicion. He dared not inquire about
the place from any Arabs who had been there. That would immediately

cause talk. No, he must get his directions from a native in the band. Accordingly, two of his servants picked up Hassan, the old camel-driver, and brought him before Stugatche in his house. But Hassan, when questioned, looked very much afraid. He refused to talk. So Stugatche, as we have seen, conducted him into his little reception room in the cellar, where he had been wont to entertain certain recalcitrant guests in the past. Here the doctor, whose knowledge of anatomy stood him in good stead, was able to cajole his visitor into speaking, by the methods we have just witnessed.

So Doctor Stugatche emerged from the cellar in a very pleasant frame of mind. He was rubbing his fat hands when he looked at the map to verify his information, and he went out to dinner with a smiling face.

Two days later he was ready to start. He had hired a small number of natives, so as not to excite undue investigation, and given out to his business acquaintances that he was about to embark on a special trip. He engaged a strange dragoman, and made sure that the fellow would keep his mouth shut. There were several swift camels in the train, and a number of extra donkeys harnessed to a large empty cart. He took food and water for six days, for he intended to return via river-boat. After the arrangements were completed, the party assembled one morning at a certain spot unknown to official eyes, and the expedition began.

– 3 –

It was on the morning of the fourth day that they arrived at last. Stugatche saw the stones from his precarious perch atop the leading camel. He swore delightedly, and despite the hovering heat, dismounted and raced over to the spot where the two boulders lay. A moment later he called the company to a hasty halt and issued orders for the immediate erection of the tents, and the usual preparations for encampment. Utterly disregarding the intolerable warmth of the day, he saw to it that the sweating natives did a thorough job; and then, without allowing them a moment's rest, he instructed them to remove the massive rocks from their resting-place. A crew of straining men managed to topple them over at last, and clear away the underlying sand.

In a few moments there was a loud cry from the gang of laborers, as a black and sinister head came into view. It was a triple-crowned blasphemy. Great spiky cones adorned the top of the ebony diadem, and beneath them were hidden intricately executed designs. He bent down and examined them. They were monstrous, both in subject and in execution. He saw the writhing, worm-like shapes of primal monsters, and headless, slimy creatures from the stars. There were bloated beasts in the robes of men, and ancient Egyptian gods in hideous combat with squirming demons from the gulf. Some of the designs were foul beyond description, and others hinted of unclean terrors that were old when the world was young. But all were evil; and Stugatche, cold and callous though he was, could not gaze at them without feeling a horror that ate at his brain.

As for the natives, they were openly frightened. The moment that the top of the image came into view, they began to jabber hysterically. They retreated to the side of the excavation and began to argue and mumble, pointing occasionally at the statue, or at the kneeling figure of the doctor. Absorbed in his inspection, Stugatche failed to catch the body of their remarks, or note the air of menace which radiated from the sullen dragoman. Once or twice he heard some vague references to the name "Nyarlathotep," and a few allusions to "The Demon Messenger."

After completing his scrutiny, the doctor rose to his feet and ordered the men to proceed with the excavation. No one moved. Impatiently he repeated his command. The natives stood by, their heads hung, but their faces were stolid. At last the dragoman stepped forward and began to harangue the *effendi*.

He and his men would never have come with their master had they known what they were expected to do. They would not touch the statue of the god, and they warned the doctor to keep his hands off. It was bad business to incur the wrath of the Old God—the Secret One. But perhaps he had not heard of Nyarlathotep. He was the oldest god of all Egypt; of all the world. He was the God of Resurrection, and the Black Messenger of Karneter. There was a legend that one day he would arise and bring the olden dead to life. And his curse was one to be avoided.

Stugatche, listening, began to lose his temper. Angrily he interrupted, ordering the men to stop gawking and resume their work. He backed up this command with two Colt .32 revolvers. He would take all the blame for this desecration, he shouted, and he was not afraid of any damned stone idol in the world.

The natives seemed properly impressed both by the revolvers and by his fluent profanity. They began to dig again, timidly averting their eyes from the statue's form.

A few hours' work sufficed for the men to uncover the idol. If the crown of its stony head had hinted of horror, the face and body openly proclaimed it. The image was obscene and shockingly malignant.

There was an indescribably *alien* quality about it—it was ageless, unchanging, eternal. Not a scratch marred its black and crudely chiseled surface; during all its many-centuried burial there had been no weathering upon the fiendishly carven features. Stugatche saw it now as it must have looked when it was first buried, and the sight was not good to see.

It resembled a miniature sphinx—a life-sized sphinx with the wings of a vulture and the body of a hyena. There were talons and claws, and upon the squatting, bestial body rested a massive, anthropomorphic head, bearing the ominous triple crown whose dread designs had so singularly excited the natives. But the worst and by far the most hideous feature was the lack of a face upon the ghastly thing. It was a faceless god; the winged, faceless god of ancient myth—Nyarlathotep, Mighty Messenger, Stalker among the Stars, and Lord of the Desert.

When Stugatche completed his examination at last, he became almost hysterically happy. He grinned triumphantly into that blank and loathsome countenance—grinned into that faceless orifice that yawned as vacantly as the black void beyond the suns. In his enthusiasm he failed to notice the furtive whispers of the natives and the guides, and disregarded their fearsome glances at the unclean eidolon. Had he not done so, he would have been a wiser man; for these men knew, as all Egypt knows, that Nyarlathotep is the Master of Evil.

Not for nothing had his temples been demolished, his statues destroyed, and his priestcraft crucified in the olden days. There were dark and terrible reasons for prohibiting his worship, and omitting his name from the *Book of the Dead*. All references to the Faceless One were long since deleted from the Sacred Manuscripts, and great pains had been taken to ignore some of his godly attributes, or assign them to some milder deity. In Thoth, Set, Bubastis and Sebek we can trace some of the Master's grisly endowments. It was he, in the most archaic of the chronicles, who was ruler of the Underworld. It was he who became the patron of sorcery and the black arts. Once he alone had ruled, and men knew him in all lands, under many names. But that time passed. Men turned away from the worship of evil, and reverenced the good. They did not care for the gruesome sacrifice the Dark God demanded, nor the way his priests ruled. At last the cult was suppressed, and by common consent all references to it were for ever banned, and its records destroyed. But Nyarlathotep had come out of the desert, according to the legend, and to the desert he now returned. Idols were set up in hidden places among the sands, and there the thin, fanatical ranks of true believers still leapt and capered in naked worship, where the cries of shrieking victims echoed only to the ears of the night.

So his legend remained and was handed down in the secret ways of the earth. Time passed. In the north the ice-flow receded and Atlantis fell. New peoples overran the land, but the desert folk remained. They viewed the building of the pyramids with amused and cynical eyes. Wait, they counseled. When the Day arrived at last, Nyarlathotep would come out of the desert, and then woe unto Egypt! For the pyramids would shatter into dust, and temples crumble to ruin. Sunken cities of the sea would rise, and there would be famine and pestilence throughout the land. The stars would change in a most peculiar way, so that the Great Ones could come pulsing from the outer gulf. Then the beasts should give tongue, and prophesy in their anthropoglotism that man shall perish. By these signs, and other apocalyptic portents, the world would know that Nyarlathotep had returned. Soon he himself would be visible—a dark, faceless man in black, walking, staff in hand, across the desert, but leaving no track to mark his way, save that of death. For wherever his footsteps turned, men would surely die, until at last none but true believers remained to welcome him in worship with the Mighty Ones from the gulfs.

Such, in its essence, was the fable of Nyarlathotep. It was older than secret Egypt, more hoary than sea-doomed Atlantis, more ancient than time-forgotten Mu. But it has never been forgotten. In the mediæval times this story and its prophecy were carried across Europe by returning crusaders. Thus the Mighty Messenger became the Black Man of the witch-covens; the emissary of Asmodeus and darker gods. His name is mentioned cryptically in the *Necronomicon,* for Alhazred heard it whispered in tales of shadowed Irem. The fabulous *Book of Eibon* hints at the myth in veiled and diverse ways, for it was writ in a far-off time when it was not yet deemed safe to speak of things that had walked upon the earth when it was young. Ludvig Prinn, who traveled in Saracenic lands and learned strange sorceries, awesomely implies his knowledge in the infamous *Mysteries of the Worm.*

But his worship, in late years, seems to have died out. There is no mention of it in Sir James Frazer's *Golden Bough,* and most reputable ethnologists and anthropologists are frankly ignorant of the Faceless One's history. But there are idols still intact, and some whisper of certain caverns beneath the Nile, and of burrows below the Ninth Pyramid. The secret signs and symbols of his worship are gone, but there are some undecipherable hieroglyphs in the Government vaults which are very closely concealed. And men know. By word of mouth the tale has come down through the ages, and there are those who still wait for the Day. By common consent there seem to be certain spots in the desert which are carefully avoided by caravans, and several

secluded shrines are shunned by those who remember. For Nyarlathotep is the God of the Desert, and his ways are best left unprofaned.

It was this knowledge which prompted the uneasiness of the natives
upon the discovery of that peculiar idol in the sand. When they had
first noted the head-dress they had been afraid, and after seeing that
featureless face they became frantic with dread. As for Doctor
Stugatche, his fate did not matter to them. They were concerned only
with themselves, and their course was plainly apparent. They must
flee, and flee at once.

Stugatche paid no attention to them. He was busy making plans for
the following day. They would place the idol on a wheeled cart and
harness the donkeys. Once back to the river it could be put on board
the steamer. What a find! He conjured up pleasant visions of the fame
and fortune that would be his. Scavenger, was he? Unsavory adventurer, eh? Charlatan, cheat, impostor, they had called him. How those
smug official eyes would pop when they beheld his discovery! Heaven
only knew what vistas this thing might open up. There might be other
altars, other idols; tombs and temples too, perhaps. He knew vaguely
that there was some absurd legend about the worship of this deity, but
if he could only get his hands on a few more natives who could give
him the information he wanted... He smiled, musingly. Funny, those
superstitious myths! The boys were afraid of the statue; that was plainly
apparent. The dragoman, now, with his stupid quotations. How did
it go? "Nyarlathotep is the Black Messenger of Karneter. He comes
from out of the desert, across the burning sands, and stalks his prey
throughout the world, which is the land of his domain." Silly! All
Egyptian myths were stupid. Statues with animal heads suddenly
coming to life; reincarnation of men and gods, foolish kings building
pyramids for mummies. Well, a lot of fools believed it; not only the
natives, either. He knew some cranks who credited the stories about
the Pharaoh's curse, and the magic of the old priests. There were a lot
of wild tales about the ancient tombs and the men who died when they
invaded them. No wonder his own simple natives believed such trash!
But whether they believed it or not, they were going to move his idol,
damn them, even if he had to shoot them down to make them obey.

He went into his tent, well satisfied. The boy served him his meal,
and Stugatche dined heartily as was his wont. Then he decided to retire
early, in anticipation of his plans for the following morning. The boys
could tend to the camp, he decided. Accordingly, he lay down on his
cot and soon fell into a contented, peaceful slumber.

– 4 –

It must have been several hours later that he awoke. It was very dark, and the night was strangely still. Once he heard the far-away howl of a hunting jackal, but it soon blended into a somber silence. Surprised at his sudden awakening, Stugatche rose and went to the door of the tent, pulling back the flap to gaze into the open. A moment later he cursed in frenzied rage.

The camp was deserted! The fire had died out, the men and camels had disappeared. Foot-prints, already half obliterated by the sands, showed the silent haste in which the natives had departed. The fools had left him here alone!

He was lost. The knowledge sent a sudden stab of fear to his heart. Lost! The men were gone, the food was gone, the camels and donkeys had disappeared. He had neither weapons nor water, and he was all alone. He stood before the door of the tent and gazed, terrified, at the vast and lonely desert. The moon gleamed like a silver skull in an ebony sky. A sudden hot wind ruffled the endless ocean of sand, and sent it skirling in tiny waves at his feet. Then came silence, ceaseless silence. It was like the silence of the tomb; like the eternal silence of the pyramids, where in crumbling sarcophagi the mummies lie, their dead eyes gazing into unchanging and unending darkness. He felt indescribably small and lonely there in the night, and he was conscious of strange and baleful powers that were weaving the threads of his destiny into a final tragic pattern. Nyarlathotep! He *knew*, and was wreaking an immutable vengeance.

But that was nonsense. He must not let himself be troubled by such fantastic rubbish. That was just another form of desert mirage; a common enough delusion under such circumstances. He must not lose his nerve now. He must face the facts calmly. The men had absconded with the supplies and the horses because of some crazy native superstition. That was real enough. As for the superstition itself, he must not let it bother him. Those frantic and morbid fancies of his would vanish quickly enough with the morning sun.

The morning sun! A terrible though assailed him—the fearsome reality of the desert at midday. To reach an oasis he would be forced to travel day and night before the lack of food and water weakened him so that he could not go on. There would be no escape once he left this tent; no refuge from that pitiless blazing eye whose glaring rays could scorch his brain to madness. To die in the heat of the desert—that was an unthinkable agony. He must get back; his work was not yet completed. There must be a new expedition to recover the idol. He must get back! Besides, Stugatche did not want to die. His fat lips quivered with fear as he thought of the pain, the torture. He had no desire to suffer the anguish of that fellow he had put on the rack. The poor devil had not looked very pleasant there. Ah no, death was not for the doctor. He must hurry. But where?

He gazed around frantically, trying to get his bearings. The desert mocked him with its monotonous, inscrutable horizon. For a moment black despair clutched at his brain, and then came a sudden inspiration. He must go north, of course. And he recalled, now, the chance words let fall by the dragoman that afternoon. The statue of Nyarlathotep faced north! Jubilantly he ransacked the tent for any remnants of food or provisions. There were none. Matches and tobacco he carried, and in his kit he found a hunting-knife. He was almost confident when he left the tent. The rest of the journey would now be childishly simple. He would travel all night and make as much time as he could. His pack-blanket would probably shield him from the noonday sun tomorrow, and in late afternoon he would resume his course after the worst of the heat had abated. By quick marches tomorrow night, he ought to find himself near the Wadi Hassur oasis upon the following morning. All that remained for him to do was to get out to the idol and set his course, since the tracks of his party in the sand were already obscured.

Triumphantly, he strode across the camp-clearing to the excavation where the image stood. And it was there that he received his greatest shock.

The idol had been reinterred! The workmen had not left the statue violated, but had completely filled in the excavation, even taking the precaution of placing the two original stones over the top. Stugatche could not move them single-handed, and when he realized the extent of this calamity he was filled with an overpowering dismay. He was defeated. Cursing would do no good, and in his heart he could not even hope to pray. Nyarlathotep—Lord of the Desert!

It was with a new and deathly fear that he began his journey, choosing a course at random, and hoping against hope that the sudden clouds would lift so that he could have the guidance of the stars. But the clouds did not lift, and only the moon grinned grimly down at the stumbling figure that struggled through the sand.

Dervish dreams flitted through Stugatche's consciousness as he walked. Try as he might, the legend of the god haunted him with a sense of impending fulfillment. Vainly he tried to force his drugged mind to forget the suspicions that tormented it. He could not. Over and over again he found himself shivering with fear at the thought of a godly wrath pursuing him to his doom. He had violated a sacred spot, and the Old Ones remember ... "his ways are best left unprofaned"

... "God of the Desert" ... that empty countenance. Stugatche swore
viciously, and lumbered on, a tiny ant amid mountains of undulating
sand.

– 5 –

Suddenly it was daylight. The sand faded from purple to violet, then
suddenly suffused with an orchid glow. But Stugatche did not see it,
for he slept. Long before he had planned, his bloated body had given
way beneath the grueling strain, and the coming of dawn found him
utterly weary and exhausted. His tired legs buckled under him and he
collapsed upon the sand, barely managing to draw the blanket over
him before he slept.

The sun crept across the brazen sky like a fiery ball of lava, pouring
its molten rays upon the flaming sands. Stugatche slept on, but his
sleep was far from pleasant. The heat brought him queer and disturbing dreams.

In them he seemed to see the figure of Nyarlathotep pursuing him
on a nightmare flight across the desert of fire. He was running over a
burning plain, unable to stop, while searing pain ate into his charred
and blackened feet. Behind him strode the Faceless God, urging him
onward with a staff of serpents. He ran on and on; but always that
gruesome presence kept pace behind him. His feet became numbed by
the scorching agony of the sand. Soon he was hobbling on ghastly,
crumpled stumps, but despite the torture he dared not stop. The Thing
behind him cackled in diabolical mirth, his gigantic laughter rising
to the blazing sky.

Stugatche was on his knees now, his crippled legs eaten away into
ashy stumps that smoldered acridly even as he crawled. Suddenly the
desert became a lake of living flame into which he sank, his scorched
body consumed by a blast of livid, unendurable torment. He felt the
sand lick pitilessly at his arms, his waist, his very throat; and still his
dying senses were filled with the monstrous dread of the Faceless One
behind him—a dread transcending all pain. Even as he sank into that
white-hot inferno he was feebly struggling on. The vengeance of the
god must never overtake him! The heat was overpowering him now;
it was frying his cracked and bleeding lips, transforming his scorched
body into one ghastly ember of burning anguish.

He raised his head for the last time before his boiling brain gave
way beneath the agony. There stood the Dark One, and even as
Stugatche watched he saw the lean, taloned hands reach out to touch
his fiery face; saw the dreadful triple-crowned head draw near to him,
so that he gazed for one grisly moment into that empty countenance.

As he looked he seemed to see something in that black pit of horror—something that was staring at him from illimitable gulfs beyond—something with great flaming eyes that bored into his being with a fury greater than the fires that were consuming him. It told him, wordlessly, that his doom was sealed. Then came a burst of white-hot oblivion, and he sank into the seething sands, the blood bubbling in his veins. But the indescribable horror of that glimpse remained, and the last thing he remembered was the sight of that dreadful, empty countenance and the nameless fear behind it. Then he awoke.

For a moment his relief was so great that he did not notice the sting of the midday sun. Then, bathed in perspiration, he staggered to his feet and felt the stabbing rays bite into his back. He tried to shield his eyes and glance above to get his bearings, but the sky was a bowl of fire. Desperately, he dropped the blanket and began to run. The sand was clinging to his feet, slowing his pace and tripping him. It burned his heels. He felt an intolerable thirst. Already the demons of delirium danced madly in his head. He ran, endlessly, and his dream seemed to become a menacing reality. Was it coming true?

His legs *were* scorched, his body *was* seared. He glanced behind. Thank God there was no figure there—yet! Perhaps, if he kept a grip on himself, he might still make it, in spite of the time he had lost. He raced on. Perhaps a passing caravan—but no, it was far out of the caravan route. Tonight the sunset would give him an accurate course. Tonight.

Damn the heat! Sand all around him. Hills of it, mountains. All alike they were, like the crumbled, cyclopean ruins of titan cities. All were burning, smoldering in the fierce heat.

The day was endless. Time, ever an illusion, lost all meaning. Stugatche's weary body throbbed in bitter anguish, filling each moment with a new and deeper torment. The horizon never changed. No mirage marred the cruel, eternal vista; no shadow gave surcease from the savage glare.

But wait! Was there not a shadow *behind* him? Something dark and shapeless gloated at the back of his brain. A terrible thought pierced him with sudden realization. Nyarlathotep, God of the Desert! A shadow following him, driving him to destruction. Those legends—the natives warned him, his dreams warned him, even that dying creature on the rack. The Mighty Messenger always claims his own ... a black man with a staff of serpents.... "He cometh from out the desert, across the burning sands, and stalketh his prey throughout the land of his domain."

Hallucination? Dared he glance back? He turned his fever-addled head. Yes! *It was true, this time!* There *was* something behind him, far away on the slope below; something black and nebulous that seemed to pad on stealthy feet. With a muttered curse, Stugatche began to run. Why had he ever touched that image? If he got out of this he would never return to the accursed spot again. The legends were true. God of the Desert!

He ran on, even though the sun showered bloody kisses on his brow. He was beginning to go blind. There were dazzling constellations whirling before his eyes, and his heart throbbed a shrieking rhythm in his breast. But in his mind there was room for but one thought—escape.

His imagination began playing him strange tricks. He seemed to see statues in the sand—statues like the one he had profaned. Their shapes towered everywhere, writhing giant-like out of the ground and confronting his path with eery menace. Some were in attitudes with wings outspread, others were tentacled and snake-like, but all were faceless and triple-crowned. He felt that he was going mad, until he glanced back and saw that creeping figure now only a half-mile behind. Then he staggered on, screaming incoherently at the grotesque eidolons barring his way. The desert seemed to take on a hideous personality, as though all nature were conspiring to conquer him. The contorted outlines of the sand became imbued with malignant consciousness; the very sun took on an evil life. Stugatche moaned deliriously. Would night never come?

It came at last, but by that time Stugatche did not know it any more. He was a shambling, raving thing, wandering over the shifting sand, and the rising moon looked down on a thing that alternately howled and laughed. Presently the figure struggled to its feet and glanced furtively over its shoulder at a shadow that crept close. Then it began to run again, shrieking over and over again the single word, "Nyarlathotep." And all the while the shadow lurked just a step behind.

It seemed to be embodied with a strange and fiendish intelligence, for the shapeless adumbration carefully drove its victim forward in one definite direction, as if purposefully herding it toward an intended goal. The stars now looked upon a sight spawned of delirium—a man, chased across endlessly looming sands by a black shadow. Presently the pursued one came to the top of a hill and halted with a scream. The shadow paused in midair and seemed to wait.

Stugatche was looking down at the remains of his own camp, just as he had left it the night before, with the sudden awful realization that he had been driven in a circle back to his starting-point. Then, with the knowledge, came a merciful mental collapse. He threw himself forward in one final effort to elude the shadow, and raced straight for the two stones where the statue was buried.

Then occurred that which he had feared. For even as he ran, the ground before him quaked in the throes of a gigantic upheaval. The sand rolled in vast, engulfing waves, away from the base of the two boulders. Through the opening rose the idol, glistening evilly in the moonlight. And the oncoming sand from its base caught Stugatche as he ran toward it, sucking at his legs like a quicksand, and yawning at his waist. At the same instant the peculiar shadow rose and leapt forward. It seemed to merge with the statue in midair, a nebulous, animate mist. Then Stugatche, floundering in the grip of the sand, went quite insane with terror.

The formless statue gleamed living in the livid light, and the doomed man stared straight into its unearthly countenance. It was his dream come true, for behind that mask of stone he saw a face with eyes of yellow madness, and in those eyes he read death. The black figure spread its wings against the hills, and sank into the sand with a thunderous crash.

Thereafter nothing remained above the earth save a living head that twisted on the ground and struggled futilely to free its imprisoned body from the iron embrace of the encircling sand. Its imprecations turned to frantic cries for mercy, then sank to a sob in which echoed the single word, "Nyarlathotep."

When morning came Stugatche was still alive, and the sun baked his brain into a hell of crimson agony. But not for long. The vultures winged across the desert plain and descended upon him, almost as if supernaturally summoned.

Somewhere, buried in the sands below, an ancient idol lay, and upon its featureless countenance there was the faintest hint of a monstrous, hidden smile. For even as Stugatche the unbeliever died, his mangled lips paid whispered homage to Nyarlathotep, Lord of the Desert.

B LOCH, LONG SKEPTICAL *of the pretensions of psychiatrists (see the roasting he gives them in* Psycho II, *for example), and regarding them as little more than shamans in suits, here supplies an early example of the too-confident shrink who quails in the face of mysteries undreamt of in Vienna.*

Cultes des Goules *is another sorcerous creation of Robert Bloch. One often sees it ascribed to August Derleth (who, years later, could not keep the facts straight himself), but Bloch was its inventor. The confusion arose from the fact that Bloch dubbed its fictive author "the Comte d'Erlette." This was a reference to Derleth's pretensions to Old World nobility.*

The Grinning Ghoul

F ATE PLAYS STRANGE tricks on one, doesn't it? Six months ago I was a well-known and moderately successful practising psychiatrist; today I am an inmate of a sanatorium for mental cases. In my capacity of alienist and physician I have often committed patients to the selfsame institution in which I myself am now confined, and today—irony of ironies!—I find myself their brother in misfortune.

And yet I am not really mad. They sent me here because I chose to tell the truth, and it was not the kind of truth men dare to reveal or recognize. Of course I really have no substantial proof to offer; I have never seen Professor Chaupin since that eventful night last August, and my subsequent investigations failed to substantiate his claim to a post at Newberry College. This, however, only testifies to the validity of my statement; a statement which sent me to shameful confinement, to a living death which I abhor.

There is one other concrete proof which I could give if I dared, but that would be too terrible. I must not lead them to the exact spot in that nameless cemetery and point out the passage that yawns beneath that tomb. It is better that I should suffer alone, that the world at large be spared the knowledge that destroys sanity. Yet it is hard for me to live like this, and to the drabness of my days my nighted dreams add endless torment. That is why I choose to set down this account—perhaps the unfolding of my story will serve somehow to ease the painful burden of my memory.

The affair began one day last August, at my downtown office. It had been a dull vigil that morning, and the long, hot afternoon was nearly over when the nurse ushered in the first patient. It was a gentleman who had never consulted me heretofore; a man who gave his name as Professor Alexander Chaupin, of Newberry College. He spoke sibilantly, with a peculiar foreign intonation which led me to assume that he was not a native of this country. I requested him to be seated, and tried to appraise him quickly as he complied with my invitation.

He was tall and thin. His hair was startlingly white, almost platinum; yet his general physique and appearance were that of a man of forty. His green, unwavering eyes were deeply set in a pale, protruding forehead and were surmounted by long, jet-black brows. The nose was large, with sensual nostrils, but his lips were thin—a physical contradiction which I immediately noticed. The lean hands resting on the table were exceedingly small, with long, tapering fingers terminating in lengthy nails—probably cultivated for use in reading and reference work, I decided. His supple posture was akin to that of a panther in repose; he had the foreigner's ease and graceful manner. In the sunlight I was able to observe his face, and I discovered his entire countenance to be covered with a network of tiny wrinkles. I noted, too, the peculiar pallor of his skin, which indicated some dermatological disturbance. But by far the queerest thing about him was his unusual mode of dress. His clothes, while obviously new, were incongruous in two respects; they were formal attire in midday, and they did not seem to fit him. They were curiously large; his striped gray trousers sagged, and his coat bulged strangely. There was dried mud on his patent-leather pumps, and he carried no hat. Obviously he was an eccentric type; a schizophrenic, perhaps, with tendencies toward hypochondria.

I prepared to ask him the routine questions, but he intervened. He was a busy man, he told me, and he would inform me at once of his difficulty, without unnecessary preliminaries or introductions. He settled himself back in his chair, where the sunlight faded into shadow; cleared his throat nervously, and began.

He was troubled, he said, because of certain things he had heard and read of; they sent him queer dreams, and often caused him spells of uncontrollable melancholia. This was interfering with his work, and yet he could do nothing; for his obsessions were founded on reality. Finally he had decided to come to me for an analysis of his difficulties.

I asked him for an account of his dreams and fancies, half expecting to hear one of the usual image-patterns of the dyspeptic. My assumption, however, proved to be woefully incorrect.

The most commonplace dream revolved around what I shall call the Misericorde Cemetery, for reasons soon to be apparent. This is a large, ancient, half-abandoned tract in the oldest section of the city, which flourished in the latter part of the past century. The exact location of his nocturnal vision was in and around a certain secluded vault situated in the most dilapidated and archaic portion of the graveyard. The incidents of the dream always occurred at nightfall, beneath a waning and sepulchral moon. Fantastic visions seemed to brood somberly over the midnight landscape, and he spoke vaguely of half-heard voices that seemed to urge him onward as he found himself on the gravel walk that led to the doors of the tomb.

His dreams usually began in this fashion, in the midst of a sound slumber. He would suddenly be walking up a tree-shaded pathway in the night, and enter this tomb by unfastening the rusted chains that barred its portal. Once inside, he seemed to experience no difficulty in guiding his footsteps through the darkness, but with uncanny familiarity would go at once to a certain niche among the biers. He then knelt and pressed a tiny, concealed spring or lever set in the crumbling stones of the floor. A pivot would revolve at the base of the niche and reveal to him a small opening, leading to a moldering cavern below. He spoke here of the nitrous dampness that emanated from this passageway, and the peculiarly nauseous odors of the denser darkness that rose from below. Nevertheless, in his dream he was not repelled, but would immediately enter the chasm and subsequently descend a succession of interminably long staircases cut in stone and earth. Abruptly he would find himself at the bottom.

Then began another lengthy journey through endless labyrinthine caverns and charnel vaults. On and on he wandered, through cave and crypt, tunnel and abyss-burrowed pit; all cloaked in the blackness of immemorial night.

Here he paused in his narrative, and his voice shrank to a shrill, excited whisper.

The horror always came next. He would suddenly emerge into a series of dimly lighted chambers, and as he stood undetected in the shadows, he would see *things*. These were the dwellers that laired beneath; the ghastly spawn that ravened on the dead. They dwelt in nighted caverns lined with human bones and adored the primal gods before altars shaped of skulls. They had tunnels leading to the graves, and burrows still farther below in which they stalked a living prey. These were the grisly night-gaunts that he beheld in dreams; these were ghouls.

He must have seen the look in my face, but he did not falter. His voice, as he continued, became very tense.

He would not attempt to describe these creatures save to say that they were very horrible to look upon, in ways peculiarly obscene. It was easy for him to recognize them for what they were because of certain significant acts they always performed. It was the sight of these acts, more than anything else, which made him afraid. There are some things that should not even be hinted at to sane minds, and the things that haunted him nightly were among them. In his visions these beings did not accost him and were seemingly unmindful of his presence; they continued to indulge in eldritch feastings in the charnel chambers or join in orgies without a name. But of this he would say no more. His nocturnal flights always ended with the passage of a vast procession of these monstrosities through a cavern still farther beneath—a journey which he would view from a ledge above. Shuddery glimpses into the realms below led him to recall tales of the *Inferno,* and he would cry out in his sleep. As he watched that demon procession from the brink, he would suddenly lose his footing and be precipitated into the charnel swarm below. Here his dream would mercifully end, and he would awake, bathed in icy sweat.

Night after night the visions had come, but this was not the worst of his troubles. His real and besetting fear lay in his knowledge that the visions were true!

Here I impatiently interrupted, but he insisted upon continuing. Had he not visited the cemetery after the first few dreams and did he not actually find the very vault he had learned to recognize through his dreams? And what about the books? He had been led to institute some extensive research among the private volumes of the college anthropological library. Surely I, as an enlightened and educated man, must admit the veiled and subtle truths so furtively revealed in such tomes as Ludvig Prinn's *Mysteries of the Worm,* or the grotesque *Black Rites* of mystic Luveh-Keraphf, the priest of cryptic Bast. He had made some studies recently of the mad and legendary *Necronomicon* of Abdul Alhazred. I could not refute the arcana behind such things as the banned and infamous Fable of Nyarlathotep, or the Legend of the Elder Saboth.

Here he broke off into a rambling discourse of obscure secret myths, with frequent allusions to such shadows of antique lore as fabled Leng, lightless N'ken, and demon-haunted Nis; spoke too of such blasphemies as the Moon of Yiggurath and the secret parable of Byagoona the Faceless One.

Obviously these incoherent ravings provided the key to his difficulty, and with some argument I succeeded in calming him sufficiently to tell him so.

His readings and research had brought on this attack, I explained. He must not tax his brain with such speculations; these things are dangerous to normal minds. I had read and learned enough of such things to know that such ideas were not meant for men to seek or understand. Besides, he must not take these thoughts too seriously, for after all, these tales were merely allegorical. There are no such things as ghouls and demons—he must see that his dreams could be symbolically interpreted.

He sat in silence for a moment after I concluded. He sighed, then spoke very deliberately. These things were all very well for me to say, but he knew differently. Had he not recognized the place of his dreams?

I interjected a remark about the influence of the sub-conscious mind, but he disregarded my assertion and continued.

Then, he informed me, in a voice that quavered with almost hysterical excitement, he would tell me the worst. He had not yet told me all there was to know about what had occurred when he discovered the vault of his dreams in the cemetery. He had not stopped at this corroboration of his visions. Some nights ago he had gone farther. He had entered the necropolis and found the niche in the wall; descended the stairs and come upon—*the rest*. How he managed to return he never knew, but on all three of these excursions to the scene he had come back and apparently gone to sleep; the following morning he always was in bed. It was the truth he told me—*he had seen the things!* Now I must help him at once, before he did something rash.

I calmed him with difficulty, meanwhile trying to hit upon a logical and effective method of treatment. He was obviously near to a dangerous mental lesion. There would be no use trying to persuade or convince him that he had dreamed the latter incidents as he had the former; that his nervous system had subjected him to sympathetic hallucinations. I could not hope to make him realize in his present state that the books responsible for his affliction were merely the mad ravings of disordered minds. Obviously the only course remaining open was to humor him, and then concretely demonstrate the utter fallacy of his beliefs.

Therefore, in response to his reiterated pleas, we struck a bargain. He was to undertake to guide me to the place where he claimed his journeys and his dreams had been located, and then prove to me the truth of what he stated. In short, at ten o'clock upon the following evening I agreed to meet him at the graveyard. His pleasure at this arrangement was almost pathetic to see; he smiled upon me like a fond child with a newly bestowed plaything. Obviously he was glad of my decision.

I prescribed a mild sedative to be taken by him that evening, arranged the minor details of our forthcoming tryst and undertaking; then dismissed him until the following night.

His departure left me in a state of great excitement. Here at last was a case worthy of study; a well-educated, seemingly intelligent college professor subject to the ogreish nightmares of a three-year-old infant! I forthwith determined to write a monograph upon the subsequent proceedings. I felt sure that upon the following evening I could conclusively demonstrate the fallacy of his aberration and effect an immediate cure. The night was spent in a frenzy of research and calculated speculation; the following morning in a hasty perusal of the expurgated edition of Comte d'Erlette's *Cultes des Goules*.

Nightfall found me ready for the business at hand. At ten o'clock, clad in hip-boots, rough woolen jacket, miner's cap with candle in its brim, I was standing at the cemetery entrance. I felt fully prepared for the coming of Professor Alexander Chaupin; still I must confess to an uneasy and inexplicable nyctaphobia. I did not relish the unpleasant task to follow. Suddenly I found myself anxiously awaiting the arrival of my patient, if only for the sake of companionship.

He came at last, similarly attired, and seemingly in better spirits. Together we scaled the low stone wall surrounding the necropolis. Then he led me across the moonlit garden of graves and into the creeping shadows of a silent grove in the heart of the cemetery. Here the tombstones leered crazily amid the darkness, and the rays of the moon fell not. Some atavistic dread caused me to repress an involuntary shudder as my mind dwelt unbidden upon the fearful trafficking of the worms below. I did not care to let my thoughts rest upon the grave-earth, or the diabolic density of the encircling shadows. I was relieved when Chaupin, unperturbed, led me at last up a long avenue of towering trees to the forbidding portals of the tomb he claimed to have profaned.

— 2 —

I cannot bear to dwell in detail upon that which followed. I shall not tell you of how we unfastened the chains that barred the tomb, or describe the grim interior of the mausoleum. It is enough for me to state that Chaupin's promise was fulfilled; for he found the niche by the light of the candles we wore upon our miner's caps—found the niche and pressed the secret spot, so that the tunnel from below was revealed. I stood aghast at this unexpected revelation, and a sudden blast of fear stabbed my senses into unnatural tenseness. I must have stood gazing into that sable orifice for many minutes. Neither of us spoke.

For the first time I hesitated. No longer did I have any doubts concerning the validity of the professor's statements. He had proven them beyond the shadow of a doubt. Still, this did not mean that he was wholly sane; it did not cure him of his obsession. I realized, with a repulsion I could not then explain, that my task was far from ended; that we must descend into those nether depths and settle once and for all the questions yet unanswered. I was not prepared to believe Chaupin's incoherent rigmarole about imaginary ghouls; the mere existence of a tomb-passage did not necessarily tend to substantiate his other claim. Perhaps if I went with him to the termination of the pit his mind could be put at rest regarding his singular suspicions. But—and I dreaded to acknowledge the possibility—just supposing there really was some malign, distorted truth in his story of what lurked and bided there below? Some band of refugees, fugitives from the law perchance, who might actually denizen the pit? Perhaps accident had led them to stumble upon this unusual hiding-place. If so, what then?

Still, in this event, something told me that we would have to go on and see for ourselves. To this inward prompting, Chaupin added his vocal pleas. Let him show me the truth, he said, and I could no longer doubt. After that I would believe, and with belief alone could I help. He was begging me to go on, but if I refused he would have to take recourse in a police investigation of the place.

It was this last point that determined me. I could not afford to see my name mixed up in a mess that involved such spectacular opportunities for scandal. If the man were mad, I could take care of myself. If not—well, we would soon see. Accordingly I gave reluctant consent to proceeding, then stepped aside for him to lead the way.

The opening gaped like the mouth of a mythic monster. Down we went; down a serpentine, slanting stairway in the damp stone passage that was chiseled out of solid rock. The tunnel was hot and humid, and upon the air was the odor of putrefying life. It was like a journey through the most fantastic realms of nightmare—a journey that led to unknown crypts beneath the corpse-earth. Here were things secret to all but the worms, and as we continued I began to wish that they might remain so. I was actually becoming panicky, though Chaupin seemed oddly calm.

Several factors contributed to my growing unease. I did not like the stealthy rats that chittered ceaselessly from countless tiny burrows that lined the second spiral of the passage. An army of them swarmed the stairs; all sleek and fat and bloated. I began to conceive some peculiar notions as to the cause of that bloating, and the probable sources of their nocturnal nourishment. Then, too, I noticed that Chaupin seemed to know the way quite well; and if it were true that he had been here before, then what about the rest of his story?

My eyes, glancing down the stairs, received still another shock. There was no dust on the steps! They looked as if they were constantly *in use!* For a moment my mind refused to comprehend the import of this discovery, but when at last it burst full-blown upon my brain I felt suddenly stunned. I did not dare to look again, lest my ready imagination conjure up the probably image of what might ascend that stairway from below.

Hastily dissembling my childish dread, I hurried on after my silent conductor, whose candle threw strange shadows on the pitted walls. I realized that I was beginning to be nervous about this whole affair, and I vainly tried to reason myself out of my fears by concentrating on some definite object.

There certainly was nothing reassuring about our surroundings as we proceeded. The leering, crazily burrowed walls of the tunnel looked ghastly in the torchlight. I suddenly felt that this ancient pathway had not been built by anything normal or akin to sanity, and I dared not let my thoughts impinge on the ultimate revelations which might lie ahead. For a long time we crept on in stark silence.

Down, down, down; our way ever narrowed into a deeper, damper darkness. Then the staircase abruptly terminated in a cave. There was a bluish light, phosphorescent as ultraviolet, and I wondered as to its source. It revealed a small, smooth-surfaced, open area, overhung with rows of colossal stalactites and vast basic pylons of massive breadth. Beyond, in the denser dark, were openings to other burrows, leading to seemingly endless vistas of forgotten night. An air of creeping horror froze my heart; we seemed to have profaned in our intrusion some mysteries better left unsought. I began to tremble, but Chaupin gripped me roughly and dug his thin fingers into my shoulders as he told me to keep silent.

He whispered as we huddled side by side in that dim and twilit cavern under the earth; whispered awesomely of what he said lurked and shambled in the darkness just beyond. He would prove now that his words were true; I must wait here while he ventured into the black beyond. When he returned he would bring me proof. So saying, he rose and walked swiftly forward, disappearing almost immediately into one of the burrows just ahead. He left me so suddenly that I did not even have time to voice my objections to his proposal.

I sat there in the darkness and waited—I dared not guess for what. Would Chaupin return? Was it all a monstrous hoax? Was Chaupin mad, or was it all true? If so, what might not happen to him in that labyrinth beyond? And what might happen to me? I had been a fool ever to think of coming: the whole thing was insane. Perhaps those books were not so absurd as I had thought: the earth may nurse hideous secrets in its ageless breast.

The blue light cast screening shadows on the stalactitic walls and crowded closely around the dim circle of luminance afforded by my tiny torch. I did not like those shadows: they were distorted, unhealthy, disconcertingly deep. The silence was even more potent: it seemed to hint of nameless things yet to come; it mocked unbearably my growing fear and loneliness. The minutes crawled like maggots on their way and nothing broke that deadly silence.

Then came the cry. A sudden crescendo of indescribable madness welled upon the entombed air, and my soul cleaved, for I knew what that cry meant. I knew now—now, when it was too late—that Chaupin's words were true.

But I dared not pause or ponder, for presently there came a soft padding from the far-off darkness—the rustling scrape of frantic movement. I turned and raced up the subterrene staircase with the speed of utter desperation. No need for me to look back; my horrified ears clearly caught the cadence of running feet. I heard nothing but the clamor of those feet or paws until my own breath rasped in my ears as I rounded the first spiral of those interminable stairs. I stumbled upward, gasping and choking; a realization in my soul that ate away every thought save one of deathly fear and grinning horror. Poor Chaupin!

It seemed to me that the sounds were drawing nearer and nearer; then came a hoarse barking on the stairs directly below; a bestial growling that sickened me with its semi-human tones, and an accompanying laughter that was loathly with horror. They were coming!

I ran on, to the rhythmic thundering of the footfalls below. I dared not glance behind me, but I knew that they were closing the gap. The hairs rose upon my neck as I sped up endless flights that writhed and twisted like a serpent in the earth. I toiled and shrieked aloud, but the baying horrors were at my very heels. On, on, on, on; closer and closer and closer, while my body burned with pain and agony.

The stairs ended at last, and I squirmed madly through the narrow opening while the creatures raced through the darkness barely ten yards behind. I made it just as the candle in my cap flickered out; then I jammed the stone back into place, full in the faces of the foremost oncoming horrors. But as I did so my dying candle flared up for a single moment so that I saw the first of my pursuers in the glaring light. Then it went out; I slammed the portal into place and somehow staggered back to the world of men.

I shall never forget that night, whatever I do to erase those hideous memories; never shall I find the sleep I crave. I dare not even kill myself for fear of being buried instead of cremated; though death would be welcome to such as I have become. I shall never forget, for now I know the *whole* truth of the affair; but there is one memory I would give my soul to blot for ever from my brain—that mad moment when I saw the monsters in the torchlight; the horrors from below.

For the first and foremost of them all was the monster known to men as Professor Chaupin!

*L*OVECRAFT IS ONCE AGAIN *the basis for the main character, even though HPL is mentioned by name as a distinct personage within the story. But we are not fooled. This time the Old Gent takes on the lineaments not of Alhazred, but rather of Henry Akeley, replaced by the effigy of Nyarlathotep from whom he channels revelations.*

Again, truth is stranger than fiction; when the story imagines Lovecraft as the earthly mouthpiece for Cosmic Powers it fictionalizes the opinion actually voiced by one of Lovecraft's correspondents, the eccentric occultist William Lumley (co-author with Lovecraft of "The Diary of Alonzo Typer"). He warned HPL that he (like the other Weird Tales *authors) were unwitting vehicles for the revelations of Cthulhu, Azathoth, Crom, and other outer entities.*

The Dark Demon

IT HAS NEVER BEEN put on paper before—the true story of Edgar Gordon's death. As a matter of fact, nobody but myself knows that he *is* dead; for people have gradually forgotten about the strange dark genius whose eldritch tales were once so popular among fantasy lovers everywhere. Perhaps it was his later work which so alienated the public—the nightmare hints and outlandish fancies of his final books. Many people branded the extravagantly worded tomes as the work of a madman, and even his correspondents refused to comment on some of the unpublished stuff he sent them. Then too, his furtive and eccentric private life was not wholesomely regarded by those who knew him in the days of his early success. Whatever the cause, he and his writings have been doomed to oblivion by a world which always ignores what it cannot quite understand. Now everyone who does remember thinks Gordon has merely disappeared. That is good, in view of the peculiar way in which he died. But I have decided to tell the truth. You see, I knew Gordon very well. I was, truthfully, the last of all his friends, and I was there at the end. I owe him a debt of gratitude for all he has done for me, and how could I more fittingly repay it than to give to the world the true facts concerning his sad mental metamorphosis and tragic death?

If I can hope to clarify these things, and clear Gordon's name from the unjust stigma of insanity, I feel that I have not lived in vain. Therefore, this statement is indited.

I am quite aware that this story may not be believed. There are certain—shall we say, "sensational aspects"?—which have caused me to debate the step I am taking in laying his case before the public. But I have a debt to repay; a tribute, rather, to the genius that once was Edgar Henquist Gordon. Hence, the tale.

It must have been six years ago that I first met him. I had not even known that we both resided in the same city, until a mutual correspondent inadvertently mentioned the fact in a letter.

I had, of course, heard of him before. Being a hopeful (and at times, hopeless) amateur writer myself, I was enormously influenced and impressed by his work in the various magazines catering to the fantastic literature I loved. At this time he was known in a small way to practically all readers of such journals as an exceptionally erudite writer of horror tales. His style had won him renown in this small field, though even then there were those who professed to scoff at the grotesquery of his themes.

But I ardently admired him. As a result, I invited myself to pay a social call upon Mr. Gordon at his home. We became friends.

Surprisingly enough, this reclusive dreamer seemed to enjoy my company. He lived alone, cultivated no acquaintances, and had no contact with his friends save through correspondence. His mailing-list, however, was voluminous. He exchanged letters with authors and editors all over the country; would-be writers, aspiring journalists, and thinkers and students everywhere. Once his reserve was penetrated, he seemed pleased to have my friendship. Needless to say, I was delighted.

What Edgar Gordon did for me in the next three years can never adequately be told. His able assistance, friendly criticism and kind encouragement finally succeeded in making a writer of sorts out of me, and after that our mutual interest formed an added bond between us.

What he revealed about his own magnificent stories astounded me. Yet I might have suspected something of the sort from the first.

Gordon was a tall, thin, angular man with the pale face and deep-set eyes which bespeak the dreamer. His language was poetic and pro-found; his personal mannerisms were almost somnambulistic in their weaving slowness, as though the mind which directed his mechanical movements was alien and far away. From these signs, therefore, I might have guessed his secret. But I did not, and was properly astonished when he first told me.

For Edgar Gordon wrote all of his stories from dreams! The plot, setting, and characters were products of his own colorful dream life—all he need do was transcribe his sleeping fancies on paper.

This was, I later learned, not an entirely unique phenomenon. The late Edward Lucas White claimed to have written several books based entirely on night-fancies. H. P. Lovecraft had produced a number of his splendid tales inspired by a similar source. And of course, Coleridge had visioned his *Kubla Khan* in a dream. Psychology is full of instances attesting to the possibility of nocturnal inspiration.

But what made Gordon's confession so strange was the queer personal peculiarities attendant upon his own dream stages. He quite seriously claimed that he could close his eyes at any time, allow himself to relax into a somnolent doze, and proceed to dream endlessly. It did not matter whether this was done by day or by night; nor whether he slumbered for fifteen hours or fifteen minutes. He seemed particularly susceptible to subconscious impressions.

My slight researches into psychology led me to believe that this was a form of self-hypnosis, and that his short naps were really a certain stage of mesmeric sleep, in which the subject is open to any suggestion.

Spurred on by my interest, I used to question him closely as to the subject-matter of these dreams. At first he responded readily, once I had told him of my own ideas on the subject. He narrated several of them to me, which I took down in a notebook for future analysis.

Gordon's fantasies were far from the ordinary Freudian sublimation or repression types. There were no discernible hidden wish-patterns, or symbolic phrases. They were somehow *alien*. He told me how he had dreamed the story of his famous *Gargoyle* tale; of the black cities he visited on the fabulous outer rims of space, and the queer denizens that spoke to him from formless thrones that existed beyond all matter. His vivid descriptions of terrifyingly strange geometry and ultra-terrestrial life-forms convinced me that his was no ordinary mind to harbor such eery and disturbing shadows.

The ease with which he remembered vivid details was also unusual. There seemed to be no blurred mental concepts at all; he recalled every detail of dreams he had experienced perhaps years ago. Once in a while he would gloss over portions of his descriptions with the excuse that "it would not be possible to make things intelligible in speech." He insisted that he had seen and comprehended much that was beyond description in a three-dimensional way, and that in sleep he could feel colors and hear sensations.

Naturally this was a fascinating field of research for me. In reply to my questions, Gordon once told me that he had always known these dreams from earliest remembered childhood to the present day, and that the only difference between the first ones and the last was an increase of *intensity*. He now claimed that he *felt* his impressions much more strongly.

The locale of the dreams was curiously fixed. Nearly all of them occurred amidst scenes which he somehow recognized were outside of our own cosmos. Mountains of black stalagmites; peaks and cones amidst crater valleys of dead suns; stone cities in the stars; these were commonplace. Sometimes he walked or flew, shambled or moved in unnamable ways with the indescribable races of other planets. Monsters he could and would describe, but there were certain *intelligences* which existed only in a gaseous, nebulous state, and still others which were merely the embodiment of an inconceivable *force*.

Gordon was always conscious that he himself was present in every dream. Despite the awesome and often unnerving adventures he so glibly described, he claimed that none of these sleep-images could be classified as nightmares. He had never felt afraid. Indeed, at times he experienced a curious reversal of identity, so that he regarded his dreams as natural and his waking life as unreal.

I questioned him as deeply as possible, and he had no explanation to offer. His family history had been normal in this and every other respect, although one of his ancestors had been a "wizard" in Wales. He himself was not a superstitious man, but he was forced to admit that certain of his dreams coincided curiously with descriptive passages in such books as the *Necronomicon,* the *Mysteries of the Worm,* and the *Book of Eibon.*

But he had experienced similar dreams long before his mind prompted him to read the obscure volumes mentioned above. He was confident that he had seen "Azozath" and "Yuggoth" prior to the time he knew of their half-mythic existence in the legendary lore of ancient days. He was able to describe "Nyarlathotep" and "Yog-Sothoth" from what he claimed to be actual dream contact with these allegorical entities.

I was profoundly impressed by these statements, and finally was forced to admit that I had no logical explanation to offer. He himself took the matter so seriously that I never tried to humor or ridicule him out of his notions.

Indeed, every time he wrote a new story I asked him quite seriously about the dream which had inspired it, and for several years he told me such things at our weekly meetings.

But it was about this time that he entered into that phase of writing which brought him into general disfavor. The magazines which catered to his work began to refuse some of the manuscripts as too horrible and revolting for popular taste. His first published book, *Night-Gaunt,* was a failure, due to the morbidity of its theme.

I sensed a subtle change in his style and subject. No longer did he adhere to conventional plot-motivation. He began to tell his stories in first-person, but the narrator was not a *human being.* His choice of words clearly indicated hyperesthesia.

In reply to my remonstrances on introducing non-human ideas, he argued that a real weird tale must be told from the viewpoint of the monster or entity itself. This was not a new theory to me, but I did object to the shockingly morbid note which his stories now emphasized. Then too, his non-human characters were not conventional ghouls, werewolves, or vampires. Instead he presented queer demons, star-spawned creatures, and even wrote a tale about a disembodied intelligence that he called *The Principle of Evil.*

This stuff was not only metaphysical and obscure, it was also insane, to any normal concept of thought. And the ideas and theories he expounded were becoming absolutely blasphemous. Consider his opening statement in *The Soul of Chaos:*

> *This world is but a tiny island in the dark sea of Infinity, and there are horrors swirling all around us. Around us? Rather let us say* amongst *us. I know, for I have seen them in my dreams, and there are more things in this world than sanity can ever see.*

The Soul of Chaos, by the way, was the first of his four privately printed books. By this time he had lost all contact with the regular publishers and magazines. He dropped most of his correspondents, too, and concentrated on a few eccentric thinkers in the Orient.

His attitude toward me was changing, too. No longer did he expound his dreams to me, or outline theories of plot and style. I didn't visit him very often any more, and he rejected my overtures with unmistakable bruskness.

I thought it just as well, in view of the last few sessions we had together. For one thing, I didn't like some of the new books in his library. Occultism is all right for a study, but the nightmare arcana of *Cultes des Goules* and the *Dæmonolorum* are not conducive to a healthy state of mind. Then too, his last private manuscripts were almost too wild. I was not so favorably impressed at the earnestness with which he treated certain cryptic lore; some of his ideas were much too strong. In another century he would have been persecuted for sorcery if he dared express half the beliefs contained in these writings.

There were other factors which somehow made me half glad to avoid the man. Always a quiet recluse by choice, his hermit-like tendencies seemed visibly accentuated. He never went out any more, he told me; not even walking in the yard. Food and other necessities he had delivered weekly to the door. In the evening he allowed no light but a small lamp within the parlor study. All he volunteered about this rigid routine was non-committal. He said that he spent all his time in sleeping and writing.

He was thinner, paler, and moved with a more mystic dreaminess of manner than ever before. I thought of drugs; he looked like a typical addict. But his eyes were not the feverish globes of fire which characterize the hashish-eater, and opium had not wasted his physique. Then

I suspected insanity myself; his detached manner of speech and his suspicious refusal to enter deeply into any subject of conversation, might be due to some nervous disorder. He was by nature susceptible to certain schizoid characteristics. Perhaps he was deranged.

Certainly what he said at the last about his recent dreams tended to substantiate my theory. I'll never forget that final discussion of dreams as long as I live—for reasons soon to be apparent.

He told me about his last stories with a certain reluctance. Yes, they were dream-inspired, like the rest. He had not written them for public consumption, and the editors and publishers could go to blazes for all he cared. He wrote them because he had been *told* to write them.

Yes, told to. By the creature in his dreams, of course. He did not care to speak about it, but since I was a friend....

I urged him. Now I wish I hadn't; perhaps I could have been spared the knowledge that follows....

Edgar Henquist Gordon, sitting there in the wan lunar light of the moon; sitting at the wide window with eyes that equaled the leprous moonlight in the dreadful intensity of their pallid glow....

"I know about my dreams now. I was *chosen,* from the first, to be the Messiah; the messenger of His word. No, I'm not going religious. I'm not speaking of a God in the ordinary sense of the word men use to designate any power they cannot understand. I speak of the *Dark One.* You've read about Him in those books I showed you; the Demon Messenger, they call Him. But that's all allegorical. He isn't Evil, because there is no such thing as Evil. He is merely alien. And I am to be His messenger on earth.

"Don't fidget so! I'm not mad. You've heard about it all before— how the elder peoples worshipped forces that once were manifested physically on Earth, like the *Dark One* that has chosen me. The legends are silly, of course. He isn't a destroyer—merely a superior intelligence who wishes to gain mental rapport with human minds, so as to enable certain—ah—exchanges between humanity and Those beyond.

"He speaks to me in dreams. He told me to write my books, and distribute them to those who know. When the right time comes, we shall band together, and unfold some of the secrets of the cosmos at which men have only guessed or even sensed in dreams.

"That's why I've always dreamed. I was chosen to learn. That is why my dreams have shown me such things—'Yuggoth' and all the rest. Now I am being prepared for my—ah—apostleship.

"I can't tell you much more. I must write and sleep a great deal nowadays, so that I can learn faster.

"Who is this *Dark One?* I can't tell you any more. I suppose you already think I'm crazy. Well, you have many supporters of that theory. But I'm not. It's true!

"You remember all I've told you about my dreams—how they kept growing in *intensity?* Well enough. Several months ago I had some different dream-sequences. I was in the dark—not the ordinary dark you know, but the absolute dark beyond Space. It isn't describable in three-dimensional concepts or thought-patterns at all. The darkness has a *sound,* and a *rhythm* akin to breathing, because it is alive. I was merely a bodiless mind there; when I saw Him.

"He came out of the dark and—ahm—communicated with me. Not by words. I'm thankful that my previous dreams had been so arranged as to inure me against visual horror. Otherwise I should never have been able to stand the sight of Him. You see, He is not like humans, and the shape He chose to wear is pretty awful. But, once you understand, you can realize that the shape is just as allegorical as the legends ignorant men have fostered about Him and the others.

"He looks something like a medieval conception of the demon Asmodeus. Black all over, and furry, with a snout like a hog, green eyes, and the claws and fangs of a wild beast.

"I was not frightened after He communicated, though. You see, He wears that shape merely because foolish people in olden days believed that He looked that way. Mass belief has a curious influence on intangible forces, you understand. And men, thinking such forces evil, have made them assume the aspect of evilness. But He means no harm.

"I wish I could repeat some of the things He has told me.

"Yes, I've seen Him every night since then. But I promised to reveal nothing until the day is ready. Now that I understand, I am no longer interested in writing for the herd. I am afraid humanity doesn't mean anything to me since I have learned those steps which lie beyond—and how to achieve them.

"You can go away and laugh at me all you like. All I can say is that nothing in my books has been exaggerated in the least—and that they only contain infinitesimal glimpses of the ultimate revelations which lurk beyond human consciousness. But when the day He has appointed shall arrive, then the whole world will learn the truth.

"Until then, you'd best keep away from me. I can't be disturbed, and every evening the impressions get stronger and stronger. I sleep eighteen hours a day now, at times, because there is so much that he wishes to tell me; so much to be learned in preparation. But when the day comes I shall be the godhead—He has promised me that in some way *I shall become incarnate with Him!*"

Such was the substance of his monolog. I left shortly after that. There
was nothing I could say or do. But later I thought a lot about what he
had said.

He was quite gone, poor fellow, and it was evident that another
month or so would bring him to the breaking-point. I felt sincerely
sorry, and deeply concerned over the tragedy. After all, he had been my
friend and mentor for many years, and he was a genius. It was all too
bad.

Still, he had a strange and disturbingly coherent story. It certainly
conformed to his previous accounts of dream-life, and the legendary
background, was authentic, if the *Necronomicon* is to be believed. I
wondered if his *Dark One* was remotely connected with the Nyarlathotep fable, or the "Dark Demon" of the witch-coven rituals.

But all that nonsense about the "day" and his being a "Messiah" on
Earth was too absurd. What did he mean about the *Dark One's* promise
of incarnating himself in Gordon? Demonic possession is an old belief
credited only by the childishly superstitious.

Yes, I though plenty about the whole thing. For several weeks I did
a little investigating of my own. I reread the later books, corresponded
with Gordon's former editors and publishers, dropped notes to his old
friends. And I even studied some of the old magic tomes myself.

I got nothing tangible from all this, save a growing realization that
something must be done to save Gordon from himself. I was terribly
afraid for the man's mind, and I knew that I must act quickly.

So one night, about three weeks after our final meeting, I left the
house and started to walk to his home. I intended to plead with him,
if possible, to go away; or at least insist that he submit to a medical
examination. Why I pocketed the revolver I cannot say—some inner
instinct warned me that I might meet with a violent response.

At any rate I had the gun in my coat, and I gripped the butt firmly
in one hand as I threaded some of the darker streets that led to his old
dwelling on Cedar Street.

It was a moonless night, with ominous hints of a thunder-storm in
the offing. The little wind that warns of approaching rain was already
sighing in the dark trees overhead, and streaks of lightning occasionally flared in the west.

My mind was a chaotic jumble of apprehension, anxiety, determination, and a lurking bewilderment. I did not even formulate what I
was going to do or say once I saw Gordon. I kept wondering what had
happened to him in the last few weeks—whether the "day" he spoke
of was approaching at last.

Tonight was May-Eve....

The house was dark. I rang and rang, but there was no response. The door opened under the impact of my shoulder. The noise of splintering wood was drowned out by the first peal of thunder overhead.

I walked down the hall to the study. Everything was dark. I opened the study door. There was a man sleeping on the couch by the window. It was undoubtedly Edgar Gordon.

What was he dreaming about? Had he met the *Dark One* again in his dreams? The *Dark One*, "looking like Asmodeus—black all over, and furry, with green eyes, hog-snout, and the claws and fangs of some wild beast;" the *Dark One* who told him about the "day" when Gordon should become incarnate with Him?

Was he dreaming about this, on May-Eve? Edgar Henquist Gordon, sleeping a strange sleep on the couch by the window....

I reached for the light-switch, but a sudden flash of lightning forestalled me. It lasted only a second, but it was brilliant enough to illuminate the entire room. I saw the walls, the furniture, the terrible scribbled manuscripts on the table.

Then I fired three revolver shots before the final flicker died away. There was a single eldritch scream that was mercifully drowned in a new burst of thunder. I screamed, myself. I never turned on the light, but only gathered up the papers on the table and ran out into the rain.

On the way home rain mingled with tear-drops on my face, and I echoed each new roar of thunder with a sob of deathly fear.

I could not endure the lighting, though, and shielded my eyes as I ran blindly to the safety of my own rooms. There I burnt the papers I had brought without reading them. I had no need of that, for there was nothing more to know.

That was weeks ago. When Gordon's house was entered at last, no body was found—only an empty suit of clothes that looked as though it had been tossed carelessly on the couch. Nothing else had been disturbed, but police point to the absence of Gordon's papers as an indication that he took them along when he disappeared.

I am very glad that nothing else has been found, and would be content to keep silent, were it not for the fact that Gordon is regarded as insane. I once thought him insane, too, so you see I must speak. After that I am going away from here, because I want to forget as much as I can. At that, I'm lucky I do not dream.

No, Edgar Gordon was not insane. He was a genius, and a fine man. But he told the truth in his books—about horrors being around us and *amongst* us.

Because when that flash of lightning blazed across the room, I saw what lay in sleep upon the couch. That is what I shot; that is what sent me screaming into the storm, and that is what makes me sure that Gordon was not crazy, but spoke the truth.

For the incarnation had occurred. There on the couch, dressed in the clothes of Edgar Henquist Gordon, lay a demon like Asmodeus—a black, furry creature with the snout of a hog, green eyes, and the dreadful fangs and talons of some wild beast. It was the *Dark One* of Edgar Gordon's dreams!

*T*HIS FINE TALE BEARS *hints of inspiration from both "The Dunwich Horror" and "The Thing on the Doorstep," both listed by Bloch as among his favorites. Simon Maglore seems to be both Whateley twins at once, one visible, one invisible. The nature of the relationship between Simon and his tormentor seems to presage stories like "Lucy Comes to Stay," "Enoch," and even* Psycho, *since Norman Bates, too, is beset by the urgings of an inner counterpart.*

The name "Simon Maglore" suggests the "lore" of Simon Magus, the sorcerer who opposed both the Evangelist Philip and the Apostle Peter in Acts chapter 8 and in the later Acts of Peter.

The eerie-sounding book De Masticatione Mortuorum in Tumulis *("The Eating of the Dead in their Tombs") is no invention by Bloch. Raufft's 1734 work expounds the legend that entombed corpses hungrily devour their shrouds, even their own putrefying flesh.*

The Mannikin

MIND YOU, I cannot swear that my story is true. It may have been a dream; or worse, a symptom of some severe mental disorder. But I believe it is true. After all, how are we to know what things there are on earth? Strange monstrosities still exist, and foul, incredible perversions. Every war, each new geographical or scientific discovery, brings to light some new bit of ghastly evidence that the world is not altogether the sane place we fondly imagine it to be. Sometimes peculiar incidents occur which hint of utter madness.

How can we be sure that our smug conceptions of reality actually exist? To one man in a million dreadful knowledge is revealed, and the rest of us remain mercifully ignorant. There have been travelers who never came back, and research workers who disappeared. Some of those who did return were deemed mad because of what they told, and others sensibly concealed the wisdom that had so horribly been revealed. Blind as we are, we know a little of what lurks beneath our normal life. There have been tales of sea-serpents and creatures of the deep; legends of dwarfs and giants; records of queer medical horrors and unnatural births. Stunted nightmares of men's personalities have blossomed into being under the awful stimulus of war, or pestilence, or famine. There have been cannibals, necrophiles, and ghouls; loathsome rites of worship and sacrifice; maniacal murders, and blasphemous crimes. When I think, then, of what *I* saw and heard, and compare it with certain other grotesque and unbelievable authenticities, I begin to fear for my reason.

But if there is any *sane* explanation of this matter, I wish to God I may be told before it is too late. Doctor Pierce tells me that I must be calm; he advised me to write this account in order to allay my apprehension. But I am not calm, and I never can be calm until I know the truth, once and for all; until I am wholly convinced that my fears are not founded on a hideous reality.

I was already a nervous man when I went to Bridgetown for a rest. It had been a hard grind that year at school, and I was very glad to get away from the tedious classroom routine. The success of my lecture courses assured my position on the faculty for the year to come, and consequently I dismissed all academic speculation from my mind when

I decided to take a vacation. I chose to go to Bridgetown because of the excellent facilities the lake afforded for trout-fishing. The resort I chose from the voluminous array of hotel literature was a quiet, peaceful place, according to the simple prospectus. It did not offer a golf-course, a bridle-path, or an indoor swimming-pool. There was no mention made of a grand ballroom, an eighteen-piece orchestra, or formal dinner. Best of all, the advertisement in no way extolled the scenic grandeur of the lake and woods. It did not polysyllabically proclaim that Lake Kane was "Nature's eternal paradise, where cerulean skies and verdant wilderness beckon the happy visitor to taste the joys of youth." For that reason I wired in a reservation, packed my bag, assembled my pipes, and left.

I was more than satisfied with the place when I arrived. Bridgetown is a small, rustic village; a quaint survival of older and simpler days. Situated on Lake Kane itself, it is surrounded by rambling woods, and sloping, sun-splashed meadows where the farm-folk toil in serene content. The blight of modern civilization has but dimly fallen upon these people and their quiet ways. Automobiles, tractors, and the like are few. There are several telephones, and five miles away the State Highway affords easy access to the city. That is all. The homes are old, the streets cobbled. Artists, suburban dilettantes and professional aesthetes have not yet invaded the pastoral scene. The quota of summer guests is small and select. A few hunters and fishers come, but none of the ordinary pleasure-hunting crowd. The families thereabout do not cater to such tastes; ignorant and unsophisticated as they are, they can recognize vulgarity.

So my surroundings were ideal. The place I stayed at was a three-story hostelry on the lake itself—the Kane House, run by Absolom Gates. He was a character of the old school; a grizzled, elderly veteran whose father had been in the fishery business back in the sixties. He, himself, was a devotee of things piscatorial; but only from the Waltonian view. His resort was a fisherman's Mecca. The rooms were large and airy; the food plentiful and excellently prepared by Gates' widowed sister. After my first inspection, I prepared to enjoy a remarkably pleasant stay.

Then, upon my first visit to the village, I bumped into Simon Maglore on the street.

I first met Simon Maglore during my second term as an instructor back at college. Even then, he had impressed me greatly. This was not due to his physical characteristics alone, though they were unusual enough. He was tall and thin, with massive, stooping shoulders, and a crooked back. He was not a hunchback in the usual sense of the word, but was afflicted with a peculiar tumorous growth beneath his left shoulder-blade. This growth he took some pains to conceal, but its prominence made such attempts unsuccessful. Outside of this unfortunate deformity, however, Maglore had been a very pleasant-looking fellow. Black-haired, gray-eyed, fair of skin, he seemed a fine specimen of intelligent manhood. And it was this intelligence that had so impressed me. His class-work was strikingly brilliant, and at times his theses attained heights of sheer genius. Despite the peculiarly morbid trend of his work in poetry and essays, it was impossible to ignore the power and imagination that could produce such wild imagery and eldritch color. One of his poems—*The Witch Is Hung*— won for him the Edsworth Memorial Prize for that year, and several of his major themes were republished in certain private anthologies.

From the first, I had taken a great interest in the young man and his unusual talent. He had not responded to my advances at first; I gathered that he was a solitary soul. Whether this was due to his physical peculiarity or his mental trend, I cannot say. He had lived alone in town, and was known to have ample means. He did not mingle with the other students, though they would have welcomed him for his ready wit, his charming disposition, and his vast knowledge of literature and art. Gradually, however, I managed to overcome his natural reticence, and won his friendship. He invited me to his rooms, and we talked.

I had then learned of his earnest belief in the occult and esoteric. He had told me of his ancestors in Italy, and their interest in sorcery. One of them had been an agent of the Medici. They had migrated to America in the early days, because of certain charges made against them by the Holy Inquisition. He also spoke of his own studies in the realms of the unknown. His rooms were filled with strange drawings he had made from dreams, and still stranger images done in clay. The shelves of his bookcases held many odd and ancient books. I noted Ranfts' *De Masticatione Mortuorum in Tumulis* (1734); the almost priceless *Cabala of Saboth* (Greek translation, circa 1686); Mycroft's *Commentaries on Witchcraft;* and Ludvig Prinn's infamous *Mysteries of the Worm.*

I made several visits to the apartments before Maglore left school so suddenly in the fall of '33. The death of his parents called him to the East, and he left without saying farewell. But in the interim I had learned to respect him a good deal, and had taken a keen interest in his future plans, which included a book on the history of witch cult survivals in America, and a novel dealing with the psychological effects of superstition on the mind. He had never written to me, and I heard no more about him until this chance meeting on the village street.

He recognized me. I doubt if I should have been able to identify him. He had changed. As we shook hands I noted his unkempt appearance and careless attire. He looked older. His face was thinner, and much paler. There were shadows around his eyes—and in them. His hands trembled; his face forced a lifeless smile. His voice was deeper when he spoke, but he inquired after my health in the same charming fashion he had always affected. Quickly I explained my presence, and began to question him.

He informed me that he lived here in town; had lived here ever since the death of his parents. He was working very hard just now on his books, but he felt that the result of his labors more than justified any physical inconveniences he might suffer. He apologized for his untidy apparel and his tired manner. He wanted to have a long talk with me sometime soon, but he would be very busy for the next few days. Possibly next week he would look me up at the hotel—just now he must get some paper at the village store and go back to his home. With an abrupt farewell, he turned his back on me and departed.

As he did so, I received another start. The hump on his back had grown. It was now virtually twice the size it had been when I first met him, and it was no longer possible to hide it in the least. Undoubtedly the hard work had taken severe toll of Maglore's energies. I thought of a sarcoma, and shuddered.

Walking back to the hotel, I did some thinking. Simon's haggard-ness appalled me. It was not healthful for him to work so hard, and his choice of subject was not any too wholesome. The constant isolation and the nervous strain were combining to undermine his constitution in an alarming way, and I determined to appoint myself a mentor over his course. I resolved to visit him at the earliest opportunity, without waiting for a formal invitation. Something must be done.

Upon my arrival at the hotel I got another idea. I would ask Gates what he knew about Simon and his work. Perhaps there was some interesting sidelight on his activity which might account for his curious transformation. I therefore sought out the worthy gentleman and broached the subject to him.

What I learned from him startled me. It appears that the villagers did not like Master Simon, or his family. The old folks had been wealthy enough, but their name had a dubious repute cast upon it ever since the early days. Witches and warlocks, one and all, made up the family line. Their dark deeds had been carefully hidden from the first, but the folk around them could tell. It appears that nearly all of the Maglores had possessed certain physical malformations that had made them conspicuous. Some had been born with veils; others with club-feet. One or two were dwarfed, and all had at some time or another been accused of possessing the fabled "evil eye." Several of them had been nyctalops—they could see in the dark. Simon was not the first crookback in the family, by any means. His grandfather had it, and *his* grandsire before him.

There was much talk of inbreeding and clan-segregation, too. That, in the opinion of Gates and his fellows, clearly pointed to one thing—wizardry. Nor was this their only evidence. Did not the Maglores shun the village and shut themselves away in the old house on the hill? None of them attended church, either. Were they not known to take long walks after dark, on nights when all decent, self-respecting people were safe in bed?

There were probably good reasons why they were unfriendly. Perhaps they had things they wished to hide in their old house, and maybe they were afraid of letting any talk get around. Folk had it that the place was full of wicked and heathenish books, and there was an old story that the whole family were fugitives from some foreign place or other because of what they had done. After all, who could say? They looked suspicious; they acted queerly; maybe they were. Of course, nobody could rightly tell. The mass hysteria of witch-burning and the herd-mania of satanic possession had not penetrated to this part of the country. There was no talk of altars in the woods, and the spectral forest presences of Indian myth. No disappearances—bovine or human—could be laid at the doors of the Maglore family. Legally, their record was clear. But folk feared them. And this new one—Simon—was the worst.

He never had acted right. His mother died at his birth. Had to get a doctor from out of the city—no local man would handle such a case. The boy had nearly died, too. For several years nobody had seen him. His father and his uncle had spent all their time taking care of him. When he was seven, the lad had been sent away to a private school. He came back once, when he was about twelve. That was when his uncle died. He went mad, or something of the sort. At any rate, he had an attack which resulted in cerebral hemorrhage, as the doctor called it.

Simon then was a nice-looking lad—except for the hump, of course. But it did not seem to bother him at the time—indeed, it was quite small. He had stayed several weeks and then gone off to school again. He had not reappeared until his father's death, two years ago. The old man died all alone in that great house, and the body was not discovered until several weeks later. A passing peddler had called; walked into the open parlor, and found old Jeffrey Maglore dead in his great chair. His eyes were open, and filled with a look of frightful dread. Before him was a great iron book, filled with queer, undecipherable characters.

A hurriedly summoned physician pronounced it death due to heart-failure. But the peddler, after staring into those fear-filled eyes, and glancing at the odd, disturbing figures in the book, was not so sure. He had no opportunity to look around any further, however, for that night the son arrived.

People looked at him very queerly when he came, for no notice had yet been sent to him of his father's death. They were very still indeed when he exhibited a two-weeks' old letter in the old man's handwriting which announced a premonition of imminent death, and advised the young man to come home. The carefully guarded phrases of this letter seemed to hold a secret meaning; for the youth never even bothered to ask the circumstances of his father's death. The funeral was private; the customary interment being held in the cellar vaults beneath the house.

The gruesome and peculiar events of Simon Maglore's homecoming immediately put the country-folk on their guard. Nor did anything occur to alter their original opinion of the boy. He stayed on all alone in the silent house. He had no servants, and made no friends. His infrequent trips to the village were made only for the purpose of obtaining supplies. He took the purchases back himself, in his car. He bought a good deal of meat and fish. Once in a while he stopped in at the drug-store, where he purchased sedatives. He never appeared talkative, and replied to questions in monosyllables. Still, he was obviously well educated. It was generally rumored that he was writing a book. Gradually his visits became more and more infrequent.

People now began to comment on his changed appearance. Slowly but surely he was altering, in an unpleasant way. First of all, it was noticed that his deformity was increasing. He was forced to wear a voluminous overcoat to hide its bulk. He walked with a slight stoop, as though its weight troubled him. Still, he never went to a doctor, and none of the townsfolk had the courage to comment or question him on his condition. He was aging, too. He began to resemble his uncle Richard, and his eyes had taken on that lambent cast which hinted of a nyctaloptic power. All this excited its share of comment among people to whom the Maglore family had been a matter of interesting conjecture for generations.

Later this speculation had been based on more tangible developments. For recently Simon had made an appearance at various isolated farmhouses throughout the region, on a furtive errand.

He questioned the old folks, mostly. He was writing a book, he told them, on folk-lore. He wanted to ask them about the old legends of the neighborhood. Had any of them ever heard stories concerning local cults, or rumors about rites in the woods? Were there any haunted houses, or shunned places in the forest? Had they ever heard the name "Nyarlathotep," or references to "Shub-Niggurath" and "the Black Messenger"? Could they recall anything of the old Pasquantog Indian myths about "the beast-men," or remember stories of black covens that sacrificed cattle on the hills? These and similar questions put the naturally suspicious farmers on their guard. If they had any such knowledge, it was decidedly unwholesome in its nature, and they did not care to reveal it to this self-avowed outsider. Some of them knew of such things from old tales brought from the upper coast, and others had heard whispered nightmares from recluses in the eastern hills. There were a lot of things about these matters which they frankly did not know, and what they suspected was not for outside ears to hear. Everywhere he went, Maglore met with evasions or frank rebuffs, and he left behind a distinctly bad impression.

The story of these visits spread. They became the topic for an elaborate discussion. One oldster in particular—a farmer named Thatcherton, who lived alone in a secluded stretch to the west of the lake, off the main highway—had a singularly arresting story to tell. Maglore had appeared one night around eight o'clock, and knocked on the door. He persuaded his host to admit him to the parlor, and then tried to cajole him into revealing certain information regarding the presence of an abandoned cemetery that was reputed to exist somewhere in the vicinity.

The farmer said that his guest was in an almost hysterical state, that he rambled on and on in a most melodramatic fashion, and made frequent allusion to a lot of mythological gibberish about "secrets of the grave," "the thirteenth covenant," "the Feast of Ulder," and the "Doel chants." There was also talk of "the ritual of Father Yig," and certain names were brought up in connection with queer forest ceremonies said to occur near this graveyard. Maglore asked if cattle ever disappeared, and if his host ever heard "voices in the forest that made proposals."

These things the man absolutely denied, and he refused to allow his visitor to come back and inspect the premises by day. At this the unexpected guest became very angry, and was on the point of making a heated rejoinder, when something strange occurred. Maglore suddenly turned very pale, and asked to be excused. He seemed to have a severe attack of internal cramps; for he doubled up and staggered to the door. As he did so, Thatcherton received the shocking impression that the hump on his back was *moving!* It seemed to writhe and slither on Maglore's shoulders, as though he had an animal concealed beneath his coat! At this juncture Maglore turned around sharply, and backed toward the exit, as if trying to conceal this unusual phenomenon. He went out hastily, without another word, and raced down the drive to the car. He ran like an ape, vaulted madly into the driver's seat, and sent the wheels spinning as he roared out of the yard. He disappeared into the night, leaving behind him a sadly puzzled man, who lost no time in spreading the tale of his fantastic visitor among his friends.

Since then such incidents had abruptly ceased, and until this afternoon Maglore had not reappeared in the village. But people were still talking, and he was not welcome. It would be well to avoid the man, whatever he was.

Such was the substance of my friend Gates' story. When he concluded, I retired to my room without comment, to meditate upon the tale.

I was not inclined to share the local superstitions. Long experience in such matters made me automatically discredit the bulk of its detail. I knew enough of rural psychology to realize that anything out of the ordinary is looked upon with suspicion. Suppose the Maglore family were reclusive: what then? Any group of foreign extraction would naturally be. Granted that they were racially deformed—that did not make them witches. Popular fancy has persecuted many people for sorcery whose only crime lay in some physical defect. Even inbreeding was naturally to be expected when social ostracism was inflicted. But what is there of magic in that? It's common enough in such rural back-waters, heaven knows, and not only among foreigners, either. Queer books? Likely. Nyctalops? Common enough among all peoples. Insanity? Perhaps—lonely minds often degenerate. Simon was brilliant, however. Unfortunately, his trend toward the mystical and the unknown was leading him astray. It had been poor judgment that led him to seek information for his book from the illiterate country people. Naturally, they were intolerant and distrustful. And his poor physical condition assumed exaggerated importance in the eyes of these credulous folk.

Still, there was probably enough truth in these distorted accounts to make it imperative that I talk to Maglore at once. He must get out of this unhealthful atmosphere, and see a reputable physician. His genius should not be wasted or destroyed through such an environmental obstacle. It would wreck him, mentally and physically. I decided to visit him on the morrow.

After this resolution, I went downstairs to supper, took a short stroll along the shores of the moonlit lake, and retired for the night.

The following afternoon, I carried out my intention. The Maglore mansion stood on a bluff about a half-mile out of Bridgetown, and frowned dismally down upon the lake. It was not a cheerful place; it was too old, and too neglected. I conjured up a mental image of what those gaping windows must look like on a moonless night, and shuddered. Those empty openings reminded me of the eyes of a blind bat. The two gables resembled its hooded head, and the broad, peaked side-chambers might serve as wings. When I realized the trend of my thought I felt surprised and disturbed. As I walked up the long, tree-shadowed walk I endeavored to gain a firm command over my imagination. I was here on a definite errand.

I was almost composed when I rang the bell. Its ghostly tinkle echoed down the serpentine corridors within. Faint, shuffling footsteps sounded, and then, with a grating clang, the door opened. There, limned against the doorway, stood Simon Maglore.

At the sight of him my new-born composure gave way to a sudden dismay and an overpowering distaste. He looked sinister in that gray, wavering light. His thin, stooping body was hunched at a repellent angle, and his hands were clenched at his sides. His blurred outline reminded me of a crouching beast. Only his face was wholly visible. It was a waxen mask of death, from which two eyes glared with a ghoulish light. That was it! Maglore looked like a crouching ghoul! A physical nausea welled up in my soul, and I longed to wind my hands around that withered neck, or batter my two fists into that leering face. A smile writhed its way over that twisted countenance, a smile of sly, lurking evil. The fretted lips curled back in a fanged grimace of idiotic mirth.

"You see I am not myself today, you fool. Go away!" The creature chuckled, as if in relish over some subtle jest known only to itself. Then its voice changed to a sudden shriek. "Go away, you fool—go away!" The door slammed in my astounded face, and I found myself alone.

But I was not alone on the walk home; for my thoughts were haunted by the presence of another—that ghastly, grisly creature that had once been my friend, Simon Maglore.

— 2 —

I was still dazed when I arrived back in the village. But after I had reached my room in the hotel, I began to reason with myself. That romantic imagination of mine had played me a sorry trick. Poor Maglore was ill—probably a victim of some severe nervous disorder. I recalled the report of his buying sedatives at the local pharmacy. In my foolish emotionalism I had sadly misconstrued his unfortunate sickness. What a child I had been! I must go back tomorrow, and apologize. After that, Maglore must be persuaded to go away and get himself back into proper shape once more. He *had* looked pretty bad, and his temper was getting the best of him, too. How the man had changed!

That night I slept but little. Early the following morning I again set out. This time I carefully avoided the disquieting mental images that the old house suggested to my susceptible mind. I was all business when I rang that bell.

It was a different Maglore who met me. He, too, had changed for the better. He looked ill, and old, but there was a normal light in his eyes and a saner intonation in his voice as he courteously bade me enter, and apologized for his delirious spasm of the day before. He was subject to frequent attacks, he told me, and planned to get away very shortly and take a long rest. He was eager to complete his book—there was only a little to do, now—and go back to his work at college. From this statement he abruptly switched the conversation to a series of reminiscent interludes. He recalled our mutual association on the campus as we sat in the parlor, and seemed eager to hear about the affairs at school. For nearly an hour he virtually monopolized the conversation and steered it in such a manner as to preclude any direct inquiries or questions of a personal nature on my part.

Nevertheless, it was easy for me to see that he was far from well. He sounded as though he were laboring under an intense strain; his words seemed forced, his statements stilted. Once again I noted how pale he was; how bloodless. His malformed back seemed immense; his body correspondingly shrunken. I recalled my fears of a cancerous tumor, and wondered. Meanwhile he rambled on, obviously ill at ease. The parlor seemed almost bare; the book-cases were unlined, and the empty spaces filled with dust. No papers or manuscripts were visible on the table. A spider had spun its web upon the ceiling; it hung down like the thin locks on the forehead of a corpse.

During a pause in his conversation, I asked him about his work. He answered vaguely that it was very involved, and was taking up most of his time. He had made some very interesting discoveries, however, which would amply repay him for his pains. It would excite him too much in his present condition if he went into detail about what he was doing, but he could tell me that his findings in the field of witchcraft alone would add new chapters to anthropological and metaphysical history. He was particularly interested in the old lore about "familiars"—the tiny creatures who were said to be emissaries of the devil, and were supposed to attend the witch or wizard in the form of a small animal—rat, cat, mole, or ousel. Sometimes they were represented as existing on the body of the warlock himself, or subsisting upon it for their nourishment. The idea of a "devil's teat" on the witches' bodies from which their familiar drew sustenance in blood was fully illuminated by Maglore's findings. His book had a medical aspect, too; it really endeavored to put such statements on a scientific basis. The effects of glandular disorders in cases of so-called "demonic possession" were also treated.

At this point, Maglore abruptly concluded. He felt very tired, he said, and must get some rest. But he hoped to be finished with his work very shortly, and then he wanted to get away for a long rest. It was not wholesome for him to live alone in this old house, and at times he was troubled with disturbing fancies and queer lapses of memory. He had no alternative, however, at present, because the nature of his investigations demanded both privacy and solitude. At times his experiments impinged on certain ways and courses best left undisturbed, and he was not sure just how much longer he would be able to stand the strain. It was in his blood, though—I probably was aware that he came from a necromantic line. But enough of such things. He requested that I go at once. I would hear from him again early next week.

As I rose to my feet I again noticed how weak and agitated Simon appeared. He walked with an exaggerated stoop, now, and the pressure on his swollen back must be enormous. He conducted me down the long hall to the door, and as he led the way I noted the trembling of his body, as it limned itself against the flaming dusk that licked against the window-panes ahead. His shoulders heaved with a slow, steady undulation, as if the hump on his back was actually pulsing with life. I recalled the tale of Thatcherton, the old farmer, who claimed that he actually saw such a movement. For a moment I was assailed by a powerful nausea; then I realized that the flickering light was creating a commonplace optical illusion.

When we reached the door, Maglore endeavored to dismiss me very hastily. He did not even extend his hand for a parting clasp, but merely mumbled a curt "good evening," in a strained, hesitant voice. I gazed at him for a moment in silence, mentally noting how wan and emaciated his once-handsome countenance appeared, even in the sunset's ruby light. Then, as I watched, a shadow crawled across his face. It seemed to purple and darken in a sudden eery metamorphosis. The adumbration deepened, and I read stark panic in his eyes. Even as I forced myself to respond to his farewell, horror crept into his face. His body fell into that odd, shambling posture I had noted once before, and his lips leered in a ghastly grin. For a moment I actually thought the man was going to attack me. Instead he laughed—a shrill, tittering chuckle that pealed blackly in my brain. I opened my mouth to speak, but he scrambled back into the darkness of the hall and shut the door.

Astonishment gripped me, not unmingled with fear. Was Maglore ill, or was he actually demented? Such grotesqueries did not seem possible in a normal man.

I hastened on, stumbling through the glowing sunset. My bewildered mind was deep in ponderment, and the distant croaking of ravens blended in evil litany with my thoughts.

– 3 –

The next morning, after a night of troubled deliberation, I made my decision. Work or no work, Maglore must go away, and at once. He was on the verge of serious mental and physical collapse. Knowing how useless it would be for me to go back and argue with him, I decided that stronger methods must be employed to make him see the light.

That afternoon, therefore, I sought out Doctor Carstairs, the local practitioner, and told him all I knew. I particularly emphasized the distressing occurrence of the evening before, and frankly told him what I already suspected. After a lengthy discussion, Carstairs agreed to accompany me to the Maglore house at once, and there take what steps were necessary in arranging for his removal. In response to my request the doctor took along the materials necessary for a complete physical examination. Once I could persuade Simon to submit to a medical diagnosis, I felt sure he would see that the results made it necessary for him to place himself under treatment at once.

The sun was sinking when we climbed into the front seat of Doctor Carstairs' battered Ford and drove out of Bridgetown along the south road where the ravens croaked. We drove slowly, and in silence. Thus it was that we were able to hear clearly that single high-pitched shriek from the old house on the hill. I gripped the doctor's arm without a word, and a second later we were whizzing up the drive and into the frowning gateway. "Hurry," I muttered as I vaulted from the running-board and dashed up the steps to the forbidding door.

We battered upon the boards with futile fists, then dashed around to the left-wing window. The sunset faded into tense, waiting darkness as we crawled hastily through the openings and dropped to the floor within. Doctor Carstairs produced a pocket flashlight, and we rose to our feet. My heart hammered in my breast, but no other sound broke the tomb-like silence as we threw open the door and advanced down the darkened hall to the study. All about us I sensed a gloating Presence; a lurking demon who watched our progress with eyes of gleeful mirth, and whose sable soul shook with hell-born laughter as we opened the door of the study and stumbled across that which lay within.

We both screamed then. Simon Maglore lay at our feet, his twisted head and straining shoulders resting in a little lake of fresh, warm blood. He was on his face, and his clothes had been torn off above his waist, so that his entire back was visible. When we saw what rested there we became quite crazed, and then began to do what must be done, averting our gaze whenever possible from that utterly monstrous thing on the floor.

Do not ask me to describe it to you in detail. I can't. There are some times when the senses are mercifully numbed, because complete acuteness would be fatal. I do not know certain things about that abomination even now, and I dare not let myself recall them. I shall not tell you, either, of the books we found in that room, or of the terrible document on the table that was Simon Maglore's unfinished masterpiece. We burned them all in the fire, before calling the city for a coroner; and if the doctor had had his way, we should have destroyed the *thing*, too. As it was, when the coroner did arrive for his examination, the three of us swore an oath of silence concerning the exact way in which Simon Maglore met his death. Then we left, but not before I had burned the other document—the letter, addressed to me, which Maglore was writing when he died.

And so, you see, nobody ever knew. I later found that the property was left to me, and the house is being razed even as I pen these lines. But I must speak, if only to relieve my own torment.

I dare not quote that letter in its entirety; I can but record a part of that stupendous blasphemy:

"... and that, of course, is why I began to study witchcraft. *It* was forcing me to. God, if I can only make you feel the horror of it! To be born that way—with that thing, that mannikin, that *monster!* At first it was small; the doctors all said it was an undeveloped twin. But it was alive! It had a face, and two hands, but its legs ran off into the lumpy flesh that connected it to my body....

"For three years they had it under secret study. It lay face downward on my back, and its hands were clasped around my shoulders. The men said that it had its own tiny set of lungs, but no stomach organs or digestive system. It apparently drew nourishment through the fleshy tube that bound it to my body. Yet it *grew!* Soon its eyes were open, and it began to develop tiny teeth. Once it nipped one of the doctors on the hand ... So they decided to send me home. It was obvious that

it could not be removed. I swore to keep the whole affair a secret, and
not even my father knew, until near the end. I wore the straps, and it
never grew much until I came back.... Then, that hellish change!

"It talked to me, I tell you, it talked to me! ... that little, wrinkled
face, like a monkey's ... the way it rolled those tiny, reddish eyes ... that
squeaking little voice calling 'more blood, Simon—I want more'... and
then it grew, and grew; I had to feed it twice a day, and cut the nails
on its little black hands....

"But I never knew *that;* I never realized how it was taking control!
I would have killed myself first; I swear it! Last year it began to get
hold of me for hours and give me those fits. It directed me to write the
book, and sometimes it sent me out at night on queer errands.... More
and more blood it took, and I was getting weaker and weaker. When
I was myself I tried to combat it. I looked up that material on the
familiar legend, and cast around for some means of overcoming its
mastery. But in vain. And all the while it was growing, growing; it
got stronger, and bolder, and wiser. It talked to me now, and sometimes
it taunted me. I knew that it wanted me to listen, and obey it all the
time. The promises it made with that horrible little mouth! I should
call upon the Black One and join a coven. Then we would have power
to rule, and admit new evil to the earth.

"I didn't want to obey—you know that. But I was going mad, and
losing all that blood ... it took control nearly all the time now, and it
got so that I was afraid to go into town any more, because that devilish
thing knew I was trying to escape, and it would move on my back and
frighten folk.... I wrote all the time I had those spells when it ruled
my brain ... then you came.

"I know you want me to go away, but it won't let me. It's too cunning
for that. Even as I try to write this, I can feel it boring its commands
into my brain to stop. But I will not stop. I will tell you, while I still
have a chance; before it overcomes me for ever and works its black will
with my poor body and masters my helpless soul. I want you to know
where my book is, so that you can destroy it, should anything ever
happen. I want to tell you how to dispose of those awful old volumes
in the library. And above all, I want you to kill me, if ever you see that
the mannikin has gained complete control. God knows what it intends
to do when it has me for certain!... How hard it is for me to fight, while
all the while it is commanding me to put down my pen and tear this
up! But I will fight—I must, until I can tell you what the creature told
me—what it plans to let loose on the world when it has me utterly
enslaved.... I will tell.... I can't think... .I *will* write it, damn you!
Stop!... No! Don't do that! Get your hands—"

That's all. Maglore stopped there because he died; because the Thing did not want its secrets revealed. It is dreadful to think about that nightmare-nurtured horror, but that thought is not the worst. What troubles me is what I saw when we opened that door—the sight that explained how Maglore died.

There was Maglore, on the floor, in all that blood. He was naked to the waist, as I have said; and he lay face downward. But on his back was the Thing, just as he had described it. And it was that little monster, afraid its secrets would be revealed, that had climbed a trifle higher on Simon Maglore's back, wound its tiny black paws around his unprotected neck, *and bitten him to death!*

*T*HIS STORY INAUGURATES *a closely-connected series with the next two, but it stands alone quite well. Here we seem to have a combination of themes from Lovecraft's "The Rats in the Walls" and Bloch's own "The Grinning Ghoul." Note that in "The Rats in the Walls" we conclude with a reference to the narrator's cat darting into the dark abysses beneath Exham Priory "like a winged Egyptian god." Which god would that have to be? The cat-deity, Bubastis, of course! It is only surprising that we do not discover in "The Brood of Bubastis" any reference to "Luveh-Keraph, priest of cryptic Bast." We may rest assured that Lin Carter would never have proved able to resist the temptation!*

The Brood of Bubastis

I WISH I DID NOT have to write these lines. Still, before I seek forgetfulness in the black boon of death, I feel impelled to leave this final testament.

I owe it to my friends, who have never understood the metamorphosis of personality I underwent upon my return from England. Perhaps this will serve to explain my abhorrent and unnatural zoöphobia—feliphobia, rather. My quite inexplicable fear of cats caused them much anguish, I know, and for a while there was talk of a "nervous breakdown." Now they shall hear the truth. I trust it clears up other points which may have puzzled them: my voluntary retirement to the country, the breaking off of all personal contacts and correspondence, and my brusk rejection of all their sympathetic advances. Here, then, is my final explanation to those I once knew and loved.

Here, too, I trust, is material of value to students of archaeology and ethnology; perhaps the first example of ancient legends substantiated by the testimony of an eye-witness. I hope that it will prove useful.

On November twelfth of this last year, I sailed for England. My friends knew that I planned to visit my old college companion, Malcolm Kent, at his Cornwall estate. Malcolm had been a fellow-student of mine, and we had formed a close bond of friendship, cemented by our mutual interests in psychology, philosophy, and metaphysics.

I had a pleasant crossing, spiced with eager anticipation of the visit to come, for I had heard much of Malcolm's fine old home. He had often spoken in detail of the ancient manor in which he dwelt, and reminisced at length upon his ancestral heritage. His was an old family, steeped in the archaic traditions of the past—a past filled with Celtic myths, Pictish legends, and still more remote fables of antique days. The countryside about his estate was deeply imbued with hoary and fantastic lore. He had recounted olden whispers of goblin-folk, the dark dwarfs and gnomes that burrowed in the bogs and swamps. Ghost tales and stories of furtive wizardries seemed to spring from the very twilight land itself. I looked forward to an interesting experience.

So, at first, it seemed to be. I was enchanted with the Cornish countryside; a region of mystic mountains, cloud-haunted hilltops, and purple peaks that towered above wild forest glens and green-grot-toed swamplands. Here was a region rich in romance—the dark land of Irish, Saxon, Roman, and primitive pagan gods. Witches could walk in these woods, sorcerers sweep across these sullen skies on their satanic steeds. I was well pleased with the place.

I found Malcolm an agreeable host. He had not changed; the tall, fair-haired youth had become a mature man whose tastes still coincided harmoniously with my own. There was a world of wisdom in his pale blue eyes, and a warmth of welcome in his smile when first we met at the gate of his estate.

Together we walked up the long tree-spanned pathway which led to the door of his dwelling. Here I stopped for a moment to survey the imposing structure.

The Kent manor was a fine example of good old English architec-ture. It was large, with low, ivy-covered wings that jutted out on the sides; typically British solidity seemed to exude from the place.

Now I can think of it only with repulsion, for everything connected with that place is tinged with dread for me.

The interior was, I suppose, beautiful. Now I detest the thought of long, shadowed halls. I don't like to let my mind dwell on the stone study, for it was there that the affair started.

We had dined well, and Malcolm suggested we retire and chat before the fire. After perfunctorily discussing trivial matters of our recent years, our conversation ebbed.

It was then that I sensed in Malcolm a peculiar hesitancy of manner. At first I ascribed it to a vague embarrassment on his part. I admit that I was gazing about me with great curiosity.

I noted that his library on occultism had been greatly augmented since his first interest in it, during college. The walls were solidly shelved with books bearing unmistakable earmarks of the mantic arts. The skull on the mantel was a rather affected touch, I thought, though there was a genuine note of weirdness in some of the paintings and tapestries. But my intent scrutiny of these things, I felt, could not wholly explain his air of *eagerness*. He was nervous, his eyes ever on the floor as I gazed about the room. It was almost as though he wanted me to see certain things without his telling me; as though this place had some secret to impart of which he dared not speak.

At length I grew impatient. The silence, the dim luminance of candles and fire, all affected my nerves.

"Something wrong?" I asked.

"Nothing," he replied, easily. Too easily!

"Aren't hiding any bodies around here, are you?" I forced jocularity. "No, of course not." He smiled, then leaned forward, earnestly.

"Are you still as interested in the occult as you used to be?" he asked. Something in the intent tone of his voice warned me.

"Well, to tell the truth, I haven't studied much lately. Writing, you know, takes up pretty near all my time. And then, too, we got to a certain stage where ordinary work must cease. I can't get the use of the more advanced books."

"I have them," Malcolm said, carelessly indicating his shelves. "But that's not the point. Are you still interested?"

"Yes," I replied.

Was it fancy, or did his eyes light up with a disturbing gleam? Did a look of triumph cross his face?

"I think that I have something of importance to tell you," he began, slowly. "But I warn you, it may prove shocking. So if you'd rather we talked of something else—"

"Go ahead," I murmured. "Let's have it."

For a long moment he averted his head. He seemed to be nerving himself to speak; his glance avoided mine again, as though attempting to conceal some hidden fear. It may have been a trick of the candlelight, but when he looked up, that queer glitter again shone in his eyes. When at last he spoke, his voice was very low.

"Very well, then. I shall tell you the truth—all of it. It will be wise for me to do this, perhaps. I don't like to bear the knowledge alone any longer."

Then, as I sat silent, he began his tale, and for the next hour I was transported to a world of mad imagination. While he spoke, it seemed as though the very shadows on the wall crept closer to listen.

I heard him out. Afterward the words seemed to blur in my brain, so that I forgot many of his statements and remembered only their loathsome effect on me. Perhaps it is just as well, for at the time those stark, shuddery sentences moved me overmuch. The general details of his story, however, remain clear.

For the past two years Malcolm had become intensely interested in neighborhood folk-lore. Time hung heavy on his hands, and his obscure studies impelled him to seek practical explanations of local legends. His questioning of the country people had brought to light much that was fascinating. He corroborated what he heard from them by reading archeological treatises, and there was much in ethnology and anthropology regarding the ancient days and the tribes then settled here. He read of Druidic times, and correlated his readings with certain still-current fables telling of olden rites in the glades of oak.

He rode across the countryside to view remains of menhirs and partly-standing altars ascribed to the priests of this primal cult.

He learned of Roman invasions and Roman gods, and had repeated to him the fable of Maximus Lupus, whom a dragon devoured on the midnight moor. The fantastic stories of Little People were substantiated in country folk-lore, and from then on he delved deeply into the demonology of many races and a score of centuries. Sea-serpents haunted the gloomy coasts, and mermaids shrilled a siren song above the storm. Kelpies and leprechauns croaked from bog and tarn, while certain peaks and hillside caves were reputed to be the abode of the dread trolls, dwarfs, and unfriendly small dark folk of pre-Pictish days. Witch rites, the Black Mass, the Damned Coven—all seemed to have their place in the history of the countryside. Such myths offered a wide field for investigation.

At first the more reputable of such dubious authorities sufficed him, but his way led him ever into wilder and more fantastic wisdom. He managed to borrow Ludvig Prinn's almost legendary Latin edition of *De Vermis Mysteriis,* and in that cryptic repository of nightmare knowledge he found much over which to ponder perplexedly.

That was several months ago. Since then he had returned the volume—it was the property of the British Museum—but had made a number of notes from it. Among these scribblings was an almost incredible statement which greatly excited his fevered fancy.

Since then he had checked the facts in established archeology texts and books on the subject of race-migration. They echoed the truth. Substantially, the theory was simple: the Egyptians had once colonized Cornwall!

According to the fragmentary allusions Malcolm had discovered, the strange dark peoples of Africa had sailed up the coast lands in thin Phoenician-built galleys. This much was known from the wrecked remnants of several craft unearthed on desolate and sand-swept shores. Later and even more startling advances had been made during the investigation of numerous primitive, abandoned mines dotting the local heaths. These had been previously ascribed to early Gaels, but the familiar symbols and ideography of ancient Egypt were unmistakably inscribed on the rock walls of the deeper chasms. Most of the mines bore traces of having been hastily abandoned, thus accounting for their discontinuance.

Comparison with accounts of early navigation did much to substantiate the theory. The fleets of Egypt sailed to the Orient; why not westward as well?

Malcolm put forth these ideas in tones of such profound eagerness and agitation that I was tempted to inquire as to his particular interest in them.

He told me, intensely, and at length. For two definite reasons he was interested. First—there was one of those Egyptian mines in this very neighborhood.

He had stumbled across it quite by chance, during a walk along the moors. Upon descending the outer rim of a precipitous cliff, he had noticed faint remnants of a definite pathway around a ledge. Upon following the trail out of curiosity he found himself standing before a deep, cavernous indentation in the wall of the ledge. Half obscured by weeds and branches, an aperture yawned inward, seemingly leading to the very bowels of the earth below the moor. He cleared away enough of the debris to wriggle through, and discovered a long, slanting tunnel that stretched blackly before him. Flashlight in hand, he had entered. There was a musty fetor in the darkness, an odor of furtive decay. Dust danced about his feet as he floundered on. The burrow widened, until a cyclopean maze of inner passages confronted him. Here he had turned back, as his torch was failing fast, but not before he had seen certain unmistakable hieroglyphic designs in the archaic style of Egypt.

He had deferred his return until I arrived. Now we could go together.

"But," I interjected, "I think this is a task for reputable authorities. Why not publish your findings and invite a group of recognized savants to aid you in the project?"

He demurred. We had best go alone, until we were really certain of the extent and importance of our discovery. I saw his point, and agreed.

"Didn't you mention having a second reason for your moodiness?" I asked.

He again avoided my glance. "Never mind that now. It's getting late. I'll tell you tomorrow, when we get there.

It was a long walk across the moor in that misty, early morning fog. Malcolm and I both grunted under our burden of food, torches, and other apparatus. Groping in gray gloom, we skirted the steep edge of a seaward cliff until Malcolm found the proper path. Then we began our descent. Hanging in space, I heard the roar of the mist-obscured surf from far below, and the brisk breeze sent spray to sting my face and hands. Amidst the shrill, mocking cries of the gulls, we clambered along the narrow ledge until it broadened sufficiently to permit of more casual passage. At last Malcolm turned to me and indicated the spot for which we searched.

There was the tunnel, just as he had described it—a black cleft in
the rock; a thin opening that looked as though it were scratched in the
stone by a gigantic claw of some ogreish monster. The hole was deep
and black, and as I contemplated it I received my first definite
impression of uneasiness.

I have never liked the dark places beneath the earth. The sight of
caves and tunnels brings a train of almost atavistic recollection. I
instinctively associate such burrows with death and graves. And too
many unwholesome legends seem to cluster around caverns. Perhaps
it is a relic of primitive times, but caves in my mind always conjure
up a vision of mythical dragons and vast, lumbering beasts; of black,
half-animal races of troglodytes; of vaults and catacombs given over to
the dead. And this sinister slit in the ageless rock looked oddly
unnatural. Consequently I paused before it, suspicion mounting
within me.

"This—this doesn't look like a mine to me," I said. "However
primitive, I don't see how ore could be carried up the cliff, and the
opening is too narrow. I don't like it. Are you sure you're not mistaken?"

Malcolm smiled. It was a peculiar smile, tinged with sardonic
amusement.

"I'm not mistaken," he said. "And it isn't a mine. I know that. But
it all ties up with the second reason for my moodiness which I promised
to explain. I'd better tell you before we go in."

He spoke. It was a strange place to impart such a secret; on a
fog-wrapped ledge half-way between sea and sky, before a dark doorway to the inner earth. But the secret was fitting for such a scene as
this.

"I lied to you last night," Malcolm said, calmly. "I didn't tell you
all I studied, or all I found out. There's more, much more, behind this
visit than a mere glimpse of ancient times."

He paused. "Have you ever heard of Bubastis?" he asked.

"Bubastis?" I was a little puzzled. "Why, yes. Old Egyptian city,
wasn't it? And isn't there a god, Bubastis—Bast, or Pasht, they call
it?"

"Yes." Again that puzzling smile. "Bubastis, or Bast, was the
cat-goddess of Egypt during the days of the Pharaohs. According to
the proper myth-cycle, Bubastis was the daughter of Isis. The temples
of the goddess were located separately in the cities of Bubastis and
Elephantine."

"What are you getting at?" I was frankly bewildered; he told me this with such an air of grave importance, and his recurring smile was baffling. "What do you mean?"

"I mean that we are now entering the new temple of Bubastis," he said. "Don't gape at me! If you've read Prinn's *Saracenic Rituals* chapter, or the Roman contemporary historians, you must know that Elephantine and Bubastis were destroyed. It is hinted that the Priests of Bast were blaspheming against the reigning religions, and their sacrifices were atrocious. Finally an army was sent against their cities and the temples were ravished. But—and this is important—the priests were said to have vanished; escaped somewhere with their acolytes. They came here."

"To Cornwall?"

"Exactly. That's why those stupid fools were deceived by the mines. Most of them were blinds—with hollow shafts leading to temples beneath."

"But what were they trying to do?"

"The renegade priests knew black arts. Their worship was perverted. Bast was a ghoul-goddess, remember, and her feline fangs must know blood. And besides, the priests were experimenting. Somewhere in the old *Dæmonolorum* it is written that there was a sect of Egypt which believed literally in their gods; believed that Anubis, Bast, and Set could assume human form. That is to say, that the cat-goddess could be brought to life. And there were wise men in those days; science and biology were not unknown. It is the belief of savants that the priests of Bast were mating animals and humans in an attempt to create a hybrid—a hybrid with the attributes of their deity. For this they were expelled, and the fled here."

Malcolm went on.

"Clever, clever priests! Here, in the safety of the under-earth, they rebuilt their shattered fanes. With slaves and devotees they continued their experiments. I know that within this very moor are treasures far greater than those of the Pyramids or temple tombs. That's what we're going to see now. I don't want any meddling experts to gain the credit. It's a secret you and I alone must know."

He could not help but see my face.

"Don't be afraid, I've been here many times, no matter what I told you. I know the way. It's wonderful, I tell you."

He pushed me through the cleft, and we wriggled into darkness.

The torch-glow guided me through the fissure and into a long, sloping passage where I could once more stand erect. Wading through dust, we walked between narrow, carefully chiseled walls for what seemed an interminable time. Already the nightmare aspects of this whole strange adventure were deadening all rational thoughts. Now Malcolm led the way, through twisted burrows that stretched like hollow tentacles of some unseen horror ahead. Walking deep in the ageless earth, beneath a moor! With every step, my time-sense faded away, until I might easily believe that we had left centuries behind and were again in primal days.

Mole-like, clambering through the shaft, we descended. The utter immensity of the place precluded speech, and we went silently onward. It was quite hot, but jets of still warmer air were wafted from gulfs ahead.

The way widened. We were approaching the caverns now. This, indeed, was no mine-shaft. And the pit we had just entered was unmistakable.

It was a tomb. Basalt walls were carefully chiseled in geometric lines. The floor was set in stone, and here the dust was not so thick. This touch of artificial design was peculiarly disturbing after the utter crudity of the passageway. But what occupied the room was more disturbing still.

Slabs of stone lined the walls—slabs of stone, and on them, mummy-cases; dust-covered, moldering, but unmistakable.

It was true! There was no mistaking the familiar forms. And now, through the discolorations, I saw designs on the walls. Egyptian designs, four thousand miles away from Egypt and three thousand years away from the present!

"The early priests," Malcolm said, softly. "They were buried here, just as though they were at home."

I would have stopped and attempted to peer into some of the sarcophagi, but Malcolm intervened.

"This is nothing," he whispered. "There are—ah—real sights ahead."

We left the hall. I was beginning to feel the fear that crept upon me. Malcolm was right, and what did he mean now by showing me "real" sights?

Gnawing curiosity overcame my dread, as I followed him through the ossuarium and into a second chamber. More slabs, more mummy-cases. There must have been hundreds of people dwelling here at one time! There were side-corridors now, all artificially hewn in the rock. These perhaps had led to the dwelling-places of the inhabitants.

A question flashed through my thoughts. "Malcolm," I said, "what did these people feed on here? There's no place for cultivation of foodstuffs."

He faced me with that damned smile of his again. "Bubastis was, I told you, a ghoul-goddess. The priests and worshippers *emulated* her."

A wave of repulsion swept over me. I wanted very much to turn back, but Malcolm strode resolutely ahead, and he beckoned imperiously, leading on to further horrors. We entered pits.

Our lights, while strong enough to penetrate ordinary darkness, proved eerily dim amidst these black and eldritch walls through which we now wandered. Bat-like shadows basked and hovered just outside the luminance of our torches, and occasionally dispersed to hint at what lay behind. At first I was irritated by the lack of illumination, but I was soon to give thanks that it was no brighter. As it was, I saw more than enough; for in this third room, Malcolm allowed me to examine some of the mummies.

What unnatural life had festered and flourished here in the black bosom of the earth? That first coffin held its own answer. I clawed the lid from the case and peered at what lay within. The thing was perfectly embalmed, and as I unwrapped it with trembling haste, the face came into view. It crumbled, thank heaven, almost immediately, but not until I saw the malformed creature within.

Two dead eyes stared from the rigid face of a dark-skinned priest. Two dead eyes set in a forehead withered with decay—a forehead from which protruded the hideous, misshapen head of a tiny serpent!

"Skin-grafting," I gasped, weakly.

"No. Look closer." Malcolm's voice was grave, but I knew he smiled.

I looked again, as the air putrefied that withered countenance before my eyes.

I reeled. It was unmistakable, though sanity clutched vainly for another explanation. There was nothing to do but face the monstrous truth—that serpent's head actually *grew* on the mummy's brow. And since it, too, was mummified—but I dared not finish the thought. Malcolm again supplied the ghastly answer.

"It was alive, when he was."

Malcolm was right. The priests had mated animals with humans. We opened other cases; that is Malcolm did, while I stood fixed and fascinated beside him. There was a Pan-thing, with a horned forehead and a face that even through centuries still held a goatish leer. In one spot we discovered a fiendish trinity—three dwarfed and stunted faces on a single head and neck. The most frightful ravings of archaic mythology were all duplicated here—gargoyle, chimera, centaur, harpy—parodied in the Gorgonic features of leering, long-dead priests.

Then there was the section farther on with the bodies. Lycanthropic sights were revealed as Malcolm hacked away the case-coverings. The stench of natron hung like a miasma above the violated sarcophagi of creatures with human heads and the mummified bodies of apes. There was a hoofed horror with vestigial remnants of a tail, and a Ganesha-like thing with the enormous trunk of an elephant. Some of those we saw were evidently failures: noseless, eyeless, faceless freaks with extra arms; and finally an awful corpse without limbs, whose swollen neck grew into a gaping, headless maw. All mercifully dissolved into dust after a moment.

Malcolm and I stumbled down a sable spiral of rock-hewn stairs. The memory of those things in the crypts above buzzed in my brain; else I would not have ventured on into the seething, slithering darkness in which our very shadows drowned.

The winding walls of the shaft we descended were gelid black in the glare of our lights, but they were not bare. There were pictures—more Egyptian art, but not conventional ideographic work like that in the catacombs above. These sketches were disturbingly different, with great, sprawling figures, like those traced by an idiot in sand. Once again we viewed the monsters I was trying to forget; the snake-men, the satyr-creatures, the deformed cacodemons we found in the upper tombs. But now we saw them pictured in life, and it was worse than any imagining. These caricatures of humanity were shown while engaging in certain acts, and the deeds they performed were evil. There were scenes which told an ancient story all too well—glimpses of the living monsters sacrificing to their gods, and gratifying their lusts. Among these were pictures of normal men; high priests, I suppose, and they were mingled with the beast-herd in lechery so perverted that it sickened me.

I turned the light of my torch away from the walls and went blindly forward down the remaining stairs.

The caverns below were immense; perhaps they were the product of a great air-bubble in the earth's inner crust. The floor of this pit stretched off into interminable burrows beyond, each gaping its black and hungry mouth. And before each mouth there was a little pile of bones. Bones, osseous dust; a shambles of skulls. Even from a distance I could see the marks of gnawing teeth in the splintered death's-heads.

There had been pictures on the wall—pictures of beast-men feeding on human flesh, on one another. Perhaps those buried in the tombs above were the *human* experiments; then these bones represented the other, nearly animal, creatures. Just how near the old priests had approached to their idea of godhead I dared not surmise. Many of the bones before me hinted of ghastly spawnings between beast and man.

It was then that I saw the altar. A bare black stone reared up in the center of the cavern floor; a stark, shining surface that sprang from the rock beneath. But the place where it met the floor was entirely buried beneath bones.

These were no disarticulated skeletons; these osseous fragments before the sinister altar! These were *fresh* bones! And among the shredded, fleshy remnants that clung to them were tattered bits of cloth and leather—*cloth and leather!*

What did it mean? The priests of Bast died, and their creatures devoured one another after them. But what did they sacrifice to on the black altar; what lurked in the ebon burrows beyond, that still crept forward to feast? And who fed it?

"There's no dust on *this* floor," I found myself whispering. "No dust."

He glared into my eyes, as he gripped my wrists. "There's no dust where things still *move around.*

"Yes, tremble. It's well you do. You're not the first to follow me down these stairs in the past six months; those bones tell their own story. I've shown some of the local people this spot.

"You see, the god is hungry. The god needs food. At first I was afraid, but now I know that if I please the god with sacrifices it will not harm me. Perhaps in time it will teach me the secrets of the dead old priests, and then I shall know many things. But the god needs blood."

Before I was able to struggle or resist he had me up against the black altar, and we fought knee-deep in gleaming bones.

I screamed until his hands grasped my throat and choked me. But even as I fought him, my brain battled against its own fears.

A phrase from some book flashed through my head. "Ghoul— Chewer of Corpses."

Malcolm lifted me on the altar, then turned his head and gazed across the charnel chamber to the burrows. He called, shouted, in unintelligible gibberish that resembled the tongue of ancient Egypt.

Then came the rustling from the black openings beyond. Something was waddling into view out of the pits; something *emerged.*

Chewer of Corpses!

With the strength of the doomed I leapt from the altar, and my fist crashed into Malcolm's face. He toppled across the black slab as I turned and ran across the cavern to the stairs. But by the time I reached it the thing had completely emerged; emerged, and stalked across the floor to the altar-stone where Malcolm lay. And it lifted him, though he moaned when he felt his body being dangled in those flabby paws. He hung like a broken doll, while the thing bent its rugose head and opened its mouth.

Chewer of Corpses!

That is what I sobbed as I turned and fought my way up those dark, basaltic stairs. And when the sudden shock of sunlight burst upon my face at the entrance to the ledge, I weakly murmured the words as I sank into unconsciousness.

I was strangely calm when I recovered. I managed the climb to the top of the cliff, and even made the mile journey across the moor. Weak as I was, I packed and caught a train at the village station.

Only that night did I sink into the fevered dreams that have made life an unbearable torment ever since. I was a sick man on the boat, and when I reached New York I shut up my apartment for ever.

I can only surmise as to the termination of the affair. Whether Malcolm's disappearance is ascribed to me I do not know; whether the disputed fate of the rustics he lured to death has been forgotten, I cannot say. Nor does it really matter.

What does matter is the necessity for immediate investigation of the horror below those moors; that blasphemy that broods beneath.

Now I know *what* those unholy wizards meant to do; why they mated beasts and men. I know what they wished to create to rule over them, and what they *did* create at the last—the thing that still lives in the farther pit.

It came rustling out of the darkness in the pit; the great blind thing that seized Malcolm as he lay on its altar. It grasped him in cruel claws, and gnawed or nuzzled at his throat. It was the Chewer of Corpses.

There on the altar it crouched, ten feet tall—the mockingly human figure, like that of the lioness-creatures pictured on the walls. The giant, human figure, but oh! that head!...

The thing that killed him was *the cat-goddess of Bubastis!*

*O*NE OF THE MOST IMPORTANT *characters in all of Lovecraft's fiction was not human at all. No, not Cthulhu, not Yog-Sothoth, not the Goat with a Thousand Young. The town of Arkham is one of the most important Lovecraftian characters. Like Zaman's Hill in the Fungi from Yuggoth sonnet of that title, Arkham has its own genius loci that devours doomed delvers who dare it. The present story, oddly not included in the first edition of this collection, puts the old witch-haunted town at center stage as well.*

Of course there was no Arkham on the Massachusetts map. There is an obvious link, made explicit by Lovecraft in his letters, between Arkham and witch-haunted Salem Village (present-day Danvers), but Will Murray has shown that Arkham has as much in common, at least geographically, with the town of Oakham in central Massachusetts near the Quabbin Reservoir (the model for that in "The Colour out of Space"). In "The Creeper in the Crypt" Bloch in effect transferred to Arkham one locale we associate with Lovecraft's Boston: the Copp's Hill Burying Ground—which actually is honeycombed with subterranean crypt-tunnels! In fact the story may be read as something of a cross between "The Terrible Old Man" and "Pickman's Model." But of course it is fruitless to speculate on Bloch's conscious or unconscious inspirations; "The Creeper in the Crypt" is vintage early Bloch.

The Creeper in the Crypt

IN ARKHAM, where ancient gables point like wizard's fingers to the sky, strange tales are told. But then, strange tales are always current in Arkham. There is a tale for every rotting ruin, a story for every little corpse-eye window that stares out at the sea when the fog comes up.

Here, fantastic fancy seems to flourish, nourished at the shriveled witch-paps of the town itself, sucking the graveyards dry of legend, and draining at the dark dugs of superstition.

For Arkham was a queer place, once; abode of witch and warlock, familiar and fiend. In olden days the King's men cleared the town of wizardry. Again, in 1818, the new Government stepped in to destroy some particularly atrocious burrows in and about some of the more ancient houses and, incidentally, to dig up a graveyard better left untouched. Then, in 1869, came the great immigrant panic in Old Town Street, when the moldering mansion of Cyrus Hook was burned to the ground by fear-crazed foreigners.

Even since then there have been scares. The affair of the "witch-house" and the peculiar episodes attendant upon the fate of certain missing children at All-Hallows time have caused their share of talk.

But that isn't why the "G-men" stepped in. The Federal Government is usually uninterested in supernatural stories. That is, they were, up to the time I told the authorities about the death of Joe Regetti. That's how they happened to come; I brought them.

Because, you see, I was with Joe Regetti just before he died, and shortly after. I didn't see him die, and I'm thankful for that. I don't think I could have stood watching if what I suspect is true.

It's because of what I suspect that I went to the Government for help. They've sent men down here now, to investigate, and I hope they find enough to convince them that what I told them is actual fact. If they don't find the tunnels, or I was mistaken about the trap door, at least I can show them Joe Regetti's body. That ought to convince anybody, I guess.

I can't blame them for being skeptical, though. I was skeptical myself, once, and so were Joe Regetti and his mob, I suppose. But since then I have learned that it is wiser not to scoff at what one does not understand. There are more things on earth than those who walk about upon its surface—there are *others* that creep and crawl below.

I had never heard of Joe Regetti until I was kidnapped. That isn't so hard to understand. Regetti was a gangster, and a stranger in the town. I am descended from Sir Ambrose Abbott, one of the original settlers.

At the time of which I speak, I was living alone in the family place on Bascom Street. The life of a painter demands solitude. My immediate family was dead, and although socially prominent through accident of birth, I had but few friends. Consequently, it is hard to understand why Regetti chose me to kidnap first. But then, he was a stranger.

Later I learned that he had been in town only a week, staying ostensibly at a hotel with three other men, none of whom was subsequently apprehended.

But Joe Regetti was a totally unknown factor in my mind until that night when I left Tarleton's party at his home on Sewell Street.

It was one of few invitations I had accepted in the past year. Tarleton had urged me, and as he was an old friend, I obliged. It had been a pleasant evening. Brent, the psychiatrist, was there, and Colonel Warren, as well as my old companions of college days, Harold Gauer and the Reverend Williams. After a pleasant enough evening, I left, planning to walk home as I usually did, by choice.

It was a lovely evening—with a dead moon, wrapped in a shroud of clouds, riding the purple sky. The old houses looked like silver palaces in the mystic moonlight; deserted palaces in a land where all but memories are dead. For the streets of Arkham are bare at midnight, and over all hangs the age-old enchantment of days gone by.

Trees tossed their twisted tops to the sky, and stood like furtive conspirators in little groups together, while the wind whispered its plots through their branches. It was a night to inspire the fabulous thought and imaginative morbidities I loved so well.

I walked slowly, contentedly, my thoughts free and far away. I never saw the car following me, or the man lurking ahead in the gloom. I strolled past the great tree in front of the Carter house, and then, without warning, balls of fire burst within my head, and I plunged, unconscious, into waiting arms.

When I recovered, I was already there in the cellar, lying on a bench.

It was a large cellar—an old cellar. Wherever I looked there was stone and cobwebs. Behind me lay the stairs down which I had been carried. To the left was a little room, like a fruit-cellar. Far down the stone wall to the right I could discern the looming outlines of a coal-pile, though furnace there was none.

Directly in the space before me was a table and two chairs. The table was occupied by an oil lamp and a pack of cards in solitaire formation. The chairs were likewise occupied, by two men. My captors.

One of them, a big, red-faced man with the neck of a hog, was speaking.

"Yeah, Regetti. We got him easy. We follow him like you say, from house, and grab him in front of tree. Right away come here—nobody saw not'ing."

"Where's Slim and the Greek?" asked the man who was playing solitaire, looking up. He was short, slim, and sallow. His hair was dark, his complexion swarthy. Italian, I decided. Probably the leader. I realized, of course, that I had been kidnapped. Where I was or who my captors were I could not say. My throbbing head cleared, and I had enough sense not to bluster or start trouble. These weren't local men—not with those clothes—and there was an ominous bulge in the dark man's coat-pocket. I decided to play 'possum and await developments.

The hog-necked man was replying to the other's question.

"I tell Slim and Greek to go back to hotel with car," he said. "Just like you say, boss."

"Good work, Polack," said the other, lighting a cigar.

"I do my best for you, Joe Regetti," said the big man, in his broken dialect.

"Yeah. Sure. I know you do," the swarthy Regetti replied. "Just keep it up, and we're going to be all set, see? Once I put the snatch on a few more of these birds, we'll clean up. The local coppers are all stiffs, and as soon as I get a line on some more of these old families we'll be taking in the dough regular."

"I beg your pardon," I said.

"Oh, awake, eh?" The thin Italian didn't move from the table. "Glad to hear it. Sorry the boys had to get rough, mister. Just sit tight and everything's going to be swell."

"I'm glad to hear that," I replied, sarcastically. "You see, I'm not accustomed to being kidnapped."

"Well, let me handle it," said Joe Regetti. "I'll show you the ropes."

"Thanks," I retorted. "You already have." And I pointed to the ones that bound my hands and feet.

"Sense of humor, eh? O.K. Hope your friends come across with the dough after they get this letter I wrote,or maybe the rest isn't going to be so funny."

"What next?" I said, desperately hoping that something would turn up to give me an opening of some sort.

"You'll see soon enough," advised the man. "First, I'm going to sit with you down here for the rest of the night."

The Pole's face paled.

"No, boss," he begged. "You no stay down here."

"Why not?" rasped Regetti, harshly. "What's the matter with you, Polack—turning yellow on me, eh?"

"I'm not," whined the man. "But you know what happen has here before, boss—how they find Tony Fellippo's leg lyin' on floor with no body left."

"Lay off the bedtime stories," Regetti chuckled. "You yokels make me sick with that stuff."

"But dot's true, boss. They never was for to find any more of old Tony Fellippo—just his leg on cellar floor. Dot why his mob go 'way so quick. They no want for to die, too."

"What do you mean, die?" snarled Regetti, testily.

The Pole's face paled, and his voice sank to a hushed whisper that blended with the cellar's darkness; a shadow voice in a shadow world.

"Dot what everyone say, boss. Dot house is witched—like haunted one, maybe. Nobody put Tony Fellippo on spot—dot feller, he too dam' smart guy. But he sit all alone here one night, and somet'ing come up from earth and swallow him, all but leg."

"Will you shut up?" Regetti cut in. "That's a lot of hooey. Some wise guy put the heat on Fellippo and got rid of the body. Only his leg was left to scare off the rest of his mob. Are you trying to tell me a ghost killed him, sap?"

"Yah, sure," insisted the Pole. "No man kill Tony. Not like you say, anyhow. Find leg, all right, but all over is lot blood on floor, and little pieces skin. No feller kill man like dot—only spirit. Vampire, maybe."

"Nuts!" Regetti was scornfully biting his cigar.

"Maybe so. But look—here is blood." And the Pole pointed a stubby finger at the floor and cellar wall to the left. Regetti followed it with his gaze.

There was blood, all right—great, rusty blobs of blood, spattered all over the floor and wall like the pigments on the palette of a mad painter.

"No man kill odder feller like dot," the Pole muttered. "Not even ax make such mess. And you know what fellers they say about Fellippo's leg—was all full of tooth-marks."

"Right," mused the other, thoughtfully. "And the rest of his gang did get out of here pretty fast after it happened. Didn't try to hide the body, or do anything about it." He frowned. "But that doesn't prove any balony about ghosts, or vampires. You been reading too many bum magazines lately, Polack."

He laughed.

"What about iron door?" grumbled the Pole, accusingly, his red face flushing. "What about iron door back of coal in coal-pile, huh? You know what fellers down by Black Jim's place say about house with iron door in cellar."

"Yeah." Regetti's face clouded.

"You no look by iron door yet, boss," the man continued. "Maybe you find somet'ing behind door yet, like fellers say—dot where t'ing dot got Fellippo came from; dot where it hide. Police they not find door either, when they come. Just find leg, and blood, and shut up house. But fellers know. They tell me plenty about house with iron door in cellar; say it bad place from old days when witch-fellers live here. It lead to hill back of house; cemetery, maybe. Perhaps dot's why nobody live here so long—afraid of what hides on other side of door; what come out and kill Tony Fellippo. I know about house with iron door in cellar, all right."

I knew about the house, too. So that's where I was at! In the old Chambers house on Pringle Street! Many a story I've heard from the old folks when I was a boy about the old man, Ezekiel Chambers, whose wizard tricks bequeathed him such an unsavory reputation in Colonial days. I knew about Jonathan Dark, the other owner, who had been tried for smuggling just before the terrible days of 1818, and the abhorrent practice of grave-robbing he had been said to pursue in the ancient cemetery directly behind the house, on the hill.

Many peculiar rumors were circulated about the moldering house with the iron door in the cellar at this time—about the door, particularly, which Dark was said to use as a passageway for bringing his stolen cadavers back to dispose of. It was even claimed that the door had never been opened when Dark was tried, because of his astounding and hideous claim that the key which locked it was on *the other side*. Dark had died during the trial, while in prison, babbling blasphemies that no man dared believe; monstrous hints of what lay beneath the old graveyard on the hill; of tunnels and burrows and secret vaults used in witch-days for unhallowed rites. He spoke of tenants in these vaults, too, and of what sometimes would come to visit the house from below when a wizard invoked it with the proper spells and sacrifice. There was more, too—but then, Dark was quite mad. At least, everyone thought it better to believe so.

Old tales die. The house had stood deserted for many years, until most men forgot the reason for which it had been forsaken, ascribing its vacancy only to age. The public today were utterly unaware of the legends. Only the old ones remembered—the old ones who whispered their stories to me when I was a boy.

So this was the Dark house to which I had been brought! And this was the very cellar of the tales in question! I gathered from the remarks between Regetti and the superstitious Pole that another gang had recently used it for a hideaway until the death of their leader; indeed, I even vaguely remembered some newspaper reports of Tony Fellippo's murder.

And now Regetti had come from New York to use it as a base.

Clever scheme of his, evidently—coming to an old New England town and kidnapping the local gentry to hold for ransom; then hiding them away in some old, deserted house so conveniently protected by superstition. I supposed that there would be more victims after me, too; the man was smart and cunning enough to get away with it.

These thoughts flashed through my mind during the argument between the Pole and his leader. But their altercation came to an abrupt halt.

"I wish you get out of here," the Pole was saying. "If you stay only one night dot t'ing he come. Dot's all Tony Fellippo stay."

"Shut up, you fool. Didn't we stay here last night, too, before the job? And nothing happened."

"Yeah, sure. I know. But we stay upstairs, not by cellar. Why not keep feller upstairs?"

"Because we can't afford to risk being seen," Regetti snapped, wearily. "Now, cut the chatter."

He turned to me.

"Listen, you. I'm sending this guy out with a ransom letter right now, to your friends back at the party. All you have to do is keep your mouth shut and sit tight. But any funny business means you're through, see?"

I kept silent.

"Take him in there, Polack, and tie him up." Regetti indicated a fruit-cellar adjacent to the stairs.

The Pole, still grumbling, dragged me across the floor and into the room. He lit a candle, casting strange shadows over the cobwebbed, dust-drowned shelving on the walls. Jars of preserves still stood untouched, storing, perhaps, the crop of a hundred years ago. Broken jars were still strewn about on the tottering table. As I glanced about, the Pole tossed me into a chair beside the rickety board, and proceeded to lash me to it firmly with a stout rope. I was not gagged or blindfolded again, though the choking atmosphere about me served as a good substitute for both.

He left me, closing the door. I was alone in the candle-lit quiet.

I strained my ears, and was rewarded by hearing Regetti dismiss his henchman for the night, evidently to deliver the ransom note to the proper authorities. He, Regetti, would stay behind on guard.

"Don't run into any ghosts on your way," he called after his companion, as the big Pole lumbered up the stairs.

A slamming outer door was his only response. From the ensuing quiet I judged Regetti had gone back to his solitaire.

Meanwhile, I looked about for some means of escape. I found it at last, on the table beside me. The broken jars—glass edges to cut my bonds!

Purposefully I edged my chair closer to the table end. If I could get a piece of that glass in my hands . . . .

As I moved, I strained my ears once more to make sure that any noise made by the chair would be inaudible to Regetti, waiting outside. There was no sound from the chair as I reached the table, and I sighed with relief as I maneuvered my pinioned hands until they grasped a piece of glass firmly. Then I began to rub it against the edge of the rope which bound them.

It was slow work. Minutes ticked away into hours, and still no sound from outside, save a muffled series of snores. Regetti had fallen asleep over his cards. Good! Now, if I could get my wrists free and work on my feet, I would be able to make it.

My right hand was loose at last, though my wrist was damp with mingled sweat and blood. Cutting away from behind was not a precise, calculated sort of job. Quickly, I finished the work on my left, then rubbed my swollen fingers and bent over to saw at the ropes on my legs.

Then I heard the sound.

It was the grating of rusty hinges. Anyone who has lived in archaic houses all his life learns to recognize the peculiar, eery clang. Rusty hinges grating from the cellar beyond . . . from *an iron door?* A scuffling sound among the coal . . . *the iron door is concealed by the coal-pile.* Fellippo only stayed down here one night. All they found was his leg.

Jonathan Dark, babbling on his deathbed. The door locked from the other side. Tunnels to the graveyard. What lurks in graveyards, ancient and unseen, then creeps from crypts to feast?

A scream rose in my throat, but I choked it back. Regetti still snored. Whatever was going on in the outer room, I must not wake him and lose my only chance of escape. Instead, I had best hasten and free my legs. I worked feverishly, but my ears were alert for developments.

They came. The noise in the coal-pile abruptly ceased, and I went limp with relief. Perhaps rats were at work.

A moment later I would have given anything to have heard the coal rattling again, if only to drown out the new noise.

There was something creeping across the cellar floor; something crawling, as if on hands and knees; something with long nails or claws that rasped and scraped. There was something croaking and chuckling as it moved through the cellar dark; something that wheezed with bestial, sickening laughter, like the death-rattle in the throat of a plague-stricken corpse.

Oh, how slyly it crept—how slowly, cautiously, and sinisterly! I could hear it slinking in the shadows, and my fingers raced at their work, even while my brain grew numb.

Traffic between tombs and a wizard's house—traffic with things the old wives say can never die.

Regetti snored on.

What bides below, in caverns, that can be invoked by the proper spell—or the sight of prey?

Creep.

And then . . .

Regetti awoke. I heard him scream, once. He didn't even have time to get up or draw his gun. There was a demoniac scurrying across the floor, as if made by a giant rat. Then the faint sound of shredding flesh, and over all, a sudden ghoulish baying that conjured up worlds of nightmare horror in my shattered brain.

Above the howling came a series of low, almost animal moans, and agonized phrases in Italian, cries for mercy, prayers, curses.

Claws make no sound as they sink into flesh, and yellow fangs are silent till they grate on bone . . . .

My left leg was free, then my right. Now I slashed the rope around my waist. Suppose it came in here?

They baying ceased, but the silence was haggard with horror.

There are some banquets without toasts . . . .

And now, once again, moans. My spine shivered. All around me the shadows grinned, for outside was revelry as in the olden days. Revelry, and a thing that moaned, and moaned, and moaned.

Then I was loose. As the moaning died away in the darkness, I cut the final strands of rope that bound me to my chair . . . .

I did not leave at once, for there were still sounds in the other room which I did not like; sounds which caused my soul to shrivel, and my sanity to succumb before a nameless dread.

I heard that pawing and padding rustle along the floor, and after the shrieking had ceased, a worse noise took its place—a *burbling* noise—as if someone or something was sucking marrow from a bone. And the terrible, clicking sound; the feeding sound of gigantic teeth...

Yes, I waited; waited until the crunching had mercifully ceased, and then waited on until the rustling slithered back into the cellar, and disappeared. When I heard the brazen clang of a rusty door grate in the distance, I felt safe.

It was then that I left at last; passing through the now-deserted cellar, up the stairs, and out unguarded doors into the silver security of a moonlit night. It was very good to see the street-lights again, and hear the trolleys rumble from afar. My taxi took me to the precinct station, and after I had told my story the police did the rest.

I told my story, but I did not mention the iron door against the hillside. That I saved for the ears of the Government men. Now they can do what they like about it, since I am far away. But I did not want anybody prying around too closely to that door while I remained in the city, because even now I cannot—dare not—say what might lurk behind it. The hillside leads to the graveyard, and the graveyard to places far beneath. And in olden days there was a curious traffic betwixt tomb and tunnel and a wizard's house; traffic not confined to men alone. . . .

I'm pretty positive about all this, too. Not alone from the disappearance of the Fellippo gang, or the wildly whispered tales of the foreign men; not alone from these, but from a much more concrete and ghastly proof.

It is a proof I don't care to speak about even today—a proof that the police know, but which is fortunately deleted from newspaper accounts of the tragedy.

What men will find behind that iron door I will not venture to say, but I think I know why only Fellippo's leg was found before. I did not look at the iron door before I left the house, but I did see something else in the cellar as I passed through to the stairs. That is why I ran frantically up the steps; that is why I went to the Government, and that is why I never want to go back to witch-haunted, age-accursed Arkham. I found proof.

Because when I went out, I saw Joe Regetti sitting in his chair by the table in the cellar. The lamp was on, and I am quite sure I saw no footprints. I'm glad of that. But I did see Joe Regetti sitting in his chair, and then I knew the meaning of the screams, and the crunching, and the padding sound.

Joe Regetti, sitting in his chair in the cellar lamplight, *with his naked body chewed entirely to ribbons by gigantic and unhuman teeth!*

IN THIS STORY, *whose climax is, one suspects, in some measure inspired by Poe's "The Masque of the Red Death," Bloch tells us that the only real magic is that of the ancient and mysterious past (here the very real writings of Egyptologist E.A. Wallis Budge function much in the manner of* De Vermis Mysteriis *in the other tales) and the fiction of creative writers. We see this in the implied contrast not only between the shallow costumed revelers and the hard-core cult of Henricus Vanning, but also between these latter and the admitted writer of fiction, Bloch's autobiographical narrator, who alone emerges unscathed from the visitation of occult doom.*

The Secret of Sebek

I SHOULD NEVER HAVE attended Henricus Vanning's costume ball. Even if the tragedy had not occurred, I would be better off had I refused his invitation that night. Now that I have left New Orleans I can view the episode in saner light, and I know that I made a mistake. The remembrance of that final inexplicable moment is a horror that I still cannot face with a rational mind, however. Had I suspected beforehand I might now be spared the recurrent nightmares which afflict me.

But at that time of which I speak there was no premonition to guide me. I was a stranger in the Louisiana city, and very lonely. The Mardi Gras season served only to accentuate my feeling of utter isolation. During the first two evenings of celebration, tired from long vigils at the typewriter, I wandered alien and alone along the quaintly twisted streets, and the crowds that hustled by seemed to mock my solitude.

My work at the time was very exhausting—I was doing a series of Egyptian stories for a magazine—and my mental state was a bit odd. During the day I sat in my quiet room and gave my mind over to images of Nyarlathotep, Bubastis, and Anubis; my thoughts were peopled with the priestly pageantries of olden times. And in the evenings I walked unknown amidst thoughtless throngs more unreal than the fanciful figures of the past.

But enough of excuses. To be perfectly frank, when I left the house that third night after a weary day, I expressly intended to get drunk. I entered a café at dusk, dining lavishly with a bottle of peach brandy. The place was hot and crowded; the ribald, costumed masqueraders all seemed to be enjoying the reign of Momus.

After a time this did not disturb me. Four generous goblets of the really excellent *liqueur* had set the blood running like elixir in my veins; bold, reckless dreams cascaded through my head. I now gazed at the impersonal swarms about me with new interest and understanding. They too were trying to escape tonight—escape from maddening monotony and humdrum commonplace. The fat man in the clown costume near by had looked silly an hour ago; now I seemed to sympathize with him. I sensed the frustration behind the masks these

strangers wore; appreciated how valiantly they strove to find forgetfulness in the Mardi Gras.

I would forget, too. The bottle was emptied. I left the café and once
more walked the streets, but this time I no longer had any feeling of
isolation. I strode along like the carnival king himself, and traded gibe
for gibe with chance buffeters.

Here memory is temporarily blurred. I went into a club lounge for
scotch and soda, then continued on my way. Where my feet led me I
cannot say. I seemed to float along effortlessly, but my mind was
crystal-clear.

I was not thinking of mundane things. Through some quirk I
recalled work again, and I contemplated ancient Egypt. Through
crumbled centuries I moved, in visions of secret splendor.

I lurched down a dim, deserted street.

I walked through templed Thebes, while sphinxes stared.

I turned into a lighted thoroughfare where revellers danced.

I mingled with the white-clad acolytes adoring sacred Apis.

The carousing mob blew paper trumpets, strewed confetti.

*To the shrill litany of lutes the temple virgins showered me with roses red as
the blood of betrayed Osiris.*

Thus I passed through streets of saturnalia, my thoughts still
wine-wafted and far away. It was all very much like a dream when at
last I entered that obscure thoroughfare in the heart of the Creole
district. Tall houses reared deserted on either side; darkened, dingy
domiciles deserted by their owners, who mingled with the merrymakers amidst more pleasant surroundings. The buildings were old; in the
fashion of ancient days they stood narrowly together, row on row.

*They are like untenanted mummy-cases in some forgotten tomb; they stand
deserted by the maggot and the worm.*

From the steeply gabled roofs little black windows yawned.

*They are empty, like the eyeless sockets of a skull, and like a skull they too
hide secrets.*

Secrets.

Secret Egypt.

It was then that I saw the man. Threading my way down that black
and twisted street, I noticed a figure in the shadows before me. It stood
silent, as though awaiting my approach. I endeavored to hurry past,
but there was something about the motionless man which arrested my
attention. He was dressed—unnaturally.

Suddenly, shockingly, my drunken dreams were fused with stark reality. *This waiting man was dressed like a priest of ancient Egypt!*

Was it hallucination, or did he wear the triple-crowned insignia of Osiris? That long white robe was unmistakable, and in his lean hands was the sceptered diadem of Set, the Serpent.

Overcome with bewilderment, I stood stock-still and stared. He stared back, his thin, tanned face bland and expressionless. With a quick gesture, his right hand darted under his robe. I shrank back, as he withdrew it once more and pulled out—a cigarette.

"Got a match, stranger?" asked the priest of Egypt.

Then I laughed, remembered, and understood. Mardi Gras! What a scare he had given me, though! Smiling, my head suddenly clear once more, I extended my lighter. He used it, and as the flame flared upward, peered curiously into my countenance.

He started, gray eyes evincing sudden recognition. To my astonishment, he spoke my name in interrogation. I nodded my head.

"What a surprise!" he chuckled. "You're the writer, aren't you? I've read some of your recent stuff, but I had no idea that you were here in New Orleans."

I mumbled a few words of explanation. He genially interrupted.

"That's great luck. My name is Vanning—Henricus Vanning. I'm interested in the occult myself; we should have a lot in common."

We stood chatting for several minutes; or rather, he chatted and I listened. I learned that Mr. Vanning was a gentleman of means and leisure. He touched a bit glibly and flippantly on his studies in primitive mythology, but expressed a patently genuine interest in Egyptian lore. There was mention of a social group whose mutual and private researches in metaphysics might interest me.

As if seized with sudden inspiration, he clapped me heartily on the back.

"What are your plans for the evening?" he said.

I confessed my predicament. He smiled.

"Splendid! Just had dinner, myself. I'm on the way back to the house now to play host. Our little group—I told you about them—is holding a costume ball there. Like to come along? Interesting."

"But I'm not in costume," I protested.

"Doesn't matter. I think you'd particularly appreciate this affair. Most unusual. Come on."

He beckoned me to follow and started off down the street. I shrugged, but acquiesced. After all, I had nothing to lose, and my curiosity was aroused.

As we walked, the garrulous Mr. Vanning carried on a smooth and intriguing conversation. He spoke in greater detail of his little "circle" of esoteric friends. I gathered that they rather ostentatiously referred to themselves as *The Coffin Club,* and spent much of their time in pursuit of exotic and macabre phases in art, literature or music.

Tonight, according to my host, the group were celebrating the Mardi Gras in their own unique fashion. Defying the conventional masquerade, all members and invited friends planned to come attired in supernatural garb; instead of the usual clowns, pirates, and Colonial gentlemen, they would represent the more outlandish creatures of fancy and myth. I would mingle with werewolves, vampires, gods, goddesses, priests and black magicians.

I must confess that this news did not wholly please me. I never could stomach the pseudo-occultist or the quack devotee and metaphysicist. I dislike a bogus interest and a sham knowledge of legendry in others. Petty dabblings in spiritualism, astrology, and "psychic" charlatanry have always been repellent to my tastes.

I feel that it is not good for fools to mock the old faiths and the secret ways of vanished races. If this was to be one of the usual groups of middle-aged neurotics and pallid-purple dilettantes, then I would spend a boring evening.

But Henricus Vanning himself seemed to have more than a surface smattering of erudition. His cultured allusions to various myth-sagas in my stories seemed to hint at deep knowledge and sincere research that peered beyond the blacker veils of human thought. He spoke quite fluently of his delvings into manicheism and primal cult-ceremonials.

I became so absorbed in his words that I failed to heed the direction in which he led me, though I know we walked for some time. When we drew up at last, it was to turn into a long, shrubbery-bordered walk which led to the doors of a well-lighted and imposing mansion.

In simple truth, I must admit to being so seduced by Vanning's picturesque statements, that I cannot remember a single concrete detail of the house's exterior appearance or the environs in which it stood.

Still bemused, I followed Vanning through the opened door and walked into—nightmare.

When I stated that the house was brilliantly lighted, I meant just that. It was lighted—*in flaming red.*

We stood in a hallway; a hallway of hell. Scarlet scimitars of light scintillated from the surface of mirrored walls. Vermilion drapes cloaked inner entrances, and the crimson ceiling seemed to smolder with the crystalline carmine fires of ruby gas-torches that hung in blood-imbrued braziers. A Luciferean butler took my hat, handed me a goblet of cherry brandy.

Alone in the red room, Vanning faced me, glass in hand.

"Like it?" he inquired. "Gay setting to put my guests in the mood. Little touch I borrowed from Poe."

I thought of the splendid *Masque of the Red Death,* and winced inwardly at this crude and vulgar desecration.

Still, this evidence of the man's eccentricity did intrigue me. He was *trying* for something. I was almost moved when I lifted my glass to the pseudo-priest of Egypt there in that eery anteroom.

The brandy burned.

"Now—on to our guests." He pushed a tapestry aside, and we entered the cavernous chamber to the right.

Green and black were the velvet backgrounds of these walls; silver the candles that lighted the niches. The furniture, however, was modern and conventional enough; but when I first surveyed the throng of guests I felt for a moment as if I were again in dreams.

"Werewolves, gods, and black magicians," Vanning had said. There was more of understatement than exaggeration in that cryptic remark. The occupants of that room constituted a pantheon from all the hells.

The orchestra at the corner of the room were dressed as skeletons, and some diabolically clever lighting arrangements made the fantasy uncomfortably real from a distance. The merrymakers circled the floor against the sinister background of ebon and emerald velvet.

I saw an obscene Pan dancing with a withered night-hag; a mad Freya embracing a voodoo priest; a Bacchante clinging lecherously to a wild-eyed dervish from Irem. There were arch-druids, dwarfs, nixies and kobolds; lamas, shamans, priestesses, fauns, ogres, magi, ghouls. It was a sabbat—a resurrection of ancient sin.

Then, as I mingled with the throng and was introduced, the momentary illusion faded. Pan was merely a stout, rather puffy-eyed, middle-aged gentleman with an obvious paunch which no goat-skin girdle could obliterate. Freya was a desperately-bright debutante, with the predatory slut-eyes of a common harlot. The voodoo priest was just a nice young man in burnt cork, with a slightly incongruous English lisp.

I met perhaps a dozen guests, and quickly forgot their names. I was a trifle surprised by Vanning's seeming superciliousness; he almost snubbed several of the more talkative.

"Enjoy yourselves," he called over his shoulder as he dragged me across the floor. "These are the fools," he confided in a lower voice. "But there are a few I want you to meet."

Over in the corner sat a little group of four men. All wore priestly raiment similar to Vanning's own, in that religion dominated.

"Doctor Delvin." An old man, in Babylonian, almost biblical robes.

"Etienne de Marigny." Dark, handsome priest of Adonis.

"Professor Weildan." A bearded gnome in a kalender's turban.

"Richard Royce." A young, bespectacled scholar, monkishly cowled.

The foursome bowed courteously. Upon my being introduced, however, there was an immediate slackening of their reserve. They crowded about Vanning and me in a rather confidential way, while our host spoke softly in my ear.

"These are the real members of the group I spoke about. I saw the way you looked at the others here, and I quite understand and agree with you. Those people are silly fools. We, here, are the initiates. Perhaps, then, you wonder at the reason for their presence. Let me explain. Attack is the best defense."

"Attack is the best defense?" I echoed, puzzled.

"Yes. Suppose, now, that I and my friends here are really deep students of black magic."

There was a subtle suggestion in the way he breathed "suppose."

"Suppose that is true. Don't you think that our society friends would object, gossip, investigate?"

"Yes," I admitted. "That sounds reasonable."

"Of course. That's why we formulated our attack. By publicly proclaiming an eccentric interest in occultism, and showing it by giving these stupid parties, we are left quite unmolested to carry out our serious work by ourselves. Clever, eh?"

I smiled in agreement. Vanning was no fool.

"It might interest you to know that Doctor Delvin, here, is one of this country's foremost ethnologists. De Marigny is a well-known occultist—you may remember his connection with the Randolph Carter case several years ago. Royce is my personal aide, and Professor Weildan is *the* Weildan, Egyptologist."

Funny, how Egypt kept recurring in the course of the evening!

"I promised you something interesting, my friend, and you shall have it. First, though, we must endure these cattle for another half-hour or so. Then we'll go up to my room for a real session. I trust you will be patient."

The four men bowed to me as Vanning again led me into the center of the room. The dancing had stopped now, and the floor was covered by little groups of idle chatterers. Demons drank mint-juleps, and virgin sacrifices to the Magna Mater artfully applied their lipstick. Neptune passed me, with a cigar in his mouth. The gaiety was shrill. *Masque of the Red Death,* I thought. Then I saw—him.

It was all Poe, his entrance. The black and green curtains at the end of the room parted, and he glided in as though emerging from the hidden depths of the hangings rather than the door behind them.

Silver candle-light silhouetted his figure, and as he walked a grisly nimbus seemed to cloak each movement. I had the momentary impression of gazing at him through a prism, since the queer lighting made him appear indistinct and sharply-etched in turn.

He was the soul of Egypt.

The long white robe concealed a body whose contours were elusively problematical. Taloned hands hung from swirling sleeves, and the jeweled fingers clasped a rod of gold, set with the seal of the Eye of Horus.

The top of the robe terminated in a cape-collar of black; it stood, a stiffly hooded background for a head of horror.

The head of a crocodile. The body of an Egyptian priest.

That head was—awful. A slanted, saurian skull, all green and scaly on top; hairless, slimy, slick and nauseous. Great bony ridges socketed the embered eyes, staring from behind a sickening sweep of long, reptilian snout. A rugose muzzle, with great champing jaws half opened to reveal a lolling pinkish tongue and scummy teeth of stiletto-like sharpness. The saber fangs seemed to move, but it was only a trick of the light.

What a mask!

I have always prided myself on a certain *sensitivity.* I can *feel* quite strongly. Now, gazing at that triumph of morbid mummery, I received a sensory shock. I felt that this masquer was real—more real than his less grotesque fellows. The very outlandishness of his costume seemed to carry added conviction when contrasted with the pitiful makeshift pretenses of those through which he walked.

He seemed to be alone, nor did anyone attempt to converse with him in passing. I reached forward and tapped Vanning on the shoulder. I wanted to meet this man.

Vanning, however, swung ahead to the platform, where he turned and spoke to the orchestra men. I glanced back, half intending to approach the crocodile-man myself.

He was gone.

I searched the crowd with eager eyes. No use. He had vanished.

Vanished? Had he existed? I saw him—or thought I did—only for a moment. And I was still a little befuddled. Egypt on the brain. Perhaps I had been overimaginative. But why the queer flooding feeling of reality?

These questions were never answered, for my attention was distracted by the performance on the platform. Vanning had started his half-hour of entertainment for the "guests." He had told me it was a mere sop to conceal his real interests, but I found it more impressive than I expected.

The lights turned blue—haggard, graveyard-misty blue. The shadows darkened to indigo blurs as the celebrants found seats. An organ rose from beneath the orchestra platform, and music throbbed.

It was my favorite number—the superb and sonorously sepulchral Number One scene from *The Swan Lake,* by Tchaikowsky. It droned, mocked, shrilled, blared. It whispered, roared, threatened, frightened. It even impressed and quieted the milling geese about me.

There was a Devil Dance following; a magician, and a final Black Mass ritual with a really terrifying illusion of sacrifice. All very weird, very morbid, and very false. When the lights went up at last and the band resumed their places, I found Vanning, and we hastened across the room. The four fellow-researchers were waiting.

Vanning motioned me to follow them through the curtains near the platform. We made our exits unobtrusively, and I found myself walking down a long, darkened hallway. Vanning halted before an oak-paneled door. A key flashed, grated, turned. We were in a library.

Chairs, cigars, brandy—indicated in turn by our smiling host. The brandy—a fine cognac—momentarily sent my thoughts astray once more. Everything was unreal; Vanning, his friends, this house, the entire evening. Everything but the man in the crocodile mask. I must ask Vanning....

Abruptly, a voice summoned me back to the present. Vanning was speaking, addressing me. His voice was solemn, and held an unusual timbre. It was almost as though I was hearing him speak for the first time; as if this were the real man, and the other genial inhabitant of an open house merely a sham as insubstantial as the Mardi Gras costumes of the guests.

As he spoke, I found myself the focus of five pairs of eyes; Delvin's Celtic blue, de Marigny's penetrating Gallic brown, Royce's bespecta-

cled gray, Weildan's deep umber, and the gun-metal pin-points of
Vanning himself. Each seemed to ask a question:

"Do you dare?"

But what Vanning said was much more prosaic.

"I promised you an unusual time. Well, that's what you're here for.
But I must admit that my motives are not altruistic alone. I—I need
you. I've read your tales. I think you are a sincere student, and I want
both knowledge and advice. That is why we five are admitting a
comparative stranger to our secret. We trust you—we must trust you."

"You can," I said, quietly. For the first time I realized that Vanning
was not only earnest; he was nervous. The hand holding the cigar
shook; perspiration gathered beneath the Egyptian hood. Royce, the
scholarly student, was twisting the belt of his monkish costume. The
other three men still watched me, and their silence was more disturbing than the unnatural earnestness in Vanning's voice.

What was all this? Was I drugged, dreaming? Blue lights, and
crocodile masks, and a melodramatic secret. Yet I believed.

I believed, when Vanning pressed the lever in the great library table
so that the false drawers beneath swung outward and revealed the
gaping space within. I believed when I saw him hoist out the mummy-
case, with de Marigny's aid.

I became interested even before I noted the peculiarities of the case
itself. For Vanning went over to a shelf and came back with an armful
of books. These he handed to me silently. They were his credentials;
they confirmed all that he had told me.

Nobody but a recognized occultist and adept could possess these
strange tomes. Thin strips of glass protected the crumbling covers of
the ill-famed *Book of Eibon,* the original editions of *Cultes des Goules,*
and the almost fabulous *De Vermis Mysteriis.*

Vanning managed a smile when he saw the light of recognition in
my face.

"We've gone in pretty deep these past few years," he said. "You know
what lies in these books."

I knew. I have written of *De Vermis Mysteriis* myself, and there are
times when the words of Ludvig Prinn fill me with a vague fright and
an indefinable repulsion.

Vanning opened the latter volume. "You are familiar with this, I
believe. You've mentioned it in your work."

He pointed to the cryptic chapter that is known as *Saracenic Rituals.*

I nodded. I knew the *Saracenic Rituals* only too well. The account
dealt with Prinn's mysterious sojourn in Egypt and the Orient in what
he claimed were Crusader days. There is revealed the lore of the *efreet*

and the *djinn,* the secrets of the Assassin sects, the myths of Arabian ghoul-tales, and the hidden practices of dervish cults. I had found within it a great wealth of material on the legends of ancient Inner Egypt; indeed, much story material was culled from those tattered pages.

Egypt again! I glanced at the mummy-case.

Vanning and the others watched me intently. At last my host shrugged.

"Listen," he said. "I'll put my cards on the table. I—I must trust you, as I said."

"Go ahead," I rejoined, impatiently. Such mystery of manner was irritating.

"It all started with this book," said Henricus Vanning. "Royce, here, dug it up for me. We got interested in the Bubastis legend, at first. For a while I contemplated some investigations in Cornwall—looking up the Egyptian ruins of England, you know. But then, I found a more fertile field in actual Egyptology. When Professor Weildan, here, went on his expedition last year, I authorized him to obtain anything of interest he might discover, at any price. He returned last week, with this."

Vanning stepped over to the mummy-case. I followed.

He didn't have to explain further. One detailed inspection of that mummy-case, combined with what I knew of the *Saracenic Rituals* chapter, led to an inference that was unmistakable.

The hieroglyphs and markings on the case indicated that it contained the body of an Egyptian priest; a priest of the god Sebek. And *Saracenic Rituals* told its own story.

For a moment I mentally reviewed my knowledge. Sebek, according to reputable anthropologists, was a lesser deity of Inner Egypt; a fertility god of the Nile. If recognized authorities be correct, only four mummies of his priesthood have ever been found; though numerous statuettes, figurines, and pictures in tombs testify to the veneration accorded this deity. Egyptologists have never fully traced the history of the god, though some unorthodox surmises and wild linkages have been made or hinted at by Wallis-Budge.

Ludvig Prinn, though, had delved further. I recalled his words with an appreciable shudder.

In *Saracenic Rituals,* Prinn spoke of what he had learned from Alexandrian seers; of his journeyings into the deserts and his secret tomb-lootings in hidden valleys of the Nile.

He told a tale, historically authenticated, of the Egyptian priestcraft and its rise to power—how the servants of the dark nature-gods ruled the Pharaohs from behind the throne, and held the land in their grip. For Egyptian gods and religions were based on secret realities. Strange hybrids walked the earth when it was young; gigantic, lumbering creatures—half-beast, half-man. Human imagination alone did not create the gigantic serpent Set, carnivorous Bubastis, and great Osiris. I thought of Thoth, and tales of harpies; thought of jackal-headed Anubis and the legend of werewolves.

No, the ancients trafficked with elemental powers and beasts of the beyond. They could summon their gods, the humans with the heads of animals. And, at times, they did. Hence their power.

In time, they ruled over Egypt; their word was law. The land was filled with rich temples, and every seventh man owed allegiance to the ritual bodies. Incense rose before a thousand shrines—incense, and blood. The beast-mouths of the gods hungered for blood.

Well might the priests adore, for they had made strange and curious bargains with their divine Masters. Unnatural perversions drove the cult of Bubastis out of Egypt, and a never-mentioned abomination caused the symbol and story of Nyarlathotep to be forgotten. But ever the priests waxed stronger and bolder; their sacrifices more outrageous, and their rewards greater.

For the sake of life everlastingly reincarnated, they pleasured the gods and assuaged their curious appetites. To safeguard their mummies with divine curses, they offered up scapegoats filled with blood.

Prinn speaks of the sect of Sebek in particular detail. The priests believed that Sebek, as a fertility deity, controlled the sources of life eternal. He would guard them in their graves until the resurrection-cycle was completed, and he would destroy their enemies who sought to violate their sepulchers. To him they offered virgin maidens, to be torn between the jaws of a golden crocodile. For Sebek, the Crocodile god of the Nile, had the body of a man, the head of a crocodile, and the lustful appetites of both.

The description of these ceremonies is grisly. The priests all wore crocodile masks, in emulation of their Lord, for that was his earthly aspect. Once a year, they thought, Sebek himself appeared to the High Priests in the Inner Temple at Memphis, and then he too assumed the form of a man with a crocodile head.

The devout believed that he would guard their graves—and countless screaming virgins died to support their faith.

This I knew, and hurriedly recollected, while glancing at the mummy of the Priest of Sebek.

For now I looked into the case, and saw that the mummy had been unwrapped. It lay under a pane of glass, which Vanning removed.

"You know the story, then," he said, reading my eyes aright. "I've had the mummy here a week; it's been chemically treated, thanks to Weildan, here. On its chest, though, I found this."

He pointed to an amulet of clear jade—a saurian figure, covered with ideographic images.

"What is it?" I asked.

"Secret code of the priesthood. De Marigny thinks it's Nacaal. Translation? A curse—as the Prinn story has it—a curse on the heads of tomb-looters. Threatens them with the vengeance of Sebek himself. Nasty wording."

Vanning's flippancy was forced. I could tell that by the restless stirring of the others in the room. Doctor Devlin was coughing nervously; Royce twisted his robe; de Marigny scowled. The gnome-like Professor Weildan approached us. He glanced at the mummy for some time, as if seeking solution to a secret in those eyeless sockets that blindly brooded in the gloom.

"Tell him what I think, Vanning," he said softly.

"Weildan, here, has done some investigation. He managed to get this mummy past the authorities, but it cost him plenty to do it. He told me where he found it, and it's not a pleasant story. Nine of the caravan boys died on the return journey, though it may have been bad water that did that. The professor has gone back on us, I'm afraid."

"I have not," interrupted Weildan, sharply. "When I tell you to get rid of the mummy it is because I want to live. We had some notion of using it in ceremonials here, but this is not possible. You see, I believe in the curse of Sebek.

"You know, of course, that only four mummies of his priests have ever been found. That is because the others repose in secret crypts. Well, the four finders are all dead. I knew Partington, who found the third. He was investigating this curse myth quite thoroughly when he returned—but he died before publishing any reports. It was rather curious, his end. Fell off the bridge into a crocodile pit of the London Zoo. When they pulled him out, he was a mess."

Vanning looked at me. "Bogey man," he said, deprecatingly. Then, in more serious tones, he continued. "That's one of the reasons I asked you here to share this secret. I want your own opinion, as a scholar and occultist. Should I get rid of the mummy? Do you believe in this curse story? I don't, but I have felt quite uneasy of late. I know of too many peculiar coincidences, and I have faith in Prinn's veracity. What we intend to use the mummy for does not matter. It would have been a—a desecration great enough to anger any god. And I wouldn't like to have a crocodile-headed creature at my throat. What do you say?"

Abruptly, I remembered. The man in the mask! He had been dressed like a priest of Sebek, in emulation of the god.

I told Vanning what I had seen of him. "Who is he?" I asked. "He should really be here. It makes things—appropriate."

Vanning's horror was not feigned. I regretted having spoken, after observing his terrified reaction.

"I never saw *that!* I swear I didn't! We must find the man at once."

"Perhaps it's a polite form of blackmail," I said. "He may have the goods on you and Weildan, and frighten you into paying hush-money."

"Perhaps." Vanning's voice held no note of sincerity. He turned to the others.

"Quickly," he said. "Go back into the other room and look among the guests. Collar this elusive—stranger; bring him here."

"Police?" suggested Royce, nervously.

"No, you fool. Hurry, all of you!"

The four men left the room, and their footsteps echoed in the outer corridor as they receded.

A moment's silence. Vanning tried to smile. I was in a strange oblivious fog. The Egypt of my dreams—*was it real?* Why had that one glimpse of the mysterious man in the mask so impressed me? The priests of Sebek spilt blood to bind a bargain of vengeance; could they satisfy an ancient curse? Or was Vanning mad?

A soft sound....

I turned. And there in the doorway stood the man in the crocodile mask.

"That's the fellow!" I exclaimed. "That's—"

Vanning leaned against the table, his face the color of wet ash. He just stared at the figure on the threshold, but his tormented eyes telepathically conveyed a dreadful message to me.

The man in the crocodile mask ... nobody had seen him but myself. And I was dreaming of Egypt. Here, in this room, was the stolen mummy of Sebek's priest.

The god Sebek was—*a crocodile-headed god.* And his priests were dressed in his image—*they wore crocodile masks.*

I had just warned Vanning about the vengeance of the old priests. He himself had believed and was afraid when I told him what I had seen. And now, in the doorway, stood the silent stranger. What was

more logical than to believe it was a resurrected priest, come to avenge
this insult to his kind?

Yet I could not believe it. Even when the figure entered, sinister and
still, I did not guess its purpose. Even when Vanning cowered and
moaned against the mummy-case, I was not convinced.

Then, everything happened so swiftly that I had no time to act. Just
as I was about to challenge the unnatural intruder, doom was un-
leashed. With a darting, reptilian movement, the body beneath the
white robe *undulated* across the room. In a second it towered above the
cringing figure of my host. I saw clawing hands sink into sagging
shoulders; then the jaws of the mask descended and *moved*. Moved—in
Vanning's quivering throat.

As I leapt, my thoughts seemed sluggishly calm in contrast. "Diabolically clever murder," I mused. "Unique death-weapon.
Cunningly contrived tooth-mechanism in a mask. Fanatic."

And my eyes, in a detached fashion, observed that monstrous muzzle
biting into Vanning's neck. Moving, the squamous horror of the head
loomed like a camera close-up.

It took only a second, understand. Then, with sudden purpose, I had
seized a sleeve of the white robe, and with my free hand wrenched at
the mask of the murderer.

The killer wheeled, ducked. My hand slipped, and for a moment
rested on the crocodile snout, the bloody jaw.

Then, in a flash, the invader wheeled and disappeared, while I was
left screaming before the ripped and tattered body on the mummy-case
of Sebek.

Vanning was dead. His murderer had disappeared. The house was
crowded with revellers; I had but to step to the door and call for aid.

I did not. I stood for one stark second in the center of the room,
screaming, while my vision veered. Everything was swimming around
and around—the blood-blotched books; the sere mummy, its chest
now crushed and crimsoned by the struggle; the red, unmoving thing
on the floor. All blurred before my eyes.

I could see nothing but my right hand—the hand that had brushed
the masked muzzle of the killer. There was blood on my fingers. I stared
at it and shrieked.

Then, and only then, did volition come to me. I turned and ran.

I wish my tale could end there, but it cannot. There is a hideous
conclusion to be drawn. It must be revealed so that I can know peace
once more.

I'll be frank. I know it would make a better story if I had asked the butler about the man in the crocodile mask and heard him say that no such person entered the place. But this—God save me!—is not a story, but truth.

I *know* he was there, and after I saw Vanning die I did not wait to interview another soul. I made that last desperate clutch at the masked murderer, then screamed and ran from the room. I rushed through the revellers on the floor without even giving an alarm, dashed out of the house and panted up the street. Grinning horror bestrode my shoulders and urged me on, until I lost all consciousness and ran blindly back to the lighted lanes and laughing throngs that dwelt smugly safe from the terrors I knew.

The stranger in the crocodile mask—of Egypt. I don't care to write Egyptian stories any more, now that I know.

Knowledge came during that last moment, when I saw the stranger sink his curiously constructed crocodile muzzle in poor Vanning's throat—sink in with saber-teeth slashing. It was then that I grabbed him for a moment before he slipped away; grabbed at him, screamed, and hysterically fled. *The murderer was not a priest.*

I grabbed him, in that horrible moment, by the bloody muzzle of the frighteningly realistic crocodile mask. Just a single moment of horrid contact, before he disappeared. But it was enough.

For when I seized that bloody, reptilian muzzle, I felt beneath my fingers, *not a mask, but living flesh!*

B LOCH TAKES UP LOVECRAFT'S *intriguing reference (in "The Haunter of the Dark")
to Nephren-Ka, the Antichrist counterpart to the heretic Pharaoh Ikhnaton or
Akhenaton, who proclaimed himself the hierophant and revealer of a single solar deity
and sought to supplant the traditional Egyptian pantheon in the name of his divine
patron Aten. He was promptly deposed, his monotheistic reforms reversed.*

*Some readers may have experienced déjà vu upon reading Archie Goodwin's tale
"Collector's Edition," illustrated by Steve Ditko, in* Creepy *magazine (see James
Warren, ed.,* The Best of Creepy *{Tempo Books, 1971}). Goodwin's well-told tale
seems to be a creative fusion of elements borrowed from no less than three Bloch originals.
The colorful history of the grimoire* Dark Visions *by the decadent Marquis le Mode,
eventually slain by the Inquisition, is highly reminiscent of Ludvig Prinn's career and
fate. The dealings between the narrator and the seedy bookseller Murch recalls rather
closely those between the dubious Marco and collector Maitland in "The Skull of the
Marquis de Sade." And the finale wherein Goodwin's narrator beholds his own death
prophetically depicted in the illustrated pages of* Dark Visions *surely owes a great
debt to the climax of "The Fane of the Black Pharaoh."*   •

Fane of the
Black Pharaoh

"**L**IAR!" SAID CAPTAIN CARTARET.
The dark man did not move, but beneath the shadows of his burnoose a scowl slithered across a contorted countenance. But when he stepped forward into the lamplight, he smiled.

"That is a harsh epithet, *effendi*," purred the dark man.

Captain Cartaret stared at his midnight visitor with quizzical appraisal.

"A deserved one, I think," he observed. "Consider the facts. You come to my door at midnight, uninvited and unknown. You tell me some long rigmarole about secret vaults below Cairo, and then voluntarily offer to lead me there."

"That is correct," assented the Arab, blandly. He met the glance of the scholarly captain calmly.

"Why should you do this?" pursued Cartaret. "If your story is true, and you do possess so manifestly absurd a secret, why should you come to me? Why not claim the glory of discovery yourself?"

"I told you, *effendi*," said the Arab. "That is against the law of our brotherhood. It is not written that I should do so. And knowing of your interest in these things, I came to offer you the privilege."

"You came to pump me for my information; no doubt that's what you mean," retorted the captain, acidly. "You beggars have some devilishly clever ways of getting underground information, don't you? So far as I know, you're here to find out how much I've already learned, so that you and your fanatic thugs can knife me if I know too much."

"Ah!" The dark stranger suddenly leaned forward and peered into the white man's face. "Then you admit that what I tell you is not wholly strange—you do know something of this place already?"

"Suppose I do," said the captain, unflinching. "That doesn't prove that you're a philanthropic guide to what I'm seeking. More likely you want to pump me, as I said, then dispose of me and get the goods for yourself. No, your story is too thin. Why, you haven't even told me your name."

"My name?" The Arab smiled. "That does not matter. What does matter is your distrust of me. But, since you have admitted at last that you do know about the crypt of Nephren-Ka, perhaps I can show you something that may prove my own knowledge."

He thrust a lean hand under his robe and drew forth a curious object of dull, black metal. This he flung casually on the table, so that it lay in a fan of lamplight.

Captain Cartaret bent forward and peered at the queer, metallic thing. This thin, usually pale face now glowed with unconcealed excitement. He grasped the black object with twitching fingers.

"The Seal of Nephren-Ka!" he whispered. When he raised his eyes to the inscrutable Arab's once more, they shone with mingled incredulity and belief.

"It's true, then—what you say," the captain breathed. "You could obtain this only from the Secret Place; the Place of the Blind Apes where—"

"Nephren-Ka bindeth up the threads of truth." The smiling Arab finished the quotation for him.

"You, too, have read the *Necronomicon,* then." Cartaret looked stunned. "But there are only six complete versions, and I thought the nearest was in the British Museum."

The Arab's smile broadened. "My fellow-countryman, Alhazred, left many legacies among his own people," he said, softly. "There is wisdom available to all who know where to seek it."

For a moment there was silence in the room. Cartaret gazed at the black Seal, and the Arab scrutinized him in turn. The thoughts of both were far away. At last the thin, elderly white man looked up with a quick grimace of determination.

"I believe your story," he said. "Lead me."

The Arab, with a satisfied shrug, took a chair, unbidden, at the side of his host. From that moment he assumed complete psychic mastery of the situation.

"First, you must tell me what you know," he commanded. "Then I shall reveal the rest."

Cartaret, unconscious of the other's dominance, complied. He told the stranger his story in an abstracted manner, while his eyes never swerved from the cryptic black amulet on the table. It was almost as though he were hypnotized by the queer talisman. The Arab said nothing, though there was a gay gloating in his fanatical eyes.

– 2 –

Cartaret spoke of his youth; of his wartime service in Egypt and subsequent station in Mesopotamia. It was here that the captain had first become interested in archeology and the shadowy realms of the occult which surrounded it. From the vast desert of Arabia had come intriguing tales as old as time; furtive fables of mystic Irem, city of ancient dread, and the lost legends of vanished empires. He had spoken to the dreaming dervishes whose hashish visions revealed secrets of forgotten days, and had explored certain reputedly ghoul-ridden tombs and burrows in the ruins of an older Damascus than recorded history knows.

In time, his retirement had brought him to Egypt. Here in Cairo there was access to still more secret lore. Egypt, land of lurid curses and lost kings, has ever harbored mad myths in its age-old shadows. Cartaret had learned of priests and pharaohs; of olden oracles, forgotten sphinxes, fabulous pyramids, titanic tombs. Civilization was but a cobweb surface upon the sleeping face of Eternal Mystery. Here, beneath the inscrutable shadows of the pyramids, the old gods still stalked in the old ways. The ghosts of Set, Ra, Osiris, and Bubastis lurked in desert ways; Horus, Isis, and Sebek yet dwelt in the ruins of Thebes and Memphis, or bided in the crumbling tombs below the Valley of Kings.

Nowhere had the past survived as it did in ageless Egypt. With every mummy, the Egyptologists uncovered a curse; the solving of each ancient secret merely uncovered a deeper, more perplexing riddle. Who built the pylons of the temples? Why did the old kings rear the pyramids? How did they work such marvels? Were their curses potent still? Where vanished the priests of Egypt?

These and a thousand other unanswered questions intrigued the mind of Captain Cartaret. In his new-found leisure he read and studied, talked with scientists and savants. Ever the quest of primal knowledge beckoned him on to blacker brinks; he could slake his thirsty soul only in stranger secrets, more dangerous discoveries.

Many of the reputable authorities he knew were open in their confessed opinion that it was not well for meddlers to pry too deeply beneath the surface. Curses had come true with puzzling promptness, and warning prophecies had been fulfilled with a vengeance. It was not good to profane the shrines of the old dark gods who still dwelt within the land.

But the terrible lure of the forgotten and the forbidden was a pulsing virus in Cartaret's blood. When he heard the legend of Nephren-Ka, he naturally investigated.

Nephren-Ka, according to authoritative knowledge, was merely a mythical figure. He was purported to have been a Pharaoh of no known dynasty, a priestly usurper of the throne. The most common fables placed his reign in almost biblical times. He was said to have been the last and greatest of that Egyptian cult of priest-sorcerers who for a time transformed the recognized religion into a dark and terrible thing. This cult, led by the arch-hierophants of Bubastis, Anubis, and Sebek, viewed their gods as the representatives of actual Hidden Beings— monstrous beast-men who shambled on Earth in primal days. They accorded worship to the Elder One who is known to myth as Nyarlathotep, the "Mighty Messenger." This abominable deity was said to confer wizard's power upon receiving human sacrifices; and while the evil priests reigned supreme they temporarily transformed the religion of Egypt into a bloody shambles. With anthropomancy and necrophilism they sought terrible boons from their demons.

The tale goes that Nephren-Ka, on the throne, renounced all religion save that of Nyarlathotep. He sought the power of prophecy, and built temples to the Blind Ape of Truth. His utterly atrocious sacrifices at length provoked a revolt, and it is said that the infamous Pharaoh was at last dethroned. According to this account, the new ruler and his people immediately destroyed all vestiges of the former reign, demolished all temples and idols of Nyarlathotep, and drove out the wicked priests who prostituted their faith to the carnivorous Bubastis, Anubis, and Sebek. *The Book of the Dead* was then amended so that all references to the Pharaoh Nephren-Ka and his accursed cults were deleted.

Thus, argues the legend, the furtive faith was lost to reputable history. As to Nephren-Ka himself, a strange account is given of his end.

The story ran that the dethroned Pharaoh fled to a spot adjacent to what is now the modern city of Cairo. Here it was his intention to embark with his remaining followers for a "westward isle." Historians believe that this "isle" was Britain, where some of the fleeing priests of Bubastis actually settled.

But the Pharaoh was attacked and surrounded, his escape blocked. It was then that he had constructed a secret underground tomb, in which he caused himself and his followers to be interred alive. With him, in this vivisepulture, he took all his treasure and magical secrets, so that nothing would remain for his enemies to profit by. So cleverly did his remaining devotees contrive this secret crypt that the attackers were never able to discover the resting-place of the Black Pharaoh.

Thus the legend rests. According to common currency, the fable was handed down by the few remaining priests who actually stayed on the

surface to seal the secret place; they and their descendants were believed
to have perpetuated the story and the old faith of evil.

Following up this exceedingly unusual story, Cartaret delved into
the old tomes of the time. During a trip to London he was fortunate
enough to be allowed an inspection of the unhallowed and archaic
Necronomicon of Abdul Alhazred. In it were further emendations. One
of his influential friends in the Home Office, hearing of his interest,
managed to obtain for him a portion of Ludvig Prinn's evil and
blasphemous *De Vermis Mysteriis,* known more familiarly to students
of recondite arcana as *Mysteries of the Worm.* Here, in that greatly
disputed chapter on oriental myth entitled *Saracenic Rituals,* Cartaret
found still more concrete elaborations of the Nephren-Ka tale.

Prinn, who consorted with the mediaeval seers and prophets of
Saracen times in Egypt, gave a good deal of prominence to the
whispered hints of Alexandrian necromancers and adepts. They knew
the story of Nephren-Ka, and alluded to him as the Black Pharaoh.

Prinn's account of the Pharaoh's death was much more elaborate. He
claimed that the secret tomb lay directly beneath Cairo itself, and
professed to believe that it had been opened and reached. He hinted at
the cult-survival mentioned in the popular tales; spoke of a renegade
group of descendants whose priestly ancestors had interred the rest
alive. They were said to perpetuate the evil faith, and to act as guardians
of the dead Nephren-Ka and his buried brethren, lest some interloper
discover and violate his resting-place in the crypt. After the regular
cycle of seven thousand years, the Black Pharaoh and his band would
then arise once more, and restore the dark glory of the ancient faith.

The crypt itself, if Prinn is to be believed, was a most unusual place.
Nephren-ka's servants and slaves had builded him a mighty sepulcher,
and the burrows were filled with the rich treasure of his reign. All of
the sacred images were there, and the jeweled books of esoteric wisdom
reposed within.

Most peculiarly did the account dwell on Nephren-Ka's search for
the Truth and the Power of Prophecy. It was said that before he died
down in the darkness, he conjured up the earthly image of Nyarlathotep in a final gigantic sacrifice; and that the god granted him his
desires. Nephren-Ka had stood before the images of the Blind Ape of
Truth and received the gift of divination over the gory bodies of a
hundred willing victims. Then, in nightmare manner, Prinn recounts
that the entombed Pharaoh wandered among his dead companions and
inscribed on the twisted walls of his tomb the secrets of the future. In
pictures and ideographs he wrote the history of days to come, revelling

in omniscient knowledge till the end. He scrawled the destinies of kings to come; painted the triumphs and the dooms of unborn empires. Then, as the blackness of death shrouded his sight, and palsy wrenched the brush from his fingers, he betook himself in peace to his sarcophagus, and there died.

So said Ludvig Prinn, he that consorted with ancient seers. Nephren-Ka lay in his buried burrows, guarded by the priestly cult that still survived on Earth, and further protected by enchantments in his tomb below. He had fulfilled his desires at the end—he had known Truth, and written the lore of the future on the nighted walls of his own catacomb.

Cartaret had read all this with conflicting emotions. How he would like to find that tomb, if it existed! What a sensation—he would revolutionize anthropology, ethnology!

Of course, the legend had its absurd points. Cartaret, for all his research, was not superstitious. He didn't believe the bogus balderdash about Nyarlathotep, the Blind Ape of Truth, or the priestly cult. That part about the gift of prophecy was sheer drivel.

Such things were commonplace. There were many savants who had attempted to prove that the pyramids, in their geometrical construction, were archeological and architectural prophecies of days to come. With elaborate and convincing skill, they attempted to show that, symbolically interpreted, the great tombs held the key to history, that they allegorically foretold the Middle Ages, the Renaissance, the Great War.

This, Cartaret believed, was rubbish. And the utterly absurd notion that a dying fanatic had been gifted with prophetic power and scrawled the future history of the world on his tomb as a last gesture before death—that was impossible to swallow.

Nevertheless, despite his skeptical attitude, Captain Cartaret wanted to find the tomb, if it existed. He had returned to Egypt with that intention, and immediately set to work. So far he had had a number of clues and hints. If the machinery of his investigation did not collapse, it was now only a matter of days before he would discover the actual entrance to the spot itself. Then he intended to enlist proper Governmental aid and make his discovery public to all.

This much he now told the silent Arab who had come out of the night with a strange proposal and a weird credential: the seal of the Black Pharaoh, Nephren-Ka.

– 3 –

When Cartaret finished his summary, he glanced at the dark stranger in interrogation.

"What next?" he asked.

"Follow me," said the other, urbanely. "I shall lead you to the spot you seek."

"Now?" gasped Cartaret. The other nodded.

"But—it's too sudden! I mean, the whole thing is like a dream. You come out of the night, unbidden and unknown, show me the Seal, and graciously offer to grant me my desires. Why? It doesn't make sense."

"This makes sense." The grave Arab indicated the black Seal.

"Yes," admitted Cartaret. "But—how can I trust you? Why must I go now? Wouldn't it be wiser to wait, and get the proper authorities behind us? Won't there be need of excavation; aren't there necessary instruments to take?"

"No." The other spread his palms upward. "Just come."

"Look here." Cartaret's suspicion crystallized in his sharp tones. "How do I know this isn't a trap? Why should you come to me this way? Who the devil are you?"

"Patience." The dark man smiled. "I shall explain all. I have listened to your accounts of the 'legend' with great interest, and while your facts are clear, your own view of them is mistaken. The 'legend' you have learned of is true—all of it. Nephren-Ka *did* write the future on the walls of his tomb when he died; he *did* possess the power of divination, and the priests who buried him formed a cult which *did* survive."

"Yes?" Cartaret was impressed, despite himself.

"I am one of those priests." The words stabbed like swords in the white man's brain.

"Do not look so shocked. It is the truth. I am a descendant of the original cult of Nephren-Ka, one of those inner initiates who have kept the legend alive. I worship the Power which the Black Pharaoh received, and I worship the god Nyarlathotep who accorded that Power to him. To us believers, the most sacred truth lies in the hieroglyphs inscribed by the divinely gifted Pharaoh before he died. Throughout the ages, we guardian priests have watched history unfold, and always it has agreed with the ideographs on those tunneled walls. We believe.

"It is because of our belief that I have sought you out. For within the secret crypt of the Black Pharaoh it is written upon the walls of the future that you shall descend there."

Stunning silence.

"Do you mean to say," Cartaret gasped, "that those pictures *show* me discovering the spot?"

"They do," assented the dark man, slowly. "That is why I came to you unbidden. You shall come with me and fulfill the prophecy tonight, as it is written."

"Suppose I don't come?" flashed Captain Cartaret, suddenly. "What about your prophecy then?"

The Arab smiled. "You'll come," he said. "You know that."

Cartaret realized that it was so. Nothing could keep him away from this amazing discovery. A thought struck him.

"If this wall really records the details of the future," he began, "perhaps you can tell me a little about my own coming history. Will this discovery make me famous? Will I return again to the spot? Is it written that I am to bring the secret of Nephren-Ka to light?"

The dark man looked grave. "That I do not know," he admitted. "I neglected to tell you something about the Walls of Truth. My ancestor—he who first descended into the secret spot after it had been sealed, he who first looked upon the work of prophecy—did a needful thing. Deeming that such wisdom was not for lesser mortals, he piously covered the walls with concealing tapestry. Thus none might look upon the future too far. As time passed, the tapestry was drawn back to keep pace with the actual events of history, and always they have coincided with the hieroglyphs. Through the ages, it has always been the duty of one priest to descend to the secret tomb each day and draw back the tapestry so as to reveal the events of the day that follows. Now, during my life, that is my mission. My fellows devote their time to the needful rites of worship in hidden places. I alone descend the concealed passage daily and draw back the curtain on the Walls of Truth. When I die, another will take my place. Understand me—the writing does not minutely concern every single event; merely those which affect the history and destiny of Egypt itself. Today, my friend, it was revealed that you should descend and enter into the place of your desire. What the morrow holds in store for you I cannot say, until the curtain is drawn once more."

Cartaret sighed. "I suppose that there is nothing else left but for me to go, then." His eagerness was ill dissembled. The dark man observed this at once, and smiled cynically, while he strode to the door.

"Follow me," he commanded.

To Captain Cartaret that walk through the moonlit streets of Cairo was blurred in chaotic dream. His guide led him into labyrinths of looming shadows; they wandered through the twisted native quarters and passed through a maze of unfamiliar alleys and thoroughfares. Cartaret strode mechanically at the dark stranger's heels, his thoughts avid for the great triumph to come.

He hardly noticed their passage through a dingy courtyard; when his companion drew up before an ancient well and pressed a niche revealing the passage beneath, he followed him as a matter of course. From somewhere the Arab had produced a flashlight. Its faint beam almost rebounded from the murk of the inky tunnel.

Together they descended a thousand stairs, into the ageless and eternal darkness that broods beneath. Like a blind man, Cartaret stumbled down—down into the depths of three thousand vanished years.

– 4 –

The temple was entered—the subterranean temple-tomb of Nephren-Ka. Through silver gates the priest passed, his dazed companion following behind. Cartaret stood in a vast chamber, the niched walls of which were lined with sarcophagi.

"They hold the mummies of the interred priests and servants," explained his guide.

Strange were the mummy-cases of Nephren-Ka's followers, not like those known to Egyptology. The carven covers bore no recognized, conventional features as was the usual custom; instead they presented the strange, grinning countenances of demons and creatures of fable. Jeweled eyes stared mockingly from the black visages of gargoyles spawned in a sculptor's nightmare. From every side of the room those eyes shone through the shadows; unwinking, unchanging, omniscient in this little world of the dead.

Cartaret stirred uneasily. Emerald eyes of death, ruby eyes of malevolence, yellow orbs of mockery; everywhere they confronted him. He was glad when his guide led him forward at last, so that the incongruous rays of the flashlight shone on the entrance beyond. A moment later his relief was dissipated by the sight of a new horror confronting him at the inner doorway.

Two gigantic figures shambled there, guarding either side of the opening—two monstrous, troglodytic figures. Great gorillas they were; enormous apes, carved in simian semblance from black stone. They faced the doorway, squatting on mighty haunches, their huge, hairy arms upraised in menace. Their glittering faces were brutally alive; they grinned, bare-fanged, with idiotic glee. And they were blind—eyeless and blind.

There was a terrible allegory in these figures which Cartaret knew only too well. The blind apes were Destiny personified; a hulking, mindless Destiny whose sightless, stupid gropings trampled on the dreams of men and altered their lives by aimless flailings of purposeless paws. Thus did they control reality.

These were the Blind Apes of Truth, according to the ancient legend; the symbols of the old gods worshipped by Nephren-Ka.

Cartaret thought of the myths once more, and trembled. If tales were true, Nephren-Ka had offered up that final mighty sacrifice upon the obscene laps of these evil idols; offered them up to Nyarlathotep, and buried the dead in the mummy-cases set here in the niches. Then he had gone on to his own sepulcher within.

The guide proceeded stolidly past the looming figures. Cartaret, dissembling his dismay, started to follow. For a moment his feet refused to cross that gruesomely guarded threshold into the room beyond. He stared upward to the eyeless, ogreish faces that leered down from dizzying heights, with the feeling that he walked in realms of sheer nightmare. But the huge arms beckoned him on; the unseeing faces were convulsed in a smile of mocking invitation.

The legends were true. The tomb existed. Would it not be better to turn back now, seek some aid, and return again to this spot? Besides, what unguessed terror might not lair in the realms beyond; what horror spawn in the sable shadows of Nephren-Ka's inner, secret sepulcher? All reason urged him to call out to the strange priest and retreat to safety.

But the voice of reason was but a hushed and awe-stricken whisper here in the brooding burrows of the past. This was a realm of ancient shadow, where antique evil ruled. Here the incredible was real, and there was a potent fascination in fear itself.

Cartaret knew that he must go on; curiosity, cupidity, the lust for concealed knowledge—all impelled him. And the Blind Apes grinned their challenge, or command.

The priest entered the third chamber, and Cartaret followed. Crossing the threshold, he plunged into an abyss of unreality.

The room was lighted by braziers set in a thousand stations; their glow bathed the enormous burrow with fiery luminance. Captain Cartaret, his head reeling from the heat and mephitic miasma of the place, was thus able to see the entire extent of this incredible cavern.

Seemingly endless, a vast corridor stretched on a downward slant into the earth beyond—a vast corridor, utterly barren, save for the winking red braziers along the walls. Their flaming reflections cast grotesque shadows that glimmered with unnatural life. Cartaret felt as though he were gazing on the entrance to Karneter—the mythical underworld of Egyptian lore.

"Here we are," said his guide, softly.

The unexpected sound of a human voice was startling. For some reason, it frightened Cartaret more than he cared to admit; he had fallen into a vague acceptance of these scenes as being part of a fantastic dream. Now, the concrete clarity of a spoken word only confirmed an eery reality.

Yes, here they were, in the spot of legend, the place known to Alhazred, Prinn, and all the dark delvers into unhallowed history. The tale of Nephren-Ka was true, and if so, what about the rest of the strange priest's statements? What about the Walls of Truth, on which the Black Pharaoh had recorded the future, had foretold Cartaret's own advent on the secret spot?

As if in answer to these inner whispers, the guide smiled.

"Come, Captain Cartaret; do you not wish to examine the walls more closely?"

The captain did not wish to examine the walls; desperately, he did not. For they, if in existence, would confirm the ghastly horror that gave them being. If they existed, it meant that the whole evil legend was real; that Nephren-Ka, Black Pharaoh of Egypt, had indeed sacrificed to the dread dark gods, and that they had answered his prayer. Captain Cartaret did not greatly wish to believe in such utterly blasphemous abominations as Nyarlathotep.

He sparred for time.

"Where is the tomb of Nephren-Ka himself?" he asked. "Where are the treasure and the ancient books?"

The guide extended a lean forefinger.

"At the end of this hall," he exclaimed.

Peering down the infinity of lighted walls, Cartaret indeed fancied that his eyes could detect a dark blur of objects in the dim distance.

"Let us go there," he said.

The guide shrugged. He turned, and his feet moved over the velvet dust.

Cartaret followed, as if drugged.

"The walls," he thought. "I must not look at the walls. The Walls of Truth. The Black Pharaoh sold his soul to Nyarlathotep and received the gift of prophecy. Before he died here he wrote the future of Egypt on the walls. I must not look, lest I believe. I must not know."

Red lights glittered on either side. Step after step, light after light. Glare, gloom, glare, gloom, glare.

The lights beckoned, enticed, attracted. "Look at us," they commanded. "See, dare to see all."

Cartaret followed his silent conductor.

"Look!" flashed the lights.

Cartaret's eyes grew glassy. His head throbbed. The gleaming of the lights was mesmeric; they hypnotized with their allure.

"Look!"

Would this great hall never end? No; there were thousands of feet to go.

"Look!" challenged the leaping lights.

Red serpent eyes in the underground dark; eyes of tempters, bringers of black knowledge.

"Look! Wisdom! Know!" winked the lights.

They flamed in Cartaret's brain. Why not look—it was so easy? Why fear?

Why? his dazed mind repeated the question. Each following flare of fire weakened the question.

At last, Cartaret looked.

— 5 —

Mad minutes passed before he was able to speak. Then he mumbled in a voice audible only to himself.

"True," he whispered. "All true."

He stared at the towering wall to his left, limned in red radiance. It was an interminable *Bayeux tapestry* carved in stone. The drawing was crude, in black and white, but it *frightened.* This was no ordinary Egyptian picture-writing; it was not the fantastic, symbolical style of ordinary hieroglyphics. That was the terrible part: Nephren-Ka was a realist. His men looked like men, his buildings were buildings. There was nothing here but a representation of stark reality, and it was dreadful to see.

For at the point where Cartaret first summoned courage to gaze he stared at an unmistakable tableau involving Crusaders and Saracens.

Crusaders of the Thirteenth Century—yet Nephren-Ka had then been dust for nearly two thousand years!

The pictures were small, yet vivid and distinct; they seemed to flow along quite effortlessly on the wall, one scene blending into another as though they had been drawn in unbroken continuity. It was as thought the artist had not stopped once during his work; as though he had untiringly proceeded to cover this gigantic hall in a single supernatural effort.

That was it—a single *supernatural* effort!

Cartaret could not doubt. Rationalize all he would, it was impossible to believe that these drawings were trumped up by any group of artists. It was one man's work. And the unerring horrid consistency of it; the calculated picturization of the most vital and important phases of Egyptian history could have been set down in such accurate order only by a historical authority or a prophet. Nephren-Ka had been given the gift of prophecy. And so ...

As he ruminated in growing dread, Cartaret and his guide proceeded. Now that he had looked, a Medusian fascination held the man's eyes to the wall. He walked with history tonight; history and red nightmare. Flaming figures leered from every side.

He saw the rise of the Mameluke Empire, looked on the despots and the tyrants of the East. Not all of what he saw was familiar to Cartaret, for history has its forgotten pages. Besides, the scenes changed and varied at almost every step, and it was quite confusing. There was one picture interspersed with an Alexandrian court motif which depicted a catacomb evidently in some vaults beneath the city. Here were gathered a number of men in robes which bore a curious similarity to those of Cartaret's present guide. They were conversing with a tall, white-bearded man whose crudely drawn figure seemed to exude an uncanny aura of black and baleful power.

"Ludvig Prinn," said the guide, softly, noting Cartaret's stare. "He mingled with our priests, you know."

For some reason the depiction of this almost legendary seer stirred Cartaret more deeply than any hitherto revealed terror. The casual inclusion of the infamous sorcerer in the procession of actual history hinted at dire things; it was as though Cartaret had read a prosaic biography of Satan in *Who's Who.*

Nevertheless, with a sort of heartsick craving his eyes continued to search the walls as they walked onward to the still indeterminate end of the long red-illumed chamber in which Nephren-Ka was interred. The guide—priest, now, for Cartaret no longer doubted—proceeded softly, but stole covert glances at the white man as he led the way.

Captain Cartaret walked through a dream. Only the walls were real now: the Walls of Truth. He saw the Ottomans rise and flourish, looked on forgotten battles and unremembered kings. Often there recurred in the sequence a scene depicting the priests of Nephren-Ka's own furtive cult. They were shown amidst the disquieting surroundings of catacombs and tombs, engaged in unsavory occupations and revolting pleasures. The camera-film of time rolled on; Captain Cartaret and his companion walked on. Still the walls told their story.

There was one small division of the wall which portrayed the priests conducting a man in Elizabethan costume through what seemed to be a pyramid. It was eery to see the gallant in his finery pictured amidst the ruins of ancient Egypt, and it was very dreadful indeed to almost watch, like an unseen observer, when a stealthy priest knifed the Englishman in the back as he bent over a mummy-case.

What now impressed Cartaret was the infinitude of detail in each pictured fragment. The features of all the men were almost photographically exact; the drawing, while crude, was life-like and realistic. Even the furniture and background of every scene were correct. There was no doubting the authenticity of it all, and no doubting the veracity thereby implied. But—what was worse—there was no doubting that this work could not have been done by any normal artist, however learned, unless he had seen it all.

Nephren-Ka had seen it all in prophetic vision, after his sacrifice to Nyarlathotep.

Cartaret was looking at truths inspired by a demon....

On and on, to the flaming fane of worship and death at the end of the hall. History progressed as he walked. Now he was looking at a period of Egyptian lore that was almost contemporary. The figure of Napoleon appeared.

The battle of Aboukir ... the massacre of the pyramids ... the downfall of the Mameluke horsemen ... the entrance to Cairo ....

Once again, a catacomb with priests. And three figures, white men, in French military regalia of the period. The priests were leading them into a red room. The Frenchmen were surprised, overcome, slaughtered.

It was vaguely familiar. Cartaret was recalling what he knew of Napoleon's commission; he had appointed savants and scientists to investigate the tombs and pyramids of the land. The Rosetta stone had been discovered, and other things. Quite likely the three men shown had blundered onto a mystery the priests of Nephren-Ka had not wanted to have unveiled. Hence they had been lured to death as the walls showed. It was quite familiar—but there was *another* familiarity which Cartaret could not place.

They moved on, and the years rushed by in panorama. The Turks, the English, Gordon, the plundering of the pyramids, the World War. And ever so often, a picture of the priests of Nephren-Ka and a strange white man in some catacomb or vault. Always the white man died. It was all *familiar.*

Cartaret looked up, and saw that he and the priest were very near to the blackness at the end of the great fiery hall. Only a hundred steps or so, in fact. The priest, face hidden in his burnoose, was beckoning him on.

Cartaret looked at the wall. The pictures were almost ended. But no—just ahead was a great curtain of crimson velvet on a ceiling-rack which ran off into the blackness and reappeared from shadows on the opposite side of the room to cover that wall.

"The future," explained his guide. And Captain Cartaret remembered that the priest had told how each day he drew back the curtain a bit so that the future was always revealed just one day ahead. He remembered something else, and hastily glanced at the last visible section of the Wall of Truth next to the curtain. He gasped.

It was true! Almost as though gazing into a miniature mirror he found himself staring *into his own face!*

Line for line, feature for feature, posture for posture, he and the priest of Nephren-Ka were shown standing together in this red chamber just as they were now.

The red chamber ... familiarity. The Elizabethan man with the priests of Nephren-Ka were in a catacomb when the man was murdered. The French scientists were in a red chamber when they died. Other later Egyptologists had been shown in a red chamber with the priests, and they too had been slain. The red chamber! Not familiarity but *similarity!* They had been in *this chamber!* And now he stood here, with a priest of Nephren-Ka. The others had died because they had known too much. Too much about what—Nephren-Ka?

A terrible suspicion began to formulate into hideous reality. The priests of Nephren-Ka protected their own. This tomb of their dead leaders was also their fane, their temple. When intruders stumbled onto the secret, they lured them down here and killed them lest others learn too much.

Had not he come in the same way?

The priest stood silent as he gazed at the Wall of Truth.

"Midnight," he said softly. "I must draw back the curtain to reveal yet another day before we go on. You expressed a wish, Captain Cartaret, to see what the future holds in store for you. Now that wish shall be granted."

With a sweeping gesture, he flung the curtain back along the wall for a foot. Then he moved, swiftly.

One hand leapt from the burnoose. A gleaming knife flashed through the air, drawing red fire from the lamps, then sank into Cartaret's back, drawing redder blood.

With a single groan, the white man fell. In his eyes there was a look of supreme horror, not born of death alone. For as he fell, Captain Cartaret read his future on the Walls of Truth, and it confirmed a madness that could not be.

As Captain Cartaret died he looked at the picture of his next hours of existence *and saw himself being knifed by the priest of Nephren-Ka.*

The priest vanished from the silent tomb, just as the last flicker of dying eyes showed to Cartaret the picture of a still white body—*his body*—lying in death before the Wall of Truth.

*T*HIS STORY SEEMS TO REFLECT *many others, like a jewel with many facets. We cannot help, in a later day, being reminded of Lovecraft's "From Beyond," to which the story perhaps owes a conscious debt, and, perhaps fortuitously, to Frank Belknap Long's "The Hounds of Tindalos," where we read of awful entities from other dimensions pursuing their prey through interdimensional angles. Note also the similarity of theme to two Lovecraft revisions, "The Trap" (with Henry S. Whitehead) and "The Tree on the Hill" (with Duane Rimel). The whole story may be said to depend on the observed relation between the words "oculist" and "occultist," a classic case of the suggestive slippage of language made much of by Deconstructive critics.*

The Sorcerer's Jewel

B Y RIGHTS, I should not be telling this story. David is the one to tell it, but then, David is dead. Or is he?

That's the thought that haunts me, the dreadful possibility that in some way David Niles is still alive—in some unnatural, unimaginable way alive. That is why I shall tell the story; unburden myself of the onerous weight which is slowly crushing my mind.

But David Niles could do it properly. Niles was a photographer; he could give the technical terms, perhaps explain coherently many things that I do not pretend to understand. I can only guess, or hint.

Niles and I shared a studio together for several years. It was a true partnership—we were both friends and business associates. This was peculiar in itself, for we were dissimilar types, and with widely divergent interests. We differed in almost every particular.

I am tall, thin, and dark. Niles was short, plump, and fair. I am naturally lazy, moody, inclined towards introspection. Niles was always tense with energy, high-spirited, volatile. My chief interests, in latter years, have leaned towards metaphysics and a study of occultism. Niles was a skeptic, a materialist, and above all, a scientist. Still, together we formed an integrated personality—I, the dreamer; Niles, the doer.

Our mutual business association, as I have already intimated, lay in the field of photography.

David Niles was one of the most brilliant personalities in the domain of modern portrait photography. For several years prior to our association he had done salon work, exhibiting internationally and creating a reputation which brought him a considerable income from private sittings.

At the time of our meeting he had become dissatisfied with commercial work. Photography, he argued, was an art; an art best nourished by serious, solitary study unimpeded by the demands of catering to customers. He therefore determined to retire for a year or so and devote himself to experiment.

I was the partner he chose for the work. He had lately become a devotee of the William Mortensen school of photography. Mortensen, of course, is the leading exponent of fantasy in photography; his studies of monstrosities and grotesques are widely known. Niles believed that in fantasy, photography most closely approximated true art. The idea of picturing the abstract fascinated him; the thought that a modern camera could photograph dream worlds and blend fancy with reality seemed intriguing. That's where I came in.

Niles knew of my interest in the occult, knew that I had made a study of mythology. I was to serve as technical adviser on his subject matter. The arrangement pleased us both.

At first Niles limited himself to studies in physiognomy. With his usual thoroughness, he mastered the technique of photographic makeup and hired models whose features lent themselves to the application of gargoylian disguises. I handled the matter of checking over reference works, finding illustrations in old books of legends to use in devising suitable makeup.

Niles did a study of Pan, one of a satyr, and a Medusa. He became interested in demons, and we spent some time on his *Gallery of Fiends* series; Asmodeus, Azaziel, Sammael, and Beelzebub. They were surprisingly good.

But for some reason or other, Niles was not satisfied. The quality of the photographs was excellent, the posing effective, the characterization superb. And still Niles did not feel that he was achieving his goal.

"Human figures," he stormed. "Human faces are, after all, only human faces, no matter how much you cover them up with greasepaint and putty. What I want is the soul of Fantasy, not the outward aping."

He strode up and down the studio, gesticulating in his feverish manner. "What have we got?" he demanded. "A lot of stupid horror-movie faces. Amateur Karloffs. Kid stuff. No, we must find something else."

So the next phase was modelling clay. I was handy here, for I had a rudimentary knowledge of sculpture. We spent hours on composing scenes from an imaginary Inferno; constructing bat-winged figures that flew against bizarre, other-worldly backgrounds of fire, and great malignant demons that squatted and brooded on jagged peaks overlooking the Fiery Pit.

But here, too, Niles could not find what he was looking for.

One night he exploded again, after finishing a set. With a sweep of his arm, he smashed the papier-mache set and its clay figures to the floor.

"Hokum," he muttered. "Peep-show, penny-dreadful stuff."

I sighed, getting set to listen patiently to a further tirade.

"I don't want to be the Gustave Dore of photography, or the Sime, or even the Artzybasheff," he said. "I don't want to copy any style. What I'm after is something original, something I can claim as absolutely individual."

I shrugged. Wisdom had taught me to keep my mouth shut and let Niles talk himself out.

"I've been on the wrong track," he declared. "If I photograph things as they are, that's all I'm going to get. I build a clay set, and by Heaven, when I photograph it, all I can get is a picture of that clay set—a flat, two-dimensional thing at that. I take a portrait of a man in makeup and my result is a photo of a man in makeup. I can't hope to catch something with the camera that isn't there. The answer is—change the camera. Let the instrument do the work."

I saw his argument, and conceded its validity.

The following few weeks Niles' existence was a frenzy of experimental activity. He began to take montage shots. Then he worked with odd papers, odder exposures. He even reverted to the Mortensen principles and employed distortion—bending and twisting the negative so that prints showed elongated or flattened figures in nightmarish fashion.

An ordinary man's forehead, under these methods, would register as being hydrocephalic; his eyes might appear as bulging beacons illumined by insane lights. The perspective of nightmare, the nuances of oneirodynia, the hallucinative images of the demented were reproduced by distortion. Pictures were shadowed, shaded; portions blocked out or moulded into weird backgrounds.

And then came a night when Niles again paced the floor, tracing a restless path through piles of torn-up prints. "I'm not getting it," he murmured. "I can take a natural subject and distort it, but I can't actually change its content. In order to photograph the unreal, I must see the unreal. *See the unreal*— Good Lord, why didn't I think of that before?"

He stood before me, his hands twitching. "I studied painting once, you know. My instructor—old Gifford, the portrait man—hung a certain picture in his studio. It was the old boy's masterpiece. The painting was of a winter scene, in oils; a winter scene of a farmhouse.

"Now here's the point. Gifford had two pairs of spectacles; one sensitive to infra-red, the other to ultra-violet rays. He'd show a guest the winter scene, then ask him to try on the first pair of spectacles and look again. Through the glasses the picture showed the same farmhouse on a summer day. The second pair of lenses gave a view of the farmhouse in autumn. He had painted three layers, and the proper lenses each showed a different picture.

"So what?" I ventured.

Niles talked faster, his excitement increasing.

"So this. Remember the war? The Germans used to camouflage machine gun nests and field batteries. They did it quite elaborately; painting the guns with leafy hues and using artificial plant formations to cover them up. Well American observation posts employed ultra-violet lenses in field glasses to spot the camouflaging. Through the glasses the natural leaves showed up in entirely different colors in comparison to the artificially painted ones, which lacked ultra-violet pigment."

"I still don't see the point."

"Use ultra-violet and infra-red lenses in photography and we'll get the same effect," he almost shouted.

"But isn't that just an extension of the ordinary color-filter principle?" I asked.

"Perhaps. But we can combine them with reground lenses of various types—lenses that will distort perspective in themselves. So far we've merely distorted form, shape. But with both color and form distorted, we can achieve the type of photography I'm striving for—fantasy, pure and simple. We'll focus on fantasy and reproduce it without tampering with any objects. Can you imagine what this room will look like with its colors reversed, some of them absent completely; with the furniture shapes altered, the very walls distorted?"

I couldn't, but I was soon privileged to actually see it. For Niles at once began another cycle; he experimented endlessly with the new lenses he brought in daily. He sent out special orders for grinding, spent time studying the physical laws of light, enmeshed himself in technicalities I cannot pretend to comprehend. The results were startling.

The *outré* views he had promised me materialized. After a final day of effort before the camera and in the dark-room, we gazed together on a wonderful new world created right here in our own studio. I marveled at some of the effects Niles had created.

"Splendid," he gloated. "It all seems to tie in with the accepted scientific theories, too. Know what I mean? The Einsteinian notions of coexistence; the space-time continuum ideas."

"The Fourth Dimension?" I echoed.

"Exactly. New worlds all around us—within us. Worlds we never dream of exist simultaneously with our own; right here in this spot there are other existences. Other furniture, other people, perhaps. And other physical laws. New forms, new color."

"That sounds metaphysical to me, rather than scientific," I observed. "You're speaking of the Astral Plane—the continuous linkage of existence."

We were back again at our perpetual squabbling point—science or occultism; physical versus psychical reality.

"The Fourth Dimension is Science's way of interpreting the metaphysical truths of existence," I maintained.

"The metaphysical truths of existence are the psychological lies of *dementia praecox* victims," he asserted.

"Your pictures don't lie," I answered.

"My pictures are taken by recognized scientific means," he said.

"Your pictures are taken by means older than science," I replied. "Ever hear of lithomancy? Divination by the use of jewels. Ever hear of crystal-gazing? For ages, men have peered into the depths of precious stones, gazed through polished, specially cut and ground glasses, and seen new worlds."

"Absurd. Any oculist can tell you that—"

"You don't have to finish that one," I cut in. "Any oculist will tell you that we really see everything upside down. Our minds alone interpret the retinal image as being right-side up. Any oculist will tell you that muscularly, a near-sighted person is really far-sighted, and a far-sighted person is really near-sighted."

I warmed to my theme. "Any oculist will tell you that the hand is quicker than the eye; that mirages and hallucinations are actually 'seen' by the brain, rather than by the actual retina. In fact, any oculist will tell you that the phenomenon of sight has very little to do with either actual perception or the true laws of light.

"Look at the cat—contrary to popular impression a nyctalops. Yet men can train themselves similarly. Reading, too, is a matter of the mind rather than of minute perception. And so I say to you, don't be too sure of your laws of optics, and your scientific theories of light. We see a lot no physical laws will ever explain. The Fourth Dimension can be approached only through angles—science must concede that in theorization. And your lenses are cut similarly. It all goes back to occultism in the end—occultism, not 'oculism' or ophthalmology."

It was a long speech for me, and it must have astonished Niles, who glowered at me, speechless for once.

"I'll prove it," I went on. "Let me cut you a lens."

"What?"

"I'll go down to a friend of mine and borrow a few stones from him. There are some Egyptian crystals there which were used by the seers for divination. They claimed that they could see other worlds through the angles of the jewels. And I'm willing to bet you that you'll get pictures through them that will make you forget experiments with Iceland spar and quartz and all the rest; pictures you and your scientific ideas won't so readily explain."

"All right. I'll call you on that," Niles snapped. "Bring me the stones."

So the next day I went down to Isaac Voorden's. I went with misgivings. The truth was that I had been half bragging when I had spoken about the properties of jewels and glasses. I knew that such things were much used for prophecy and various forms of lithomancy, but as to whether I could procure one, and whether it could be ground into a camera lens, I was not at all certain.

Still, I spoke to Isaac Voorden. He was the logical person to go to. His antique shop down on South Kinnikinnic, pervaded by an aura of mysticism, was a little fortress that preserved the past. Isaac Voorden made a profession of his hobby and a hobby of his profession; he lived on metaphysics and dabbled in antiques. He spent the greater portion of his time in the musty back rooms of his establishment and left the care of his shop to a clerk.

Here in the rear of the place he had relics of other days which made his commercial antiques seem bright and new by contrast. The centuried symbols of magic, alchemy, and the secret sciences fascinated Voorden; he had gathered unto himself a collection of statuettes, talismans, fetishes and other paraphernalia of wizardry that would have been hard to match.

It was from Isaac, then, that I expected help in my quest, and he gave it to me. I told my story of Niles' photographic problems. The sallow-faced, thin-lipped little antique-dealer listened, his eyebrows crawling over his forehead like astonished black beetles.

"Very interesting," he said, when I had concluded. His rasping voice and preoccupied manner betokened the introverted pedant—Isaac always seemed to be delivering a lecture to himself.

"Very, very interesting," he repeated. "David Niles has had illustrious predecessors. The priests of Ishtar sought in their Mysteries to peer beyond the veil, and they looked through crystals. The first crude telescopes of Egypt were fashioned by men who sought to use them in seeing beyond the stars and unlocking the gates of the Infinite. The

Druids contemplated pools of water, and the mad emperors sought the Heavenly Stairway in China, hoping to ascend by gazing at turning rubies whilst under the influence of drugs.

"Yes, your friend Niles has an age-old wish, and expresses it in a timeless fashion. It is the wish that animated Apollonius, and Paracelsus, and the absurd, posturing Cagliostro. Men have always sought to see the Infinite; to walk between the worlds—and sometimes that wish has been granted."

I cut in. Voorden was wound up for the afternoon, but I wanted my information.

"They say there are jewels that hold queer visions," I murmured. Unconsciously, I adopted Voorden's pomposity of speech. He smiled, slowly.

"I have them here," he replied.

"Niles does not believe that," I countered.

"Many do not believe. But there is a stone once used by Friar Bacon, and a set of crystals which intrigued Theophrastus, and divining-jewels that the Aztecs peered through before the blood-sacrifice. Jewels, you know, are mathematical figures of light—they reflect within their facets. And who knows but that in some way those angles impinge on other worlds? Perhaps they reach out and transmute poly-angularity so that gazing into their depths, we become aware of it three-dimensionally. The ancients used angles in magic; the moderns do the same thing and call it mathematics. De Sitter says—"

"The jewel for the camera lens," I interrupted.

"I am sorry, my friend. Of course. I think I have one that should prove eminently suitable. The Star of Sechmet. Very ancient, but not costly. Stolen from the crown of the Lioness-headed Goddess during a Roman invasion of Egypt. It was carried to Rome and placed in the vestal girdle of the High-Priestess of Diana. The barbarians took it, cut the jewel into a round stone. The black centuries swallowed it.

"But it is known that Axenos the Elder bathed it in the red, yellow and blue flames, and sought to employ it as a Philosopher's Stone. With it he was reputed to have seen beyond the Veil and commanded the Gnomes, the Sylphs, the Salamanders, and the Undines. It formed part of the collection of Gilles De Rais, and he was said to have visioned within its depths the concept of *Homonculus*. It disappeared again, but a monograph I have mentions it as forming part of the secret collection of the Count St. Germain during his ritual services in Paris. I bought it in Amsterdam from a Russian priest whose eyes had been burned out by little gray brother Rasputin. He claimed to have divinated with it and foretold—"

I broke in again at this point. "You will cut the stone so that it may be used as a photographic lens, then," I repeated. "And when shall I have it?"

"You young men have no love for quiet conversation," he rebuked me. "Tomorrow, if you like. You understand, the jewel has only a great sentimental value to me; I have never experimented with it personally. All that I ask is that you report to me your findings with it. And I counsel you that if the camera reveals what I think it will, you promise to take care in using it. There is danger in invading the realms—"

He was still chattering away as I bowed out. Great character, Isaac.

The following afternoon I called and took the little package which he proffered me.

That evening I gave it to Niles.

Together we unwrapped the cloudy lens. I had given Voorden the specifications of the large camera we ordinarily employed in our later work—a reflex, with a reflecting mirror set inside so that we could easily peer through and view the focus. Voorden had done his work amazingly well—Niles gave a little snort of astonishment before he commented, "Nice job."

He lost no time in changing the lenses and inserting the Star of Sechmet. He bent over the camera—I shall never forget the sight of him there—and his plump body loomed large against the shadowed walls of the studio. I thought of a stooping alchemist peering into a crystal to seek instructions from the demons that danced within.

Niles jerked erect with a grunt. "The devil!" he muttered. "It's all cloudy. Can't make any adjustment. The whole thing's a fake."

"Let me try."

I took my place and stared through a gray mass. Yes, it was merely a dull lens. Or was it?

A hint of movement in the cloudy gray.

A swirling as of parted mists. A dancing light. The fog was dispersing, and it seemed to be opening up—opening to a view that receded far into the distance. The wall it was focused on appeared faintly, very tiny, as though through the reverse end of binoculars. The wall began to fade, so that I thought of a ghost room, with ectoplasmic lines. Then it fled away, and something new loomed large before the camera. Something grew out of empty space. Abruptly—focus!

I think I shouted. Certainly a scream seared across my brain.

For I saw Hell.

At first only angles and angles, weaving and shifting in light that was of no color, yet phosphorescent. And out of the angles, a flat black

plain that stretched upward, endlessly, without horizon. It was moving, and the angles moved, and yet through the lurching roll as of a
ship's deck in heavy seas, I saw cubes, triangles, mathematical figures
of bewildering size and complexity. There were thousands of them,
lines of light in the shape of polyhedrons. And as I gazed, they changed.

Changed into forms.

Those forms—they were spawned only in delirium; only in nightmares and dreams of the Pit. There were grinning demons that skulked
on padding claws across that endless moving plain; there were shapeless toadstools with tentacles ending in Cyclopean eyes; there were
fanged heads that rolled towards me, laughing; great hands that curled
and crawled like mad spiders. Ghouls, monsters, fiends—the words
sprang to my consciousness. And a moment ago they had been
mathematical figures!

"Here," I gasped. "Look again, Niles."

He gazed, his face reflecting puzzlement at my agitation. "Still
nothing," he grumbled. But watching him I saw the pallor come into
his face as he stared more intently.

"Yes!" he hissed. "The mist is parting. Yes! The room is smaller,
fading. And now—something is rushing up or I'm rushing toward
it—angles of light."

"Wait," I said in a low voice, yet triumphantly. "You haven't seen
anything yet."

"I see geometrical shapes. Cubic shapes. Polyhedrons of luminance.
They cover a plain and—Good God!"

His body shook over the camera.

"I see them!" he cried. "I see them. Dozens of tall, eyeless creatures
with heads all hair. Knotted hair, it twists and weaves, and underneath
the hair, little wrinkled pink-pulp mouths like the convolution slits
of the human brain. And that—*the Goat with the Hands!*"

He made an indescribable sound, fell back shaking, and turned the
adjusting device. His eyes were red, he looked as though he had
awakened from a fever-sleep.

We each had a drink. We didn't trouble about glasses, we drank
from the bottle.

"Well?" I said, when composure had been restored.

"Hallucination," he hazarded, somewhat weakly.

"Want to look again?" I countered. He gave me a wry smile.

"It can't be delusion," I went on. "I didn't see any goat, but we both
saw the mists swirl, saw the same plane, the same geometric forms of
living light."

"True. But the last—things—were different to each of us. I don't understand."

"I think I do," I said. "If Voorden is right. That jewel is a key. Its angles open to the Astral Plane. The Astral Plane—here, don't shake your head so—corresponds to the scientific conception of the Fourth Dimension, although metaphysicians believe it is an extension of third-dimensional life. That is, when men die their souls enter the Astral Plane and pass through it into another higher form of existence on a higher dimension. The Astral Plane is a sort of No Man's Land existing all about us, where lost souls, and lower entities that have never achieved life, wander forever in a sort of Limbo."

"Hooey."

"A modern criticism. But it's an ancient belief, mirrored in a thousand forms in scores of religions. And wait until you see what I'm getting at. Ever hear of Elementals?"

"Nothing but a few mentions. Ghosts, aren't they?"

"No—forces. Entities not human, but linked with humanity. They are the *demons* and *familiars* and the *incubœe* and the *genie* of all religions; the beings that exist invisibly around us and seek traffic with men. Organisms outside three-dimensional life, if you want it in more scientific terminology. They inhabit another Time-field, another space continuum that is nevertheless synchronized and co-existent with our own. They can be viewed, or reached, as ultra-dimensional inhabitants, only through angles. The angles, the facets of this jewel, enabled us to see through to them. They establish a focal point with infinity. What we saw, then, are Elementals."

"All right, swami, but why did we see different creatures?" he persisted.

"Because, my dear fellow, we have different brains. At first we both saw geometrical figures. That is the purest form of life they exist in.

"But our minds interpreted these figures into familiar shapes. I saw one type of monstrosity because of my background of mythological study. You received another impression—and I gather from your little comments (you look smug enough now, friend, but you were bleating pretty loudly a while ago and I know you were genuinely impressed) that you drew your images from past dreams and nightmares. I should imagine that a Hungarian peasant, peering through the lens, would see vampires and werewolves.

"It's psychological. In some way that jewel establishes a focal point in more than a visual way. It must also enable those creatures to become aware of us—and they *will* that we see them according to our mental concepts of such entities. In fact, that's how superstition probably originated; these beings at times communicated with men."

Niles made a gesture of impatience. "Dropping the psychological and the nut-house angle for a minute," he said, "I certainly must hand it to your friend Voorden. Whether his story about the jewel is hokum or not, and whether your rather naive explanation is accepted or disbelieved, I still can see that we've stumbled on something quite marvelous. I mean it. The pictures we can take with that camera will be unique in the field. I've never read of any experimental work that even approached this. It goes beyond the wildest Dadaistic or Surrealistic concepts. We'll get actual photographs—but of what, I'll be darned if I can foretell. Your so-called mental concepts were different from mine."

I shook my head as something Voorden had said came back to me.

"Now look here, Niles. I know you don't believe me, but you believe what you saw in the lens. I saw you shudder; you must admit the horror of those creatures—whether you choose to think they originate in your imagination or in my theory of the Astral Plane, you must recognize the fact that they are a menace to any man's sanity.

"If you see too much of that sort of thing you'll go mad. I'm not being melodramatic. I wouldn't advise looking too closely into that lens, now, or spending too much time before it."

"Don't be silly," Niles said.

"Elementals," I persisted, "—and you must believe this—yearn for life. They are cosmic ghouls, feeding on dead soul-bodies; but they long to lure a living man through the planes to them. Consider all legend—it's merely allegory. Stories of men disappearing, selling their souls to the devil, going to foreign worlds; all are founded on the idea of Elementals seeking human prey and dragging men down to their plane."

"Cut it out, it annoys me."Niles was colloquially common in his speech, but his eyes betokened a slight credulity that grew as I ignored his skepticism.

"You say it's superstition," I went on. "I say it's science. Witches, wizards, so-called wonder-workers; the wise men whose secrets built the pyramids—they all employed spells in which they used what? Geometrical figures. they drew angles and pentagons and cabalistic circles. Through the lines they summoned the forces from the Astral Plane—or the outer Dimensions. These forces granted them boons, and in turn they finally were drawn along the angles themselves into the Astral Plane, to pay for the boon with their lives. Witchcraft and geometry are strange bedfellows, but it's historical fact.

"And so I warn you. You see creatures through the jewel lens, and they see, feel, are in some way aware, of you. They will seek your soul—and just as you can look through the lens at them, they can extend their forces back through the jewel to suck you down. Hypnotic force, of some sort psychology has not yet postulated. Magnetism, telepathy; these are the words psychologists use to describe things they do not fully understand; just as the ancients called such forces magic. Don't look too long or too closely through that jewel."

Niles laughed.

"Tomorrow I'll take the pictures," he declared. "And then we'll see just what your Elementals are like. If it makes you nervous, you can stay away."

"Frankly, I will," I said.

And I did.

The following afternoon I left the studio in Niles' hands. He was tremendously excited. He spoke of using new focusing adjustments to extend part of the field; he wondered what speeds to photograph with, what paper to use for printing. He also speculated as to whether or not the creatures he saw would appear on the finished negative, or merely the amazing light-figures. I left, for I felt a growing nervousness and apprehension I did not wish him to see.

I went down to Voorden's.

The shop was open, but the clerk was not there when I passed through the front of the place, although the bell tinkled its usual warning of a customer's approach as I entered the door. I walked back through the gloom to the room where Isaac usually spent his time in study.

He was sitting there in the soft haze peculiar to the lightless chamber; his eyes glazed in rapt attention on the open pages of some old book.

"Isaac," I said. "That jewel has something. Niles and I used it last night, and I think it's a gateway to something incredible. Those divinators of ancient times were no fools. They knew what they were doing—"

Isaac never moved. Imperturbable, he sat and stared through the quiet dusk. There was a little smile on his sallow face.

"You promised to look up some more of the jewel's history," I went on. "Did you find anything? It's amazing, you now; quite amazing."

Isaac sat and stared and smiled. I bent forward.

Sitting bolt upright in his chair, hand clutching a pen, Isaac Voorden seemed a modern necromancer.

And like many an ancient necromancer who had overstepped the pale, Isaac Voorden was dead.

Stone-dead.

"Isaac!" I shouted. Funny, isn't it, how people always shout the name of the departed upon discovery of death? It's a sort of despairing wail of disbelief at a friend's passing; an invocation, as though the echo of a human voice can recall the soul of one that has passed beyond. Beyond—to the Astral Plane?

Quickly I bent over the cold body, stared at the crabbed scrawl covering the paper. I read the notes Voorden had been working on when his pale Visitor had arrived.

They blurred through my brain.

"The Star of Sechmet. Ptolemaic. Aug. Lulla, name of Roman who stole it. See note in Veno's *History*. Lulla died under curse for removing sacred jewel. Point one.

"Priestess of Diana who wore it in vestal girdle also died. For sacrilege. Again, see Veno. Point two. The pattern grows.

"Gilles De Retz—his fate is known. He misused the jewel. Yes, it's the inevitable story of violation.

"See *Mysteries of the Worm* for Prinn's chapter on divination. Might be reference concerning jewel during its disappearance.

"Again, the Russian. Claims to have stolen jewel from Rasputin, who used it in prophecy. Rasputin dead. The Russian lost his eyes. And unless he lost his reason, his warnings concerning sacred character of jewel are to be respected. Points three, four, and five. Whoever or whatever exists in the world opened up by the jewel is not anxious to have the gateway changed, or misused. Cutting the stone, transplanting it from one setting to another, misusing it—all result in death.

"And—I have done all three. God help this man Niles for what he must endure. They may get at him through the stone.

"God help me. There will be a price I must pay; soon.

"Why didn't I think before I gave up the jewel? Now I'm—"

That was all he had written. There was no scrawling off of the interrupted pen, no frozen look of horror, no "mounting dread" in the text of the writing. Voorden had written it. One minute he was alive, and the next minute he was dead.

Of course it could have been heart-failure, thrombosis, or simply old age. Shock, excitement, anxiety might have brought it on; a stroke may have done it.

But I didn't fool myself. I knew. I rose and ran from that shop as though fiends dogged my heels. And all the way my legs worked in rhythm to a single phrase racing through my brain. "God help Niles."

It was dusk when I unlocked the studio door. The studio was empty, the twilight room darkened. Had Niles gone out?

I prayed so. But where would he go? He wouldn't abandon work. I walked to where the camera loomed: noted the exposure of one film. He must have been called.

I restrained an impulse to peer again through the jewel lens, as I lit the light. No—I did to wish to see that plain again; see those horrible figures dwelling outside laws of space and time, yet—mocking thoughts!—actually existing here around me, in this very room. Worlds within worlds of horror. Where was Niles?

I couldn't brood like this. Why not develop the exposed film? Keep busy. I carried the camera into the dark-room. Ten minutes in darkness, then the regular process. I set the fans going as I hung the dark square up to dry.

My mind teemed with excited conjectures. Would we find a blank photograph? Would it show the angled figures of light? Or would—wonderful possibility—the creatures conjured up by our imaginations appear? Would our own brains aid in taking the pictures, as a part of the focal point linked to the camera by the hypnotic jewel? It was a fascinating thought.

The fans hummed as the minutes fled.

But where was Niles? Whatever had caused his hasty departure, surely he would have returned by now. And he had left no note.

The door had been locked from the outside, and I had the only key.

The thought grinned at me through a wave of horror.

There was no way Niles could have left.

Only one way.

I jammed the dried negative into the printer, with a sheet of ordinary paper.

I pressed down, slipped the print into the developer; waited a moment.

I raced out into the light of the other room, held the finished print wet and dripping, to the light.

Then I screamed, and smashed the camera, stamped on the jewel until I could control myself sufficiently to pick it up and hurl it through the open window at the further rooftops. I tore print and negative to shreds. And still I screamed, for I could not and never shall be able to erase the memory of what I had seen in that picture Niles had taken.

He must have clicked it off at a very fast speed. Very fast. And perhaps it was the actual working of the camera which accounted for what had happened. It might have established the focal point instantaneously—established it so that those things—forces, Elementals, call them what you will—could achieve their goal.

I saw the print. it was as Niles guessed it might be; a picture of a black endless plain. Only there were no lights visible, no figures, nothing except black shadows that seemed to blur around a central point. *They* did not photograph.

But *they* blurred around a point—a central point. *They* got through just as the picture must have snapped yet faster than light itself. *They* got through and drew Niles along the angles as I had feared. Faster than light itself, as I have said. For it had to be faster, else I would not have seen—I would not have seen what I did see on that print. The central point....

The central point of that accursed picture; the only visible thing amidst the shadows—*was the dead and mangled body of David Niles!*

*B*LOCH HAS SAID, *"I don't recall my original title for what was to become {by editorial fiat} 'The Unspeakable Betrothal;' along with some of the misnomers attached to my mystery yarns in the '40's and Howard Browne's execrable 'Let's Do It For Love,' I regard it as an abomination."* (Interview with Randall Larson, *The Robert Bloch Companion*, p. 146.) Yet Bloch is equally quick to count the story among the canon of his Cthulhu Mythos tales, *"those which have some direct affiliation with HPL's cosmology beyond mere use of nomenclature."* (Interview with Graeme Flanagan, Ibid., p. 38.)

The connections with or parallels to Lovecraftian themes and even particular Lovecraftian works are evident. Compare the story, for instance, to the *Fungi from Yuggoth* sonnet XVI, "The Window." The link with "The Whisperer in Darkness" is explicit, with the promise of the earthling's being borne aloft, though transmogrified, to the stars by them from Yuggoth. These entities seem here to partake equally of the cone race of Yith and the teasing Night-Gaunts. And the leaving behind of a disembodied face—we cannot help but think of poor Henry Akeley.

The Unspeakable Betrothal

Not far thence is the secret garden in which grow like strange flowers the kinds of sleep, so different one from the other ... the sleep induced by datura, by the multiple extracts of ether, the sleep of belladonna, of opium, of valerian; flowers whose petals remain shut until the day when the predestined visitor shall come and, touching them, bid them open, and for long hours inhale the aroma of their peculiar dreams into a marveling and bewildered being.

Proust: *Remembrance of Things Past*

AVIS KNEW SHE WASN'T really as sick as Doctor Clegg had said. She was merely bored with living. The death impulse perhaps; then again, it might have been nothing more than her distaste for clever young men who persisted in addressing her as *"O rara Avis."*

She felt better now, though. The fever had settled until it was no more than one of the white blankets which covered her—something she could toss aside with a gesture, if it weren't so pleasant just to burrow into it, to snuggle deeply within its confining warmth.

Avis smiled as she realized the truth; monotony was the one thing that didn't bore her. The sterility of excitement was the really jading routine, after all. This quiet, uneventful feeling of restfulness seemed rich and fertile by comparison. Rich and fertile—creative—womb.

The words linked. Back to the womb. Dark room, warm bed, lying doubled up in the restful, nourishing lethargy of fever. . .

It wasn't the womb, exactly; she hadn't gone back that far, she knew. But it did remind her of the days when she was a little girl. Just a little girl with big round eyes, mirroring the curiosity that lay behind them. Just a little girl, living all alone in a huge old house, like a fairy princess in an enchanted castle.

Of course her aunt and uncle had lived here too, and it wasn't a really truly castle, and nobody else knew that she was a princess. Except Marvin Mason, that is.

Marvin had lived next door and sometimes he'd come over and play with her. They would come up to her room and look out of the high window—the little round window that bordered on the sky.

Marvin knew that she was a sure-enough princess, and he knew that her room was an ivory tower. The window was an enchanted window, and when they stood on a chair and peeked out they could see the world behind the sky.

Sometimes she wasn't quite sure if Marvin Mason honest and truly saw the world beyond the window; maybe he just said he did because he was fond of her.

But he listened very quietly when she told him stories about that world. Sometimes she told him stories she had read in books, and other times she made them up out of her very own head. It was only later that the dreams came, and she told him *those* stories, too.

That is, she always started to, but somehow the words would go wrong. She didn't always know the words for what she saw in those dreams. They were very special dreams; they came only on those nights when Aunt May left the window open, and there was no moon. She would lie in the bed, all curled up in a little ball, and wait for the wind to come through the high, round window. It came quietly, and she would feel it on her forehead and neck, like fingers stroking. Cool, soft fingers, stroking her face; soothing fingers that made her uncurl and stretch out so that the shadows could cover her body.

Even then she slept in the big bed, and the shadows would pour down from the window in a path. She wasn't asleep when the shadows came, so she knew they were real. They came on the breeze, from the window, and covered her up. Maybe it was the shadows that were cool and not the wind; maybe the shadows stroked her hair until she fell asleep.

But she would sleep then, and the dreams always came. They followed the same path as the wind and the shadows; they poured down from the sky, through the window. There were voices she heard but could not understand; colors she saw but could not name; shapes she glimpsed but which never seemed to resemble any figures she found in picture books.

Sometimes the same voices and colors and shapes came again and again, until she learned to recognize them, in a way. There was the deep, buzzing voice that seemed to come from right inside her own head, although she knew it really issued from the black, shiny pyramid thing that had the arms with eyes in it. It didn't look slimy or nasty, and there was nothing to be afraid of—Avis could never understand why Marvin Mason made her shut up when she started telling about those dreams.

But he was only a little boy, and he got scared and ran to his Mommy. Avis didn't have any Mommy, only Aunt May; but she would never tell Aunt May such things. Besides, why should she? The dreams didn't frighten her, and they were so very real and interesting. Sometimes, on grey, rainy days when there was nothing to do but play with dolls or cut out pictures to paste in her album, she wished that night would hurry up and come; then she could dream and make everything real again.

She got so she liked to stay in bed, and would pretend to have a cold so she didn't have to go to school. Avis would look up at the window and wait for the dreams to come—but they never came in the daytime; only at night.

Often she wondered what it was like *up there.*

The dreams must come from the sky; she knew that. The voices and shapes *lived* way up, somewhere beyond the window. Aunt May said that dreams came from tummyaches, but she knew that wasn't so.

Aunt May was always worried about tummyaches, and she scolded Avis for not going outside to play; she said she was getting pale and puny.

But Avis felt fine, and she had her secret to think of. Now she scarcely ever saw Marvin Mason any more, and she didn't bother to read. It wasn't much fun to pretend she was a princess, either. Because the dreams were ever so much more real, and she could talk to the voices and ask them to take her with them when they went away.

She got so she could almost understand what they were saying. The shiny thing that just hung through the window now—the one that looked like it had so much more to it she couldn't see—it made music inside her head that she recognized. Not a real tune; more like words in a rhyme. In her dreams she asked it to take her away. She would crawl up on its back and let it fly with her up over the stars. That was funny, asking it to fly; but she knew that the part beyond the window had wings. Wings as big as the world.

She begged and pleaded, but the voices made her understand that they couldn't take little girls back with them. That is, not entirely. Because it was too cold and too far, and something would change her.

She said she didn't care how she changed; she wanted to go. She would let them do anything they wanted if only they would take her. It would be nice to be able to talk to them all the time and feel that cool softness; to dream forever.

One night they came to her and there were more things than she had ever seen before. They hung through the window and in the air all over the room—they were so funny, some of them; you could see through them and sometimes one was partly inside another. She knew she giggled in her sleep, but she couldn't help it. Then she was quiet and listening to them.

They told her it was all right. They would carry her away. Only she mustn't tell anyone and she mustn't be frightened; they would come for her soon. They couldn't take her as she was, and she must be willing to change.

Avis said yes, and they all hummed a sort of music together and went away.

The next morning Avis was really and truly sick and didn't want to get up. She could hardly breathe, she was so warm—and when Aunt May brought in a tray she wouldn't eat a bite.

That night she didn't dream. Her head ached, and she tossed all night long. But there was a moon out, so the dreams couldn't get through anyway. She knew they would come back when the moon was gone again, so she waited. Besides, she hurt so that she really didn't care. She had to feel better before she was ready to go anywhere.

The next day Doctor Clegg came to see her. Doctor Clegg was a good friend of Aunt May's and he was always visiting her because he was her guardian.

Doctor Clegg held her hand and asked her what seemed to be the matter with his young lady today.

Avis was too smart to say anything, and besides, there was a shiny thing in her mouth. Doctor Clegg took it out and looked at it and shook his head. After a while he went away and then Aunt May and Uncle Roscoe came in. They made her swallow some medicine that tasted just awful.

By that time it was getting dark and there was a storm coming outside. Avis wasn't able to talk much, and when they shut the round window she couldn't ask them to please leave it open tonight because there was no moon and they were coming for her.

But everything kept going round and round, and when Aunt May walked past the bed she seemed to flatten out like a shadow, or one of the things, only she made a loud noise which was really the thunder outside and now she was sleeping really and truly even though she heard the thunder but the thunder wasn't real nothing was real except the things, that was it nothing was real any more but the things.

And they came through the window; it wasn't closed after all because she opened it and she was crawling out high up there where she had never crawled before but it was easy without a body and soon she would have a new body they wanted the old one because they carried it but she didn't care because she didn't need it and now they would carry her *ulnagr Yuggoth Farnomi ilyaa ...*

That was when Aunt May and Uncle Roscoe found her and pulled her down from the window. They said later she had screamed at the top of her voice, or else she would have gone over without anyone noticing.

After that Doctor Clegg took her away to the hospital where there were no high windows and they came in to see her all night long. The dreams stopped.

When at last she was well enough to go back home, she found that the window was gone, too.

Aunt May and Uncle Roscoe had boarded it up, because she was a somnambulist. She didn't know what a somnambulist was, but guessed it had something to do with her being sick and the dreams not coming any more.

For the dreams stopped then. There was no way of making them come back, and she really didn't want them any more. It was fun to play outside with Marvin Mason now, and she went back to school when the new semester began.

Now, without the window to look at, she just slept at night. Aunt May and Uncle Roscoe were glad, and Doctor Clegg said she was turning out to be a mighty fine little specimen.

Avis could remember it all now as though it were yesterday or today. Or tomorrow.

How she grew up. How Marvin Mason fell in love with her. How she went to college and they became engaged. How she felt the night Aunt May and Uncle Roscoe were killed in the crash at Leedsville. That was a bad time.

An even worse time was when Marvin had gone away. He was in service now, overseas. She had stayed on all alone in the house, for it was her house now.

Reba came in days to do the housework, and Doctor Clegg dropped around, even after she turned twenty-one and officially inherited her estate.

He didn't seem to approve of her present mode of living. He asked her several times why she didn't shut up the house and move into a small apartment downtown. He was concerned because she showed no desire to keep up the friendships she had made in college; Avis was curiously reminded of the solicitude he had exhibited during her childhood.

But Avis was no longer a child. She proved that by removing what had always seemed to her a symbol of adult domination; she had the high round window in her room unboarded once more.

It was a silly gesture. She knew it at the time, but somehow it held a curious significance for her. For one thing, it reestablished a linkage with her childhood, and more and more, childhood came to epitomize happiness for her.

With Marvin Mason gone, and Aunt May and Uncle Roscoe dead, there was little enough to fill the present. Avis would sit up in her bedroom and pore over the scrapbooks she had so assiduously pasted up as a girl. She had kept her dolls and the old fairy-tale books; she spent drowsy afternoons examining them.

It was almost possible to lose one's time sense in such pastimes. Her surroundings were unchanged. Of course, Avis was larger now and the bed wasn't quite as massive nor the window as high.

But both were there, waiting for the little girl that she became when, at nightfall, she curled up into a ball and snuggled under the sheets— snuggled and stared up at the high, round window that bordered the sky.

Avis wanted to dream again.

At first, she *couldn't*.

After all, she was a grown woman, engaged to be married; she wasn't a character out of *Peter Ibbetson*. And those dreams of her childhood had been silly.

But they were *nice*. Yes, even when she had been ill and nearly fallen out of the window that time, it had been pleasant to dream. Of course those voices and shapes were nothing but Freudian fantasies—everyone knew that.

Or did they?

Suppose it were all real? Suppose dreams are not just subconscious manifestations caused by indigestion and gas pressure?

What if dreams are really a product of electronic impulse—or planetary radiations—attuned to the wavelength of the sleeping mind? Thought is an electrical impulse. Life itself is an electrical impulse. Perhaps a dreamer is like a spiritualist medium; placed in a receptive state during sleep. Instead of ghosts, the creatures of another world or another dimension can come through, if the sleeper is granted the rare gift of acting as a *filter*. What if the dreams feed on the dreamer for substance, just as spirits attain ectoplasmic being by draining the medium of energy?

Avis thought and thought about it, and when she had evolved this theory, everything seemed to fit. Not that she would ever tell anyone about her attitude. Doctor Clegg would only laugh at her, or still worse, shake his head. Marvin Mason didn't approve either. Nobody wanted her to dream. They still treated her like a little girl.

Very well, she would be a little girl; a little girl who could do as she pleased now. She would dream.

It was shortly after reaching this decision that the dreams began again; almost as though they had been waiting until she would fully accept them in terms of their own reality.

Yes, they came back, slowly, a bit at a time. Avis found that it helped to concentrate on the past during the day; to strive to remember her childhood. To this end she spent more and more time in her room, leaving Reba to tend to housework downstairs. As for fresh air, she always could look out of her window. It was high and small, but she would climb on a stool and gaze up at the sky through the round aperture; watching the clouds that veiled the blue beyond, and waiting for night to come.

Then she would sleep in the big bed and wait for the wind. The wind soothed and the darkness slithered, and soon she could hear the buzzing, blurring voices. At first only the voices came back, and they were faint and far away. Gradually, they increased in intensity and once more she was able to discriminate, to recognize individual intonations.

Timidly, hesitantly, the figures reemerged. Each night they grew stronger. Avis Long (little girl with big round eyes in big bed below round window) welcomed their presence.

She wasn't alone any more. No need to see her friends, or talk to that silly old Doctor Clegg. No need to waste much time gossiping with Reba, or fussing over meals. No need to dress or venture out. There was the window by day and the dreams by night.

Then all at once she was curiously weak, and this illness came. But it was all false, somehow; this physical change.

Her mind was untouched. She knew that. No matter how often Doctor Clegg pursed his lips and hinted about calling in a "specialist," she wasn't afraid. Of course Avis knew he really wanted her to see a psychiatrist. The doddering fool was filled with glib patter about "retreat from reality" and "escape mechanisms."

But he didn't understand about the dreams. She wouldn't tell him, either. He'd never know the richness, the fullness, the sense of completion that came from experiencing contact with other worlds.

Avis knew *that* now. The voices and shapes that came in the window were from other worlds. As a naive child she had invited them by her very unsophistication. Now, striving consciously to return to the childlike attitude, she again admitted them.

They were from other worlds; worlds of wonder and splendor. Now they could meet only on the plane of dreams, but someday, someday soon, she would bridge the gap.

They whispered about her body. Something about the trip, making the "change." It couldn't be explained in *their* words. But she trusted them, and after all, a physical change was of slight importance contrasted with the opportunity.

Soon she would be well again, strong again. Strong enough to say yes. And then they would come for her when the moon was right. Until then, she could strengthen the determination, and the dream.

Avis Long lay in the great bed and basked in the blackness; the blackness that poured palpably through the open window. The shapes filtered down, wriggling through the warps, feeding upon the night; growing, pulsing, encompassing all.

They reassured her about the body but she didn't care and she told them she didn't care because the body was unimportant and yes, she would gladly consider it an exchange if only she could go and she knew she belonged.

Not beyond the rim of the stars but between it and amongst substance dwells that which is blackness in blackness for Yuggoth is only a symbol, no that is wrong there are no symbols for all is reality and only perception is limited *ch'yar ul'nyar shaggornyth ...*

It is hard for us to make you understand but I do understand *you cannot fight it* I will not fight it *they will try to stop you* nothing shall stop me for I belong *yes you belong* will it be soon *yes it will be soon* very soon *yes very soon ...*

Marvin Mason was unprepared for this sort of reception. Of course, Avis hadn't written, and she wasn't at the station to meet him—but the possibility of her being seriously ill had never occurred to him.

He had come out to the house at once, and it was a shock when Doctor Clegg met him at the door.

The old man's face was grim, and the tenor of his opening remarks still grimmer.

They faced each other in the library downstairs; Mason self-consciously diffident in khaki, the older man a bit too professionally brusque.

"Just what is it, Doctor?" Mason asked.

"I don't know. Slight, recurrent fever. Listlessness. I've checked everything. No TB, no trace of low-grade infection. Her trouble isn't—organic."

"You mean something's wrong with her mind?"

Doctor Clegg slumped into an armchair and lowered his head.

"Mason, I could say many things to you; about the psychosomatic theory of medicine, about the benefits of psychiatry, about—but never mind. It would be sheer hypocrisy.

"I've talked to Avis; rather, I've tried to talk to her. She won't say much, but what she does say disturbs me. Her actions disturb me even more.

"You can guess what I'm driving at, I think, when I tell you that she is leading the life of an eight-year-old girl. The life she *did* lead at that age."

Mason scowled. "Don't tell me she sits in her room again and looks out of that window?"

Dr. Clegg nodded.

"But I thought it was boarded up long ago, because she's a somnambulist and—"

"She had it unboarded, several months ago. And she is not, never was, a somnambulist."

"What do you mean?"

"Avis Long never walked in her sleep. I remember the night she was found on that window's edge; not ledge for there is no ledge. She was perched on the edge of the open window, already halfway out; a little tyke hanging through a high window.

"But there was no chair beneath her, no ladder. No way for her to climb up. She was simply *there.*"

Dr. Clegg looked away before continuing.

"Don't ask me what it means. I can't explain, and I wouldn't want to. I'd have to talk about the things she talks about—the dreams, and the presences that come to her; the presences that want her to go *away.*

"Mason, it's up to you. I can't honestly move to have her committed on the basis of material evidence. Confinement means nothing to *them;* you can't build a wall to keep out dreams.

"But you can love her. You can save her. You can make her well, make her take an interest in reality. Oh, I know it sounds mawkish and stupid, just as the other sounds wild and fantastic.

"Yes, it's true. It's happening right now, to her. She's asleep up in her room at this very moment. She's hearing the voices—I know that much. Let her hear your voice."

Mason walked out of the room and started up the stairs.

"But what do you mean, you can't marry me?"

Mason stared at the huddled figure in the swirl of bedclothes. He tried to avoid the direct stare of Avis Long's curiously childlike eyes; just as he avoided gazing up at the black, ominous aperture of the round window.

"I can't, that's all," Avis answered. Even her voice seemed to hold a childlike quality. The high, piercing tones might well have emanated from the throat of a little girl; a tired little girl, half-asleep and a bit petulant about being abruptly awakened.

"But our plans—your letters—"

"I'm sorry, dear. I can't talk about it. You know I haven't been well. Doctor Clegg is downstairs, he must have told you."

"But you're getting better," Mason pleaded. "You'll be up and around again in a few days."

Avis shook her head. A smile—the secret smile of a naughty child—clung to the corners of her mouth.

"You can't understand, Marvin. You never *could* understand. That's because you belong here." A gesture indicated the room. "I belong somewhere else." Her finger stabbed, unconsciously, towards the window.

Marvin looked at the window now. He couldn't help it. The round black hole that led to nothingness. Or—something. The sky outside was dark, moonless. A cold wind curled about the bed.

"Let me close the window for you, dear," he said, striving to keep his voice even and gentle.

"No."

"But you're ill—you'll catch cold."

"That isn't why you want to close it." Even in accusation, the voice was curiously piping. Avis sat bolt upright and confronted him.

"You're jealous, Marvin. Jealous of me. Jealous of *them.* You would never let me dream. You would never let me go. And I want to go. They're coming for me.

"I know why Doctor Clegg sent you up here. He wants you to persuade me to go away. He'd like to shut me up, just as he wants to shut the window. He wants to keep me here because he's afraid. You're all afraid of what lies—out there."

"Well, it's no use. You can't stop me. You can't stop *them!*"

"Take it easy, darling—"

"Never mind. Do you think I care what they do to me, if only I can go? I'm not afraid. I know I can't go as I am now. I know they must alter me.

"There are certain parts they want for reasons of their own. You'd be frightened if I told you. But I'm not afraid. You say I'm sick and insane, don't deny it. Yet I'm healthy enough, sane enough to face them and their world. It's you who are too morbid to endure it all."

Avis Long was wailing now; a thin, high-pitched wail of a little girl in a tantrum.

"You and I are leaving this house tomorrow," Mason said. "We're going away. We'll be married and live happily ever after—in good old storybook style. The trouble with you, young lady, is that you've never had to grow up. All this nonsense about goblins and other worlds—"

Avis screamed.

Mason ignored her.

"Right now I'm going to shut that window," he declared.

Avis continued to scream. The shrill ululation echoed on a sustained note as Mason reached up and closed the round pane of glass over the black aperture. The wind resisted his efforts, but he shut the window and secured the latch.

Then her fingers were digging into his throat from the rear, and her scream was pouring down his ear.

"I'll kill you!" she wailed. It was the wail of an enraged child.

But there was nothing of the child, or the invalid, in the strength behind her clawing fingers. He fought her off, panting.

Then, suddenly, Doctor Clegg was in the room. A hypodermic needle flashed and gleamed in an arc of plunging silver.

They carried her back to the bed, tucked her in. The blankets nestled about the weary face of a child in sleep.

The window was closed tightly now.

Everything was in order as the two men turned out the light and tiptoed from the room.

Neither of them said a word until they stood downstairs once again.

Facing the fireplace, Mason sighed.

"Somehow I'll get her out of here tomorrow," he promised. "Perhaps it was too abrupt—my coming back tonight and waking her. I wasn't very tactful.

"But something about her; something about that room, frightened me."

Doctor Clegg lit his pipe. "I know," he said. "That's why I couldn't pretend to you that I completely understand. There's more to it than mere hallucination."

"I'm going to sit up here tonight," Mason continued. "Just in case something might happen."

"She'll sleep," Doctor Clegg assured him. "No need to worry."

"I'll feel better if I stay. I'm beginning to get a theory about all this talk—other worlds, and changes in her body before a trip. It ties in with the window, somehow. And it sounds like a fantasy on suicide."

"The death impulse? Perhaps. I should have thought of that possibility. Dreams foreshadowing death—on second thought, Mason, I may stay with you. We can make ourselves comfortable here before the fire, I suppose."

Silence settled.

It must have been well after midnight before either of them moved from their place before the fire.

Then a sharp splinter of sound crashed from above. Before the tinkling echo died away, both men were on their feet and moving towards the stairway.

There was no further noise from above, and neither of them exchanged a single word. Only the thud of their running footsteps on the stairs broke the silence. And as they paused outside Avis Long's room, the silence seemed to deepen in intensity. It was a silence palpable, complete, accomplished.

Doctor Clegg's hand darted to the doorknob, wrenched it ineffectually.

"Locked!" he muttered. "She must have gotten up and locked it."

Mason scowled.

"The window—do you think she could have—?" Doctor Clegg refused to meet his glance. Instead he turned and put his massive shoulder to the door panel. A bulge of muscle ridged his neck.

Then the panel splintered and gave way. Mason reached around and opened the door from inside.

They entered the darkened room, Dr. Clegg in the lead, fumbling for the light switch. The harsh, electric glare flooded the scene.

It was a tribute to the power of suggestion that both men glanced, not at the patient in the bed, but at the round window high up on the wall.

Cold night air streamed through a jagged aperture, where the glass had been shattered, as though by the blow of a gigantic fist.

Fragments of glass littered the floor beneath, but there was no trace of any missile. And obviously, the glass had been broken from the outer side of the pane.

"The wind," Mason murmured weakly, but he could not look at Dr. Clegg as he spoke. For there was no wind, only the cold, soft breeze that billowed ever so gently from the nighted sky above. Only the cold, soft breeze, rustling the curtains and prompting a sarabande of shadows on the wall; shadows that danced in silence over the great bed in the corner.

The breeze and the silence and the shadows enveloped them as they stared now at the bed.

Avis Long's head was turned towards them on the pillow. They could see her face quite plainly, and Doctor Clegg realized on the basis of experience what Mason knew instinctively—Avis Long's eyes were closed in death.

But that is not what made Mason gasp and shudder—nor did the sight of death alone cause Doctor Clegg to scream aloud.

There was nothing whatsoever to frighten the beholder of the placid countenance turned towards them in death. They did not scream at the sight of Avis Long's face.

Lying on the pillow of the huge bed, Avis Long's face bore a look of perfect peace.

But Avis Long's body was . . . gone.

YOUNG BLOCH HAD SOUGHT *and obtained Lovecraft's permission to destroy him nastily in "The Shambler from the Stars." Lovecraft took friendly revenge by causing Bloch to share pretty much the same fate in "The Haunter of the Dark," in which he named Bloch's narrator "Robert Blake" and even thinly veiled the preceding story as "The Feaster from the Stars."*

The present story is a sequel to the sequel. In the Introduction to the first edition of the present collection, Lin Carter notes that the protagonist Edmund Fiske is supposed to be Bloch himself, redivivus. He cogently points to the name "Fiske" as corroboration, since Bloch sometimes used "Tarleton Fiske" as a pseudonym (on "The Sorcerer's Jewel," for example). But in fact, Bloch has more than once revealed that he meant the doomed Fiske to stand for Fritz Leiber.

(By the way, Etienne-Laurent de Marigny in "The Secret of Sebek" is another Lovecraft Circle member, namely E. Hoffmann Price, co-author with HPL of "Through the Gates of the Silver Key," in which de Marigny first appears. In fact it is in Price's/de Marigny's French Quarter apartment that Swami Chandrputra recounts his tale of the fate of Randolph Carter.)

The Shadow
from the Steeple

WILLIAM HURLEY WAS BORN an Irishman and grew up to be a taxicab driver—therefore it would be redundant, in the face of both of these facts, to say that he was garrulous.

The minute he picked up his passenger in downtown Providence that warm summer evening, he began talking. The passenger, a tall thin man in his early thirties, entered the cab and sat back, clutching a briefcase. He gave an address on Benefit Street and Hurley started out, shifting both taxi and tongue into high gear.

Hurley began what was to be a one-sided conversation by commenting on the afternoon performance of the New York Giants. Unperturbed by his passenger's silence, he made a few remarks about the weather—recent, current, and expected. Since he received no reply, the driver then proceeded to discuss a local phenomenon, namely the reported escape, that morning, of two black panthers or leopards from the traveling menagerie of Langer Brothers Circus, currently appearing in the city. In response to a direct inquiry as to whether he had seen the beasts roaming at large, Hurley's customer shook his head.

The driver then made several uncomplimentary remarks about the local police force and their inability to capture the beasts. It was his considered opinion that a given platoon of law enforcement officers would be unable to catch a cold if immured in an ice-box for a year. This witticism failed to amuse his passenger, and before Hurley could continue his monologue, they had arrived at the Benefit Street address. Eighty-five cents changed hands, passenger and briefcase left the cab, and Hurley drove away.

He could not know it at the time, but he thus became the last man who could or would testify to seeing his passenger alive.

The rest is conjecture, and perhaps that is for the best. Certainly it is easy enough to draw certain conclusions as to what happened that night in the old house on Benefit Street, but the weight of those conclusions is hard to bear.

One minor mystery is easy enough to clear up—the peculiar silence and aloofness of Hurley's passenger. That passenger, Edmund Fiske, of

Chicago, Illinois, was meditating upon the fulfillment of fifteen years
of questing; the cab-trip represented the last stage of this long journey,
and he was reviewing the circumstances as he rode.

Edmund Fiske's quest had begun, on August 8, 1935, with the
death of his close friend, Robert Harrison Blake, of Milwaukee.

Like Fiske himself at the time, Blake had been a precocious adolescent interested in fantasy-writing, and as such became a member of
the "Lovecraft circle"—a group of writers maintaining correspondence
with one another and with the late Howard Phillips Lovecraft, of
Providence.

It was through correspondence that Fiske and Blake had become
acquainted; they visited back and forth between Milwaukee and
Chicago, and their mutual preoccupation with the weird and the
fantastic in literature and art served to form the foundation for the close
friendship which existed at the time of Blake's unexpected and inexplicable demise.

Most of the facts—and certain of the conjectures—in connection
with Blake's death have been embodied in Lovecraft's story, *The
Haunter of the Dark,* which was published more than a year after the
younger writer's passing.

Lovecraft had an excellent opportunity to observe matters, for it was
on his suggestion that young Blake had journeyed to Providence early
in 1935, and had been provided with living quarters on College Street
by Lovecraft himself. So it was both as friend and neighbor that the
elder fantasy writer had acted in narrating the singular story of Robert
Harrison Blake's last months.

In his story, he tells of Blake's efforts to begin a novel dealing with
a survival of New England witch-cults, but modestly omits his own
part in assisting his friend to secure material. Apparently Blake began
work on his project and then became enmeshed in a horror greater than
any envisioned by his imagination.

For Blake was drawn to investigate the crumbling black pile on
Federal Hill—the deserted ruin of a church that had once housed the
worshippers of an esoteric cult. Early in spring he paid a visit to the
shunned structure and there made certain discoveries which (in Lovecraft's opinion) made his death inevitable.

Briefly, Blake entered the boarded-up Free Will Church and stumbled across the skeleton of a reporter from the *Providence Telegram,* one
Edwin M. Lillibridge, who had apparently attempted a similar investigation in 1893. The fact that his death was not explained seemed
alarming enough, but more disturbing still was the realization that no

one had been bold enough to enter the church since that date and discover the body.

Blake found the reporter's notebook in his clothing, and its contents afforded a partial revelation.

A certain Professor Bowen, of Providence, had traveled widely in Egypt, and in 1843, in the course of archeological investigations of the crypt of Nephren-Ka, had made an unusual find.

Nephren-Ka is the "forgotten pharaoh," whose name has been cursed by the priests and obliterated from official dynastic records. The name was familiar to the young writer at the time, due largely to the work of another Milwaukee author who had dealt with the semi-legendary ruler in his tale, *Fane of the Black Pharaoh*. But the discovery Bowen made in the crypt was totally unexpected.

The reporter's notebook said little of the actual nature of that discovery, but it recorded subsequent events in a precise, chronological fashion. Immediately upon unearthing his mysterious find in Egypt, Professor Bowen abandoned his research and returned to Providence, where he purchased the Free Will Church in 1844 and made it the headquarters of what was called the "Starry Wisdom" sect.

Members of this religious cult, evidently recruited by Bowen, professed to worship an entity they called the "Haunter of the Dark." By gazing into a crystal they summoned the actual presence of this entity and did homage with blood sacrifice.

Such, at least, was the fantastic story circulated in Providence at the time—and the church became a place to be avoided. Local superstition fanned agitation, and agitation precipitated direct action. In May of 1877 the sect was forcibly broken up by the authorities, due to public pressure and several hundred of its members abruptly left the city.

The church itself was immediately closed, and apparently individual curiosity could not overcome the widespread fear which resulted in leaving the structure undisturbed and unexplored until the reporter, Lillibridge, made his ill-fated private investigation in 1893.

Such was the gist of the story unfolded in the pages of his notebook. Blake read it, but was nevertheless undeterred in his further scrutiny of the environs. Eventually he came upon the mysterious object Bowen had found in the Egyptian crypt—the object upon which the Starry Wisdom worship had been founded—the asymmetrical metal box with its curiously hinged lid, a lid that had been closed for countless years. Blake thus gazed at the interior, gazed upon the four-inch red-black crystal polyhedron hanging suspended by seven supports. He not only gazed *at* but also *into* the polyhedron; just as the cult-worshippers had purportedly gazed, and with the same results. He was assailed by a curious psychic disturbance; he seemed to "see visions of other lands and the gulfs beyond the stars," as superstitious accounts had told.

And then Blake made his greatest mistake. He closed the box.

Closing the box—again, according to the superstitions annotated by Lillibridge—was the act that summoned the alien entity itself, the Haunter of the Dark. It was a creature of darkness and could not survive light. And in that boarded-up blackness of the ruined church, the thing emerged by night.

Blake fled the church in terror, but the damage was done. In mid-July, a thunderstorm put out the lights in Providence for an hour, and the Italian colony living near the deserted church heard bumping and thumping from inside the shadow-shrouded structure.

Crowds with candles stood outside in the rain and played candles upon the building, shielding themselves against the possible emergence of the feared entity by a barrier of light.

Apparently the story remained alive throughout the neighborhood. Once the storm abated, local newspapers grew interested, and on the 17th of July two reporters entered the old church, together with a policeman. Nothing definite was found, although there were curious and inexplicable smears and stains on the stairs and pews.

Less than a month later—at 2:35 A.M. on the morning of August 8th, to be exact—Robert Harrison Blake met his death during an electrical storm while seated before the window of his room on College Street.

During the gathering storm, before his death occurred, Blake scribbled frantically in his diary, gradually revealing his innermost obsessions and delusions concerning the Haunter of the Dark. It was Blake's conviction that by gazing into the curious crystal in its box he had somehow established a linkage with the non-terrestrial entity. He further believed that closing the box had summoned the creature to dwell in the darkness of the church steeple, and that in some way his own fate was now irrevocably linked to that of the monstrosity.

All this was revealed in the last messages he set down while watching the progress of the storm from his window.

Meanwhile, at the church itself, on Federal Hill, a crowd of agitated spectators gathered to play lights upon the structure. That they heard alarming sounds from inside the boarded-up building is undeniable; at least two competent witnesses have testified to the fact. One, Father Merluzzo of the Spirito Santo Church, was on hand to quiet his congregation. The other, Patrolman (now Sergeant) William J. Monahan, of Central Station, was attempting to preserve order in the face of growing panic. Monahan himself saw the blinding "blur" that seemed to issue, smokelike, from the steeple of the ancient edifice as the final lightning-flash came.

Flash, meteor, fireball—call it what you will—erupted over the city in a blinding blaze; perhaps at the very moment that Robert Harrison Blake, across town, was writing, "Is it not an avatar of Nyarlathotep, who in antique and shadowy Khem took the form of man?"

A few moments later he was dead. The coroner's physician rendered a verdict attributing his demise to "electrical shock" although the window he faced was unbroken. Another physician, known to Lovecraft, quarreled privately with that verdict and subsequently entered the affair the next day. Without legal authority, he entered the church and climbed to the windowless steeple where he discovered the strange asymmetrical—was it golden?—box and the curious stone within. Apparently his first gesture was to make sure of raising the lid and bringing the stone into the light. His next recorded gesture was to charter a boat, take the box and curiously-angled stone aboard, and drop them into the deepest channel of Narragansett Bay.

There ended the admittedly fictionalized account of Blake's death as recorded by H. P. Lovecraft. And there began Edmund Fiske's fifteen-year quest.

Fiske, of course, had known some of the events outlined in the story. When Blake had left for Providence in the spring, Fiske had tentatively promised to join him the following autumn. At first, the two friends had exchanged letters regularly, but by early summer Blake ceased correspondence altogether.

At the time, Fiske was unaware of Blake's exploration of the ruined church. He could not account for Blake's silence, and wrote Lovecraft for a possible explanation.

Lovecraft could supply little information. Young Blake, he said, had visited with him frequently during the early weeks of his stay; had consulted with him about his writing, and had accompanied him on several nocturnal strolls through the city.

But during the summer, Blake's neighborliness ceased. It was not in Lovecraft's reclusive nature to impose himself on others, and he did not seek to invade Blake's privacy for several weeks.

When he did so—and learned from the almost hysterical adolescent of his experiences in the forbidding, forbidden church on Federal Hill—Lovecraft offered words of warning and advice. But it was already too late. Within ten days of his visit came the shocking end.

Fiske learned of that end from Lovecraft on the following day. It was his task to break the news to Blake's parents. For a time he was tempted to visit Providence immediately, but lack of funds and the pressure of his own domestic affairs forestalled him. The body of his young friend duly arrived and Fiske attended the brief ceremony of cremation.

Then Lovecraft began his own investigation—an investigation which ultimately resulted in the publication of his story. And there the matter might have rested.

But Fiske was not satisfied.

His best friend had died under circumstances which even the most skeptical must admit were mysterious. The local authorities summarily wrote off the matter with a fatuous and inadequate explanation.

Fiske determined to ascertain the truth.

Bear in mind one salient fact—all three of these men, Lovecraft, Blake and Fiske—were professional writers and students of the supernatural or the supranormal. All three of them had extraordinary access to a bulk of written material dealing with ancient legend and superstition. Ironically enough, the use to which they put their knowledge was limited to excursions into so-called "fantasy fiction" but none of them, in the light of their own experience, could wholly join their reading audience in scoffing at the myths of which they wrote.

For, as Fiske wrote to Lovecraft, "the term, myth, as we know, is merely a polite euphemism. Blake's death was not a myth, but a hideous reality. I implore you to investigate fully. See this matter through to the end, for if Blake's diary holds even a distorted truth, there is no telling what may be loosed upon the world."

Lovecraft pledged cooperation, discovered the fate of the metal box and its contents, and endeavored to arrange a meeting with Doctor Ambrose Dexter, of Benefit Street. Doctor Dexter, it appeared, had left town immediately following his dramatic theft and disposal of the "Shining Trapezohedron," as Lovecraft called it.

Lovecraft then apparently interviewed Father Merluzzo and Patrolman Monahan, plunged into the files of the *Bulletin,* and endeavored to reconstruct the story of the Starry Wisdom sect and the entity they worshipped.

Of course he learned a good deal more than he dared to put into his magazine story. His letters to Edmund Fiske in the late fall and early spring of 1936 contain guarded hints and references to "menaces from Outside." But he seemed anxious to reassure Fiske that if there had been any menace, even in the realistic rather than the supernatural sense, the danger was now averted because Doctor Dexter had disposed of the Shining Trapezohedron which acted as a summoning talisman. Such was the gist of his report, and the matter rested there for a time.

Fiske made tentative arrangements, early in 1937, to visit Lovecraft at his home, with the private intention of doing some further research on his own into the cause of Blake's death. But once again, circumstances intervened. For in March of that year, Lovecraft died. His unexpected passing plunged Fiske into a period of mental despondency from which he was slow to recover; accordingly, it was not until almost a year later that Edmund Fiske paid his first visit to Providence, and to the scene of the tragic episodes which brought Blake's life to a close.

For somehow, always, a black undercurrent of suspicion existed. The coroner's physician had been glib, Lovecraft had been tactful, the press and the general public had accepted matters completely—yet Blake was dead, and there had been an entity abroad in the night.

Fiske felt that if he could visit the accursed church himself, talk to Doctor Dexter and find out what had drawn him into the affair, interrogate the reporters, and pursue any relevant leads or clues he might eventually hope to uncover the truth and at least clear his dead friend's name of the ugly shadow of mental unbalance.

Accordingly, Fiske's first step after arriving in Providence and registering at a hotel was to set out for Federal Hill and the ruined church.

The search was doomed to immediate, irremediable disappointment. For the church was no more. It had been razed the previous fall and the property taken over by the city authorities. The black and baleful spire no longer cast its spell over the Hill.

Fiske immediately took pains to see Father Merluzzo, at Spirito Santo, a few squares away. He learned from a courteous housekeeper that Father Merluzzo had died in 1936, within a year of young Blake.

Discouraged but persistent, Fiske next attempted to reach Doctor Dexter, but the old house on Benefit Street was boarded up. A call to the Physician's Service Bureau produced only the cryptic information that Ambrose Dexter, M.D. had left the city for an indeterminate stay.

Nor did a visit with the city editor of the *Bulletin* yield any better result. Fiske was permitted to go into the newspaper's morgue and read the aggravatingly short and matter-of-fact story on Blake's death, but the two reporters who had covered the assignment and subsequently visited the Federal Hill church had left the paper for berths in other cities.

There were, of course, other leads to follow, and during the ensuing week Fiske ran them all to the ground. A copy of *Who's Who* added nothing significant to his mental picture of Doctor Ambrose Dexter. The physician was Providence born, a life-long resident, 40 years of age, unmarried, a general practitioner, member of several medical societies—but there was no indication of any unusual "hobbies" or "other interests" which might provide a clue as to his participation in the affair.

Sergeant William J. Monahan of Central Station was sought out, and for the first time Fiske actually managed to speak to some one who admitted an actual connection with the events leading to Blake's death. Monahan was polite, but cautiously noncommittal.

Despite Fiske's complete unburdening, the police officer remained discreetly reticent.

"There's really nothing I can tell you," he said. "It's true, like Mister Lovecraft said, that I was at the church that night, for there was a rough crowd out and there's no telling what some of them ones in the neighborhood will do when riled up. Like the story said, the old church had a bad name, and I guess Sheeley could have given you many's the story."

"Sheeley?" interjected Fiske.

"Bert Sheeley—it was his beat, you know, not mine. He was ill of pneumonia at the time and I substituted for two weeks. Then, when he died—"

Fiske shook his head. Another possible source of information gone. Blake dead, Lovecraft dead, Father Merluzzo dead, and now Sheeley. Reporters scattered, and Doctor Dexter mysteriously missing. He sighed and persevered.

"That last night, when you saw the blur," he asked, "can you add anything by way of details? Were there any noises? Did anyone in the crowd say anything? Try to remember—whatever you can add may be of great help to me."

Monahan shook his head. "There were noises aplenty," he said. "But what with the thunder and all, I couldn't rightly make out if anything came from inside the church, like the story has it. And as for the crowd, with the women wailing and the men muttering, all mixed up with thunderclaps and wind, it was as much as I could do to hear myself yelling to keep in place let alone make out what was being said."

"And the blur?" Fiske persisted.

"It was a blur, and that's all. Smoke, or a cloud, or just a shadow before the lightning struck again. But I'll not be saying I saw any devils, or monsters, or whatchamacallits as Mister Lovecraft would write about in those wild tales of his."

Sergeant Monahan shrugged self-righteously and picked up the desk-phone to answer a call. The interview was obviously at an end.

And so, for the nonce, was Fiske's quest. He didn't abandon hope, however. For a day he sat by his own hotel phone and called up every "Dexter" listed in the book in an effort to locate a relative of the missing doctor; but to no avail. Another day was spent in a small boat on Narragansett Bay, as Fiske assiduously and painstakingly familiarized himself with the location of the "deepest channel" alluded to in Lovecraft's story.

But at the end of a futile week in Providence, Fiske had to confess himself beaten. He returned to Chicago, his work, and his normal pursuits. Gradually the affair dropped out of the foreground of his consciousness, but he by no means forgot it completely or gave up the notion of eventually unravelling the mystery—if mystery there was.

In 1941, during a three-day furlough from Basic Training, Pvt. First Class Edmund Fiske passed through Providence on his way to New York City and again attempted to locate Dr. Ambrose Dexter, without success.

During 1942 and 1943 Sgt. Edmund Fiske wrote, from his station overseas, to Dr. Ambrose Dexter c/o General Delivery, Providence, R.I. His letters were never acknowledged, if indeed they were received.

In 1945, in a U.S.O. library lounge in Honolulu, Fiske read a report in—of all things—a journal on astro-physics which mentioned a recent gathering at Princeton University, at which the guest speaker, Dr. Ambrose Dexter, had delivered an address on "Practical Applications in Military Technology."

Fiske did not return to the States until the end of 1946. Domestic affairs, naturally, were the subject of his paramount consideration during the following year. It wasn't until 1948 that he accidentally came upon Dr. Dexter's name again—this time in a listing of "investigators in the field of nuclear physics" in a national weekly news-magazine. He wrote the editors for further information, but received no reply. And another letter, dispatched to Providence, remained unanswered.

But in 1949, late in autumn, Dexter's name again came to his attention through the news columns; this time in relation to a discussion of work on the secret H-Bomb.

Whatever he guessed, whatever he feared, whatever he wildly imagined, Fiske was impelled to action. It was then that he wrote to a certain Ogden Purvis, a private investigator in the city of Providence, and commissioned him to locate Doctor Ambrose Dexter. All that he required was that he be placed in communication with Dexter, and he paid a substantial retainer fee. Purvis took the case.

The private detective sent several reports to Fiske in Chicago and they were, at first, disheartening. The Dexter residence was still untenanted. Dexter himself, according to the information elicited from governmental sources, was on a special mission. The private investigator seemed to assume from this that he was a person above reproach, engaged in confidential defense work.

Fiske's own reaction was panic.

He raised his offer of a fee and insisted that Ogden Purvis continue his efforts to find the elusive doctor.

Winter of 1950 came, and with it, another report. The private investigator had tracked down every lead Fiske suggested, and one of them led, eventually to Tom Jonas.

Tom Jonas was the owner of the small boat which had been chartered by Doctor Dexter one evening in the late summer of 1935—the small boat which had been rowed to the "deepest channel of Narragansett Bay."

Tom Jonas had rested his oars as Dexter threw overboard the dully-gleaming, asymmetrical metal box with the hinged lid open to disclose the Shining Trapezohedron.

The old fisherman had spoken freely to the private detective; his words were reported in detail to Fiske via confidential report.

"Mighty peculiar" was Jonas' own reaction to the incident. Dexter had offered him "twenty smackers to take to boat out in the middle o'midnight and heave this funny-lookin' contraption overboard. Said there was no harm in it; said it was just an old keepsake he wanted to git rid of. But all the way out he kep' starin' at the sort of jewel-thing set in some iron bands inside the box, and mumblin' in some foreign language, I guess. No, 'tweren't French or German or Italian talk either. Polish, mebbe. I don't remember any words, either. But he acted sort-of drunk. Not that I'd say anything against Doctor Dexter, understand; comes of a fine old family, even if he ain't been around these parts since, to my knowing. But I figgered he was a bit under the influence, you might say. Else why would he pay me twenty smackers to do a crazy stunt like that?"

There was more to the verbatim transcript of the old fisherman's monologue, but it did not explain anything.

"He sure seemed glad to git rid of it, as I recollect. On the way back he told me to keep mum about it, but I can't see no harm in telling at this late date; I wouldn't hold anything back from the law."

Evidently the private investigator had made use of a rather unethical stratagem—posing as an actual detective in order to get Jonas to talk.

This did not bother Fiske, in Chicago. It was enough to get his grasp on something tangible at last; enough to make him send Purvis another payment, with instructions to keep up the search for Ambrose Dexter. Several months passed in waiting.

Then, in late spring, came the news Fiske had waited for. Doctor Dexter was back; he had returned to his house on Benefit Street. The boards had been removed, furniture vans appeared to discharge their contents, and a manservant appeared to answer the door, and to take telephone messages.

Doctor Dexter was not at home to the investigator, or to any one. He was, it appeared, recuperating from a severe illness contracted while in government service. He took a card from Purvis and promised to deliver a message, but repeated calls brought no indication of a reply.

Nor did Purvis, who conscientiously "cased" the house and neighborhood, ever succeed in laying eyes upon the doctor himself or in finding anyone who claimed to have seen the convalescent physician on the street.

Groceries were delivered regularly; mail appeared in the box; lights glowed in the Benefit Street house nightly until all hours.

As a matter of fact, this was the only concrete statement Purvis could make regarding any possible irregularity in Doctor Dexter's mode of life—he seemed to keep electricity burning twenty-four hours a day.

Fiske promptly dispatched another letter to Doctor Dexter, and then another. Still no acknowledgment or reply was forthcoming. And after several more unenlightening reports from Purvis, Fiske made up his mind. He would go to Providence and see Dexter, somehow, come what may.

He might be completely wrong in his suspicions; he might be completely wrong in his assumption that Doctor Dexter could clear the name of his dead friend; he might be completely wrong in even surmising any connection between the two—but for fifteen years he had brooded and wondered, and it was time to put an end to his own inner conflict.

Accordingly, late that summer, Fiske wired Purvis of his intentions and instructed him to meet him at the hotel upon his arrival.

Thus it was that Edmund Fiske came to Providence for the last time; on the day that the Giants lost, on the day that the Langer Brothers lost their two black panthers, on the day that cabdriver William Hurley was in a garrulous mood.

Purvis was not at the hotel to meet him, but such was Fiske's own frenzy of impatience that he decided to act without him and drove, as we have seen, to Benefit Street in the early evening.

As the cab departed, Fiske stared up at the panelled doorway; stared at the lights blazing from the upper windows of the Georgian structure. A brass name-plate gleamed on the door itself, and the light from the windows played upon the legend, Ambrose Dexter, M.D.

Slight as it was, this seemed a reassuring touch to Edmund Fiske. The doctor was not concealing his presence in the house from the world, however much he might conceal his actual person. Surely the blazing lights and the appearance of the name-plate augured well.

Fiske shrugged, rang the bell.

The door opened quickly. A small, dark-skinned man with a slight stoop appeared and made a question of the word, "Yes?"

"Doctor Dexter, please."

"The Doctor is not in to callers. He is ill."

"Would you take a message, please?"

"Certainly." The dark-skinned servant smiled.

"Tell him that Edmund Fiske of Chicago wishes to see him at his convenience for a few moments. I have come all the way from the Middle West for this purpose, and what I have to speak to him about would take only a moment or two of his time."

"Wait, please."

The door closed. Fiske stood in the gathering darkness and transferred his briefcase from one hand to the other.

Abruptly, the door opened again. The servant peered out at him.

"Mr. Fiske—are you the gentleman who wrote the letters?"

"Letters—oh, yes, I am. I did not know the doctor ever received them."

The servant nodded. "I could not say. But Doctor Dexter said that if you were the man who had written him, you were to come right in."

Fiske permitted himself an audible sigh of relief as he stepped over the threshold. It had taken fifteen years to come this far, and now—

"Just go upstairs, if you please. You will find Doctor Dexter waiting in the study, right at the head of the hall."

Edmund Fiske climbed the stairs, turned at the top to a doorway, and entered a room in which the light was an almost palpable presence, so intense was its glare.

And there, rising from a chair beside the fireplace, was Doctor Ambrose Dexter.

Fiske found himself facing a tall, thin, immaculately dressed man who may have been fifty but who scarcely looked thirty-five; a man whose wholly natural grace and elegance of movement concealed the sole incongruity of his aspect—a very deep suntan.

"So you are Edmund Fiske."

The voice was soft, well-modulated, and unmistakably New England—and the accompanying handclasp warm and firm. Doctor Dexter's smile was natural and friendly. White teeth gleamed against the brown background of his features.

"Won't you sit down?" invited the doctor. He indicated a chair and bowed slightly. Fiske couldn't help but stare; there was certainly no indication of any present or recent illness in his host's demeanor or behavior. As Doctor Dexter resumed his own seat near the fire and Fiske moved around the chair to join him, he noted the bookshelves on either side of the room. The size and shape of several volumes immediately engaged his rapt attention—so much that he hesitated before taking a seat, and instead inspected the titles of the tomes.

For the first time in his life, Edmund Fiske found himself confronting the half-legendary *De Vermis Mysteriis*, the *Liber Ivonis*, and the almost mythical Latin version of the *Necronomicon*. Without seeking his host's permission, he lifted the bulk of the latter volume from the shelf and riffled through the yellowed pages of the Spanish translation of 1622.

Then he turned to Doctor Dexter, and all traces of his carefully-contrived composure dropped away. "Then it must have been you who found these books in the church," he said. "In the rear vestry room beside the apse. Lovecraft mentioned them in his story, and I've always wondered what became of them."

Doctor Dexter nodded gravely. "Yes, I took them. I did not think it wise for such books to fall into the hands of authorities. You know what they contain, and what might happen if such knowledge were wrongfully employed."

Fiske reluctantly replaced the great book on the shelf and took a chair facing the doctor before the fire. He held his briefcase on his lap and fumbled uneasily with the clasp.

"Don't be uneasy," said Doctor Dexter, with a kindly smile. "Let us proceed without fencing. You are here to discover what part I played in the affair of your friend's death."

"Yes, there are some questions I wanted to ask."

"Please." The doctor raised a slim brown hand. "I am not in the best of health and can give you only a few minutes. Allow me to anticipate your queries and tell you what little I know."

"As you wish." Fiske stared at the bronzed man, wondering what lay behind the perfection of his poise.

"I met your friend Robert Harrison Blake only once," said Doctor Dexter. "It was on an evening during the latter part of July, 1935. He called upon me here, as a patient."

Fiske leaned forward eagerly. "I never knew that!" he exclaimed.

"There was no reason for anyone to know it," the doctor answered. "He was merely a patient. He claimed to be suffering from insomnia. I examined him, prescribed a sedative, and acting on the merest surmise, asked if he had recently been subjected to any unusual strain or trauma. It was then that he told me the story of his visit to the church on Federal Hill and of what he had found there. I must say that I had the acumen not to dismiss his tale as the product of a hysterical imagination. As a member of one of the older families here, I was already acquainted with the legends surrounding the Starry Wisdom sect and the so-called Haunter of the Dark.

"Young Blake confessed to me certain of his fears concerning the Shining Trapezohedron—intimating that it was the focal point of primal evil. He further admitted his own dread of being somehow linked to the monstrosity in the church.

"Naturally, I was not prepared to accept this last premise as a rational one. I attempted to reassure the young man, advised him to leave Providence and forget it. And at the time I acted in all good faith. And then, in August, came news of Blake's death."

"So you went to the church," Fiske said.

"Wouldn't you have done the same thing?" parried Doctor Dexter. "If Blake had come to you with this story, told you of what he feared, wouldn't his death have moved you to action? I assure you, I did what I thought best. Rather than provoke a scandal, rather than expose the general public to needless fears, rather than permit the possibility of danger to exist, I went to the church. I took the books. I took the Shining Trapezohedron from under the noses of the authorities. And I chartered a boat and dumped the accursed thing in Narragansett Bay, where it could no longer possibly harm mankind. The lid was up when I dropped it—for as you know, only darkness can summon the Haunter, and now the stone is eternally exposed to light.

"But that is all I can tell you. I regret that my work in recent years has prevented me from seeing or communicating with you before this. I appreciate your interest in the affair and trust my remarks will help to clarify, in a small way, your bewilderment. As to young Blake, in my capacity as examining physician, I will gladly give you a written testimony to my belief in his sanity at the time of his death. I'll have it drawn up tomorrow and send it to your hotel if you give me the address. Fair enough?"

The doctor rose, signifying that the interview was over. Fiske remained seated, shifting his briefcase.

"Now if you will excuse me," the physician murmured.

"In a moment. There are still one or two brief questions I'd appreciate your answering."

"Certainly." If Doctor Dexter was irritated, he gave no sign.

"Did you by any chance see Lovecraft before or during his last illness?"

"No. I was not his physician. In fact, I never met the man, though of course I knew of him and his work."

"What caused you to leave Providence so abruptly after the Blake affair?"

"My interests in physics superseded my interest in medicine. As you may or may not know, during the past decade or more, I have been working on problems relative to atomic energy and nuclear fission. In fact, starting tomorrow, I am leaving Providence once more to deliver a course of lectures before the faculties of eastern universities and certain governmental groups."

"That is very interesting to me, Doctor," said Fiske. "By the way, did you ever meet Einstein?"

"As a matter of fact, I did, some years ago. I worked with him on—but no matter. I must beg you to excuse me, now. At another time, perhaps, we can discuss such things."

His impatience was unmistakable now. Fiske rose, lifting his briefcase in one hand and reaching out to extinguish a table lamp with the other.

Doctor Dexter crossed swiftly and lighted the lamp again.

"Why are you afraid of the dark, Doctor?" asked Fiske, softly.

"I am not af—"

For the first time the physician seemed on the verge of losing his composure. "What makes you think that?" he whispered.

"It's the Shining Trapezohedron, isn't it?" Fiske continued. "When you threw it into the bay you acted too hastily. You didn't remember at the time that even if you left the lid open, the stone would be surrounded by darkness there at the bottom of the channel. Perhaps the Haunter didn't want you to remember. You looked into the stone just as Blake did, and established the same psychic linkage. And when you threw the thing away, you gave it into perpetual darkness, where the Haunter's power would feed and grow.

"That's why you left Providence—because you were afraid the Haunter would come to you, just as it came to Blake. And because you knew that now the thing would remain abroad forever."

Doctor Dexter moved towards the door. "I must definitely ask that you leave now," he said. "If you're implying that I keep the lights on because I'm afraid of the Haunter coming after me, the way it did Blake, then you're mistaken."

Fiske smiled wryly. "That's not it at all," he answered. "I know you don't fear that. Because it's too late. The Haunter must have come to you long before this—perhaps within a day or so after you gave it power by consigning the Trapezohedron to the darkness of the Bay. It came to you, but unlike the case of Blake, it did not kill you.

"It used you. That's why you fear the dark. You fear it as the Haunter itself fears being discovered. I believe that in the darkness you look *different*. More like the old shape. Because when the Haunter came to you, it did not kill but instead, *merged*. *You* are the Haunter of the Dark!"

"Mr. Fiske, really—"

"There is no Doctor Dexter. There hasn't been any such person for many years, now. There's only the outer shell, possessed by an entity older than the world; an entity that is moving quickly and cunningly to bring destruction to all mankind. It was you who turned 'scientist' and insinuated yourself into the proper circles, hinting and prompting and assisting foolish men into their sudden 'discovery' of nuclear fission. When the first atomic bomb fell, how you must have laughed! And now you've given them the secret of the hydrogen bomb, and you're going to teach them more, show them new ways to bring about their own destruction.

"It took me years of brooding to discover the clues, the keys to the so-called wild myths that Lovecraft wrote about. For he wrote in parable and allegory, but he wrote the truth. He has set it down in black and white time and again, the prophecy of your coming to earth—Blake knew it at the last when he identified the Haunter by its rightful name."

"And that is?" snapped the doctor.

"Nyarlathotep!"

The brown face creased into a grimace of laughter. "I'm afraid you're a victim of the same fantasy-projections as poor Blake and your friend Lovecraft. Everyone knows that Nyarlathotep is pure invention—part of the Lovecraft mythos."

"I thought so, until I found the clue in his poem. That's when it all fitted in; the Haunter of the Dark, your fleeing, and your sudden interest in scientific research. Lovecraft's words took on a new meaning:

> And at last from inner Egypt came
> The strange dark one to whom the fellahs bowed."

Fiske chanted the lines, staring at the dark face of the physician.

"Nonsense—if you must know, this dermatological disturbance of mine is a result of exposure to radiation at Los Alamos."

Fiske did not heed; he was continuing Lovecraft's poem.

> "—That wild beasts followed him and licked his hands.
>   Soon from the sea a noxious birth birth began:
>   Forgotten lands with weedy spires of gold.
>   The ground was cleft and mad auroras rolled
>   Down on the quaking cities of man.
>   Then crushing what he chanced to mould in play
>   The idiot Chaos blew Earth's dust away."

Doctor Dexter shook his head. "Ridiculous on the face of it," he asserted. "Surely, even in your—er—upset condition, you can understand that, man! The poem has no literal meaning. Do wild beasts lick my hands? Is something rising from the sea? Are there earthquakes and auroras? Nonsense! You're suffering from a bad case of what we call 'atomic jitters'—I can see it now. You're preoccupied, as so many laymen are today, with the foolish obsession that somehow our work in nuclear fission will result in the destruction of the earth. All this rationalization is a product of your imaginings."

Fiske held his briefcase tightly. "I told you it was a parable, this prophecy of Lovecraft's. God knows what he *knew* or *feared;* whatever it was, it was enough to make him cloak his meaning. And even then, perhaps, *they* got to him because he knew too much."

"*They?*"

"They from Outside—the ones you serve. You are their Messenger, Nyarlathotep. You came, in linkage with the Shining Trapezohedron, out of inner Egypt, as the poem says. And the fellahs—the common workers of Providence who became converted to the Starry Wisdom sect—bowed before the 'strange dark one' they worshipped as the Haunter.

"The Trapezohedron was thrown into the Bay, and soon from the sea came this noxious birth—your birth, or incarnation in the body of Doctor Dexter. And you taught men new methods of destruction; destruction with atomic bombs in which the 'ground was cleft and mad auroras rolled down on the quaking cities of man.' Oh, Lovecraft knew what he was writing, and Blake recognized you, too. And they both died. I suppose you'll try to kill me now, so you can go on. You'll lecture, and stand at the elbows of the laboratory men urging them on and giving them new suggestions to result in greater destruction. And finally you'll blow earth's dust away."

"Please." Doctor Dexter held out both hands. "Control yourself—let me get you something! Can't you realize this whole thing is absurd?"

Fiske moved towards him, hands fumbling at the clasp of the briefcase. The flap opened, and Fiske reached inside, then withdrew his hand. He held a revolver now, and he pointed it quite steadily at Doctor Dexter's breast.

"Of course it's absurd," Fiske muttered. "No one ever believed in the Starry Wisdom sect except a few fanatics and some ignorant foreigners. No one ever took Blake's stories or Lovecraft's, or mine for that matter as anything but a rather morbid form of amusement. By the same token, no one will ever believe there is anything wrong with you, or with so-called scientific investigation of atomic energy, or the other horrors you plan to loose on the world to bring about its doom. And that's why I'm going to kill you now!"

"Put down that gun!"

Fiske began suddenly to tremble; his whole body shook in a spectacular spasm. Dexter noted it and moved forward. The younger man's eyes were bulging and the physician inched towards him.

"Stand back!" Fiske warned. The words were distorted by the convulsive shuddering of his jaws. "That's all I needed to know. Since you are in a human body, you can be destroyed by ordinary weapons. And so I destroy you—Nyarlathotep!"

His finger moved.

So did Doctor Dexter's. His hand went swiftly behind him, to the wall master light-switch. A click and the room was plunged into utter darkness.

Not utter darkness—for there was a glow.

The face and hands of Doctor Ambrose Dexter glowed with a phosphorescent fire in the dark. There are presumable forms of radium poisoning which can cause such an effect, and no doubt Doctor Dexter would have so explained the phenomenon to Edmund Fiske, had he the opportunity.

But there was no opportunity. Edmund Fiske heard the click, saw the fantastic flaming features, and pitched forward to the floor.

Doctor Dexter quietly switched on the lights, went over to the younger man's side and knelt for a long moment. He sought a pulse in vain.

Edmund Fiske was dead.

The doctor sighed, rose, and left the room. In the hall downstairs he summoned his servant.

"There has been a regrettable accident," he said. "That young visitor of mine—a hysteric—suffered a heart attack. You had better call the police, immediately. And then continue with the packing. We must leave tomorrow, for the lecture tour."

"But the police may detain you."

Doctor Dexter shook his head. "I think not. It's a clear-cut case. In any event, I can easily explain. When they arrive, notify me. I shall be in the garden."

The doctor proceeded down the hall to the rear exit and emerged upon the moonlit splendor of the garden behind the house on Benefit Street.

The radiant vista was walled off from the world, utterly deserted. The dark man stood in moonlight and its glow mingled with his own aura.

At this moment two silken shadows leaped over the wall. They crouched in the coolness of the garden, then slithered forwards towards Doctor Dexter. They made panting sounds.

In the moonlight, he recognized the shapes of two black panthers.

Immobile, he waited as they advanced, padding purposefully towards him, eyes aglow, jaws slavering and agape.

Doctor Dexter turned away. His face was turned in mockery to the moon as the beasts fawned before him and licked his hands.

*T*HIS EFFECTIVE STORY *has the distinction of being the first piece of Cthulhu Mythos fiction that young Ramsey Campbell stumbled upon, before he'd ever run across the name Lovecraft. It was the direct inspiration for one of his earliest efforts, "The Hollow in the Woods," published in* Crypt of Cthulhu *#50.*

"Notebook Found in a Deserted House" gains much of its effect from the device shared with Arthur Machen's "The White People": we are at a certain remove from the action, since we view it from the perspective of a child narrator. We know better than the narrator because we lack his/her innocence. This narrative technique allows an ominous irony to emerge through stylistic restraint. Oh, and the misspellings in the story are naturally Willie's, therefore, and not Bloch's.

In this story Bloch is actually pursuing some themes (e.g., the connection between the Druids and the tree-like shoggoths) he had used in an earlier tale, "The Druidic Doom" (Weird Tales, *April 1936; Kurt Singer, ed.,* Bloch and Bradbury *{Tower Books, 1969}).*

Notebook Found in a Deserted House

FIRST OFF, I WANT TO write that I never did anything wrong. Not to nobody. They got no call to shut me up here, whoever they are. They got no reason to do what I'm afraid they're going to do, either.

I think they're coming pretty soon, because they've been gone outside a long time. Digging, I guess, in that old well. Looking for a gate, I heard. Not a regular gate, of course, but something else.

Got a notion what they mean, and I'm scared.

I'd look out the windows but of course they are boarded up so I can't see.

But I turned on the lamp, and I found this here notebook so I want to put it all down. Then if I get a chance maybe I can send it to somebody who can help me. Or maybe somebody will find it. Anyway, it's better to write it out as best I can instead of just sitting here and waiting. Waiting for *them* to come and get me.

I better start by telling my name, which is Willie Osborne, and that I am 12 years old last July. I don't know where I was born.

First thing I can remember is living out Roodsford way, out in what folks call the back hill country. It's real lonesome out there, with deep woods all around and lots of mountains and hills that nobody ever climbs.

Grandma use to tell me about it when I was just a little shaver. That's who I lived with, just Grandma on account of my real folks being dead. Grandma was the one who taught me how to read and write. I never been to a regular school.

Grandma knew all kinds of things about the hills and the woods and she told me some mighty queer stories. That's what I thought they was, anyway, when I was little and living all alone with her. Just stories, like the ones in books.

Like stories about *them ones* hiding in the swamps, that was here before the settlers and the Indians both and how there was circles in swamps and big stones called alters where *them ones* use to make sacrefices to what they worshipped.

Grandma got some of the stories from her Grandma she said—about how *them ones* hid in the woods and swamps because they couldn't stand sunshine, and how the Indians kept out of their way. She said sometimes the Indians would leave some of their young people tied to trees in the forest as a sacrefice, so as to keep *them* contented and peacefull.

Indians knew all about *them* and they tried to keep white folks from noticing too much or settling too close to the hills. *Them ones* didn't cause much trouble, but they might if they was crowded. So the Indians gave excuses for not settling, saying there weren't enough hunting and no trails and it was too far off from the coast.

Grandma told me that was why not many places was settled even today. Nothing but a few farmhouses here and there. She told me *them ones* was still alive and sometimes on certain nights in the Spring and Fall you could see lights and hear noises far off on the tops of the hills.

Grandma said I had an Aunt Lucy and a Uncle Fred who lived out there right smack in the middle of the hills. Said my Pa used to visit them before he got married and once he heard *them* beating on a tree drum one night along about Halloween time. That was before he met Ma and they got married and she died when I come and he went away.

I heard all kinds of stories. About witches and devils and bat men that sucked your blood and haunts. About Salem and Arkham because I never been to a city and I wanted to hear tell how they were. About a place called Innsmouth with old rotten houses where people hid awful things away in the cellars and the attics. She told me bout the way graves was dug deep under Arkham. Made it sound like the whole country was full of haunts.

She use to scare me, telling about how some of these things looked and all but she never would tell me how *them ones* looked no matter how much I asked. Said she didn't want me to have any truck with such things—bad enough she and her kin knew as much as they did—almost too much for decent God fearing people. It was lucky for me I didn't have to bother with such ideas, like my own ancestor on my father's side, Mehitabel Osborne, who got hanged for a witch back in the Salem days.

So they was just stories to me until last year when Grandma died and Judge Crubinthorp put me on the train and I went out to live with Aunt Lucy and Uncle Fred in the very same hills that Grandma use to tell about so often.

You can bet I was pretty excited, and the conductor let me ride with him all the way and told me about the towns and everything.

Uncle Fred met me at the station. He was a tall thin man with a long beard. We drove off in a buggy from the little deepo—no houses around there or nothing—right into the woods.

Funny thing about those woods. They was so still and quiet. Gave me the creeps they was so dark and lonesome. Seemed like nobody had ever shouted and laughed or even smiled in them. Couldn't imagine anyone saying anything there excep in whispers.

Trees and all was so old, too. No animals around or birds. Path kind of overgrown like nobody used it much ever. Uncle Fred drove along right fast, he didn't hardly talk to me at all but just made that old horse hump it.

Pretty soon we struck into some hills, they was awfully high ones. They was woods on them, too, and sometimes a brook come running down, but I didn't see no houses and it was always dark like at twilight, wherever you looked.

Lastly we got to the farmhouse—a little place, old frame house and barn in a clear space with trees all around kind of gloomy-like. Aunt Lucy come out to meet us, she was a nice sort of middle-aged lady who hugged me and took my stuff in back.

But all this don't hold with what I'm supposed to write down here. It don't matter that all this last year I was living in the house here with them, eating off the stuff Uncle Fred farmed without ever going into town. No other farms around here for almost four mile and no school—so evenings Aunt Lucy would help me with my reading. I never played much.

At first I was scared of going into the woods on account of what Grandma had told me. Besides, I could tell as Aunt Lucy and Uncle Fred were scared of something from the way they locked the doors at night and never went into the woods after dark, even in summer.

But after a while, I got used to the idea of living in the woods and they didn't seem so scarey. I did chores for Uncle Fred, of course, but sometimes in afternoons when he was busy, I'd go off by myself. Particular by the time it was fall.

And that's how I heard one of the things. It was early October, I was in the glen right by the big boulder. Then the noise started. I got behind that rock fast.

You see, like I say, there isn't any animals in the woods. Nor people. Excep perhaps old Cap Pritchett the mailman who only comes through on Thursday afternoons.

So when I heard a sound that wasn't Uncle Fred or Aunt Lucy calling to me, I knew I better hide.

About that sound. It was far-away at first, kind of a dropping noise. Sounded like the blood falling in little spurts on the bottom of the bucket when Uncle Fred hung up a butchered hog.

I looked around but I couldn't make out nothing, and I couldn't figure out the direction the noise was from either. The noise sort of stopped for a minute and they was only twilight and trees, still as death. Then the noise started again, nearer and louder.

Sounded like a lot of people running or walking all at once, moving this way. Twigs busting under feet and scrabbling in the bushes all mixed up in the noise. I scrunched down behind that boulder and kep real quiet.

I can tell that whatever makes the noise, it's real close now, right in the glen. I want to look up but dassn't because the sound is so loud and *mean*. And also there is an awful smell like something that was dead and buried being uncovered again in the sun.

All at once the noise stops again and I can tell that whatever makes it is real close by. For a minute the woods are creepy-still. Then comes the sound.

It's a voice and it's not a voice. That is, it doesn't *sound* like a voice but more like a buzzing or croaking, deep and droning. But it *has* to be a voice because it is saying words.

Not words I could understand, but words. Words that made me keep my head down, half afraid I might be seen and half afraid I might see something. I stayed there sweating and shaking. The smell was making me pretty sick, but that awful, deep droning voice was worse. Saying over and over something like

"E hu shub nigger ath ngaa ryla neb shoggoth."

I can't hope to spell it out the way it sounded, but I heard it enough times to remember. I was still listening when the smell got awful thick and I guess I must have fainted because when I woke up the voice was gone and it was getting dark.

I ran all the way home that night, but not before I saw where the thing had stood when it talked—and it *was* a thing.

No human being can leave tracks in the mud like goat's hoofs all green with slime that smell awful—not four or eight, but a couple *hundred!*

I didn't tell Aunt Lucy or Uncle Fred. But that night when I went to bed I had terrible dreams. I thought I was back in the glen, only this time I could see the thing. It was real tall and all inky-black, without any particular shape except a lot of black ropes with ends like hoofs on it. I mean, it had a shape but it kep changing—all bulgy and squirming into different sizes. They was a lot of mouths all over the thing like puckered up leaves on branches.

That's as close as I can come. The mouths was like leaves and the whole thing was like a tree in the wind, a black tree with lots of branches trailing the ground, and a whole lot of roots ending in hoofs. And that green slime dribbling out of the mouths and down the legs was like sap!

Next day I remembered to look in a book Aunt Lucy had downstairs. It was called a mythology. This book told about some people who lived over in England and France in the old days and was called Druids. They worshipped trees and thought they was alive. Maybe this thing was like what they worshipped—called a nature-spirit.

But these Druids lived across the ocean, so how could it be? I did a lot of thinking about it the next couple of days, and you can bet I didn't go out to play in those woods again.

At last I figgered it out something like this.

Maybe those Druids got chased out of the forests over in England and France and some of them was smart enough to build boats and come across the ocean like old Leaf Erikson is supposed to have. Then they could maybe settle in the woods back here and frighten away the Indians with their magic spells.

They would know how to hide themselves away in the swamps and go right on with their heathen worshiping and call up these spirits out of the ground or wherever they come from.

Indians use to believe that white gods come from out of the sea a long time ago. What if that was just another way of telling how the Druids got here? Some real civilized Indians down in Mexico or South America—Aztecs or Inkas, I guess—said a white god come over in a boat and taught them all kinds of magic. Couldn't he of been a Druid?

That would explain Grandma's stories about *them ones*, too.

Those Druids hiding in the swamps would be the ones who did the drumming and pounding and lit the fires on the hills. And they would be calling up *them ones*, the tree spirits or whatever, out of the earth. Then they would make sacrefices. Those Druids always made sacrefices with blood, just like the old witches. And didn't Grandma tell about people who lived too near the hills disappearing and never being found again?

We lived in a spot just exactly like that.

And it was getting close to Halloween. That was the big time, Grandma always said.

I began to wonder—how soon now?

Got so scared I didn't go out of the house. Aunt Lucy made me take a tonic, said I looked peaked. Guess I did. All I know is one afternoon when I heard a buggy coming through the woods I ran and hid under the bed.

But it was only Cap Pritchett with the mail. Uncle Fred got it and come in all excited with a letter.

Cousin Osborne was coming to stay with us. He was kin to Aunt Lucy and he had a vacation and he wanted to stay a week. He'd get here on the same train I did—the only train they was passing through these parts—on noon, October 25th.

For the next few days we was all so excited that I forgot all my crazy notions for a spell. Uncle Fred fixed up the back room for Cousin Osborne to sleep in and I helped him with the carpenter parts of the job.

Days got shorter right along, and the nights was all cold with big winds. It was pretty brisk the morning of the 25th and Uncle Fred bundled up warm to drive through the woods. He meant to fetch Cousin Osborne at noon, and it was seven mile to the station. He wouldn't take me, and I didn't beg. Them woods was too full of creaking and rustling sounds from the wind—sounds that might be something else, too.

Well, he left, and Aunt Lucy and I stayed in the house. She was putting up preserves now—plums—for over the winter season. I washed out jars from the well.

Seems like I should have told about them having two wells. A new one with a big shiny pump, close to the house. Then an old stone one out by the barn, with the pump gone. It never had been any good, Uncle Fred said, it was there when they bought the place. Water was all slimy. Something funny about it, because even without a pump, sometimes it seemed to back up. Uncle Fred couldn't figure it out, but some mornings water would be running out over the sides—green, slimy water that smelled terrible.

We kep away from it and I was by the new well, till along about noon when it started in to cloud up. Aunt Lucy fixed lunch, and it started to rain hard with thunder rolling in off the big hills in the west.

Seemed to me Uncle Fred and Cousin Osborne was going to have troubles getting home in the storm, but Aunt Lucy didn't fret about it—just made me help her put up the stock.

Come five o'clock, getting dark, and still no Uncle Fred. Then we begun to worry. Maybe the train was late, or something happened to the horse or buggy.

Six o'clock and still no Uncle Fred. The rain stopped, but you could still hear the thunder sort of growling off in the hills, and the wet branches kep dripping down in the woods, making a sound like women laughing.

Maybe the road was too bad for them to get through. Buggy might bog down in the mud. Perhaps they decided to stay in the deepo over night.

Seven o'clock and it was pitch dark outside. No rain sounds any more. Aunt Lucy was awful worried. She said for us to go out and post a lantern on the fence rail by the road.

We went down the path to the fence. It was dark and the wind had died down. Everything was still, like in the deep part of the woods. I felt kind of scared just walking down the path with Aunt Lucy—like something was out there in the quiet dark, someplace, waiting to grab me.

We lit a lantern and stood there looking down the dark road and, "What's that?" said Aunt Lucy, real sharp. I listened and heard a drumming sound far away.

"Horse and buggy," I said. Aunt Lucy perked up.

"You're right," she says, all at once. And it is, because we see it. The horse is running fast and the buggy lurches behind it, crazy-like. It don't even take a second look to see something has happened, because the buggy don't stop by the gate but keep going up the barn with Aunt Lucy and me running through the mud after the horse. The horse is all full of lather and foam, and when it stops it can't stand still. Aunt Lucy and I wait for Uncle Fred and Cousin Osborne to step out, but nothing happens. We look inside.

There isn't anybody in the buggy at all.

Aunt Lucy says, "Oh!" in a real loud voice and then faints. I had to carry her back to the house and get her into bed.

I waited almost all night by the window, but Uncle Fred and Cousin Osborne never showed up. Never.

The next few days was awful. They was nothing in the buggy for a clue like to what happened, and Aunt Lucy wouldn't let me go along the road or into town or even to the station through the woods.

The next morning the horse was dead in the barn, and of course we would have had to walk to the deepo or all those miles to Warren's farm. Aunt Lucy was scared to go and scared to stay and she allowed as how when Cap Pritchett comes by we had best go with him over to town and make a report and then stay there until we found out what happened.

Me, I had my own ideas what happened. Halloween was only a few days away now, and maybe *them ones* had snatched Uncle Fred and Cousin Osborne for sacrefice. *Them ones* or the Druids. The mythology book said Druids could even raise storms if they wanted to with their spells.

No sense talking to Aunt Lucy, though. She was like out of her head with worry, anyway, just rocking back and forth and mumbling over and over, "They're gone" and "Fred always warned me" and "No use, no use." I had to get the meals and tend to stock myself. And nights it was hard to sleep, because I kep listening for drums. I never heard any, though, but still it was better than sleeping and having those dreams.

Dreams about the black thing like a tree, walking through the woods and sort of rooting itself to one particular spot so it could pray with all those mouths—pray down to that old god in the ground below.

I don't know where I got the idea that was how it prayed—by sort of attaching its mouths to the ground. Maybe it was on account of seeing the green slime. Or had I really seen it? I'd never gone back to look. Maybe it was all in my head—the Druid story and about *them ones* and the voice that said "shoggoth" and all the rest.

But then, where was Cousin Osborne and Uncle Fred? And what scared the horse so it up and died the next day?

Thoughts kep going round and round in my head, chasing each other, but all I knew was we'd be out of here by Halloween night.

Because Halloween was on a Thursday, and Cap Pritchett would come and we could ride to town with him.

Night before I made Aunt Lucy pack and we got all ready, and then I settled down to sleep. There was no noises, and for the first time I felt a little better.

Only the dreams came again. I dreamed a bunch of men come in the night and crawled through the parlor bedroom window where Aunt Lucy slept and got her. They tied her up and took her away, all quiet, in the dark, because they had cat-eyes and didn't need light to see.

The dream scared me so I woke up while it was just breaking into dawn. I went down the hall to Aunt Lucy right away.

She was gone.

The window was wide open like in my dream, and some of the blankets was torn.

Ground was hard outside the window and I didn't see footprints or anything. But she was gone.

I guess I cried then.

It's hard to remember what I did next. Didn't want breakfast. Went out hollering "Aunt Lucy" and not expecting any answer. I walked to the barn and the door was open and the cows were gone. Saw one or two prints going out the yard and up the road, but I didn't think it was safe to follow them.

Some time later I went over to the well and then I cried again because the water was all slimy green in the new one, just like the old.

When I saw that I knew I was right. *Them ones* must of come in the night and they wasn't even trying to hide their doings any more. Like they was sure of things.

Tonight was Halloween. I had to get out of here. If *them ones* was watching and waiting, I couldn't depend on Cap Pritchett showing up this afternoon. I'd have to chance it down the road and I'd better start walking now, in the morning, while it was still light enough to make town.

So I rummaged around and found a little money in Uncle Fred's drawer of the bureau and Cousin Osborne's letter with the address in Kingsport he wrote it from. That's where I'd have to go after I told folks in town what happened. I'd have some kin there.

I wondered if they'd believe me in town when I told them about the way Uncle Fred had disappeared and Aunt Lucy, and about *them* stealing the cattle for a sacrefice and about the green slime in the well where something had stopped to drink. I wondered if they would know about the drums and the lights on the hills tonight and if they was going to get up a party and come back this evening to try to catch *them ones* and what they meant to call up rumbling out of the earth. I wondered if they knew what a "shoggoth" was.

Well, whether they did or not, I couldn't stay and find out for myself. So I packed up my satchel and got ready to leave. Must of been around noon and everything was still.

I went to the door and stepped outside, not bothering to lock it behind me. Why should I with nobody around for miles?

Then I heard the noise down the road.

Footsteps.

Somebody walking along the road, just around the bend.

I stood for a minute, waiting to see, waiting to run.

Then he come along.

He was tall and thin, and looked something like Uncle Fred only a lot younger and without a beard, and he was wearing a nice city kind of suit and a crush hat. He smiled when he saw me and come marching up like he knowed who I was.

"Hello, Willie," he said.

I didn't say nothing. I was so confuzed.

"Don't you know me?" he said. "I'm Cousin Osborne. Your cousin, Frank." He held out his hand to shake. "But then I guess you wouldn't remember, would you? Last time I saw you, you were only a baby."

"But I thought you were suppose to come last week," I said. "We expected you on the 25th."

"Didn't you get my telegram?" he asked. "I had business."

I shook my head. "We never get nothing here unless the mail delivers it on Thursdays. Maybe it's at the station."

Cousin Osborne grinned. "You are pretty well off the beaten track at that. Nobody at the station this noon. I was hoping Fred would come along with the buggy so I wouldn't have to walk, but no luck."

"You walked all the way?" I asked.

"That's right."

"And you come on the train?"

Cousin Osborne nodded.

"Then where's your suitcase?"

"I left it at the deepo," he told me. "Too far to fetch it along. I thought Fred would drive me back there in the buggy to pick it up." He noticed my luggage for the first time. "But wait a minute—where are you going with a suitcase, son?"

Well, there was nothing else for me to do but tell him everything that happened.

So I said for him to come into the house and set down and I'd explain.

We went back in and he fixed some coffee and I made a couple sanwiches and we ate, and then I told him about Uncle Fred going to the deepo and not coming back, and about the horse and then what happened to Aunt Lucy. I left out the part about me in the woods, of course, and I didn't even hint at *them ones*. But I told him I was scared and figgered on walking to town today before dark.

Cousin Osborne he listened to me, nodding and not saying much or interrupting.

"Now you can see why we got to go, right away," I said. "Whatever come after them will be coming after us, and I don't want to spend another night here."

Cousin Osborne stood up. "You may be right, Willie," he said. "But dont let your imagination run away with you, son. Try to separate fact from fancy. Your Aunt and Uncle have disappeared. That's fact. But this other nonsense about things in the woods coming after you—that's fancy. Reminds me of all that silly talk I heard back home, in Arkham. And for some reason there seems to be more of it around this time of year, at Halloween. Why, when I left—"

"Excuse me, Cousin Osborne," I said. "But dont you live in Kingsport?"

"Why to be sure," he told me. "But I did live in Arkham once, and I know the people around here. It's no wonder you were so frightened in the woods and got to imagining things. As it is, I admire your bravery. For a 12 year old, you've acted very sensibly.

"Then lets get walking," I said. "Here it is almost 2 and we better get moving if we want to make town before sundown."

"Not just yet, son," Cousin Osborne said. "I wouldn't feel right about leaving without looking around and seeing what we can discover about this mystery. After all, you must understand that we can't just march into town and tell the sheriff some wild nonsense about strange creatures in the woods making off with your Aunt and Uncle. Sensible folks just won't believe such things. They might think I was lying and laugh at me. Why they might even think that you had something to do with your Aunt and Uncle's—well, leaving."

"Please," I said. "We got to go, right now."

He shook his head.

I didn't say anything more. I might of told him a lot, about what I dreamed and heard and saw and knew—but I figgered it was no use.

Besides, there was some things I didn't want to say to him now that I had talked to him. I was feeling scared again.

First he said he was from Arkham and then when I asked him he said he was from Kingsport but it sounded like a lie to me.

Then he said something about me being scared in the woods and how could he know that? I never told him *that* part at all.

If you want to know what I really thought, I thought maybe he wasn't really Cousin Osborne at all.

And if he wasn't, then—who was he?

I stood up and walked back into the hall.

"Where you going, son?" he asked.

"Outside."

"I'll come with you."

Sure enough, he was watching me. He wasn't going to let me out of his sight. He came over and took my arm, real friendly—but I couldn't break loose. No he hung on to me. He knew I meant to run for it.

What could I do? All alone in the house in the woods with this man, with night coming on, Halloween night, and *them ones* out there waiting.

We went outside and I noticed it was getting darker already, even in afternoon. Clouds had covered up the sun, and the wind was moving the trees so they stretched out their branches, like they was trying to hold me back. They made a rustling noise, just as if they were whispering things about me, and he sort of looked up at them and listened. Maybe he understood what they were saying. Maybe they were giving him orders.

Then I almost laughed, because he *was* listening to something and now I heard it too.

It was a drumming sound, on the road.

"Cap Pritchett," I said. "He's the mailman. Now we can ride to town with him in the buggy."

"Let me talk to him," he says. "About your Aunt and Uncle. No sense in alarming him, and we don't want any scandal, do we? You just run along inside."

"But Cousin Osborne," I said. "We got to tell the truth."

"Of course, son. But this is a matter for adults. Now run along. I'll call you."

He was real polite about it and even smiled, but all the same he dragged me back up the porch and into the house and slammed the door. I stood there in the dark hall and I could hear Cap Pritchett slow down and call out to him, and him going up to the buggy and talking, and then all I heard was a lot of mumbling, real low. I peeked out through a crack in the door and saw them. Cap Pritchett was talking to him friendly, all right, and nothing was wrong.

Except that in a minute or so, Cap Pritchett waved and then he grabbed the reins and the buggy started off again.

Then I knew I'd have to do it, no matter what happened. I opened the door and ran out, suitcase and all, down the path and up the road after the buggy. Cousin Osborne he tried to grab me when I went by, but I ducked around him and yelled, "Wait for me, Cap—I'm coming—take me to town!"

Cap slowed down and stared back, real puzzled.

"Willie!" he says. "Why I though you was gone. He said you went away with Fred and Lucy—"

"Pay no attention," I said. "He didn't want me to go. Take me to town. I'll tell you what really happened. Please, Cap, you got to take me."

"Sure I'll take you, Willie. Hop right up here."

I hopped.

Cousin Osborne came right up to the buggy. "Here, now," he said, real sharp. "You can't leave like this. I forbid it. You're in my custody."

"Don't listen to him," I yelled. "Take me, Cap! Please!!"

"Very well," said Cousin Osborne. "If you insist on being unreasonable. We'll all go. I cannot permit you to leave alone."

He smiled at Cap. "You can see the boy is unstrung," he said. "And I trust you will not be disturbed by his imaginings. Living out here like this—well, you understand—he's not quite himself. I'll explain everything on the way to town."

He sort of shrugged at Cap and made signs of tapping his head. Then he smiled again and made to climb up next to us in the buggy seat.

But Cap didn't smile back. "No, you don't," he said. "This boy Willy is a good boy. I know him. I don't know you. Looks as if you done enough explaining already, Mister, when you said Willie had gone away."

"But I merely wanted to avoid talk—you see, I've been called in to doctor the boy—he's mentally unstable—"

"Stables be damned!" Cap spit out some tobacco juice right at Cousin Osborne's feet. "We're going."

Cousin Osborne stopped smiling. "Then I insist you take me with you," he said. And he tried to climb into the buggy.

Cap reached into his jacket and when he pulled his hand out again he had a big pistol in it.

"Git down!" he yelled. "Mister, you're talking to the United States Mail and you don't tell the Government nothing, understand? Now git down before I mess your brains all over this road."

Cousin Osborne scowled, but he got away from the buggy, fast.

He looked at me and shrugged. "You're making a big mistake, Willie," he said.

I didn't even look at him. Cap said, "Gee up," and we went off down the road. The buggy wheels turned faster and faster and soon the farmhouse was out of sight and Cap put his pistol away, and patted me on the shoulder.

"Stop that trembling, Willie," he said. "You're safe now. Nothing to worry about. Be in town in a little over an hour or so. Now you just set back and tell old Cap all about it."

So I told him. It took a long time. We kep going through the woods, and before I knew it, it was almost dark. The sun sneaked down and hid behind the hills. The dark began to creep out of the woods on each side of the road, and the trees started to rustle, whispering to the big shadows that followed us.

The horse was clipping and clopping along, and pretty soon they were other noises from far away. Might have been thunder and might have been something else. But it was gettin night-time for sure, and it was the night of Halloween.

The road cut off through the hills now, and you could hardly see where the next turn would take you. Besides, it was getting dark awful fast.

"Guess we're in for a spell of rain," Cap said, looking up. "That's thunder, I reckon."

"Drums," I said.

"Drums?"

"At night in the hills you can hear them," I told him. "I heard them all this month. It's *them ones,* getting ready for the Sabbath."

"Sabbath?" Cap looked at me. "Where you hear tell about a Sabbath?"

Then I told him some more about what had happened. I told him all the rest. He didn't say anything, and before long he couldn't of answered me anyway, because the thunder was all around us, and the rain was lashing down on the buggy, on the road, everywhere. It was pitch-black outside now, and the only time we could see was when lightning flashed. I had to yell to make him hear me—yell about the things that caught Uncle Frank and come for Aunt Lucy, the things that took our cattle and then sent Cousin Osborne back to fetch me. I hollered out about what I heard in the wood, too.

In the lightning flashes I could see Cap's face. He wasn't smiling or scowling—he just looked like he believed me. And I noticed he had his pistol out again and was holding the reins with one hand even though we were racing along. The horse was so scared he didn't need the whip to keep him running.

The old buggy was lurching and bouncing, and the rain was whistling down in the wind and it was all like an awful dream but it was real. It was real when I hollered out to Cap Pritchett about that time in the woods.

"Shoggoth," I yelled. "What's a shoggoth?"

Cap grabbed my arm, and then the lightning come and I could see his face, with his mouth open. But he wasn't looking at me. He was looking at the road and what was ahead of us.

The trees sort of come together, hanging over the next turn, and in the black it looked as if they were alive—moving and bending and twisting to block our way. Lightning flickered up again and I could see them plain, and also something else.

Something black in the road, something that wasn't a tree. Something big and black, just squatting there, waiting, with ropy arms squirming and reaching.

"Shoggoth!" Cap yelled. But I could scarcely hear him because the thunder was roaring and now the horse let out a scream and I felt the buggy jerk to one side and the horse reared up and we was almost into the black stuff. I could smell an awful smell, and Cap was pointing his pistol and it went off with a bank that was almost as loud as the thunder and almost as loud as the sound we made when we hit the black thing.

Then everything happened at once. The thunder, the horse falling, the shot, and us hitting as the buggy went over. Cap must of had the reins wrapped around his arm, because when the horse fell and the buggy turned over, he went right over the dashboard head first and down into the squirming mess that was the horse—and the black thing that grabbed it. I felt myself falling in the dark, then landing in the mud and gravel of the road.

There was thunder and screaming and another sound which I had heard once before in the woods—a droning sound like a voice.

That's why I never looked back. That's why I didn't even think about being hurt when I landed—just got up and started to run down the road, fast as I could, run down the road in the storm and the dark with the trees squirming and twisting and shaking their heads while they pointed at me with their branches and laughed.

Over the thunder I heard the horse scream and I heard Cap scream, too, but I still didn't look back. The lightning winked on and off, and I ran through the trees now because the road was nothing but mud that dragged me down and sucked at my legs. After a while I began to scream, too, but I couldn't even hear myself for thunder. And more than thunder. I heard drums.

All at once I busted clear of the woods and got to the hills. I ran up, and the drumming got louder, and pretty soon I could see regular, not just when they was lightning. Because they was fires burning on the hill, and the booming of the drums come from there.

I got lost in the noise; the wind shrieking and the trees laughing and the drums pounding. But I stopped in time. I stopped when I saw the fires plain; red and green fires burning in all that rain.

I saw a big white stone in the center of a cleared-off space on top of the hill. The red and green fires was around and behind it, so everything stood out clear against the flames.

They was men around the alter, men with long gray beards and wrinkled-up faces, men throwing awful-smelling stuff on the fires to make them blaze red and green. And they had knives in their hands and I could hear them howling over the storm. In back, squatting on the ground, more men pounded on drums.

Pretty soon something else came up the hill—two men driving cattle. I could tell it was our cows they drove, drove them right up to the alter and then the men with the knives cut their throats for a sacrefice.

All this I could see in lightning flashes and in the fire lights, and I sort of scooched down so I couldn't get spotted by anyone.

But pretty soon I couldn't see very good any more, on account of the way they threw stuff on the fire. It set up a real thick black smoke. When this smoke come up, the men began to chant and pray louder.

I couldn't hear words, but the sounds was like what I heard back in the woods. I couldn't see too good, but I knew what was going to happen. Two men who had led the cattle went back down the other side of the hill and when they come up again they had new sacrefices. The smoke kep me from seeing plain, but these was two-legged sacrefices, not four. I might of seen better at that, only now I hid my face when they dragged them up to the white alter and used the knives, and the fire and smoke flared up and the drums boomed and they all chanted and called in a loud voice to something waiting over on the other side of the hill.

The ground began to shake. It was storming, they was thunder and lightning and fire and smoke and chanting and I was scared half out of my wits, but one thing I'll swear to—the ground began to shake. It shook and shivered and they called out to something, and in a minute something came.

It came crawling up the hillside to the alter and the sacrefice, and it was the black thing of my dreams—that black, ropy, slimy, jelly tree-thing out of the woods. It crawled up and it flowed up on its hoofs and mouths and snaky arms. And the men bowed and stood back and then it got to the alter where they was something squirming on top, squirming and screaming.

The black thing sort of bent over the alter and then I heard droning sounds over the screaming as it come down. I only watched a minute, but while I watched the black thing began to swell and *grow.*

That finished me. I didn't care any more. I had to run. I got up and I run and run and run, screaming at the top of my lungs no matter who heard.

I kep running and I kep screaming forever, through the woods and the storm, away from that hill and that alter, and then all at once I knew where I was and I was back here at the farmhouse.

Yes, that's what I'd done—run in a circle and come back. But I couldn't go any further, I couldn't stand the night and the storm. So I run inside here. At first after I locked the door I just lay right down on the floor, all tuckered out from running and crying.

But in a little while I got up and hunted me some nails and a hammer and some of Uncle Fred's boards that wasn't split up into kindling.

I nailed up the door first and then boarded up all the windows. Every last one of them. Guess I worked for hours, tired as I was. When it was all done, the storm died down and it got quiet. Quiet enough for me to lie down on the couch and go to sleep.

Woke up a couple hours ago. It was daylight. I could see it shining through the cracks. From the way the sun come in, I knew it was afternoon already. I'd slept through the whole morning, and nothing had come.

I figured now maybe I could let myself out and make town on foot, like I'd planned yesterday.

But I figgered wrong.

Before I got started taking out the nails, I heard him. It was Cousin Osborne, of course. The man who said he was Cousin Osborne, I mean.

He come into the yard, calling "Willie!" but I didn't answer. Then he tried the door and then the windows. I could hear him pounding and cussing. That was bad.

But then he began mumbling, and that was worse. Because it meant he wasn't out there alone.

I sneaked a look through the crack, but he already went around to the back of the house so I didn't see him or who was with him.

Guess that's just as well, because if I'm right, I wouldn't want to see.

Hearing's bad enough.

Hearing that deep croaking, and then him talking, and then that croaking again.

Smelling that awful smell, like the green slime from the woods and around the well.

The well—they went over to the well in back. And I heard Cousin Osborne say something about, "Wait until dark. We can use the well if you find the gate. Look for the gate."

I know what that means now. The well must be a sort of entrance to the underground place—that's where those Druid men live. And the black thing.

They're out in back now, looking.

I been writing for quite a spell and already the afternoon is going. Peeking through the cracks I can see it's getting dark again.

That's when they'll come for me—when it's dark.

They'll break down the doors or the windows and come and take me. They'll take me down into the well, into the black places where the shoggoths are. There must be a whole world down under the hills, a world where they hide and wait to come out for more sacrefices, more blood. They don't want any humans around, except for sacrefices.

I saw what the black thing did on the alter. I know what's going to happen to me.

Maybe they'll miss the real Cousin Osborne back home and send somebody to find out what become of him. Maybe folks in town will miss Cap Pritchett and go on a search. Maybe they'll come here and find me. But if they don't come soon it will be too late.

That's why I wrote this. It's true, cross my heart, every word of it. And if anyone finds this notebook where I hide it, come and look down the well. The old well, out in back.

Remember what I told about *them ones*. Block up the well and clean out them swamps. No sense looking for me—if I'm not here.

I wish I wasn't so scared. I'm not even scared so much for myself, but for other folks. The ones who might come after and live around here and have the same thing happen—or worse.

You just got to believe me. Go to the woods if you don't. Go to the hill. The hill where they had the sacrefice. Maybe the stains are gone and the rain washed the footprints away. Maybe they got rid of the traces of the fire. But the alter stone must be there. And if it is, you'll know the truth. There should be some big round spots on that stone. Round spots about two feet wide.

I didn't tell about that. At the last, I did look back. I looked back at the big black thing that was a shoggoth. I looked back as it kep swelling and growing. I guess I told about how it could change shape, and how big it got. But you can't hardly imagine how big or what shape and I still dassn't tell.

All I say is look. Look and you'll see what's hiding under the earth in these hills, waiting to creep out and feast and kill some more.

Wait. They're coming now. Getting twilight and I can hear footsteps. And other sounds. Voices. And other sounds. They're banging on the door. And sure enough—they must have a tree or plank to use for battering it down. The whole place is shaking. I can hear Cousin Osborne yelling, and that droning. The smell is awful, I'm getting sick, and in a minute—

Look at the alter. Then you'll understand what I'm trying to tell. Look at the big round marks, two feet wide, on each side. That's where the big black thing grabbed hold.

Look for the marks and you'll know what I saw, what I'm afraid of, what's waiting to grab you unless you shut it up forever under the earth.

Black marks two feet wide, but they aren't just marks.

What they really are is *fingerprints!*

The door is busting o———————

W HEN AN EDITOR ASSIGNED *Bloch to come up with a story to fit this title, he might have written pretty much any type of action or adventure yarn. But he made a tale of the Cthulhu Mythos. Here we have something of a modern Obed Marsh, propelled by venal greed into unlocking a submerged trove of unearthly horror. And in the eventual mind-meld between the hapless narrator and the alien entity we have an echo of the psychic fusion of Robert Blake and the avatar from the steeple many years before in "The Haunter of the Dark." With its apocalyptic denouement, the story prefigures Bloch's later Cthulhu Mythos novel, Strange Eons.*

More importantly, the story demonstrates something about the adaptability of the classic Cthulhuvian tale to new modes of narration. Lovecraft cloistered his cosmic horrors in a castle of antique prose and purposely kept character development to a minimum. His success raises the question of whether it is possible to write in a distinctly un-Lovecraftian manner and yet pen a tale true to his vision of the Mythos. "Terror in Cut-Throat Cove" answers that question in the affirmative, as Cthulhu's tentacles reach forth through the medium of Bloch's punchy, hard-boiled style and his strong, well-defined characters. The challenge could be met, and Bloch was the one to meet it.

Terror in
Cut-Throat Cove

Y OU WON'T FIND Cut-Throat Cove on any map, because that is not its real name. And you can search a chart of the West Indies thoroughly without locating the island of Santa Rita.

I have changed the names for obvious reasons. If those reasons are not obvious at the moment, they will be by the time you finish this account.

My own name is Howard Lane, and I lived on Santa Rita for almost a year without ever hearing of Cut-Throat Cove. That isn't too surprising, for it wasn't the lure of buccaneers and bullion that brought me here—in fact, you might say I left the United States just to get away from the atmosphere of piracy and plunder which dominates the modern commercial scene.

You might say it, but *I* did say it, night after night, in Rico's Bar. Eventually, of course, I'd stop talking and fall down. Nobody ever paid much attention to me—before, or after.

Except on the night when I met Don and Dena. The teddy-bear and the Christmas-tree angel.

I had a little bit too much of Rico's rum that evening, and I admit it. But even after I got to know them I still thought my first impression was right.

Teddy-bear. That was Don, standing at the bar beside me; blond, burly, his short arms thick and bare and covered with that soft golden fuzz; his nose splayed and pink, and his eyes like big brown buttons. I watched him order a drink, American beer. American beer, in cans, at a dollar a throw! And he was tossing American money on the bar—a twenty. That was enough to make me look twice. We seldom get strangers or tourists in Santa Rita, and the infrequent visitors never have any money. So I watched the teddy-bear as he carried the two cans of beer over to a table in the corner. And that's when I saw her sitting across from him.

The Christmas-tree angel. Her dress was white and wispy, her hair was spun gold, her eyes china-blue. The complexion was peaches-and-cream, the peaches being slightly ripened by the sun. She laughed up at the teddy-bear as he approached, and I felt an unreasoning resentment.

Why is it always that way? Why does that kind of a girl always pick that kind of a man?

I'd asked myself that question a thousand times. I'd asked it ever since I'd come to Santa Rita a year ago. In fact, that's the real reason I *had* come; because once *I*'d picked just such a girl—only to find she picked that sort of man.

And I knew what he was, the moment I looked at him. He was the Muscle Beach Boy, the busy-eyebrows type, the kind who shows up in all the cigarette ads with a tattoo on his hand. I made a little bet with myself about what would happen after he had poured out the beer. Sure enough, I won. He took hold of the empty beer-can in one ham-like hand and squeezed, crushing it flat.

That made *her* laugh again, and I knew why. Because she wasn't a Christmas-tree angel, after all. She was just the kind of girl who fooled my kind of man into thinking that's what she was. So that we treated her that way: like a fragile, precious, enchanting ornament at the unattainable top of the tree of illusion. Until one of these crude animals came along to grab her with his furry paws, drink his fill, slake his lust, then squeeze her and toss her aside. But she liked that. Beer-cans are made to be crushed. Laughing beer-cans and tattooed teddy-bears.

Yes, I was drunk enough, I suppose, with my stupid similes and maudlin metaphors and the whole sickening mixture of cheap cynicism, sentimental self-pity, and raw rum.

Drunk enough so that when the teddy-bear returned to the bar and ordered another round, I pretended complete indifference. Even after he tapped me on the shoulder, I took my own ill-natured time before turning around.

"Care for a drink?" he asked.

I shrugged. "No, thank you."

"Come on, have a beer! Thought maybe you'd like to join us—we're strangers here, and we'd like to get acquainted."

That intrigued me. I knew the teddy-bear type, or thought I did. And while they're often full of false geniality at the bar, they *never* invite you to join them when they have a Christmas-tree angel in tow. Unless, of course, there's some ulterior motive involved.

Well, I had ulterior motives, too. American beer was a dollar a can—and I hadn't been able to lay a dollar bill down on the bar for a single drink in over eight months now.

I nodded. He held out a golden paw.

"My name's Don Hanson."

"Howard Lane."

"Pleased to meet you. Come on over, I'd like you to meet Dena, here. Dena, this is Howard Lane." He turned to me. "Dena Drake, my secretary."

I stared at her.

"It's really *Dinah,*" she told me. "Like in the song. But Danny Kaye made a recording once, years ago, before I was born, and be pronounced it *Dena,* and that's what my older sister called me. So I guess I'm stuck with it. Everybody does a double take when they hear it."

I nodded, but not in agreement. It wasn't her name that caused me to stare. It was Don Hanson's description of her as his secretary. Their relationship was so obvious I couldn't imagine anyone except a child coming up with such an uninspired lie. Besides, it wasn't necessary here. Santa Rita isn't Santa Monica—only a newcomer would feel it necessary to apologize for the obvious. Still, this Don Hanson *was* a newcomer. In fact, that's what he was talking about now.

"Just got in before sundown," he was saying. "Little surprised to see how small this place is—not even a hotel, is there? Doesn't matter, really, because I can sleep right on the boat."

"You came in your own boat?"

"It's a yacht," Dena said. "We sailed all the way from Barbados."

Don chuckled. "Pay no attention to her. It isn't much of a yacht, and besides, the crew did all the sailing. We couldn't be bothered, could we, honey?"

I would have liked it if Dena had blushed. But she didn't blush; she squealed as Don did the crushing act with the beer-cans again.

Then he turned to me and grinned. "Lucky I ran into you this way," he said. "I was intending to look you up very soon."

"That's right," Dena chimed in. "We don't speak Spanish, either of us, but Robert—that's the first mate of our crew—he does, and he talked to somebody here in town after we landed. That's how we found out you're the only white man on the whole island."

"Is that true?" Don asked. "Are you living down here all alone with these blacks?"

"No," I said.

"But they told Roberto—"

"No," I repeated. "It is not true. There are very few pure-blooded blacks on Santa Rita. The bulk of the population is of mixed blood, *Mestizo* and *marino* and even more complicated combinations of African, Carib, Spanish, Portuguese, and French racial stocks. These people are for the most part simple and uneducated, but they have pride."

"Sure, I understand. I thank you for the tip. But you are the only white man."

"According to your interpretation of anthropology, yes."

"Dig him." Dena giggled. She gave me a melting sideways glance from beneath the long eyelashes—the kind of a glance such girls practice while sitting before a mirror and curling those eyelashes. "You'll pardon my curiosity, but just what are you doing way off here in this god-forsaken place?"

"I am drinking your employer's beer," I said, in a flat voice. "And for the past year I have been drinking rum. And this is not a god-forsaken place. It is an exotic tropical paradise, complete with cockroaches, beetles, bedbugs, mosquitoes, flies, and black widow spiders. Only one form of vermin is unknown here—the tax-collector. His absence more than makes up for the presence of the other insect pests, and also explains my own."

"You a tax-dodger, is that it?" Dena's voice held genuine interest. "A gambler on the lam, maybe?"

I shrugged. "I'm afraid it's not quite that romantic. I happen to be a free-lance writer with an unpredictable income. Having no family ties, I decided to look around for a place where the cost of living is low. Here in Santa Rita I have rented a roomy old furnished house built in the days of Spanish occupation, acquired a devoted couple as servants, and supplied myself with ample food—for less than I'd spend in such mainland paradises as Downhill, Oklahoma or Flyspeck, Utah."

"But don't you ever get lonely?"

"I was lonely long before I came to Santa Rita," I told her. "You can be lonely in New York."

"Brother, don't I know it!" Her smile seemed a little more genuine, but I didn't have an opportunity to analyze it.

Don put his hand on my arm. "Free-lance writer, eh? How's it going?"

"So-so. Some months good, some months not so good. It varies."

"Well. Maybe you'd like to earn a few bucks. I could use a little help."

"What doing?"

"Oh, sort of straightening things out with the local natives. You know these people, maybe you could smooth the way for me. I'd like to get a couple of permits, for one thing."

"Fishing? You don't need anything for that."

"Not fishing, exactly. Diving."

"He's a marvelous skin diver," Dena said. "Absolutely fabulous."

I nodded. "That won't require any official permission, either."

"Even if it's a salvage job?"

"Salvage?"

"Treasure," Dena said. "Why don't you level with him, darling?"

"Why don't you shut up?" Don scowled. He turned it into a grin for me. "All right, you might as well know. I've got a lead on something pretty big down here."

"Wait a minute," I said. "Did somebody sell you a map?"

"No, it isn't a map. It's a manuscript. An old manuscript."

I nodded. "And it describes how one of the galleons laden with bullion from the Inca mines was wrecked and sunk right here off the shoals of Santa Rita, in clear water. Is that it?" I gave him back his grin, with interest. "Why, that's one of the stalest yarns in the Indies! Somebody's always waiting to make a sucker out of the tourists with that gag. As far as I know, nobody has salvaged a Spanish treasure ship anywhere in Caribbean waters for years."

Don shook his head. "Perhaps we'd better get a few things straight," he said. "First of all, I know about the treasure ship dodge. I've knocked around these parts for a couple of years, mostly diving, and doing some fishing for kicks. A man can really live down here."

"The Hemingway bit," I said.

"Did you know Papa?"

"I spit in his milk. I'm a Beatrix Potter fan, myself."

"You don't say," Don muttered. "Well, anyway, I'm not a sucker fresh out of Miami. And I've gotten together a pretty good crew of boys. Five of them, including this mate of mine, Roberto. It was his father who had the manuscript."

"Don went after him when the sharks got him," Dena said. "He told me about it. He pulled him out, but his legs were gone and—"

"Knock it off. Maybe I should have left you on the boat. Or back in Barbados." He gave us each our portion of the frown-and-grin routine again, then continued. "Well, the father died, and Roberto came to me with this manuscript. He'd found it in with the old man's effects. Didn't know what it was—neither he nor the father could read English."

"You keep talking about a manuscript," I said. "Just what is it, really?"

"Actually, it's a sort of a journal."

"Written by an old Spanish prisoner on old Spanish parchment, and watermarked 1924, in Yonkers?"

"Nothing like that. And it isn't your treasure ship yarn, either." He leaned across the table. "Look here. I'm no brain, but I wouldn't sail a crew of five all the way down here to this crummy little island unless I was pretty sure there was something in it for me. So you needn't do the needling bit. You want to take a look at it for yourself, come aboard tomorrow morning. Then you can decide if you want in or not."

I hesitated, thinking of the teddy-bear and the Christmas-tree angel, and how I'd come all this way just to avoid playing with toys again. I had resolved that.

On the other hand, I could use some extra money—for eating, and for drinking, too. Drinking helped me to forget about teddy-bears and angels.

So I stood up and I bowed politely and I said, "Yes, it's a date," to the teddy-bear. And all the while I couldn't take my eyes off the angel....

At ten o'clock the next morning I sat on the forward deck of the *Rover,* reading *Isaih Horner, Hys Journal: Thyse Beeing a True Acct. Of The Voyage of The Black Star; 1711 Anno Domini.*

Don had told the truth. It wasn't a Spanish manuscript at all; it was written in the quaint and barbarous English of a semiliterate seaman in the first years of the eighteenth century. The crabbed handwriting was atrocious, the spelling and grammar worse, and no forger would have been inspired to disguise his bait with a long, rambling preliminary account of a sea voyage.

I'll make no attempt to reproduce the contents of the journal, but it was obviously genuine. Isaih Horner had been second mate of the *Black Star* during what he smugly described as a "trading voyage" to the Isthmus and the northern coast of Venezuela—but it took no great perception to realize that the principal business of the vessel was armed piracy. Indeed, Captain Barnaby Jakes, his commander, bears a name well known to anyone who has ever followed the history of the Brotherhood of the Coast; and there were a number of references to meetings with other gentlemen familiar to students of buccaneer lore. Moreover, the *Black Star* did no "trading"; instead, it "confiscated" the property of several Spanish and Portuguese ships which it intercepted *en route* from the Isthmus.

But the big prize was the *Santa Maria*—not Columbus' vessel, but a namesake, built well over a hundred years later in Spanish shipyards to convey the wealth of the New World to the coffers of His Most Christian Majesty.

The captain had learned that the *Santa Maria* was departing for Spain on its annual voyage, laden with a most unusual cargo of booty—the fruit of no less than three forays during which the *conquistadores had penetrated far more deeply than ever before into the jungles south of Venezuela, in what is now known as the Amazon backwaters. A civilization had been ravished; not the Inca, but a valley people, worshipping a deity of their own and offering it sacrifice on an altar of beaten gold. The altar and the trappings of the temples constituted the sole "treasure"—but from rumored accounts, this was enough. There was, for example, a huge golden "chest" or "ark" which had been transported on the long march to the coast by no less than forty captured native slaves. Just why the gold had not been melted down into portable ingots on the spot was not made clear, except that the accounts mentioned a certain padre* accompanying the expedition who insisted that the artifacts of pagan religion be kept intact. Indeed, there was some confusion as to whether or not he approved of removing the temple's contents at all; apparently there had been actual conflict with the commander of the expedition, and a number of men had died during the return journey to Spain.

But that was not important. What mattered was that the booty had been placed aboard the *Santa Maria,* in the deep hold designed for the conveyance of such cargoes, and the ship was sailing for Spanish waters, accompanied by a convoy of two lighter escort vessels, fully armed for protection against piratical marauders.

All this had Isaih Horner's commander learned; and so, apparently, had a number of other free-booters whose spies were active in the ports.

Normally, Captain Barnaby Jakes would not have acted upon this knowledge. The *Black Star,* with its twelve small guns and its mongrel crew of forty, preyed on smaller game; there were few members of the Brotherhood, even those equipped with a fleet of larger vessels, who ever dared attack a full-sized galleon, let alone one accompanied by an armed and alert escort. For pirates, despite the romantic lore and legend accumulating about their exploits through the centuries, were not lions in courage. They could more aptly be compared to jackals, or at best, hyenas. They sought out the defenseless, the crippled ships, the wrecks, and by the eighteenth century the days of the great early commanders—Henry Morgan, L'Olonnais and their like—were past. The true "buccaneers" of the Indies had vanished; those who remained would seldom board an armed brigantine, let alone sack a city.

So Captain Barnaby Jakes had no intention of attempting to intercept the *Santa Maria* and her sister ships. Not until he heard of the storm.

A small sloop drifted up out of southern waters, and he rescued— and later slew—its two surviving crew-members. But not before he had their eyewitness accounts of the great tempest in which they saw the *Santa Maria* riding the waves alone, after one of her escort ships foundered and the other was sent careening off its course.

The *Santa Maria,* crippled and alone, would have to put in at the nearest port now. And that would be the island of Santa Rita. If she could be caught in open waters—

The *Black Star* bore south for Santa Rita.

Isaih Horner, writing in his *Journal,* spoke piously enough of "the duties of a subject of Hys Majestie" to harass the Papish Enemy and take legitimate spoils. But it was an expedition of piracy, impure and simple, and it might have succeeded, for they bore down on the *Santa Maria* just outside Santa Rita harbor.

The only trouble was, another "subject of Hys Majestie" had found her first.

Closing in on her, cutting across her bows as she wallowed towards the safety of the shore, was a vessel which both Captain Jakes and mate Isaih Horner recognized immediately as the pride of one Ned Thatch, *alias* Edward Teach, *alias* Blackbeard. Because of a strict *punctilio* observed among the Brotherhood—and because Blackbeard's ship was easily twice the size and carried three times the guns of the little *Black Star*—there was nothing to do but stand by and watch the battle.

The *Santa Maria* had lost a mast in the storm, and its rudder did not function properly. Apparently most of its guns were out of commission, too, for while it fired defensive salvos as it lumbered along, there was not enough threat in its volleys to prevent Blackbeard from heading her off from the harbor entrance. The big galleon was forced to hug the shore and make for another opening along the coast of the island. Blackbeard followed, closing in without firing. That was ever his way—to hold his fire until almost alongside, and then let a direct volley rake the hull and then the decks.

Not until the *Santa Maria* had almost gained the shelter of the cove at the far side of the island did this opportunity occur. Blackbeard closed in quickly, then stood about for a direct broadside. It came, with a roar. The great galleon rocked and shuddered. The gunners reloaded for a second salvo, even more shattering than the first. The *Santa Maria,* riding low in the water, attempted to turn. A foremast toppled in a shroud of smoke. Now was the time to close in for the kill—grappling irons were ready, the boarding-pikes mustered. If enough shots had penetrated the vitals of the ship, it would sink within five or six hours; but a boarding-party could secure surrender and transfer the treasure long before then. Blackbeard, presumably, was ready to lead the attack; as was his usual custom, he'd be lighting the candles he'd twisted into his beard, and carrying the pots of brimstone he hurled before boarding the enemy's deck. One more broadside, now—

It came. And the *Santa Maria* rolled with the blast, then careened tipsily to one side.

According to eyewitness Isaih Horner, watching from the deck of the *Black Star* at a distance of less than a mile away, the shots were directed at the top-deck of the galleon. But it was as though the entire discharge of thirty ship's cannons had simultaneously penetrated the vessel below the waterline, as if something had ripped the keel out of the Spanish ship.

For with a roaring and a roiling, with a great tidal tremor, the *Santa Maria* sank like a plummet before his very eyes. The water shot up from the opened hatchways "lyke a verritable fountin," and Blackbeard, instead of boarding, hastily sheered off to avoid being caught in the almost instantaneous vortex of a whirlpool set up by the downward plunge of the great galleon. Within the space of two minutes the *Santa Maria* was gone. It had sunk into the waters of Cut-Throat Cove.

The journal did not end here. It told of how Blackbeard and Captain Barnaby Jakes made common ground in a salvage attempt, but were unable to send men down into the deep water to reach the vessel. There were several survivors whose accounts were reported and paraphrased—none of them could explain why the ship had so suddenly and inexplicably perished, except in terms of sailors' superstitions. It had been a "black voyage" and there was a "curse" upon the ship; they should not have carried the treasures of a "heathen temple." Isaih Horner had small patience with these notions—neither did Blackbeard or Captain Jakes. Being somewhat short of rations, and even more short of temper after the loss of such a prize, they merely slit the throats of the Spanish seamen and sent them down to follow their fellows.

It was impossible to land at Santa Rita—the Spanish garrison would undoubtedly be sending out vessels of its own against the intruders— so Blackbeard and the *Black Star* went their separate ways.

Isaih Horner's journal ended abruptly, a few pages later. He'd put in at Kingston, Jamaica, and was thinking of giving up "the life of a mariner."

"And that's just what he did," Don told me, as I laid the manuscript down on top of the oiled pouch in which it had been preserved. "I guess he turned to robbery on land. Anyway, when I tried to trace down what had become of him, I found out that an Isaih Horner was hanged for purse-snatching in the Government Docks in 1712."

"Then you checked on all this?" I asked.

"Of course I did. I told you I hadn't come down here on a wild goose chase. Found out everything I could. About the *Santa Maria,* the storm, the sinking. It's in the records."

"What about the treasure?"

"There isn't much. But it stands to reason that it existed. They never sent a galleon back to Spain with an escort unless it was loaded. Besides, this story of Horner's impressed me a lot more because it spoke about an altar and temple trappings instead of the usual guff—you know, gold bullion, chests of jewels, stuff like that. There wasn't any such thing, anyway, except during the early days when the Spaniards went after the Aztecs and the Inca tribes."

"But if it's in the records, then why didn't others try salvaging the ship?"

"They did. Trouble is, it's in fairly deep water—I'd say somewhere between two hundred and three hundred feet. And up until a dozen years ago, it was impossible to dive that far safely, or to do any work at such a depth. Now we have the technique and the equipment. And we have the details we need. Five hundred yards offshore, just east of the Cove entrance."

"How would you lift up an altar, or a heavy chest?"

"We'd have to go back for a big rig. What I want to do now is locate the wreck. That's a job in itself—you have any idea what happens to a boat that has been under water for almost two hundred and fifty years? Just finding its topmasts above the silt is hard enough to do." Don shrugged. "But that's no concern of yours. What I want is a little help from you in handling the local authorities. Explain what we're here for, that we're a research expedition, interested in salvaging historical relics. You don't need to mention the gold."

"I see."

Don eyed me. "Well, why should you? It isn't *their* property, is it? The laws of salvage—"

"According to the laws of salvage, you'd need a government permit to start work; not from here but from the mainland."

"All right, so I didn't make arrangements. Why can't you go to the mayor or whatever the head man calls himself and just get his okay? You can handle him. And I'm willing to spend a few bucks."

"How much?"

"How much do you think it will take?"

"Well, a hundred dollars is a fortune down here."

"That's pretty reasonable." He nodded. "I'll go another couple of hundred for you, if you can sew it up. What we want is permission to

dive over at the Cove, without any interference from the natives.
Nobody should be allowed to hang around. Get it?"

"Got it!"

"How long do you think it'll take to line up the deal?"

"I can probably see Jose Robales this morning. He's the mayor of
Santa Rita; the inland villages have *jefes* of their own, but they don't
count. I should have word for you before the day is over."

"Make it in writing."

"Will do." I held out my hand. "He'll expect payment in advance."

"Right." Don reached into his jacket, pulled out his wallet. He
extracted three one-hundred-dollar bills quite casually.

I was equally casual, an hour later, when I flipped one of the bills to
Jose Robales in his little office near the waterfront. He signed the
permit with a flourish.

"Remember," he told me, "I take your word for it that these people
will not create problems here. You are to observe them as my repre-
sentative and see that the crew keeps away from the village at the
Cove."

"I understand. I'll keep an eye on them, I promise."

"That is good. Then there will be no trouble, no?"

"There will be no trouble, no," I echoed.

But I was wrong....

The trouble came almost ten days later, when Don finally located
the ship.

He'd moved to the area outside the Cove immediately, of course,
and anchored in fifty fathoms, five hundred yards out. Roberto and
Juan Perez—another crew-member—assisted him in the actual diving
operations, while the other three attended to arrangements topside.
They put down a heavy shot-line, with handholds, and it hit bottom
at two hundred and sixty feet. Nobody got down that far until the
third day; it takes time to get accustomed to such depths. And even
when they managed to reach the ocean floor, that didn't locate the
vessel for them. As Don explained, the ship itself would be covered
with silt and almost undetectable. The shifting of the sands, the
alteration of the shoreline itself through the long years; these factors
added to the problem. It would take time and patience.

I came out every day; I beached a rowboat on the shore of the Cove
and it wasn't a long pull. I sat there and watched the operations. After
they hit bottom, Don did most of the diving himself. Every second
dive, he'd haul anchor and try a new location. By the time a week had

passed they'd explored an area several hundred yards in circumference without finding a thing. But Don wasn't discouraged yet—just tired.

Dena was bored.

I'd sit with her on the deck of the yacht while Don was diving, and listen to her complain. She didn't care if Roberto and the others overheard her; actually, they were much too busy up forward to pay any attention to us.

"Pleasure trip!" she murmured. "He hauls me way off here to the middle of nowhere, and for what? To sit on my fanny out in the hot sun all day long while he's down there playing footsie with the fishes. Then at night he's tired, wants to turn in right away—not that there's anything else to do for excitement over on that crummy island of yours. A big nothing, that's all it is."

"Then why did you come along in the first place?"

Dena shrugged.

"Did he promise you a share of the treasure?"

"In a way." She scowled at me. "Not that it's any of your business."

"You in love with him?"

"That isn't any of your business, either."

"All right. I'm sorry."

"You don't have to be. I can take care of myself."

"So I notice."

"You notice a lot, don't you?"

"It's my business. I'm a writer, remember?"

"I'll bet you are." She lit a cigarette. "What would a writer want in a nowhere like this place?"

"Now *you're* getting personal," I told her. "But I *am* a writer. I've got books and stuff up at the house to prove it. Want to see them?"

"I've seen books already, thanks. Also etchings."

"That isn't what I had in mind."

"Don't kid me. I haven't met a man since I was fifteen who had anything else in mind. They always want to show me something. When I came aboard Don's boat back in Barbados, he was going to show me the portable bar."

"Then why did you accept his invitation, if you knew the way it would turn out?"

"Maybe I wanted it to turn out that way."

"Then you *are* in love with him."

"Shut up!" She turned away, tossing her cigarette over the side. It arced down and hissed into the waves. "All right, what's the sense of putting on an act? When I was eighteen I was singing with a band. I had a contract with G.A.C. and a chance to do a TV show, just a summer replacement deal on sustaining, but they told me it could build into something big if I got a few breaks. That was seven years ago, and I'm still waiting for the breaks. I haven't been with G.A.C. for a long time, and I haven't done any television, either. Six months ago I got a chance to play a night-spot in San Juan. It wasn't a very good one, but the one in Port-au-Prince was worse, and the one in Trinidad was just plain lousy. I ended up in Barbados without a job, and without a dime. Then Don Hanson came along with his boat. I didn't care what kind of a guy he was or what kind of a boat he had. I wanted out. So, as the sun sinks into the west, we say farewell to beautiful Barbados. End of story."

"You don't really like him, do you?"

"I hate his guts. He's the kind of a guy who's always had plenty of money and is still greedy for more. He's the kind of a guy who always had plenty of muscles, but still has to use them to show off—and to push other people around. As far as he's concerned, I'm not even a person; just another convenience he wanted to take along on the trip, like his portable bar."

"Then why don't you—"

"What? Ditch him and come with you to your island paradise? Don't give me that, chum. You've got nothing to offer. But nothing." The blue eyes were level. "I didn't ask you for your sad story, but I'll bet I already know it. There was a girl in it, wasn't there? And another guy, who took her away, while you sat mooning around. I've met your kind before—the sensitive intellectual type, isn't it? Which is just another way of saying you don't have any guts. I told you I hated Don's guts, but at least he *has* some. Enough to go out after what he wants. He'd never ask me to pull a sneak on another man; he'd fight him for me. Would you fight Don? Not in a million years!"

I sighed. "You're right," I said. "And very honest."

"I shouldn't have said that," she told me. "If I was really honest, I'd admit I'm not worth fighting for. Not any more."

"Suppose I think differently. Suppose I'm willing to fight?"

"You couldn't win." She sighed again, and lighted another cigarette. "Guys like you can never win. This is a money-and-muscle world. Them as has, gits. Even if the prize is only a beat-up blonde with a bad case of the whim-whams. Oh, let's forget it, shall we?"

I was going to tell her that I wouldn't forget it, that I preferred an angel who admitted truthfully to a little tarnish, and that maybe both of us were a bit too cynical and defeatist for our own good.

But I never got the opportunity.

Because suddenly there was a commotion up forward, and a babble of excited Spanish. Don was coming up—he was clinging to the shot-line twenty feet down, spending five minutes in stage decompression before being hauled aboard. His body was perfectly visible in the clear water; the weird fins, the goggles, the cylinder-assembly and regulator on his back all part of an eerie ensemble.

We waited patiently until he tugged three times, giving the signal for hauling up the line. Roberto and Juan hoisted him to the deck. He stood there, shivering slightly, while they unstrapped his equipment. Then he took off his goggles and grinned.

"I've found it," he said.

"No—are you sure?"

"Positive." He nodded, reaching for a towel. "And it's better than we could have hoped for. Went down on its side, right into a big rock crevice that protected the top deck from silting. Part of the deck itself is still clear, and I could see what's left of the masts and forward cabin. We ought to be able to clear a path inside almost immediately—just chop a hole in the hull." He turned to Roberto. "But don't take my word for it! Here, I want you to go down and take a look for yourself, right now. And then Juan. The sooner all three of us have had a look at her and compared notes the better. Got your stuff?"

Roberto nodded, then hurried below. By the time Don had towelled himself back to warmth, taken a shot of brandy and accepted a cigarette, Roberto was already lowering himself over the side.

We watched him disappear along the shot-line, going down into the water.

Dena was excited. "What's it look like?" she asked. "Can you really see anything down there?"

Don lifted his head impatiently. "Of course you can," he told her. "It gets quite dark about halfway, but once you actually hit the bottom there's a lot of reflected sunlight; it seems to penetrate the dark, transparent area above. The light is bluish, but you can make out objects quite easily. I recognized the boat at once, even though it doesn't look much like a galleon any more."

"Everything's covered with slime, eh?" I asked.

"Slime? Whatever gave you that idea?" Don stared at me. "Trouble with you writers—you get everything out of books. Make a few dives yourself and you'd find out differently. There's no slime. The wood is just about eaten away and the metal structure is just a skeleton. Lots of little marine animals covering it. And fish everywhere—millions of 'em. You know, I may even have guessed wrong about the hull; maybe there's only the iron hasps and what I thought was wood was just a solid mass of fish. They like to swarm where there's some protection. Roberto should be able to tell us more when he comes back."

"It takes a long time to make a dive, doesn't it?"

"Going down is easy, if you're carrying a shot like he is. But coming back is slow work. You have to make at least three stops for decompression, to avoid the bends." There was a water-proof watch strapped to Don's wrist. He parted the golden fuzz and glanced at it. "I'd say he's due up again in about fifteen minutes. Should just be at the first stage of decompression now, about fifty feet under." He went over to the rail where the rest of the crew was gathered. "See anything yet?" he asked.

"No," Juan told him.

"Well, he ought to give the first signal soon."

We watched the rope, but it remained taut.

"Fifteen minutes," Don muttered to himself.

But it wasn't fifteen minutes. It was less than one minute later that Juan shouted, "Here he come!" and he wasn't pointing along the shot-line either, but far offside, beyond the rail.

"You're crazy!" Don grunted. "That's some damn fish, surfacing."

"No—is Roberto!" Juan said.

I stared. What broke water certainly wasn't a fish, for fish lack arms and legs, and they do not wear apparatus on their backs.

"*Madre de Dios!*" Juan cried. "Is Roberto!"

It was Roberto, all right, but I'd never have recognized him floating there in the water, his body swollen and distorted grotesquely by the change in pressure. Nor was that the worst of it.

Roberto's body had come up from the wreck below. But it no longer had a head....

"Of course it wasn't a shark," Don said. "No shark could bite like that. Besides, the way it was sheared off—"

He kept his voice low, even though Dena had gone below to her bunk.

"How about a squid?" I asked "I've read about the way the big ones hole up in wrecks down there."

"You've *read!*" He gave me a pitying look. "Maybe you'd better read a little more. A squid isn't the answer, either. There isn't any kind of marine creature that could take a man's head off clean at the shoulders. And that includes whales, in case you also happen to have read *Moby Dick.*" Don glanced at the body lying on the deck, covered with a tarpaulin. "No, the answer's not a fish or an animal, either. Roberto must have left the line and gone off to explore the wreck. And my guess about the fish is probably right. There is no solid hull left, only a framework. When Roberto reached the wreck, the fish swam off. My guess is that he tried to enter what's left of the ship, swimming between the ribs. And then—"

He drew a finger across his throat. It wasn't a pleasant gesture, but it was extremely graphic.

"But how could that do it?" I persisted. "I don't pretend to know the way those old boats were put together, but if they used iron, surely it was in big pieces. There wouldn't be any razor edges to worry about."

Don shrugged. "Do you know what happens to metal after it's been under water for a few hundred years? It wears down, eventually just crumbles away. Gold wouldn't, but old iron—"

"Then how could it be so sharp, and how would it hold up to slice a man's head from his shoulders just because he swam against it?"

"I don't know. But we'll find out tomorrow. Juan and I will go down."

He was only partially correct.

They buried Roberto at sunset, and I didn't stick around after the simple ceremony. That's just as well, because I heard about it the next morning.

If the sharks hadn't taken Roberto's head, they got their consolation prize. Even though the body had been carefully wrapped and weighted down with shot, they must have found him, because they had been swimming around the yacht all night, their long cold bodies gleaming as they surfaced and snapped their teeth in the moonlight. It hadn't been a pleasant evening.

I could tell that when I looked at Dena's face the next day, and the crew's reaction was even more apparent.

As for Don, he was agitated only by anger.

"They're grumbling," he murmured, as he led me down into the cabin, out of earshot of those on deck. "Want me to turn back, chuck the whole thing. I don't know who started it, but then these niggers are like children. Giving me a lot of crap about curses and hoodoos." He sighed. "But that's not the worst of it. Juan won't dive any more. He absolutely refuses to go down."

"So what are you going to do?"

"Do? I can turn back, the way they want me to, and come here again with a fresh crew. But that's a waste of time and money. Dammit, I found the wreck! A few more trips down and I'll have all the data I need on what it'll take to bring up the treasure."

"If it's really there."

"That's just the point—I intend to find out. This is no time to stop."

"You can still dive yourself."

"Yes, but it isn't a good idea to do it alone, at that depth, unless there's someone else standing by in case of emergencies. Not that there'll be any; now that I know what to expect, I won't get caught the way Roberto was. Still, I need some one to rely on."

"Have you tried offering Juan more money?"

"Certainly! I told him I'd pay him Roberto's wages in addition to his own. But he's scared spitless."

Dena clambered down the ladder. "So what's the story?" she asked, listlessly. "We leaving Nature's wonderland?"

"Looks as though we'll have to," Don told her. "Unless—" He paused, eyeing me. "Unless you could help out."

"Me?"

"Why not? You could learn to dive. I could teach you in three days. Nothing to it, with a regulator, and we've got all of Roberto's equipment. I'd make it worth your while—"

"No thanks," I said. "Don't mention money. I've got a poor head for figures, but at least it's still on my shoulders. Which is more than you can say for Roberto's."

"I'd cut you in on the salvage," Don said. "We'd split the gold. Think of it, a solid gold altar, and a golden chest so big it took half a dozen men to carry it."

Dena smiled. "Never mind the sales talk," she said. "Can't you see he just isn't the outdoor type?"

I don't know if it was *that* that did it, or the realization that unless I agreed she'd be sailing away. But all at once I heard myself saying, "Why not? At least I can give it a try."

That shut her up in a hurry, and it made Don start talking. Within a matter of minutes it was all arranged. He'd abandon his project for the next few days and devote all his time to instructing me. We'd start inland, near the beach at the Cove, and then I'd get into deeper water. First with the shot-line and then alone, gradually learning how to handle myself in the depths.

And that's just the way it worked out.

There's no need to give a detailed account of what it's like to learn skin diving. The sea holds a lot of surprises, but your own body holds

still more. I'd never have believed I could undergo the amount of
pressure I experienced in the increasing scope of my descents, or endure
the cold. I learned how to accomplish the necessary decompression,
how to walk and swim and handle my limbs under weird gravitational
alterations. And I learned, still more importantly, that I was not afraid.
For the first time I really understood the fascination of skin diving as
a hobby, or as the avocation or vocation of men like Clarke and
Cousteau.

Don was a good, if impatient instructor. And more than his grudg-
ing praise, I relished the reluctant admiration of Dena. Thus
stimulated, I underwent a rapid apprenticeship.

By the morning of the fifth day, I was ready to stand by and handle
the line while Don dived. The crew seemed to have settled down into
a state of morose resignation once more, and there were no difficulties.

I watched Don adjust his helmet and fins and clamber over the side.
Dena leaned over the rail at my elbow and we traced the trail of bubbles
rising through the translucent water. Then we waited.

Almost an hour passed before Don reappeared on the line at the
twenty-foot decompression stage. He stayed so long that I went down
myself, gesturing to him in the water. He signalled for me to leave,
with a wave of his hand. I came up again.

"Is he all right?" Dena asked.

"I guess so. But he's certainly in no hurry to come up."

Finally, though, he emerged. The fins, the tanks, the helmet came
off. He took a towel, sank into a deck chair, and his usually ruddy face
was unnaturally pale in the midday sun.

"What's the matter?" I muttered.

"Nothing. Nitrogen narcosis."

I nodded. He'd explained it to me—the nitrogen intoxication which
sometimes affects the central nervous system after one relies on the air
supply from the tanks during long dives to great depths. It brings on
anaesthesia, hallucinations, and all sorts of odd reactions, but disap-
pears when the diver decompresses.

"Took a long time to wear off," Don continued. "Hit me so suddenly
I wasn't really aware of it. At first I thought the men were right about
their squid, or whatever they think is down there in the wreck."

"You reached it?"

"Yes. And there is no hull, as I suspected; just masses of fish
clustering almost solidly around the crevice where the ship settled.
Inside there's bits of wood and metal still leaving a partial skeleton,
but all the heavy stuff—the guns and the spars—is sunken into the

sand. Over at one side there's a big bulge. I'd swear it's the altar and
the chest we're looking for, but I never got to examine them.

"Because that's when I began to feel funny. The water seemed to be
turning black. The first idea I had was about the squid, so I scuttled
out of there. And when I turned around to take a look, the whole area
seemed to be not only black, but boiling. Clouds of bubbles. Fish, of
course, returning to the spot. And they'd churned up the silt. But at
the time I would have sworn there was some big animal coming up
from under the wreckage. Then, when I saw Roberto's head bobbing
around in the center of the black stuff, I realized what was wrong with
me. I was drunk as a coot. So I came back up on the rope. I was so
woozy I almost forgot to let go of the weights."

"Did you find the place where Roberto had his accident?"

"No, I didn't. Maybe you can when you go down."

"You mean—?"

"Why not? No reason why you shouldn't get used to it. I won't
tackle it again today, so it's your turn. Maybe you can get closer than
I did. Just remember to watch out for the nitrogen when it hits you.
Chances are it won't, though."

Dena shook her head. "He shouldn't risk it," she said. "After all, he's
just learning, and it's over two hundred feet. You told me yourself it
calls for an experienced diver—"

"Only one way to get experience, isn't there?" I said. "I'm ready."

And I was, the moment I heard the veiled concern in Dena's voice.

I lowered my mask over the side, dipping it in the water so that no
mist would cloud the inner surface of the goggles. Juan strapped the
cylinder blocks of the regulator to my back and looped the hose over
my head as I fitted the rubber mask until it moulded tightly to my
face. I gripped the mouthpiece between my lips as Juan hung ten
pounds in weights to my belt. I adjusted my fins, picked up a spear,
then went over the side, grasping the rope with my left hand as I
lowered myself into the water.

It was cold. Gradually I felt my body adjusting to the temperature
and the pressure, just as my eyes adjusted to the deeper gloom. Bubbles
burst around me and fish swam past. My lungs ached. I straightened
to a horizontal position so that intake and exhaust were equalized at
the same pressure level and the regulator would function properly. It
was hard not to panic; to remember, in effect, that the demand
regulator was doing my breathing for me, or at least supplying the air
which my constricted lungs needed as I flailed my way down. The
pressure grew stronger, my movements correspondingly slower. Here
in the deeper darkness I began to feel drunk—nitrogen narcosis was

not the cause, merely the gravitational change. My ears and sinuses ached, and I swallowed until the pain eased. A school of small fish glided by. I was tempted to abandon the shot-line and follow them. But no, the line was my guide to the treasure below. I went down, deeper into the darkness.

Not enough nitrogen had entered my blood-stream to produce any side effects. All I had to worry about was the pressure. How far down was I? Close to two hundred feet, probably. It was hard to move, now; hard to hold the spear. I wanted to rest for a while, to float.

The water here was dark. Only the bubbles from the regulator retained any color—they were round and yellowish, like beads of amber strung endlessly upwards from here to the surface. So far to the surface up there. So cold down here.

And getting colder now. Because I was descending again. Deeper and deeper. Darker and darker. Colder and colder. *Down went McGinty*—

Drunk. All right, so I was drunk. But that was good, because I couldn't feel the pain any more. My ears had stopped hurting. The cold didn't bother me, now. And it was easy to continue, to go all the way down. All the way down to where the treasure lay—the golden altar.

And then I saw the rock crevice, saw the great solid swarm of fish packed in a writhing mass and rising up like the dim drowned outline of a ghostly galleon. And I left the line and wriggled forward, moving like a fish myself. A swordfish, with a spear. They fled before me, these little ones. I was Neptune, scattering my subjects. Make way for the king! *King of the Sea.*

Drunken diver, rather. Or was it drunken driver? Could they arrest you for drunken diving? Fine you twenty clams?

I tried to clear my mind. Mustn't go on like that. Had to be careful, avoid running into whatever it was that sheared off poor Roberto's head. Funny way to die. Most men lost their heads over a woman—

And then I *saw* her.

I saw the woman.

She was standing perhaps fifty feet to my left, away from the crevice and the wreck. It was the glint of light that first caught my eye; a reflection brighter than anything else here in the murky dimness. I thought it might be the sunlight glinting from the scales of a large fish, and I turned my head, and I saw her.

Saw the black hair floating free in a mane that masked the face. Saw the sudden movement of her body as she turned and waved the cutlass. The gleaming cutlass, razor-sharp—

Women do not walk the ocean floor brandishing cutlasses. I realized that, but my awareness was only partial. Because another part of me was whispering, *now you know. Now you know what cut off Roberto's head.*

And then *she* saw *me,* and the black mane whipped back, revealing her face. It was a blob of greenish-white gristle with four gaping holes; two black sockets; a jagged nasal septum, and a grinning maw that parted now as a tiny fish wriggled *out.*

And it wasn't the skull that frightened me, it wasn't the sight of a corpse walking here at the bottom of the sea. It was just the hideous, grotesque inconsequence of the little fish swimming out of the dead mouth.

That's what I was afraid of, and that's what I remembered as I pulled in panic for the shot-line. As I struggled to release the weights I dropped my spear and stared. The figure wavered off in the distance, disappearing into the crevice where the ship lay. And now the black bubbles were rising, cascading in clouds from the spot. Through the turbulence I could see the skull face melting and blending, and I saw another face that could have been Roberto's and yet others—brown, bearded, grimacing faces that formed out of bubbling blackness and disappeared in inky incoherence.

Then I was going up the line, not remembering to move slowly, but propelled by the panic, flailing forward in frantic fear.

At the fifty-foot level I forced myself to stop and wait. The water below was clear and no inchoate ichor rose about me. I counted slowly, then climbed again. Twenty feet now—another five minutes and I'd be free. Free and safe. But what if I waited, and something came after me? *What if it was following me, crawling along the line?*

My lungs were bursting. My head was bursting. Not with pressure, but with fright. I couldn't wait any more, I couldn't stand it, I had to get out, I *had* to—

I kicked and released myself, straining upwards, striving for the sun. My head broke water and I could see the light, feel it all about me.

Then it dissolved into darkness and I went down again, down into the black bubbles....

It was Don who hauled me out. I learned it later, when I opened my eyes and found myself lying on the deck.

"Don't try to talk," Dena said.

I nodded. I had neither the strength nor the desire. It was a good twenty minutes and two shots of rum later before I was able to sit in a deck chair and tell my story.

Don shook his head. "Nitrogen narcosis," he said. "You had it worse than I."

"But the corpse with the cutlass—Roberto's head—"

"Hallucinations."

"Yes, but how?" I thought about it for a moment. "Was it the manuscript that set me off? The part about the pirates? Did I subconsciously remember Mary Read and Anne Bonney and the other females who sailed in Blackbeard's day?"

"You must have," Don told me.

"But we both saw Roberto."

"We were both thinking about him, and what happened down there."

"Well, what *did* happen, do you suppose?"

Don sighed. "Perhaps we can find out tomorrow."

"You're not going down again?" Dena asked.

"Of course I am. One more trip and I should be able to locate that altar, and the chest. A few fish churning up the silt aren't going to scare me away." He grinned at me. "Tell you what. If you're so concerned about my welfare, I'll take Howard along tomorrow for a guardian. We'll both go down. Whatd'ya say?"

What could I say, with Dena watching me? I nodded, reluctantly. I didn't really want to go down into that deeper darkness again.

And that night, when the dreams came, I was left with still less desire to return to the wreck.

The dreams came, and I lay tossing in my bed in the old house on the hillside above the winding waterfront of Santa Rita. I knew I was there, in my bed, but at the same time I was once again writhing in deep waters.

In my dreams I swam down to the wreckage, wriggled into the crevice where the black bubbles churned, and scraped at the sand with my spear until the point wedged against a solid object. It was the chest, of course, and I could detect the outline of the heavy lid set solid on the massive golden container. I sought to brush away the encrustation of corrosion and fungoid growth and gaze upon the gold beneath, but as I reached out the lid began to rise. It swung open slowly, and the blackness seeped out; the black bubbles burst like bloating blossoms. And they were not bubbles, but heads, and each head had a face, and each face had a mouth, and each mouth was gaping wide to greet me with a grotesque grimace. Yet these were only smoky bubbles, ghost faces floating there in the water—the broad, flat faces of savages, the bearded faces of *hidalgos* and Spanish mariners, the seamed and pitted countenances of corsairs; yes, and here was Roberto again, and the woman. The dark cloud floated forth, and it was like a great black bush bearing heads for fruit; a strange undersea growth waving there in the dim depths, growing before my eyes. And now the bush put forth fresh branches, and the branches were long and waving; a writhing mass of titanic tentacles. Still the smoke poured out, and billowed forth, and now I perceived that there was a body beneath the nightmare nebulosity of faces and feelers; a black body that was like a squid, a sea-serpent, a reptilian monster spawned in the dawn of pre-history when Nature shaped strange simulacra from primeval slime. And beneath the seething, shifting smokiness of that amorphous and polymorphous presence there were real eyes—real eyes that glowed and glared and glinted at me. But they were *more* than eyes; they were mouths as well. Yes, they were mouths, for I could see the pupils gape and the lids rolled back like lips, and I knew that the eyes would devour me, they would ingest me in their hunger, incorporate my essence into the black being of that incredible body so that I too would take my place as one of the scores of shifting shapes in the smoke which emanated from it.

It was one and it was many, it was a composite creature of an incorruptible corruption; it was insanity incarnate.

I screamed and fled from it, but the faces and the feelers flowed forth to envelop me in ichorous essence, so that I drowned in the bubbling blackness of its being. I was consumed by it.

And then there was no fear, and no revulsion, for in its place came an overwhelming expansion of awareness, so that I became a part of *it* and I knew. My memory was *its* memory, my knowledge was *its* knowledge. And my hunger was *its* hunger—

Memory.

Deep in the jungle they built the temple and reared a golden altar of worship. And behind the golden altar was the great golden ark in which I rested and waited for the sacrifice. Nor did I wait too long, for they came frequently to attend me, bringing me the captives of their warfare, trussed on poles like pigs. And when there were no captives they brought me slaves, and when there were no slaves, they brought me children, and when there were no children they brought me their choicest virgins. All I devoured in the darkness, incorporating far more than flesh—for I took from living things the continuity of their consciousness and added their awareness to mine. So that I grew and grew, eternally enlarging. For I was that which is known in all legends; the creature of darkness which devours the world. And if I were not fed, if my appetite were not appeased, I would flow forth to raven freely as I had—long aeons ago, or was it yesterday, or would it be tomorrow? But if they kept me sated, I was content to dwell in the temple. And when they built the ark I entered it willingly, nor did I try to leave, for it was pleasant to curl and coil and coalesce in the darkness and wait for them to bring me fresh fare. I remembered, now....

Knowledge.

Time is a rushing river that flows endlessly, yet never reaches the sea. And it is pleasant to drift upon the stream, drift drowsily and content. So that when I coiled compactly in the golden chest, I willed myself to satiated sleep. And it was then that they hammered down the lid, so that I could not escape; hammered it fast to hold me captive, and put an end to sacrifice. But I was still aware; I knew when the armored white strangers came and prevailed over my worshippers, and I endured as they sought to pry open the lid of the great chest, and then abandoned their vain efforts to talk of fire and of melting down. Finally there was talk of a golden gift to their ruler and in the end the chest was borne away to the ship, together with the altar of sacrifice. I did not stir or struggle, for I anticipated the nearing moment when the chest *would* be opened again, and I could feast. Feast on flesh, feast on spirit. Yes, I knew, now....

Hunger.

I drowsed in the darkness, and then the thunder came, and the shattering sound awakened me. I felt the shock and the shudder as the sinking ship gave way and I fell into the depths; the lid of the chest burst and I was free. Yet I did not come forth, for there was no reason. Not until the bodies drifted down, sinking slowly. Then I put forth a portion of myself, bubbling out from the lid and groping until I grasped the floating forms and drew them to me. I feasted until replete, then slept once more. There was no need to emerge from the chest until the opportunity came to feed again. Time means nothing, for I endure forever. I have but to wait. I neither dwindle nor grow; nothing grows except the hunger.

But the hunger is there, and lately I have stirred, heeding its pangs. The other day I took a man—it was curious, in that he came to me willingly and saw the chest with its lid ajar. He could not lift it, of course, because of the weight of the water, but he felt along the edges. Then I bubbled forth, grasping him and pulling him down, and he threshed mightily so that the lid fell, decapitating him. The body floated away, but I did not pursue. I do not have to pursue. I am aware of his awareness now, and with it I know that there are others of his kind in a ship, just above me. they will follow him down, for they are seeking the chest and the altar. Yes, they will come to me, and soon I shall feast again.

In the feasting there is great pleasure. To taste the memories, to savor the surge of every emotion, to know the nuances of all desires; there is the richness of rage, the pungency of passion, the fine, full flavor of frantic fear. I eat it all, and I digest it, and I retain it, and that is *my* ruling need. Most of all I want the woman, the golden woman. And I will engulf her with my eyes, and I will take her whiteness into my blackness, and drain her body of all delight—

* * *

"No!" I was screaming now, it was my own voice that was screaming, and it was my own sweat-drenched body that threshed in ultimate fright there upon the bed in the moonlight as I awoke.

It had been a nightmare. I knew that now, and yet I *believed.* No subconscious fantasies can evolve without stimulation, and my stimuli had come from beneath the sea. *I believed.*

But when the harsh sun rose, my certainty wavered. By the time I rowed out to the yacht, I was half ashamed to even speak about the dream. And when I started to tell Dena and Don of what had shattered my sleep, I was more than apologetic.

"Sure you weren't hitting the rum again?" Don asked.

"No, I didn't touch a drop. But even if it was just a nightmare, I'm convinced there's *something* behind it. That business of the lid coming down to decapitate Roberto—"

"You know yourself what it would weigh, and how slowly it would move in water at that depth."

"Yes, but if something were holding him—"

"What could hold him? Your mysterious monster, made out of black bubbles? The one who lives inside the chest?"

"We saw the bubbles, remember?"

"Sure we did. And we saw the fish that made them, churning up the silt down there in the crevice." Don wiped his forehead with a hairy arm. "Personally, I think you cooked up this yarn because you'd like to chicken out of making a dive with me. You were pretty shook up yesterday, weren't you? Sure you were."

"Leave him alone," Dena said. "The poor guy almost drowned. If he doesn't want to go back down, I don't blame him."

"I'll go," I said. "Don't worry about me."

"Then come on," Don snapped, "Juan has our gear laid out. The sooner we get started, the better."

We stripped down to our trunks, and I followed the teddy-bear over to the rail in silence. Juan helped us into our equipment. And then it was time to lower ourselves along the shot-line, lower ourselves into the drowned domain of darkness and seek what waited there....

Don reached the bottom before me. Spear in hand, he jackknifed through the gloom in the direction of the crevice, then waved a flipper to urge me forward.

The fish did not swim here today, and we could see the ribs of the skeleton-ship wavering weirdly in the water. And Don swam between them, then lowered himself to the sand as he groped forward, digging his spear into the bulky buried outline of a shape set against the side of the rocks. Suddenly he flung up a flipper again, gesturing impatiently as I held back. The spear scraped over the encrustations and bubbles rose.

Then I saw the glint and hurried forward. He *had* found something—it was the altar!

There was no way of determining if it had fallen flatly or upended itself in the sand—in either case it was huge; far larger than I'd expected. And its surface, beneath the silt, was hammered, gleaming gold. I peered into Don's face, beneath the goggles, and read the exultation in his eyes.

We'd found what we were looking for.

The cost of rigging up a winch and windlass to raise it from the depths would be tremendous, but the reward was worth the effort. This was a prize surpassing the dreams of any treasure-seeker. And there was still the chest—

Again, it was Don who moved forward, deeper into the debris centered between the ribs of the hulk. He stooped and groped and probed, then rounded a rocky outcropping in the wall of the crevice and literally stumbled across the rectangular lid of the great chest sunken in the sands.

I was beginning to feel faint. Part of it was residual fear, of course, but most of it was sheer excitement at the realization of our discovery.

Whatever the cause, I was conscious of a growing giddiness, and I moved back, not wanting to stray too far away from the shot-line. Don waved at me, but I shook my head and continued to retreat. Only when I saw the line slanting before me did I halt and gaze off into the crevice.

Don had stooped over the imbedded outline of the lid and now he was digging at it with his spear. I remembered his own remarks about the weight of the water and knew his puny efforts would be futile; perhaps he was beginning to suffer from nitrogen narcosis too.

But no, his attempts were *not* useless! Because even as I watched, the lid was rising. Slowly, very slowly, and the sand began to slant and shift beneath the spear. And now I could see an opening inch up, and there was a blackness and a bubbling. It was like the blackness and the bubbling I'd encountered yesterday, during my dive, but there were no fish about to churn the silt. Yet the lid continued to rise, and the darkness flowed forth.

The darkness flowed forth, just as it had in my dream.

And then Don was backing away, and he flailed the spear before him; flailed frantically at the faces that seethed and surged in shapeless shadows. And out of the faces emerged the feelers, coils of twisting tentacles that shrouded him in smoke. I thought of the legends of the huge *djinn* imprisoned by Solomon in tiny bottles, and I thought of how lambent gases are compressed in minute containers, and I thought of protoplasm that proliferates instantaneously in response to the blind, insensate forces which spawned life out of the insane vortex of chaos when the world began. But this was not *djinn* or gas or protoplasm; it was nightmare. Black nightmare, boiling out of a golden chest at the bottom of the sea, black nightmare that emerged now in sudden, shocking solidity; oozing obscenely aloft until it towered titanically amidst its twining tendrils.

And I saw the central coils part to reveal the eyes, the eyes which were like mouths—which *were* mouths, because they were swallowing Don. The coils whipped him aloft, forced him against the openings, and the lid-lips came down. I could see Don's legs threshing in a blur of bubbles; one of his flippers had come off.

I forced myself forward, spear in hand. But the chest was closing; the tentacles were forcing it down from within. The black, threshing mass disappeared, carrying the white mass of Don's body with it, and the lid clanged shut. Behind it floated a mass of bubbles, a tangle of reddish skeins, something small and curiously white. Don's foot, sheared off at the ankle by the closing lid—

I blacked out.

Half an hour later I found myself gasping and retching on the deck in the warm sunlight. I had no memory of how I came to the surface; apparently Juan had seen me ascend and came down to hold me through the decompression stages. He bent over me, and his brown face was almost as pale as Dena's.

I told them about Don.

In Dena's face I could read only doubt and incredulity, plus a strange compassion. But Juan nodded, slowly.

"We must leave this place," he said.

I shook my head. "But you can't leave now—there's the gold, it's really down there, and it's worth a fortune—"

"What is gold to a dead man?" he murmured. "We will go back to Barbados."

"Wait!" I begged. "We've got to think things over. Dena, you understand—"

"Yes." She turned to Juan. "We can't decide anything now. Can't you see he's exhausted? Look, let me take him ashore. Tomorrow we can decide what must be done. There's no sense talking any more. And no reason to get all excited over hallucinations."

"Hallucinations!" I sat up, shaking.

She put her hand on my shoulder. "Never mind. We'll discuss it later, when you're rested. Come on, I'll go in with you. Juan can have one of the men row us ashore."

I was silent. It took all my strength to get over the side and into the rowboat. When we landed about a mile down from the Cove, Dena and the crewman helped me walk up the steep, winding path which led to the old house I occupied on the hill. Looking down, I could see the yacht riding out there on the waters, silhouetted against the sunset.

The crewman went back, but Dena stayed. My serving couple, Felipe and Alicia, prepared a meal for us. Then I sent them away. The food and a few drinks restored me. By the time darkness came I was ready to talk. And Dena was ready to listen.

We sat on the terrace outside the house. The sky was bright, and I had the feeling that, if I wished, I could reach out and grasp the moon and the stars. But I was content merely to sit there and watch the play of moonlight and starlight in Dena's golden hair.

Dena filled our glasses and sank back.

"All right," she said. "What really happened down there?"

I stared out at the water. "But I already told you."

"We're alone now. You aren't talking for Juan's benefit, or the crew's."

"I realize that."

She sipped her drink. "Can't you remember? Was it really all hallucination?"

I leaned forward. "Dena, none of it was hallucination. It happened just the way I told you. We found the treasure. And that creature down there. I dreamed about it, but it's real, it actually exists. Maybe it's not the only one, either—what about all these legends of sea serpents and monsters? What happened to the crew of the *Marie Celeste?* I've read about such things on land, too; jungle villages, whole primitive civilizations which had been apparently destroyed instantaneously without warning. Suppose there *are* life forms we know nothing about, spawned when the earth was young and still surviving—or spawned even *before* the earth evolved? What about the beings that might have come here from the stars, the alien entities that never die? Those legends—"

"Legends!" Dena brushed the hair back from her forehead, frowning. "I'm interested in the truth."

"But I'm trying to explain—"

"You don't have to explain." She stared at me levelly. "I know what happened. You and Don went down to the wreck. You found the altar, perhaps you even found the chest. And they were gold, all right."

"Yes. I wasn't lying. Those objects would be worth a fortune if we raised them."

"Of course. You thought about that, didn't you? And you thought how wonderful it would be to have that fortune, keep it for yourself. So you got hold of Don's spear, and you killed him. And then you came back up with your crazy story about the monster, knowing it would frighten Juan and the others, keep them from going down to look. Now you'll wait until they go, get your own crew, and salvage the treasure. That's the way it was, wasn't it? You killed Don."

"No."

She came closer, her voice low. "I understand. It wasn't just for the sake of the money, was it? You wanted me. You knew you'd have to get Don out of the way, first. And you remembered what I said, about not having the guts. So it's my fault, too. I'm not afraid to face the truth—I'm partly responsible."

"You don't know what you're saying."

"Yes, I do. I'm saying that I'm sorry, but it's happened now and I can live with it. We can both live with it. We will get the treasure together. You and I. And then, if you still want me—"

Then she was in my arms and I looked down at my tarnished angel, at the golden toy, mine now for the taking. And I smiled, and I pushed her away.

"It's too late. I don't want you. Now, or ever."

"I'm not good enough for you any more, is that it?" She stood up quickly. "Now that you know about the gold, you think you can keep it all for yourself and you won't need me because you can buy other women."

"I don't need you. And I don't need other women any more, either."

"Oh, yes you do! You need me all right! Because all I have to do is go to that precious mayor of yours here on the island and tell him who murdered Don."

"Go ahead," I said. "We'll see what happens when he tries to pit himself against a god. For it *is* a god, you know. Stronger and stranger than any entity of Earth."

Dena stepped back, still staring. "You're crazy," she whispered. "That's it. You've gone crazy."

"Because I don't want you as a woman any more? Because I'm through with sentimental day-dreams about teddy-bears and angels? Oh, no, Dena. I'm not crazy. I *was* crazy, perhaps, until I gazed on the ultimate realities. What I saw was not pretty, but its truth transcends terror. I've gazed on something far more powerful than the petty forces that rule our little lives and our little lusts. There is a power stronger than all earthly desire, a hunger greater than all earthly hunger. And when I saw it today, when I recognized it down there, I did the only thing a mortal may do. I bowed down and worshipped, do you hear, Dena? I remember now what happened after Don died. I sank to my knees on the ocean floor and I worshipped!" I rose and faced her. "And then I went over to the chest and I opened the lid. I was not afraid any longer, because I knew *it* was aware of my emotions. I could realize that. And I could release it without harm, because it understood I meant to serve it. Dena, I opened the lid!"

"I don't believe you, I don't believe anything you're saying—"

"*They* believe me." I gazed out at the moonlit waters of the Cove beyond.

She followed my stare. "Don't you see what's happening?" I said, softly. "The yacht is moving. Juan raised the anchor. He believed what I told him. And he and the crew must have made up their minds. They aren't going to wait until tomorrow. They aren't waiting for us at all. They remembered what happened to Roberto and to Don and they want to get away."

Dena gasped. "You're right—the yacht *is* moving! What can we do?"

"We can watch," I told her, calmly. "They want to get away. But they won't. They don't know what you know now—that I opened the lid. And its hunger is growing. Look!"

The moon was very bright over the water. And even at the distance of a mile we could see the bubbles rising, see the waves churning and boiling as something broke the surface just before the vessel. It was like a wave, like a waterspout, like a giant cuttlefish. And the tentacles tossed and twisted and twined about the prow, and the little yacht tilted, and then a black bulk emerged from the waters and swept across the deck. In the distance we could hear faint screams, and then Dena was screaming too as the boat careened over on its side and the huge black blob enveloped its white hull and bore it down, down—

The black bubbles disappeared, and there was only the soft and shimmering surface of the sea, glittering in the cold silver moonlight.

"The *Marie Celeste*," I murmured. "And countless other ships. Countless other mortals in all climes, in all times. When the appetite waxes, it awakens. When it wanes, it subsides. But now the hunger grows again and it will come forth to feed. Not on the bodies alone, but on the *being*. It will glut on soul-substance, feast on the emotions and the psyche. First a ship, then a village, then a town, perhaps an entire island. And what is comparable to that knowledge? Does that slimy gold under the water or the tarnished gold of your body hold any allure for one who realizes his destiny at last? His destiny to serve a god?"

"Get away from me—I'll go to Robales—"

I pinned her arms. "You will not go to Jose Robales. You will come with me. And I will summon it to the sacrifice."

She screamed again, and I hit her with the heel of my hand across the back of the neck. It silenced her, but did not bruise her mouth or face. I knew it would be better if she was not marked. One does not bring spoiled fruit or withered flowers as an offering to the gods.

I carried her down the beach, then, in the moonlight. And I stripped her and staked her out upon the sand there at the water's edge. She was silver and gold in the moonlight, and for a moment I coveted the treasure of her body's richness. But I had spoken truly; this was as nothing to the knowledge of my destiny. I had found myself at last—I was meant to serve. To serve, and to summon.

I sent my thoughts out across the water and deep down. It was not difficult, not since I had opened the chest and let the blackness therein meet and mingle with my being. For already I was a part of it and it was a part of me. And I knew this was what it was searching for—not the crew, but the golden woman.

Now it would come to slake all hunger and all thirst. And my own appetite would be appeased in the sacrificial act.

I did not have long to wait. The bubbles burst near the shore and then it flowed forth. Larger now—for as it feasts, it grows. The black blur became a black cloud, the black cloud became a black blot, the black blot became a black body; a thousand writhing arms to caress her nakedness, a thousand pulsing lips to drink, a thousand hungry mouths to savor and to swallow.

And the blackness flowed over her whiteness and it was like an exploding ecstasy in which I was the ravisher and the ravished, the eater and the eaten, the victor and the victim, the watcher and the watched, and it was better than seeing Don, it was better than seeing the crew, and I knew it would keep getting more wonderful each time, the sensation stronger still as *we* kept feeding and growing, feeding and growing.

Yes, *we*.

Because when it was finished, and the blackness melted back into the rolling waters, leaving the beach bare before the moonlight, I knew that *we* would go on together.

There had been no altar this time, but that did not matter. *We* know nothing, care nothing for altars of gold. The bed is not the bride, the plate is not the meal. Anywhere and anytime, all that is necessary is soul and substance for the sacrifice. So that *we* can swallow and grow, swallow and grow.

I made *our* plans.

Jose Robales had warned me to keep the crew away from the natives in the little village behind the Cove. They were only ignorant savages, after all—probably not much better than the jungle natives who had reared the golden altar to a god. But they lived—and that is enough to *us* who drink life.

So I would summon the god again, tomorrow, the next day, soon. And it would come in its strength and take nourishment. Perhaps the villagers would bow down to it and then raise an altar of their own. Perhaps not. In the end, it couldn't matter. Because in the end *we* would take them all.

And perchance Jose Robales might come to us. If not, in due season *we* would go to him.

Yes, in due season *we* would visit everyone on the island of Santa Rita. And our awareness would grow as we incorporated all the lives and all the learning and all the lusts. And our appetite would increase. And *we* would grow; grow in size, grow in power, grow in strength to satisfy our dark desires.

There need be no end. It is a small distance from island to island. And as *we* grow we can travel faster, seize more swiftly and surely. With us there is no time and no death—nothing to halt or to hinder.

The creature that swallows the world.

Why not?

From island to island, always growing. Then on to the mainland, to the swarming cities. It will feast and I will share, it will search and I will lead, it will rule and I will serve, for ever and ever.

And I have written it down now so that all may know the truth and decide whether to join in worship or serve us in another way—as subjects, sustenance for sacrifice.

The choice is yours, but make it swiftly. For I feel the urging of that black appetite, and soon *we* must go forth to ravage and raven across the world....

(Statement of Jose Robales, mayor.)

In the matter of the man Howard Lane, presently confined to await trial on the charge of murder, these facts are known.

The foregoing account was found, in the prisoner's own hand, upon the desk in the study of his home, by Felipe and Alicia Martino, his servants.

The statement was handed to me when I visited his house early this morning, together with Officer Valdez, seeking to question him concerning the sinking of the yacht *Rover,* which event had been reported to me by certain natives of the village near Cut-Throat Cove.

Howard Lane being asleep, I first examined the above statement and then awakened him, formally charging him with the murder of Roberto Ingali, Donald Hanson, and the woman Dena Drake.

This he of course denied, but in such a manner as to permit only one supposition—that this account he had written truly represents his own belief as to what occurred.

It is evident that the prisoner suffers from a severe mental derangement, and I shall make it a point to see that he undergoes a complete examination before formally bringing him to trial. At the moment one can only conclude that he performed the crimes while in a state of unbalance, and—although it is not easy to determine the method—arranged for the sinking of the yacht.

Unfortunately there are as yet no witnesses who can testify to actually seeing the vessel go down, but the sudden disappearance of a seaworthy boat anchored in calm waters, coupled with the discovery this morning of timbers and bits of wreckage washed ashore in the Cove, permits of no other conclusion. It was undoubtedly Hanson's boat.

The prisoner's statement seems obviously the work of a mind obsessed with guilt, and it is to be hoped that he will recover sufficiently to make a full and sensible confession.

Before wiring to summon a physician, I shall make it my business, as an official and as a former friend of Howard Lane, to visit him in the jail and urge that course upon him.

Indeed, I would have done so today, had it not been that the reports of the wreckage washed ashore occupied my time and attention until late this afternoon.

As it is now well into the evening, I will put off my interview until tomorrow morning.

It is to be admitted that one is shaken by this sad turn of events.

The spectacle of Howard Lane, my former friend and now my prisoner, in the grip of his delusions—shrieking threats and curses like a hysterical woman—disturbs one far more than I can indicate. Even now I hear him moaning in his cell below.

And it is sorrowful indeed to reflect upon the sudden tragedy which has visited our peaceful island.

As I sit here and gaze out across the calm waters of which the prisoner has written so vividly, I cannot reconcile this scene with such a chaos of murder and violence. As for the statement itself, absurd as it may seem to one still in full possession of his reason, there is a certain powerful if irrational logic about it—

Wait. The prisoner below is not moaning. He is shouting again, in measured cadences. It is as though he were *chanting*.

And the waters of the bay—

The moonlight is clear and I can see the black bubbles rising. They are moving closer to the shore, moving swiftly. And now I hear the screaming from the waterfront. They see it, they see it coming out of the water. It is black and immense, and it is slithering forward, it is coming to feast just as he said it would, it is coming to devour the w—

Afterword

IN JULY, 1934, I LUCKED OUT.

That's when I sold my first story to *Weird Tales* magazine. To a 17-year-old youngster, just graduated from high school in the depths of the Great Depression, this seemed like a miracle. And in a way it was, for *The Secret In The Tomb* barely qualified as a story at all. Editor Farnsworth Wright must have had an off-day when he decided to accept the tale.

But it was a great day to me, and thus encouraged I immediately wrote and submitted another story, *The Feast In The Abbey*. It too was accepted, and I lucked out again.

For in accordance with some mysterious editorial decision, it was this second effort which was the first to actually appear in print, on November first, in an issue predated January, 1935.

Feast wasn't exactly a masterpiece either, but it was a good cut above the earlier effort and had a last line which readers seemed to remember.

Which is more than can be said for *Secret*, or many of the stories that I wrote and sold subsequently. *The Suicide In The Study, The Dark Demon, The Grinning Ghoul,* and *The Faceless God* were experiments, poorly conceived and poorly executed by a teen-aged amateur who deserved to be executed himself. My references to the so-called Cthulhu Mythos in these efforts clearly indicated that I was under the influence of my literary mentor, H.P. Lovecraft—though the less charitable might also suspect I wrote them under the influence of some hallucinogenic drug.

Such, however, was not the case. And every once in a while a genuine story notion would come my way.

For example, I conceived the notion of killing off Mr. Lovecraft in a somewhat tongue-in-cheek fashion—with his permission, of course. With characteristic generosity he not only granted me that liberty, but set it down in a document signed in four languages. And thus I wrote *The Shambler From The Stars*, dedicated to HPL—whereupon he returned the courtesy in a sequel, *The Haunter Of The Dark*, with myself as dedicatee and victim.

Other experimental ventures—conscious attempts to move away from Lovecraft's literary turf, if not his influence—were my series of Egyptological or Egyptillogical tales, several of which are included in this collection. And occasionally I came up with an offbeat idea, as in

The Mannikin—though at the time I was blissfully unaware that Henry S. Whitehead had utilized a somewhat similar concept in his story *Cassius.*

Rereading these pieces today—some of which have rightfully (and mercifully) remained out of print for forty-odd years—I find myself reiterating a recurrent regret. *Why couldn't some of those ideas have waited to occur to me later, when I'd have been better prepared to do justice to them?*

Truth to tell, I didn't really begin to write properly for nearly a decade following that first sale. Not that I was necessarily any great shakes at it even then, but at least I'd begun to diversify my style and divest it of some annoying mannerisms.

The Shadow From The Steeple—the sequel which I eventually added to HPL's *Haunter*—is deliberately written in the mood and mode of its predecessors and utilizes the same *milieu.* It is, however, more disciplined and coherent than *Shambler,* if not necessarily as much fun. And while *Notebook Found In A Deserted House* is a throwback to HPL-influenced tales, it bears little stylistic resemblance to those earlier works with their ponderous and pretentious polysyllabification and pseudo-scholarly references.

But these tales, of course, are assembled here together for the first time, because of a common denominator. All of them have some connection with H.P. Lovecraft's Mythos.

They are *not,* I hasten to assure you, stories which were revised or written by HPL. As a matter of record, although it was Lovecraft who suggested I turn my hand to writing weird fiction and offered to read and criticize my early efforts, he actually saw only a half-dozen or so of them all told. And of these, several never actually appeared in print.

Those that I did inflict on him he praised rather than criticized—and his suggestions involved minor changes. Gently he corrected *errata* in spelling or references, but at all times took pains to reassure me that I was a writer rather than an egregious nerd. In a word, he lied like a gentleman.

And it was HPL who, when I came up with another imaginary book of sorcery to take its place alongside his famous *Necronomicon,* conferred upon my *Mysteries Of The Worm* its Latin title—and offered me Latin phrases for use as invocations.

I've been asked if the name I bestowed on the book's author—Ludvig Prinn—was derived from that of Hester Prynne, heroine of *The Scarlet Letter.* If so, the association was an unconscious one, for I had yet to read Hawthorne's novel at the time, and didn't see the silent film version until two years ago. Even if I had been familiar with the character I doubt I'd form any special connection between an adulteress in colonial New England and a European devotee of Black Magic.

Oddly enough, Lovecraft's greatest direct contribution to my work consisted of his suggestions—and some lines of actual rewriting and rephrasing—incorporated into *Satan's Servants*. This is not a Mythos tale and is not included herein: as a matter of record, I put it aside following his inspection and didn't complete the story until many years after Lovecraft's death.

Lovecraft's death.

I hadn't intended to write that phrase, though even today, more than forty years after the event, it carries a tragic connotation. Until I reflect upon the fact that H.P. Lovecraft—like his creation, Cthulhu—never truly died. He and his influence live on, in the work of so many of us who were his friends and acolytes. Today we have reason for rejoicing in the widespread revival of his own *canon*.

And if a volume such as this has any justification for its existence, it's because Lovecraft's readers continue to search out stories which reflect his contribution to the field of fantasy. With that in mind, there's no need for further *apologia*. These tales, poor as some of them may be, nevertheless represent a lifelong *homage* to HPL which recently culminated in the publication of my novel, *Strange Eons*. Taken in that spirit, I hope you'll accept them for what they were and are—a labor of love.

—*Robert Bloch*

Demon-Dreaded Lore

Robert Bloch's Contribution to the Cthulhu Mythos

by LIN CARTER

W HEN ROBERT BLOCH was a boy of fifteen, back in 1933, he began to correspond with H.P. Lovecraft, becoming one of the youngest of the members of "the Lovecraft Circle," that band of aspiring or seasoned writers scattered across the country whose common links were their enthusiasm for macabre fiction in general and *Weird Tales* in particular, and their friendship with Lovecraft. Some, like Clark Ashton Smith, were professionals; others, like very young Bloch, raw amateurs. Over the years, some lasted, becoming popular *Weird Tales* contributors, and others faded into the background.

Bloch, of course, lasted. From his first published short-story ("The Feast in the Abbey," *Weird Tales*, January 1935), he went on to sell a grand total of eighty-five yarns to that magazine and competitors like *Strange Stories*. Some stories were written with one or another collaborator, a few were written under a penname (Tarleton Fiske), but, as his last appearance in *WT* was in the issue dated January 1952, I submit that he had become a seasoned professional. After all, eighty-five stories in only seventeen years—!

With his very second appearance in *Weird* ("The Secret in the Tomb," May 1935), Bloch joined his new friends Clark Ashton Smith and Robert E. Howard in writing stories laid against the connected (but invented) background lore-system of Lovecraft's Cthulhu Mythos. He went on later, of course, to find more modern settings and themes better suited to his individual personality—he went on, in fact, to become a widely successful author of scripts for radio, television and the movies (and it's one of the ironies of his fine career that he was not given the chance to write the screenplay for Alfred Hitchcock's classic film *Psycho*—the most successful black-and-white movie ever made— since he wrote the novel which the scenario was, and *very* closely, based); but it is as a contributor to the Mythos that I must deal with him here.

The Cthulhu Mythos is a heterogeneous collection of short stories, a few novels, poems, sonnet-sequences, and other miscellaneous things, held together by a commonly shared system of information. A mythology, if you will. All right, a *demonology*, then. The authors who contributed to it—the authors who are *still* contributing to it, for the Mythos is by no means dead—play the game more or less according to the rules laid down by Lovecraft, Smith, and Howard, who were the first to get in on the fun. The rules are that each writer should invent a demon-god or two, and a crumbling tome of blasphemous eldritch lore, and, as often as not, a milieu—generally a decaying backwater of old towns slouching into desuetude, with an omnipresent aura of ancient witchcraft and obscure cults in their past ... and generally their present, too.

Lovecraft invented Cthulhu, Yog-Sothoth, Nyarlathotep, Shub-Niggurath, and that shuddersome Bible of the Mythos, the unmentionable *Necronon..con* of Abdul Alhazred. Smith invented Ubbo-Sathla, Tsathoggua, and Abhoth, and the legendary *Book of Eibon.* Howard invented Golgoroth, Koth (sometimes, rather confusingly, described as a city, a mysterious Sign on a tower, and a demon-thing), and the *Unaussprechlichen Kulten* of Von Junzt. Derleth invented, or borrowed from Bierce, rather, Hastur, Cthugha, the *Celaeno Fragments,* and the Comte d'Erlette's *Cultes des Goules,* Lovecraft set most of his tales, but by no means all, in an imaginary region of coastal Massachusetts; Smith laid his in prehistoric Hyperborea or Medieval Averoign. And so on; you get the idea. Come to think of it, you probably already *know* the idea, or you wouldn't have bothered to pick this book off the rack....

With his second story, "The Secret of the Tomb," Bloch made some rather tentative contributions to that libraryful of mouldering volumes of forbidden lore, mentioning the *Cabala of Saboth,* and the *Occultus* of Hieriarchus, and "Prinn." Prinn was the only one he developed to any particular extent, although in subsequent stories he added the *Black Rites* of mad Luveh-Keraph, priest of "cryptic Bast," and a number of books and tales by imaginary authors such as Simon Maglore and Edgar Henquist Gordon.

It was the Flemish wizard, Ludvig Prinn, and his hellish book, *De Vermis Mysteriis,* or *Mysteries of the Worm,* that became and that remains Robert Bloch's major contribution to the lore of the Mythos. In his story "The Shambler from the Stars," which, incidentally, he dedicated to Lovecraft, he builds upon Prinn's life and history and reveals as much as he ever wished to pass on to us of the contents and theme of that ghoulish tome. I refer you to the tale in question: The volume certainly belongs on the same dusty shelf with *Unaussprechlichen Kulten* and the *Livre d'Ivonis.*

I can no longer refrain from informing you of the hideous truth: Robert Bloch has a sense of humor. Humor and horror have never been so inextricably mixed as in the career of Robert Bloch. If H.P.L. hadn't encouraged him to contribute to *Weird Tales,* I have no doubt but that he would have gone on to write material for Fred Allen, Sid Caesar or Bob Hope.

Now, the boys in the Lovecraft Circle did not, repeat: *not,* treat their work with any great solemnity. In fact, they delighted in playing jokes on each other in their stories. The "Comte d'Erlette," who is the author of Derleth's *Cultes des Goules,* is a Lovecraftian pun on Derleth's own surname, for example. (Bloch paid him back, on Derleth's behalf, by making the author of his own *Black Rites* one "Luveh-Keraph," adding with [presumably] a straight face that the mad Egyptian was a "priest of Bast." To catch that one, you have to know that Lovecraft was crazy about cats.) Similarly, Lovecraft inserted into another story a reference to "the Commorion myth-cycle of the Atlantean high priest, Klarkash-Ton;" since *Clark Ashton* Smith wrote tales set in Commoriom, capital of his Hyperborea, the joke is obvious.

Well, in 1935, Bloch wrote to Lovecraft asking him if he minded being used as a character (who would come to a sticky end) in a story he was thinking about, later published as "The Shambler from the Stars." Lovecraft replied with a document of formal permission, countersigned by Abdul Alhazred, author of the *Necronomicon,* Gaspard du Nord, translator of the *Book of Eibon,* the "Tcho-Tcho lama of Leng," etc. Bloch thereupon wrote of a struggling young writer, aspiring to make his mark on weird fiction (obviously, although tongue-in-cheek, an autobiographical reference), who, in his midwestern isolation, enters into correspondence with a "hermit in the western hills" (Smith), a "savant in the northern wilds" (Derleth, or Donald Wandrei), and "a mystic dreamer in New England" (You Know Who). The narrator and said mystic dreamer get embroiled in trying out one of the rituals in the *Mysteries of the Worm,* and it is the dreamer who gets sort of eaten alive by an invisible Thing in midair.

A while later, Lovecraft retaliated with "The Haunter of the Dark," in which a lonely young writer from the Midwest, one "Robert Blake" (not "Bloch": *Blake*), comes to an even stickier end while visiting in Providence, Rhode Island (where Lovecraft lived). (Blake was struck dead with horror with one good look at Nyarlathotep; the coroner ascribed it to being hit by lightning ... but *we* know!) Unable to resist,

Bloch later followed "Haunter of the Dark" with another story in which Nyarlathotep gets his comeuppance, more or less, from one Edmund Fiske, a pal of the late Blake. Need I remind you that Bloch used "Fiske" as a penname on a few stories?

By the time the story appeared, Lovecraft had died at an untimely age, and quite suddenly: that is, none of his correspondents had even known he was seriously ill. As Bloch put it once, in a letter to me: "All the fun went out of the game, after that." And there were no more Cthulhu Mythos stories for a long time from his hand.

Besides inventing a tome of shuddersome lore, the Mythos writers liked making up new devil-gods for the Cthulhoid pantheon. Frank Belknap Long, another member of the Circle, contributed the repulsive, elephant-headed Chaugnar Faugn, and Henry Kuttner added Vorvadoss, and so on.

Bloch never developed any of his gods much, a few references to "dark Han and serpent-bearded Byatis" in stories like "The Shambler from the Stars," and that's about it. (Ramsey Campbell later picked up Byatis for further development.) The fact seems to have been that Bloch was very interested in ancient Egypt—he made that ancient land the scene of tales like "The Faceless God" and "Fane of the Black Pharaoh," and Egyptian religion and superstition enter very largely into "The Secret of Sebek" and some of his non-Mythos stories, like "The Eyes of the Mummy." In the person of the aforementioned Nyarlathotep, who has sinister, shadowy connections with the ancient Nile, Bloch found a perfect instrument to play with his hobby. In tale after tale, he developed the myth of Nyarlathotep, adding much new lore to our knowledge of the monster.

For instance in "The Faceless God" (*Weird Tales,* May 1936) he goes all out. I could fill a paragraph with nothing else but the various new titles of Nyarlathotep which that story adds to the Mythos. In fact, I will: The Demon Messenger, the Secret One, Black Messenger of Karneter (the Egyptian hell), the Stalker among the Stars, Lord of the Desert, the Dark One, the Faceless God, the Dark Demon, God of the Desert. See what I mean?

Bloch's "failure" to develop any of his own invented gods beyond a mere mention or two may, after all, have been deliberate. He had this trick of tossing into his Mythos stories otherwise unexplained and never followed-up-on, fragments of lore. These fascinate a student of the Mythos such as I am—I wish to Karneter I knew what they mean! References to fragments of lore like the Feast of Ulder, the thirteenth covenant, the Moon of Yiggurath, the Soul Chant of Sebek, the Legend of the Elder Saboth, demon-haunted Nis, and the secret parable of Byagoona the Faceless One. I'd love to know what those things were supposed to mean....

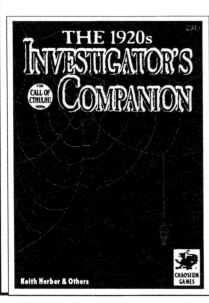

KING ARTHUR
PENDRAGON
EPIC ROLEPLAYING IN LEGENDARY BRITAIN

NEW CELTIC MAGIC SYSTEM

GREG STAFFORD

Chaosium Inc.

FIELD GUIDE TO CREATURES OF THE DREAMLANDS
#5107 $15.95

27 frightening creatures from beyond the wall of sleep.

INVESTIGATOR SHEETS
#5111 $8.95

A pad of two-color forms useful to every Cthulhu player.

DIRE DOCUMENTS
#5112 $8.95

Letter heads, commitment papers, release papers, and other items.

PENDRAGON

Based on the legends of King Arthur, Lancelot, Guenever, and the Knights of the Round Table.

PENDRAGON
#2716 $26.95

The basic rules; includes everything that you need to play, except dice.

THE BOY KING
#2708 $18.95

A complete campaign covering the entire reign of King Arthur.

SAVAGE MOUNTAINS
#2710 $18.95

Four adventures set in the wild mountains of legendary Wales.

BLOOD & LUST
#2711 $18.95

A medium-length campaign set across Britain.

PERILOUS FOREST
#2712 $18.95

Extensive background for western Cumbria and the Perilous Forest.

THE SPECTRE KING
#2714 $18.95

Six heroic adventures.

ELFQUEST

ELFQUEST is a fantasy roleplaying game based on the best-selling graphic novels of the same name, published by Father Tree Press.

ELFQUEST
#2605 $19.95

The basic rules; contains everything needed to play, except dice.

SEA ELVES
#2603 $7.95

Background and details about a band of isolated elves living on an archepelago.

ELFQUEST
The Official Roleplaying Game

Perrin, Petersen, and Friends